OTHER BOOKS BY WALTER TEVIS

The Hustler

The Man Who Fell to Earth

Mockingbird

Far from Home

Steps of the Sun

The Color of Money

Walter Tevis
THE QUEEN'S GAMBIT

"A PSYCHOLOGICAL THRILLER . . . a contest pitting human rationality against the self's unconscious urge to wipe out thought . . . thoroughly engaging."
—Christopher Lehmann-Haupt, *The New York Times*

"ABSORBING . . . SUSPENSEFUL. . . . Ultimately, this is not really a novel about chess . . . but about the human spirit, its struggles with itself and the terrible isolation it can endure. It can be read with intense enjoyment by those who know nothing about the game, as long as they are interested in what it means to be human at the deepest levels."   —*The Washington Post*

"MESMERIZING."   —*Newsweek*

"A FIRST-RATE THRILLER OF WARMLY HUMAN PROPORTIONS. *THE QUEEN'S GAMBIT* IS REWARDING FROM START TO FINISH. [It] bristle[s] with nervous excitement. . . . You'll want to sit in on this one until the final checkmate."
—*The Kansas City Star*

"It's advisable to tape your fingers before opening *The Queen's Gambit*. Otherwise, the suspense may bring on nail-chewing right to the elbow. . . . the tension builds as when any two antagonists are locked in mortal combat."
—*Houston Chronicle*

"THE ENDING IS A SERIES OF CRESCENDOS WHICH LEAVE YOU GASPING WITH PLEASURE. . . . An adult Horatio Alger tale with a heroine as plucky as you'll find anywhere. . . . ONE OF THE MOST SATISFYING NOVELS OF THE YEAR."
—*St. Louis Post-Dispatch*

THE
QUEEN'S GAMBIT

Walter Tevis

A DELL BOOK

Published by
Dell Publishing Co., Inc.
1 Dag Hammarskjold Plaza
New York, New York 10017

Dell ® TM 681510, Dell Publishing Co., Inc.

ISBN: 0-440-17183-0

Reprinted by arrangement with Random House, Inc.

Printed in the United States of America
First Dell printing—November 1984

For Eleanora

That the topless towers be burnt
And men recall that face,
Move gently if move you must
In this lonely place.
She thinks, part woman, three parts a child,
That nobody looks; her feet
Practice a tinker shuffle
Picked up on a street.
Like a long-legged fly upon the stream
Her mind moves upon silence.

—W. B. Yeats, "Long-legged Fly"

Author's Note

The superb chess of Grandmasters Robert Fischer, Boris Spassky and Anatoly Karpov has been a source of delight to players like myself for years. Since *The Queen's Gambit* is a work of fiction, however, it seemed prudent to omit them from the cast of characters, if only to prevent contradiction of the record.

I would like to express my thanks to Joe Ancrile, Fairfield Hoban and Stuart Morden, all excellent players, who helped me with books, magazines and tournament rules. And I was fortunate to have the warm-hearted and diligent help of National Master Bruce Pandolfini in proofreading the text and helping me rid it of errors concerning the game he plays so enviably well.

Chapter 1

Beth learned of her mother's death from a woman with a clipboard. The next day her picture appeared in the *Herald-Leader*. The photograph, taken on the porch of the gray house on Maplewood Drive, showed Beth in a simple cotton frock. Even then, she was clearly plain. A legend under the picture read: "Orphaned by yesterday's pile-up on New Circle Road, Elizabeth Harmon surveys a troubled future. Elizabeth, eight, was left without family by the crash, which killed two and injured others. At home alone at the time, Elizabeth learned of the accident shortly before the photo was taken. She will be well looked after, authorities say."

In the Methuen Home in Mount Sterling, Kentucky, Beth was given a tranquilizer twice a day. So were all the other children, to "even their dispositions." Beth's disposition was all right, as far as anyone could see, but she was glad to get the little pill. It loosened something deep in her stomach and helped her doze away the tense hours in the orphanage.

Mr. Fergussen gave them the pills in a little paper cup. Along with the green one that evened the disposition, there were orange and brown ones for building a strong body. The children had to line up to get them.

The tallest girl was the black one, Jolene. She was twelve. On her second day Beth stood behind her in Vitamin Line, and Jolene turned to look down at her, scowling. "You a real orphan or a bastard?"

Beth did not know what to say. She was frightened. They were at the back of the line, and she was supposed to stand there until they got up to the window where Mr. Fergussen stood. Beth had heard her mother call her father a bastard, but she didn't know what it meant.

"What's your name, girl?" Jolene asked.

"Beth."

"Your mother dead? What about your daddy?"

Beth stared at her. The words "mother" and "dead" were unbearable. She wanted to run, but there was no place to run to.

"Your folks," Jolene said in a voice that was not unsympathetic, "they dead?"

Beth could find nothing to say or do. She stood in line terrified, waiting for the pills.

"You're all greedy cocksuckers!" It was Ralph in the Boys' Ward who shouted that. She heard it because she was in the library and it had a window facing Boys'. She had no mental image for "cocksucker," and the word was strange. But she knew from the sound of it they would wash his mouth out with soap. They'd done it to her for "damn"—and Mother had said "Damn" all the time.

The barber made her sit absolutely still in the chair. "If you move, you might just lose an ear." There was nothing jovial in his voice. Beth sat as quietly as she could, but it was impossible to keep completely still. It took him a very long time to cut her hair into the bangs they all wore. She tried to occupy herself by thinking of that word, "cocksucker." All she could picture was a bird, like a woodpecker. But she felt that was wrong.

The janitor was fatter on one side than on the other. His name was Shaibel. Mr. Shaibel. One day she was sent to the basement to clean the blackboard erasers by clomping them together, and she found him sitting on a metal stool near the furnace scowling over a green-and-white checkerboard in front of him. But where the checkers should be there were little plastic things in funny shapes. Some were larger than others. There were more of the small ones than any of the others. The janitor looked up at her. She left in silence.

On Friday, everybody ate fish, Catholic or not. It came in squares, breaded with a dark, brown, dry crust and covered with a thick orange sauce, like bottled French dressing. The sauce was sweet and terrible, but the fish beneath it was worse. The taste of it nearly gagged her. But you had to eat every bite, or Mrs. Deardorff would be told about you and you wouldn't get adopted.

Some children got adopted right off. A six-year-old named Alice had come in a month after Beth and was taken in three weeks by some nice-looking people with an accent. They walked through the ward on the day they came for Alice. Beth had wanted to throw her arms around them because they looked happy to her, but she turned away when they glanced at her. Other children had been there a long time and knew they would never leave. They called themselves "lifers." Beth wondered if she was a lifer.

Gym was bad, and volleyball was the worst. Beth could never hit the ball right. She would slap at it fiercely or push at it with stiff fingers. Once she hurt her finger so much that it swelled up afterward. Most of the girls laughed and shouted when they played, but Beth never did.

Jolene was the best player by far. It wasn't just that she was older and taller; she always knew exactly what to do, and when the ball came high over the net, she could station herself under it without having to shout at the others to keep out of her way, and then leap up and spike it down with a long, smooth movement of her arm. The team that had Jolene always won.

The week after Beth hurt her finger, Jolene stopped her when gym ended and the others were rushing back to the showers.

"Lemme show you something," Jolene said. She held her hands up with the long fingers open and slightly flexed. "You do it like this." She bent her elbows and pushed her hands up smoothly, cupping an imaginary ball. "Try it."

Beth tried it, awkwardly at first. Jolene showed her again, laughing. Beth tried a few more times and did it better. Then Jolene got the ball and had Beth catch it with her fingertips. After a few times it got to be easy.

"You work on that now, hear?" Jolene said and ran off to the shower.

Beth worked on it over the next week, and after that she did not mind volleyball at all. She did not become good at it, but it wasn't something she was afraid of anymore.

Every Tuesday, Miss Graham sent Beth down after Arithmetic to do the erasers. It was considered a privilege, and Beth was the best student in the class, even though she was the youngest. She did not like the basement. It smelled musty, and she was afraid of Mr. Shaibel. But she wanted to know more about the game he played on that board by himself.

One day she went over and stood near him, waiting for him to move a piece. The one he was touching was the one with a horse's head on a little pedestal. After a second he looked up at her with a frown of irritation. "What do you *want*, child?" he said.

Normally she fled from any human encounter, especially with grownups, but this time she did not back away. "What's that game called?" she asked.

He stared at her. "You should be upstairs with the others."

She looked at him levelly; something about this man and the steadiness with which he played his mysterious game helped her to hold tightly to what she wanted. "I don't want to be with the others," she said. "I want to know what game you're playing."

He looked at her more closely. Then he shrugged. "It's called chess."

* * *

A bare light bulb hung from a black cord between Mr. Shaibel and the furnace. Beth was careful not to let the shadow of her head fall on the board. It was Sunday morning. They were having chapel upstairs in the library, and she had held up her hand for permission to go to the bathroom and then come down here. She had been standing, watching the janitor play chess, for ten minutes. Neither of them had spoken, but he seemed to accept her presence.

He would stare at the pieces for minutes at a time, motionless, looking at them as though he hated them, and then reach out over his belly, pick one up by its top with his fingertips, hold it for a moment as though holding a dead mouse by the tail and set it on another square. He did not look up at Beth.

Beth stood with the black shadow of her head on the concrete floor at her feet and watched the board, not taking her eyes from it, watching every move.

She had learned to save her tranquilizers until night. That helped her sleep. She would put the oblong pill in her mouth when Mr. Fergussen handed it to her, get it under her tongue, take a sip of the canned orange juice that came with the pill, swallow, and then when Mr. Fergussen had gone on to the next child, take the pill from her mouth and slip it into the pocket of her middy blouse. The pill had a hard coating and did not soften in the time it sat under her tongue.

For the first two months she had slept very little. She tried to, lying still with her eyes tightly shut. But she would hear the girls in the other beds cough or turn or mutter, or a night orderly would walk down the corridor and the shadow would cross her bed and she would see it, even with her eyes closed. A distant phone would ring, or a toilet would flush. But worst of all was when she heard voices talking at the desk at the end of the corridor. No matter how softly the orderly spoke to the night attendant, no matter how pleasantly, Beth immediately found herself tense and fully awake. Her stomach contracted, she tasted vinegar in her mouth; and sleep would be out of the question for that night.

Now she would snuggle up in bed, allowing herself to feel the tension in her stomach with a thrill, knowing it would soon leave her. She waited there in the dark, alone, monitoring herself, waiting for the turmoil in her to peak. Then she swallowed the two pills and lay back until the ease began to spread through her body like the waves of a warm sea.

"Will you teach me?"

Mr. Shaibel said nothing, did not even register the question with a movement of his head. Distant voices from above were singing "Bringing in the Sheaves."

She waited for several minutes. Her voice almost broke with the effort of her words, but she pushed them out, anyway: "I want to learn to play chess."

Mr. Shaibel reached out a fat hand to one of the larger black pieces, picked it up deftly by its head and set it down on a square at the other side of the board. He brought the hand back and folded his arms across his chest. He still did not look at Beth. "I don't play strangers."

The flat voice had the effect of a slap in the face. Beth turned and left, walking upstairs with the bad taste in her mouth.

"I'm not a stranger," she said to him two days later. "I live here." Behind her head a small moth circled the bare bulb, and its pale shadow crossed the board at regular intervals. "You can teach me. I already know some of it, from watching."

"Girls don't play chess." Mr. Shaibel's voice was flat.

She steeled herself and took a step closer, pointing at, but not touching, one of the cylindrical pieces that she had already labeled a cannon in her imagination. "This one moves up and down or back and forth. All the way, if there's space to move in."

Mr. Shaibel was silent for a while. Then he pointed at the one with what looked like a slashed lemon on top. "And this one?"

Her heart leapt. "On the diagonals."

You could save up pills by taking only one at night and keeping the other. Beth put the extras in her toothbrush holder, where nobody would ever look. She just had to make sure to dry the toothbrush as much as she could with a paper towel after she used it, or else not use it at all and rub her teeth clean with a finger.

That night for the first time she took three pills, one after the other. Little prickles went across the hairs on the back of her neck; she had discovered something important. She let the glow spread all over her, lying on her cot in her faded blue pajamas in the worst place in the Girls' Ward, near the door to the corridor and across from the bathroom. Something in her life was solved: she knew about the chess pieces and how they moved and captured, and she knew how to make herself feel good in the stomach and in the tense joints of her arms and legs, with the pills the orphanage gave her.

"Okay, child," Mr. Shaibel said. "We can play chess now. I play White."

She had the erasers. It was after Arithmetic, and Geography was in ten minutes. "I don't have much time," she said. She had learned all the moves last Sunday, during the hour that chapel allowed her to be in the basement. No one ever missed her at chapel, as long as she checked in, because of the group of girls that came from Children's, across town. But Geography was different. She was terrified of Mr. Schell, even though she was at the top of the class.

The janitor's voice was flat. "Now or never," he said.

"I have Geography . . ."

"Now or never."

She thought only a second before deciding. She had seen an old milk crate behind the furnace. She dragged it to the other end of the board, seated herself and said, "Move."

He beat her with what she was to learn later was called the Scholar's Mate, after four moves. It was quick, but not quick enough to keep her from being fifteen minutes late for Geography. She said she'd been in the bathroom.

Mr. Schell stood at the desk with his hands on his hips. He

surveyed the class. "Have any of you young ladies seen this young lady in the ladies'?"

There were subdued giggles. No hands were raised, not even Jolene's, although Beth had lied for her twice.

"And how many of you ladies were in the ladies' before class?"

There were more giggles and three hands.

"And did any of you see Beth there? Washing her pretty little hands, perhaps?"

There was no response. Mr. Schell turned back to the board, where he had been listing the exports of Argentina, and added the word "silver." For a moment Beth thought it was done with. But then he spoke, with his back to the class. "Five demerits," he said.

With ten demerits you were whipped on the behind with a leather strap. Beth had felt that strap only in her imagination, but her imagination expanded for a moment with a vision of pain like fire on the soft parts of herself. She put a hand to her heart, feeling in the bottom of the breast pocket of her blouse for that morning's pill. The fear reduced itself perceptibly. She visualized her toothbrush holder, the long rectangular plastic container; it had four more pills in it now, there in the drawer of the little metal stand by her cot.

That night she lay on her back in bed. She had not yet taken the pill in her hand. She listened to the night noises and noticed how they seemed to get louder as her eyes grew accustomed to the darkness. Down the hallway Mr. Byrne began talking to Mrs. Holland, at the desk. Beth's body grew taut at the sound. She blinked and looked at the dark ceiling overhead and forced herself to see the chessboard with its green and white squares. Then she put the pieces on her home squares: rook, knight, bishop, queen, king, and the row of pawns in front of them. Then she moved White's king pawn up to the fourth row. She pushed Black's up. She could do this! It was simple. She went on, beginning to replay the game she had lost.

She brought Mr. Shaibel's knight up to the third row. It stood there clearly in her mind on the green-and-white board on the ceiling of the ward.

The noises had already faded into a white, harmonious background. Beth lay happily in bed, playing chess.

The next Sunday she blocked the Scholar's Mate with her king's knight. She had gone over the game in her mind a hundred times, until the anger and humiliation were purged from it, leaving the pieces and the board clear in her nighttime vision. When she came to play Mr. Shaibel on Sunday, it was all worked out, and she moved the knight as if in a dream. She loved the feel of the piece, the miniature horse's head in her hand. When she set down the knight on the square, the janitor scowled at it. He took his queen by the head and checked Beth's king with it. But Beth was ready for that too; she had seen it in bed the night before.

It took him fourteen moves to trap her queen. She tried to play on, queenless, to ignore the mortal loss, but he reached out and stopped her hand from touching the pawn she was about to move. "You resign now," he said. His voice was rough.

"Resign?"

"That's right, child. When you lose the queen that way, you resign."

She stared at him, not comprehending. He let go of her hand, picked up her black king, and set it on its side on the board. It rolled back and forth for a moment and then lay still.

"*No,*" she said.

"Yes. You have resigned the game."

She wanted to hit him with something. "You didn't tell me that in the rules."

"It's not a rule. It's sportsmanship."

She knew now what he meant, but she did not like it. "I want to finish," she said. She picked up the king and set it back on its square.

"No."

"You've got to finish," she said.

He raised his eyebrows and got up. She had never seen him stand in the basement—only out in the halls when he was sweeping or in the classrooms when he washed the blackboards. He had to stoop a bit now to keep his head from hitting the rafters on the low ceiling. "No," he said. "You lost."

It wasn't fair. She had no interest in sportsmanship. She wanted to play and to win. She wanted to win more than she had ever wanted anything. She said a word she had not said since her mother died: "Please."

"Game's over," he said.

She stared at him in fury. "You greedy . . ."

He let his arms drop straight at his sides and said slowly, "No more chess. Get out."

If only she were bigger. But she wasn't. She got up from the board and walked to the stairs while the janitor watched her in silence.

On Tuesday when she went down the hall to the basement door carrying the erasers, she found that the door was locked. She pushed against it twice with her hip, but it wouldn't budge. She knocked, softly at first and then loudly, but there was no sound from the other side. It was horrible. She knew he was in there sitting at the board, that he was just being angry at her from the last time, but there was nothing she could do about it. When she brought back the erasers, Miss Graham didn't even notice they hadn't been cleaned or that Beth was back sooner than usual.

On Thursday she was certain it would be the same, but it wasn't. The door was open, and when she went down the stairs, Mr. Shaibel acted as though nothing had happened. The pieces were set up. She cleaned the erasers hurriedly and seated herself at the board. Mr. Shaibel had moved his king's pawn by the time she got there. She played her king's pawn, moving it two squares forward. She would not make any mistakes this time.

He responded to her move quickly, and she immediately replied. They said nothing to each other, but kept moving. Beth could feel the tension, and she liked it.

On the twentieth move Mr. Shaibel advanced a knight when he shouldn't have and Beth was able to get a pawn to the sixth rank. He brought the knight back. It was a wasted move and she felt a thrill when she saw him do it. She traded her bishop for the knight. Then, on the next move, she pushed the pawn again. It would become a queen on the next move.

He looked at it sitting there and then reached out angrily and toppled his king. Neither of them said anything. It was her first win. All of the tension was gone, and what Beth felt inside herself was as wonderful as anything she had ever felt in her life.

She found she could miss lunch on Sundays, and no one paid any attention. That gave her three hours with Mr. Shaibel, until he left for home at two-thirty. They did not talk, either of them. He always played the white pieces, moving first, and she the black. She had thought about questioning this but decided not to.

One Sunday, after a game he had barely managed to win, he said to her, "You should learn the Sicilian Defense."

"What's that?" she asked irritably.

She was still smarting from the loss. She had beaten him two games last week.

"When White moves pawn to king four, Black does this." He reached down and moved the white pawn two squares up the board, his almost invariable first move. Then he picked up the pawn in front of the black queen's bishop and set it down two squares up toward the middle. It was the first time he had ever shown her anything like this.

"Then what?" she said.

He picked up the king's knight and set it below and to the right of the pawn. "Knight to KB 3."

"What's KB 3?"

"King's bishop 3. Where I just put the knight."

"The squares have names?"

He nodded impassively. She sensed that he was unwilling to give up even this much information. "If you play well, they have names."

She leaned forward. "Show me."

He looked down at her. "No. Not now."

This infuriated her. She understood well enough that a person likes to keep his secrets. She kept hers. Nevertheless, she wanted to lean across the board and slap his face and make him tell her. She sucked in her breath. "Is that the Sicilian Defense?"

He seemed relieved that she had dropped the subject of the names of the squares. "There's more," he said. He went on with it, showing her the basic moves and some variations. But he did not use the names of the squares. He showed her the Levenfish Variation and the Najdorf Variation and told her to go over them. She did, without a single mistake.

But when they played a real game afterward, he pushed his queen's pawn forward, and she could see immediately that what he had just taught her was useless in this situation. She glared at him across the board, feeling that if she had had a knife, she could have stabbed him with it. Then she looked back to the board and moved her own queen's pawn forward, determined to beat him.

He moved the pawn next to his queen's pawn, the one in front of the bishop. He often did this. "Is that one of those things? Like the Sicilian Defense?" she asked.

"Openings." He did not look at her; he was watching the board.

"Is it?"

He shrugged. "The Queen's Gambit."

She felt better. She had learned something more from him. She decided not to take the offered pawn, to leave the tension on the board. She liked it like that. She liked the power of the pieces, exerted along files and diagonals. In the middle of the game, when pieces were everywhere, the forces crisscrossing the board thrilled her. She brought out her king's knight, feeling its power spread.

In twenty moves she had won both his rooks, and he resigned.

She rolled over in bed, put a pillow over her head to block out the light from under the corridor door and began to think how you could use a bishop and a rook together to make a sudden check on the king. If you moved the bishop, the king would be in check, and the bishop would be free to do whatever it wanted to on the next move—even take the queen. She lay there for quite a while, thinking excitedly of this powerful attack. Then she took the pillow off and rolled over on her back and made the chessboard on the ceiling and played over all her games with Mr. Shaibel, one at a time. She saw two places where she might have created the rook-bishop situation she had just invented. In one of them she could have forced it by a double threat, and in the other she could probably have sneaked it in. She replayed those two games in her mind with the new moves, and won them both. She smiled happily to herself and fell asleep.

The Arithmetic teacher gave the eraser cleaning to another student, saying that Beth needed a rest. It wasn't fair, because Beth still had perfect grades in Arithmetic, but there was nothing she could do about it. She sat in class when the little red-haired boy went out of the room each day with the erasers, doing her meaningless additions and subtractions with a trembling hand. She wanted to play chess more desperately every day.

On Tuesday and Wednesday she took only one pill and saved the other. On Thursday she was able to go to sleep after playing chess in her mind for an hour or so, and she saved the day's two pills. She did the same thing on Friday. All day Saturday, doing her work in the cafeteria kitchen and in the afternoon during the Christian movie in the library and the Personal Improvement Talk before dinner, she could feel a little glow whenever she wanted to, knowing that she had six pills in her toothbrush holder.

That night, after lights out, she took them all, one by one, and waited. The feeling, when it came, was delicious—a kind of easy sweetness in her belly and a loosening in the tight parts of her body. She kept herself awake as long as she could to enjoy the warmth inside her, the deep chemical happiness.

On Sunday when Mr. Shaibel asked where she had been, she was surprised that he cared. "They wouldn't let me out of class," she said.

He nodded. The chessboard was set up, and she saw to her surprise that the white pieces were facing her side and that the milk crate was already in place. "Do I move first?" she said, in-credulous.

"Yes. From now on we take turns. It's the way the game should be played."

She seated herself and moved the king's pawn. Mr. Shaibel wordlessly moved his queen bishop's pawn. She hadn't forgotten the moves. She never forgot chess moves. He played the Leven-fish Variation; she kept her eyes on his bishop's command of the long diagonal, the way it was waiting to pounce. And she found a way to neutralize it on the seventeenth move. She was able to trade her own, weaker bishop for it. Then she moved in with her knight, brought a rook out, and had him mated in ten more moves.

It had been simple—merely a matter of keeping her eyes open and visualizing the ways the game could go.

The checkmate took him by surprise; she caught the king on the back rank, reaching her arm all the way across the board and setting the rook crisply on the mating square. "Mate," she said levelly.

Mr. Shaibel seemed different today. He did not scowl as he always did when she beat him. He leaned forward and said, "I'll teach you chess notation."

She looked up at him.

"The names of the squares. I'll teach you now."

She blinked. "Am I good enough now?"

He started to say something and stopped. "How old are you, child?"

"Eight."

"Eight years old." He leaned forward—as far as his huge paunch would permit. "To tell you the truth of it, child, you are astounding."

She did not understand what he was saying.

"Excuse me." Mr. Shaibel reached down on the floor for a nearly empty pint bottle. He tilted his head back and drank from it.

"Is that whiskey?" Beth asked.

"Yes, child. And don't tell."

"I won't," she said. "Teach me chess notation."

He set the bottle back on the floor. Beth followed it for a moment with her eyes, wondering what whiskey would taste like and what it would feel like when you drank it. Then she turned her gaze and her attention back to the board with its thirty-two pieces, each exerting its own silent force.

Sometime in the middle of the night she was awakened. Someone was sitting on the edge of her bed. She stiffened.

"Take it easy," Jolene whispered. "It's only me."

Beth said nothing, just lay there and waited.

"Thought you might like trying something fun," Jolene said. She reached a hand under the sheet and laid it gently on Beth's belly. Beth was on her back. The hand stayed there, and Beth's body remained stiff.

"Don't be uptight," Jolene whispered. "I ain't gonna hurt nothing." She giggled softly. "I'm just horny. You know what it's like to be horny?"

Beth did not know.

"Just relax. I'm just going to rub a little. It'll feel good, if you let it."

Beth turned her head toward the corridor door. It was shut. The light, as usual, came under it. She could hear distant voices, down at the desk.

Jolene's hand was moving downward. Beth shook her head. "Don't . . ." she whispered.

"Hush now," Jolene said. Her hand moved down farther, and one finger began to rub up and down. It did not hurt, but something in Beth resisted it. She felt herself perspiring. "Ah shit," Jolene said. "I bet that feels good." She squirmed a little closer to Beth and took Beth's hand with her free one, pulling it toward her. "You touch me, too," she said.

Beth let her hand go limp. Jolene guided it up under her nightgown until the fingers grazed a place that felt warm and damp.

"Come on now, press a little," Jolene whispered. The intensity in the whispering voice was frightening. Beth did as she was told and pressed harder.

"Come on, baby," Jolene whispered, "move it up and down. Like this." She started moving her finger on Beth. It was terrifying. Beth rubbed Jolene a few times, trying hard, concentrating on just doing it. Her face was wet with sweat and her free hand was clutching at the sheet, squeezing it with all her might.

Then Jolene's face was against hers and her arm around Beth's chest. "Faster," Jolene whispered. "*Faster.*"

"No," Beth said aloud, terrified. "*No, I don't want to.*" She pulled her hand away.

"Son of a bitch," Jolene said aloud.

Footsteps came running up the hallway, and the door opened. Light streamed in. It was one of the night people whom Beth didn't know. The lady stood there for a minute. Everything was quiet. Jolene was gone. Beth didn't dare move to see if she was back in her own bed. Finally the woman left. Beth looked over and saw the outline of Jolene's body back in bed. Beth had three pills in the drawer; she took all three. Then she lay on her back and waited for the bad taste to go away.

The next day in the cafeteria, Beth felt wretched from not sleeping.

"You are the ugliest white girl *ever,*" Jolene said, in a stage whisper. She had come up to Beth in the line for the little boxes of cereal. "Your nose is ugly and your face is ugly and your skin is like sandpaper. You white trash cracker bitch."

Jolene went on, head high, to the scrambled eggs.

Beth said nothing, knowing that it was true.

King, knight, pawn. The tensions on the board were enough to warp it. Then *whack!* Down came the queen. Rooks at the bottom of the board, hemmed in at first, but ready, building pressure and then removing the pressure in a single move. In General Science, Miss Hadley had spoken of magnets, of "lines of force." Beth, nearly asleep with boredom, had waked up suddenly. Lines of force: bishops on diagonals; rooks on files.

The seats in a classroom could be like the squares. If the red-haired boy named Ralph were a knight, she could pick him up and move him two seats up and one over, setting him on the empty seat next to Denise. This would check Bertrand, who sat in the front row and was, she decided, the king. She smiled, thinking of it. Jolene and she had not spoken for over a week, and Beth had not let herself cry. She was almost nine years old, and she didn't need Jolene. It didn't matter how she felt about it. She didn't need Jolene.

"Here," Mr. Shaibel said. He handed her something in a brown paper bag. It was noon on Sunday. She slipped the bag open. In it was a heavy paperback book—*Modern Chess Openings.*

Incredulously, she began to turn the pages. It was filled with long vertical columns of chess notations. There were little chess-board diagrams and chapter heads like "Queen's Pawn Openings" and "Indian Defense Systems." She looked up.

He was scowling at her. "It's the best book for you," he said. "It will tell you what you want to know."

She said nothing but sat down on her milk crate behind the board, holding the book tightly in her lap, and waited to play.

English was the dullest class, with Mr. Espero's slow voice and the poets with names like John Greenleaf Whittier and William Cullen Bryant. "Whither, midst falling dew,/While glow the heavens with the last steps of day . . ." It was stupid. And he read every word aloud, with care.

She held *Modern Chess Openings* under her desk while Mr. Espero read. She went through variations one at a time, playing them out in her head. By the third day the notations—P-K4, N-KB3—leapt into her quick mind as solid pieces on real squares. She saw them easily; there was no need for a board. She could sit there with *Modern Chess Openings* in her lap, on the blue serge pleated skirt of the Methuen Home, and while Mr. Espero droned on about the enlargement of the spirit that great poetry gives us or read aloud lines like "To him who in the love of nature holds/communion with her visible forms, she speaks a various language," the moves of chess games clicked into place before her half-shut eyes. In the back of the book were continuations down to the very end of some of the classic games, to twenty-seventh-move resignations or to draws on the fortieth, and she had learned to put the pieces through their entire ballet, sometimes catching her breath at the elegance of a combination attack or of a sacrifice or the restrained balance of force in a position. And always her mind was on the win, or on the potential for the win.

" 'For his gayer hours she has a voice of gladness/and a smile and eloquence of beauty . . .' " read Mr. Espero, while Beth's mind danced in awe to the geometrical rococo of chess, rapt, enraptured, drowning in the grand permutations as they opened to her soul, and her soul opened to them.

"Cracker!" Jolene hissed as they left History.

"Nigger," Beth hissed back.

Jolene stopped and turned to stare at her.

The following Saturday, Beth took six pills and gave herself up to their sweet chemistry, holding one hand on her belly and the other on her cunt. That word she knew about. It was one of the few things Mother had taught her before crashing the Chevy. "Wipe yourself," Mother would say in the bathroom. "Be sure to wipe your cunt." Beth moved her fingers up and down, the way Jolene had. It didn't feel good. Not to her. She took her hand away and fell back into the mental ease of the pills. Maybe she was too young. Jolene was four years older and had fuzzy hair growing there. Beth had felt it.

"Morning, Cracker," Jolene said softly. Her face was easy.

"Jolene," Beth said. Jolene stepped closer. There was nobody around, just the two of them. They were in the locker room, after gym.

"What you want?" Jolene said.

"I want to know what a cocksucker is."

Jolene stared at her a moment. Then she laughed. "Shit," she said. "You know what a cock is?"

"I don't think so."

"That's what boys have. In the back of the health book. Like a thumb."

Beth nodded. She knew the picture.

"Well, honey," Jolene said gravely, "there's girls likes to suck on that thumb."

Beth thought about it. "Isn't that where they pee?" she said.

"I expect it wipes clean," Jolene said.

Beth walked away feeling shocked. And she was still puzzled. She had heard of murderers and torturers; at home she had seen a neighbor boy beat his dog senseless with a heavy stick; but she did not understand how someone could do what Jolene said.

The next Sunday she won five games straight. She had been playing Mr. Shaibel for three months now, and she knew that he could no longer beat her. Not once. She anticipated every feint, every threat that he knew how to make. There was no way he could confuse her with his knights, or keep a piece posted on a dangerous square, or embarrass her by pinning an important piece. She could see it coming and could prevent it while continuing to set up for attack.

When they had finished, he said, "You are eight years old?"

"Nine in November."

He nodded. "You will be here next Sunday?"

"Yes."

"Good. Be sure."

On Sunday there was another man in the basement with Mr. Shaibel. He was thin and wore a striped shirt and tie. "This is Mr. Ganz, from the chess club," Mr. Shaibel said.

"Chess club?" Beth echoed, looking him over. He seemed a little like Mr. Schell, even though he was smiling.

"We play at a club," Mr. Shaibel said.

"And I'm coach of the high school team. Duncan High," Mr. Ganz said. She had never heard of the school.

"Would you like to play me a game?" Mr. Ganz asked.

For an answer Beth seated herself on the milk crate. There was a folding chair set up at the side of the board. Mr. Shaibel eased his heavy body into it, and Mr. Ganz sat on the stool. He reached forward in quick, nervous movement and picked up two pawns: one white and one black. He cupped his hands around them, shook them together a moment and then extended both arms toward Beth with the fists clenched.

"Choose a hand," Mr. Shaibel said.

"Why?"

"You play the color you choose."

"Oh." She reached out and barely touched Mr. Ganz's left hand. "This one."

He opened it. The black pawn lay in his palm. "Sorry," he said, smiling. His smile made her uncomfortable.

The board already had Black facing Beth. Mr. Ganz put the pawns back on their squares, moved pawn to king four, and Beth relaxed. She had learned every line of the Sicilian from her book. She played the queen bishop's pawn to its fourth square. When he brought the knight out, she decided to use the Najdorf.

But Mr. Ganz was a bit too smart for that. He was a better player than Mr. Shaibel. Still, she knew after a dozen moves that he would be easy to beat, and she proceeded to do so, calmly and mercilessly, forcing him to resign after twenty-three moves.

He placed his king on its side on the board. "You certainly know the game, young lady. Do you have a team here?"

She looked at him uncomprehendingly.

"The other girls. Do they have a chess club?"

"No."

"Then where do you play?"

"Down here."

"Mr. Shaibel said you played a few games every Sunday. What do you do in between?"

"Nothing."

"But how do you keep up?"

She did not want to tell him about playing chess in her mind in class and in bed at night. To distract him she said, "Do you want to play another?"

He laughed. "All right. It's your turn to play White."

She beat him even more handily, using the Réti Opening. The book had called it a "hypermodern" system; she liked the way it used her king's bishop. After twenty moves she stopped him to point out her upcoming mate in three. It took him half a minute to see it. He shook his head in disbelief and toppled his king.

"You're astonishing," he said. "I've never seen anything like it." He stood up and walked over to the furnace, where Beth had noticed a small shopping bag. "I have to go now. But I brought you a present." He handed her the shopping bag.

She looked inside, hoping to see another chess book. Something was wrapped in pink tissue paper.

"Unwrap it," Mr. Ganz said, smiling.

She lifted it out and pulled away the loosely wrapped paper. It was a pink doll in a blue print dress, with blond hair and a puckered-up mouth. She held it a moment and looked at it.

"Well?" Mr. Ganz said.

"Do you want another game?" Beth said, holding the doll by its arm.

"I have to go," Mr. Ganz said. "Maybe I'll come back next week."

She nodded.

There was a big oilcan used for trash at the end of the hallway. As she passed it on the way to the Sunday afternoon movie, she dropped the doll into it.

During Health Class she found the picture in the back of the book. On one page was a woman and on the facing page a man. They were line drawings, with no shading. Both stood with their arms at their sides and the palms of their hands turned out. At the V below her flat belly the woman had a simple, vertical line. The man had no such line, or if he had you couldn't see it. What he had looked like a little purse with a round thing hanging down in front of it. Jolene said it was like a thumb. That was his cock.

The teacher, Mr. Hume, was saying that you should have green leafy vegetables at least once a day. He began to write the names of vegetables on the board. Outside the big windows on Beth's left, pink japonica was beginning to bloom. She studied the drawing of a naked man, trying vainly to find some secret.

*   *   *

Mr. Ganz was back the next Sunday. He had his own chessboard with him. It had black and white squares, and the pieces were in a wooden box lined with red felt. They were made of polished wood; Beth could see the grain in the white ones. She reached out while Mr. Ganz was setting them up and lifted one of the knights. It was heavier than the ones she had used and had a circle of green felt on the bottom. She had never thought about owning things, but she wanted this chess set.

Mr. Shaibel had set up his board in the usual place and got another milk crate for Mr. Ganz's board. The two boards were now side by side, with a foot of space between them. It was a sunny day, and bright light came in the window filtered through the short bushes by the walk at the edge of the building. Nobody spoke while the pieces were set up. Mr. Ganz took the knight gently from Beth's hand and put it on its home square. "We thought you could play us both," he said.

"At the same time?"

He nodded.

Her milk crate had been put between the boards. She had White for both games, and in both of them she played pawn to king four.

Mr. Shaibel replied with the Sicilian; Mr. Ganz played pawn to king four. She did not even have to pause and think about the continuations. She played both moves and looked out the window.

She beat them both effortlessly. Mr. Ganz set up the pieces, and they started again. This time she moved pawn to queen four on both and followed it with pawn to queen's bishop four—the Queen's Gambit. She felt deeply relaxed, almost in a dream. She had taken seven tranquilizers at about midnight, and some of the languor was still in her.

About midway into the games she was staring out the window at a bush with pink blooms when she heard Mr. Ganz's voice saying, "Beth, I've moved my bishop to bishop five" and she replied dreamlike, "Knight to K-5." The bush seemed to glow in the spring sunlight.

"Bishop to knight four," Mr. Ganz said.

"Queen to queen four," Beth replied, still not looking.

"Knight to queen's bishop three," Mr. Shaibel said gruffly.

"Bishop to knight five," Beth said, her eyes on the pink blossoms.

"Pawn to knight three." Mr. Ganz had a strange softness in his voice.

"Queen to rook four check," Beth said.

She heard Mr. Ganz inhale sharply. After a second he said, "King to bishop one."

"That's mate in three," Beth said, without turning. "First check is with the knight. The king has the two dark squares, and the bishop checks it. Then the knight mates."

Mr. Ganz let out his breath slowly. "Jesus Christ!" he said.

Chapter 2

They were watching the Saturday-afternoon movie when Mr. Fergussen came to take her to Mrs. Deardorff's office. It was a movie about table manners called "How to Act at Dinnertime," so she didn't mind leaving. But she was frightened. Had they found out that she never went to chapel? That she saved pills? Her legs trembled and her knees felt funny as Mr. Fergussen, wearing his white pants and white T-shirt, walked her down the long hallway, down the green linoleum with black cracks in it. Her thick brown shoes squeaked on the linoleum, and she squinted her eyes under the bright fluorescent lights. The day before had been her birthday. No one had taken any notice of it. Mr. Fergussen, as usual, had nothing to say: he walked smartly down the hall ahead of her. At the door with the frosted glass panel and the words HELEN DEARDORFF—SUPERINTENDENT he stopped. Beth pushed open the door and went inside.

A secretary in a white blouse told her to go on to the back office. Mrs. Deardorff was expecting her. She pushed open the big wooden door and walked in. In the red armchair sat Mr. Ganz, wearing a brown suit. Mrs. Deardorff was sitting behind a desk. She peered at Beth over tortoise-shell glasses. Mr. Ganz smiled self-consciously and rose halfway from the chair when she came in. Then he sat down again awkwardly.

"Elizabeth," Mrs. Deardorff said.

She had closed the door behind her and now stood a few feet away from it. She looked at Mrs. Deardorff.

"Elizabeth, Mr. Ganz tells me that you are a"—she adjusted the glasses on her nose—"a gifted child." Mrs. Deardorff looked at her for a moment as though she were expected to deny it. When Beth said nothing, she went on, "He has an unusual request to make of us. He would like you to be taken to the high school on . . ." She looked over at Mr. Ganz again.

"On Thursday," Mr. Ganz said.

"On Thursday. In the afternoon. He maintains that you are a phenomenal chess player. He would like you to perform for the chess club."

Beth said nothing. She was still frightened.

Mr. Ganz cleared his throat. "We have a dozen members, and I'd like you to play them."

"Well?" Mrs. Deardorff said. "Would you like to do that? It can be arranged as a field trip." She smiled grimly at Mr. Ganz. "We like to give our girls a chance for experience outside." That was the first time Beth had heard of it; she knew of no one who ever went anywhere.

"Yes," Beth said. "I'd like to."

"Good," Mrs. Deardorff said. "It's settled, then. Mr. Ganz and one of the girls from the high school will pick you up after lunch Thursday."

Mr. Ganz got up to go, and Beth started to follow, but Mrs. Deardorff called her back.

"Elizabeth," she said when they were alone, "Mr. Ganz informs me that you have been playing chess with our custodian."

Beth was uncertain what to say.

"With Mr. Shaibel."

"Yes, ma'am."

"That is very irregular, Elizabeth. Have you gone to the basement?"

For a moment she considered lying. But it would be too easy for Mrs. Deardorff to find out. "Yes, ma'am," she said again.

Beth expected anger, but Mrs. Deardorff's voice was surprisingly relaxed. "We can't have that, Elizabeth," she said. "As much as Methuen believes in excellence, we can't have you playing chess in the basement."

Beth felt her stomach tighten.

"I believe there are chess sets in the game closet," Mrs. Deardorff continued. "I'll have Fergussen look into it."

A phone began ringing in the outer office and a little light on the phone began flashing. "That will be all, Elizabeth. Mind your manners at the high school and be sure your nails are clean."

In "Major Hoople" in the funnies, Major Hoople belonged to the Owl's Club. It was a place where men sat in big old chairs and drank beer and talked about President Eisenhower and how much money their wives spent on hats. Major Hoople had a huge belly, like Mr. Shaibel, and when he was at the Owl's Club with a dark beer bottle in his hands, his words came from his mouth with little bubbles. He said things like "Harrumph" and "Egad!" in a balloon on top of the bubbles. That was a "club." It was like the library reading room at Methuen. Maybe she would play the twelve people in a room like that.

She hadn't told anyone. Not even Jolene. She lay in bed after lights out and thought about it with an expectant quiver in her stomach. Could she play that many games? She rolled over on her back and nervously felt the pocket of her pajamas. There were two in there. It was six days until Thursday. Maybe Mr. Ganz meant she would play one game with one person and then one game with another, if that was how you did it.

She had looked up "phenomenal." The dictionary said: "extraordinary; outstanding; remarkable." She repeated these words silently to herself now: "extraordinary; outstanding; remarkable." They became a tune in her mind.

She tried to picture twelve chessboards at once, spread out in a row on the ceiling. Only four or five were really clear. She took the black pieces for herself and assigned the whites to "them" and then had "them" move pawn to king four, and she responded with the Sicilian. She found she could keep five games going and concentrate on one at a time while the other four waited for her attention.

From out at the desk down the corridor she heard a voice say "What time is it now?" and another voice reply "It's two-twenty." Mother used to talk about the "wee, small hours." This was one of them. Beth kept playing chess, keeping five imaginary games going at once. She had forgotten about the pills in her pocket.

The next morning Mr. Fergussen handed her the little paper cup as usual but when she looked down into it there were two orange vitamin tablets and nothing else. She looked back up at him, behind the little window of the pharmacy.

"That's it," he said. "Next."

She didn't move, even though the girl behind her was pushing against her. "Where are the green ones?"

"You don't get them anymore," Mr. Fergussen said.

Beth stood on tiptoe and looked over the counter. There, behind Mr. Fergussen, stood the big glass jar, still a third full of green pills. There must have been hundreds of them in there, like tiny jellybeans. "There they are," she said and pointed.

"We're getting rid of them," he said. "It's a new law. No more tranquilizers for kids."

"It's *my* turn," said Gladys, behind her.

Beth didn't move. She opened her mouth to speak but nothing came out.

"It's my turn for vitamins," Gladys said, louder.

There had been nights when she was so involved in chess that she had slept without pills. But this wasn't one of them. She could not think about chess. There were three pills in her toothbrush holder, and that was it. Several times she decided to take one of them but then decided not to.

"I hear tell you going to *exhibit* yourself," Jolene said. She giggled, more to herself than to Beth. "Going to play chess in front of people."

"Who told you?" Beth said. They were in the locker room after volleyball. Jolene's breasts, not there a year before, jiggled under her gym shirt.

"Child, I just know things," Jolene said. "Ain't that where it's like checkers but the pieces jump around crazy? My Uncle Hubert played that."

"Did Mrs. Deardorff tell you?"

"Never go near that lady." Jolene smiled confidentially. "It was Fergussen. He told me you going to the high school downtown. Day after tomorrow."

Beth looked at her incredulously. The staff didn't trade confidences with the orphans. "Fergussen . . . ?"

Jolene leaned over and spoke seriously. "He and I been friendly from time to time. Don't want you talking about it, hear?"

Beth nodded.

Jolene pulled back and went on drying her hair with the white gym towel. After volleyball you could always stretch out the time, showering and getting dressed, before going to study hall.

Beth thought of something. After a moment she spoke in a low voice, "Jolene."

"Uh huh."

"Did Fergussen give you green pills? Extra ones?"

Jolene looked at her hard. Then her face softened. "No, honey. I wish he would. But they got the whole state after 'em for what they been doing with those pills."

"They're still there. In the big jar."

"That a fact?" Jolene said. "I ain't noticed." She kept looking at Beth. "I noticed you been edgy lately. You having withdraw symptoms?"

Beth had used her last pill the night before. "I don't know," she said.

"You look around," Jolene said. "They'll be some nervous orphans around here the next few days." She finished drying her hair and stretched. With the light coming from behind her and with her frizzy hair and her big, wide eyes, Jolene was beautiful. Beth felt ugly, sitting there on the bench beside her. Pale and little and ugly. And she was scared to go to bed tonight without pills. She had been sleeping only two or three hours a night for the past two nights. Her eyes felt gritty and the back of her neck, even right after showering, was sweaty. She kept thinking about that big glass jar behind Fergussen, filled with green pills a third of the way up—enough to fill her toothbrush holder a hundred times.

Going to the high school was her first ride in a car since she came to Methuen. That was fourteen months ago. Nearly fifteen. Mother had died in a car, a black one like this, with a sharp piece of the steering wheel in her eye. The woman with the clipboard had told her, while Beth stared at the mole on the woman's cheek and said nothing. Had felt nothing, either. Mother had passed on, the woman said. The funeral would be in three days. The coffin would be closed. Beth knew what a coffin was; Dracula slept in one. Daddy had passed on the year before, because of a "carefree life," as Mother put it.

Beth sat in the back of the car with a big, embarrassed girl named Shirley. Shirley was in the chess club. Mr. Ganz drove. There was a knot as tight as wire in Beth's stomach. She kept her knees pressed together and looked straight ahead at the back of Mr. Ganz's neck in its striped collar and at the cars and buses ahead of their car, moving back and forth outside the windshield.

Shirley tried to make conversation. "Do you play the King's Gambit?"

Beth nodded, but was afraid to speak. She hadn't slept at all the night before, and very little for nights before that. Last night she had heard Fergussen talking and laughing with the lady at Reception; his heavy laughter had rolled down the corridor and under the doorway into the ward where she lay, stiff as steel, on her cot.

But one thing had happened—something unexpected. As she was about to leave with Mr. Ganz, Jolene came running up, gave Mr. Ganz one of her sly looks and said, "Can we talk for a second?" Mr. Ganz said it was okay, and Jolene took Beth hastily aside and handed her three green pills. "Here, honey," she said, "I can tell you need these." Then Jolene thanked Mr. Ganz and skipped off to class, her geography book under one thin arm.

But there was no chance to take the pills. Beth had them in her pocket right now, but she was afraid. Her mouth was dry. She knew she could pop them down and probably no one would notice. But she was frightened. They would be there soon. Her head was spinning.

The car stopped at a light. Across the intersection was a Pure Oil station with a big blue sign. Beth cleared her throat. "I need to go to the bathroom."

"We'll be there in ten minutes," Mr. Ganz said.

Beth shook her head firmly. "I can't wait."

Mr. Ganz shrugged. When the light changed, he drove across the intersection and into the gas station. Beth went in the room marked LADIES and locked the door behind her. It was a filthy place, with smear marks on the white tiles and a chipped basin. She ran the cold-water tap for a moment and put the pills in her mouth. Cupping her hand, she filled it with water and washed them down. Already she felt better.

It was a big classroom with three blackboards across the far wall. Printed in large capitals on the center board was WELCOME BETH HARMON! in white chalk, and on the wall above this were color photographs of President Eisenhower and Vice President Nixon. Most of the regular desks had been taken out of the room and were lined along the hallway wall outside; the rest had been pushed together at the far end. Three folding tables had been set up to make a U in the center of the room, and on each of these were four green-and-beige paper chessboards with plastic pieces. Metal chairs sat inside the U, facing the black pieces, but there were no chairs facing the white ones.

It had been twenty minutes since the stop at the Pure Oil station and she was no longer trembling, but her eyes smarted and her joints felt sore. She was wearing her navy pleated skirt and a white blouse with red letters spelling *Methuen* over the pocket.

There was no one in the room when they came in; Mr. Ganz had unlocked the door with a key from his pocket. After a minute a bell rang and there were the sounds of footsteps and some shouts in the hallway, and students began to come in. They were mostly boys. Big boys, as big as men; this was senior high. They wore sweaters and slouched with their hands in their pockets. Beth wondered for a moment where she was supposed to sit. But she couldn't sit if she was going to play them all at once; she would have to walk from board to board to make the moves. "Hey, Allan. Watch out!" one boy shouted to another, jerking his thumb toward Beth. Abruptly she saw herself as a small unimportant person—a plain, brown-haired orphan girl in dull institutional clothes. She was half the size of these easy, insolent students with their loud voices and bright sweaters. She felt powerless and silly. But then she looked at the boards again, with the pieces set in the familiar pattern, and the unpleasant feelings lessened. She might be out of place in this public high school, but she was not out of place with those twelve chessboards.

"Take your seats and be quiet, please." Mr. Ganz spoke with surprising authority. "Charles Levy will take Board Number One, since he's our top player. The rest can sit where they want to. There will be no talking during play."

Suddenly everyone was quiet, and they all began to look at Beth. She looked back at them, unblinking, and she felt rising in her a hatred as black as night.

She turned to Mr. Ganz. "Do I start now?" she asked.

"With Board Number One."

"And then I go to the next one?"

"That's right," he said. She realized that he hadn't even introduced her to the class. She stepped over to the first board, the one with Charles Levy sitting behind the black pieces. She reached out, picked up the king's pawn and moved it to the fourth rank.

The surprising thing was how badly they played. All of them. In the very first games of her life she had understood more than they did. They left backward pawns all over the place, and their pieces were wide open for forks. A few of them tried crude mating attacks. She brushed those aside like flies. She moved briskly from board to board, her stomach calm and her hand steady. At each board it took only a second's glance to read the position and see what was called for. Her responses were quick, sure and deadly. Charles Levy was supposed to be the best of them; she had his pieces tied up beyond help in a dozen moves; in six more she mated him on the back rank with a knight-rook combination.

Her mind was luminous, and her soul sang to her in the sweet moves of chess. The classroom smelled of chalk dust and her shoes squeaked as she moved down the rows of players. The room was silent; she felt her own presence centered in it, small and solid and in command. Outside, birds sang, but she did not hear them. Inside, some of the students stared at her. Boys came in from the hallway and lined up along the back wall to watch the homely girl from the orphanage at the edge of town who moved from player to player with the determined energy of a Caesar in the field, a Pavlova under the lights. There were about a dozen people watching. Some smirked and yawned, but others could feel the energy in the room, the presence of something that had never, in the long history of this tired old schoolroom, been felt there before.

What she did was at bottom shockingly trivial, but the energy of her amazing mind crackled in the room for those who knew how to listen. Her chess moves blazed with it. By the end of an hour and a half, she had beaten them all without a single false or wasted move.

She stopped and looked around her. Captured pieces sat in clusters beside each board. A few students were staring at her, but most avoided her eyes. There was scattered applause. She felt her cheeks flush; something in her reached out desperately toward the boards, the dead positions on them. There was nothing left there now. She was just a little girl again, without power.

Mr. Ganz presented her with a two-pound box of Whitman's chocolates and took her out to the car. Shirley got in without a word, careful not to touch against Beth in the back seat. They drove in silence back to the Methuen Home.

Five o'clock study hall was intolerable. She tried playing chess in her mind, but it seemed for once pale and meaningless after the afternoon at the high school. She tried reading Geography, since there was a test the next day, but the big book was practically all pictures, and the pictures meant little to her. Jolene was not in the room, and she was desperate to see Jolene, to see if there were any more pills. Every now and then she touched her blouse pocket with the palm of her hand in a kind of superstitious hope that she would feel the little hard surface of a pill. But there was nothing there.

Jolene was at supper, eating her Italian spaghetti, when Beth came in and picked up her tray. She went over to Jolene's table before getting her food. There was another black girl with her. Samantha, a new one. Jolene and she were talking.

Beth walked straight up to them and said to Jolene, "Have you got any more?"

Jolene frowned and shook her head. Then she said, "How was the exhibit? You do okay?"

"Okay," Beth said. "Haven't you got just one?"

"Honey," Jolene said, turning away, "I don't want to hear about it."

The Saturday afternoon movie in the library was *The Robe*. It had Victor Mature in it and was spiritual; all the staff was there, sitting attentive in a special row of chairs at the back, near the shuddering projector. Beth kept her eyes nearly shut during the first half-hour; they were red and sore. She had not slept at all on Thursday night and had dozed off for only an hour or so Friday. Her stomach was knotted, and there was the vinegar taste in her throat. She slouched in her folding chair with her hand in her skirt pocket, feeling the screwdriver she had put there in the morning. Walking into the boys' woodworking shop after breakfast, she took it from a bench. No one saw her do it. Now she squeezed it in her hand until her fingers hurt, took a deep breath, stood up and edged her way to the door. Mr. Fergussen was sitting there, proctoring.

"Bathroom," Beth whispered.

Mr. Fergussen nodded, his eyes on Victor Mature, bare-chested in the arena.

She walked purposively down the narrow hallway, over the wavy places in the faded linoleum, past the girls' room and down to the Multi-Purpose Room, with its *Christian Endeavour* magazines and *Reader's Digest* Condensed Books and, against the far wall, the padlocked window that said PHARMACY.

There were some small wooden stools in the room; she picked up one of them. There was no one around. She could hear gladiatorial shouts from the movie in the library but nothing else except her footsteps. They sounded very loud.

She set the stool in front of the window and climbed onto it. This put her face on a level with the hasp and padlock, at the top. The window itself, made of frosted glass with chicken wire in it, was framed in wood. The wood had been thickly painted with white enamel. Beth examined the screws that held the painted hasp. There was paint in their slots. She frowned, and her heart began to beat faster.

During the rare times when Daddy had been home, and sober, he had liked to do little jobs around the house. The house was an old one, in a poorer part of town, and there was heavy paint on the woodwork. Beth, five and six years old, had helped Daddy take the old switch plates and outlet plates off the walls with his big screwdriver. She was good at it, and Daddy praised her for it. "You catch on real quick, sweetiepie," he said. She had never been happier. But when there was paint in the screw slots he would say, "Let Daddy fix that for you," and would do something to get the screw head ready so that all she had to do was put the blade in the slot and turn. But what did he do to get that paint away? And which way should you turn the screwdriver? For a moment she almost choked in a sudden flush of inadequacy. The shouts from the film arena rose to a roar, and the volume of the frenetic music rose with it. She could get down off the stool and go back and take her seat.

But if she did that, she would go on feeling the way she felt now. She would have to lie in bed at night with the light from under the door in her face and the sounds from the corridor in her ears and the bad taste in her mouth, and there would be no relief, no ease in her body. She took the screwdriver handle and banged the two big screwheads with it. Nothing happened. She gritted her teeth and thought hard. Then she nodded grimly, took a fresh purchase on the screwdriver, and using the corner of its blade, began to chisel out the paint. That was what Daddy had done. She pressed with both hands, keeping her feet firmly on the stool, and pushed along the slot. Some paint chipped loose, exposing the brass of the screw. She kept pushing with the sharp corner and more came loose. Then a big flake of paint fell off, and the slot was exposed.

She took the screwdriver in her right hand, put the blade carefully in the slot and turned—to the left, the way Daddy had taught her. She remembered it now. She was good at remembering. She twisted as hard as she could. Nothing happened. She took the screwdriver away from the slot, gripped it in both hands and put the blade back in. Then she hunched her shoulders together and twisted until her hands felt sharp pains in them. And suddenly something squeaked, and the screw loosened. She kept twisting until she could take it out the rest of the way with her finger and put it in her blouse pocket. Then she went to work on the other screw. The part of the hasp she was working on was supposed to be held by four screws—one at each corner—but only two had been put in. She had noticed this during the past several days, just as she had checked every day at Vitamin Time to see if the green pills were still there in the big jar.

She put the other screw in her pocket, and the end of the hasp came loose by itself, with the big padlock still hanging there, the other end supported by the screws that held it to the window frame. It had not taken her long to understand that you would have to remove only half a hasp, not both halves, the way it had looked at first.

She pulled open the window, leaning back so it could go by her, and put her head inside. The light bulb was off, but she could see the outline of the big jar. She put her arms inside the opening, and standing on tiptoe, pushed herself as far forward as she could. That put her belly on the sill of the window. She began to wriggle, and her feet came away from the stool. There was a slightly sharp edge along the window sill, and it felt as though it were cutting her. She ignored it and kept on wriggling, doing it methodically, inching forward. She both felt and heard her blouse ripping. She ignored it; she had another blouse in her locker and could change.

Now her hands touched the cool, smooth surface of a metal table. That was the narrow white table Mr. Fergussen stood against when he gave them their medicine. She inched forward again, and her weight came down on her hands. There were some boxes there. She pushed them aside, clearing a place for herself. Now it was easier to move. She let her weight come forward with the sill under her hips until it scraped the tops of her legs and she was able to let herself flop onto the table, twisting herself at the last second so she wouldn't fall off it. She was inside! She took a couple of deep breaths and climbed down. There was enough light for her to see all right. She walked over to the far wall of the tiny room and stopped, facing the dimly visible jar. It had a glass cover. She lifted this and set it silently on the table. Then she slowly reached inside with both hands. Her fingertips touched the smooth surface of tens of pills, hundreds of pills. She pushed her hand deeper, burying them up to the wrists. She breathed in deeply and held her breath for a long time. Finally she let it out in a sigh and removed her right hand with a fistful of pills. She did not count them, simply put them in her mouth and swallowed until they had all gone down.

Then she stuffed three handfuls of pills in her skirt pocket. On the wall to the right of the window was a Dixie cup dispenser. She was able to reach it by standing on tiptoe and stretching. She took four paper cups. She had decided on that number the night before. She carried them over, stacked, to the table that held the pill jar, set them down neatly, and filled them one at a time. Then she stood back and looked at the jar. The level had dropped to almost half what it had been. The problem seemed insoluble. She would have to wait and see what happened.

Leaving the cups, she went to the door that Mr. Fergussen used when he went to do pharmacy duty. She would leave that way, unlocking it from the inside, and make two trips to carry the pills to the metal stand by her bed. She had a nearly empty Kleenex box to put them in. She would spread a few sheets of Kleenex on top and put the box in the bottom of her enameled nightstand, under her clean underwear and socks.

But the door would not open. It was locked in some serious way. She examined the knob and latch, feeling carefully with her hands. There was a thick, heavy sensation at the back of her throat as she did this, and her arms were numb, like the arms of a dead person. What she had suspected when the door wouldn't open turned out to be true: you had to have a key even from the inside. And she could not climb back out the little window carrying four Dixie cups full of tranquilizers.

She grew frantic. They would miss her at the movie. Fergussen would be looking for her. The projector would break down and all the children would be sent into the Multi-Purpose Room, with Fergussen monitoring them, and here she would be. But deeper than that, she felt trapped, the same wretched, heart-stopping sensation she had felt when she was taken from home and put in this institution and made to sleep in a ward with twenty strangers and hear noises all night long that were, in a way, as bad as the shouting at home, when Daddy and Mother were there—the shouting from the brightly lit kitchen. Beth had slept in the dining room on a folding cot. She felt trapped then, too, and her arms were numb. There was a big space under the door that separated dining room from kitchen; the light had streamed in under it, along with the shouted words.

She gripped the doorknob and stood still for a long moment, breathing shallowly. Then her heart began beating almost normally again and feeling came back into her arms and hands. She could always get out by climbing through the window. She had a pocket full of pills. She could set the Dixie cups on the white table inside the window and then, when she was back on the stool outside, she could reach in and take them out, one at a time. She could visualize it all, like a chess position.

She carried the cups over to the table. She had begun to sense in herself an enormous calm, like the calm she had felt that day at the high school when she knew she was unbeatable. When she set down the fourth cup she turned and looked back at the glass jar. Fergussen would know that pills had been stolen. That could not be hidden. Sometimes her father had said, "In for a dime, in for a dollar."

She took the jar over to the table and poured the contents of the Dixie cups back into it, stepped back and checked. It would be simple to lean over from the outside and lift the jar out. She knew, too, where she could hide it, on the shelf of a disused janitors' closet in the girls' room. There was an old galvanized bucket up there that was never used; the jar would fit into it. There was also a short ladder in the closet, and she could use it safely because a person could lock the door on the girls' room from the inside. Then, if there was a search for the missing pills, even if they found them, they couldn't be traced to her. She would take only a few at a time and wouldn't tell anyone—not even Jolene.

The pills she had gulped down a few minutes before were beginning to reach her mind. All of her nervousness had vanished. With clear purposefulness, she climbed up on Mr. Fergussen's white table, put her head out the window and looked around her at the still-empty room. The jar of pills was a few inches from her left knee. She wriggled her way through the window and onto the stool. Standing up high there, she felt calm, powerful, in charge of her life.

She leaned forward dreamily and took the jar by its rim in both hands. A fine relaxation had spread through her body. She let herself go limp, staring down into the depths of green pills. Stately music came from the movie in the Library. Her toes were still on the stool and her body was loosely jackknifed over the window ledge; she no longer felt the sharp edge. She was like a limp rag doll. As her eyes lost focus, the green became a bright luminous blur.

"*Elizabeth!*" The voice seemed to come from a place inside her head. "*Elizabeth!*" She blinked. It was a woman's voice, harsh, like Mother's. She did not look around. Her fingers and thumbs on the side of the jar had gone loose. She squeezed them together and picked up the jar. She felt herself moving in slow motion, like slow motion in a movie where someone falls from a horse at a rodeo and you see him float gently to the ground as though it could not hurt at all. She lifted the jar with both hands and turned, and the bottom of the jar hit the window ledge with a dull ringing sound and her wrists twisted and the jar came loose from her hands and exploded on the edge of the stool at her feet. The fragments, mixed with hundreds of green pellets, cascaded to the linoleum floor. Bits of glass caught light like rhinestones and lay in place shivering while the green pills rolled outward like a bright waterfall toward Mrs. Deardorff. Mrs. Deardorff was standing a few feet away from her, saying, "Elizabeth!" over and over again. After what seemed a long time, the pills stopped moving.

Behind Mrs. Deardorff was Mr. Fergussen in his white pants and T-shirt. Next to him stood Mr. Schell, and just behind them, crowding to see what had happened, were the other children, some of them still blinking from the movie that had just ended. Every person in the room was staring at her, high on the miniature stage of her stool with her hands a foot apart as though she were still holding the glass jar.

Fergussen rode with her in the brown staff car and carried her into the hospital to the little room where the lights were bright and they made her swallow a gray rubber tube. It was easy. Nothing mattered. She could still see the green mound of pills in the jar. There were strange things happening inside her, but it didn't matter. She fell asleep and woke only for a moment when someone pushed a hypodermic needle in her arm. She did not know how long she was there, but she did not spend the night. Fergussen drove her back the same evening. She sat in the front seat now, awake and unworried. The hospital was on the campus, where Fergussen was a graduate student; he pointed out the Psychology Building as they drove past it. "That's where I go to school," he said.

She merely nodded. She pictured Fergussen as a student, taking true-false tests and holding his hand up when he wanted to leave the room. She had never liked him before, had thought of him as just one of the others.

"Jesus, kid," he said, "I thought Deardorff would *explode.*"

She watched the trees go by outside the car window.

"How many did you take? Twenty?"

"I didn't count."

He laughed. "Enjoy 'em," he said. "It'll be cold turkey tomorrow."

At Methuen she went directly to bed and slept deeply for twelve hours. In the morning, after breakfast, Fergussen, once again his usual distant self, told her to go to Mrs. Deardorff's office. Surprisingly, she wasn't afraid. The pills had worn off, but she felt rested and calm. While getting dressed she had made an extraordinary discovery. Deep in the pocket of her serge skirt, survivors of her being caught, her trip to the hospital, her undressing and then dressing again, were twenty-three tranquilizers. She had to take her toothbrush out of its holder to get them all in.

Mrs. Deardorff kept her waiting almost an hour. Beth didn't care. She read in *National Geographic* about a tribe of Indians who lived in the holes of cliffs. Brown people with black hair and bad teeth. In the pictures there were children everywhere, often snuggled up against the older people. It was all strange; she had never been touched very much by older people, except for punishment. She did not let herself think about Mrs. Deardorff's razor strop. If Deardorff was going to use it, she could take it. Somehow she sensed that what she had been caught doing was of a magnitude beyond usual punishment. And, deeper than that, she was aware of the complicity of the orphanage that had fed her and all the others on pills that would make them less restless, easier to deal with.

Mrs. Deardorff did not invite her to sit. Mr. Schell was seated on Mrs. Deardorff's little blue chintz sofa, and in the red armchair sat Miss Lonsdale. Miss Lonsdale was in charge of chapel. Before she had started slipping off to play chess on Sundays, Beth had listened to some of Miss Lonsdale's chapel talks. They were about Christian service and about how bad dancing and Communism were, as well as some other things Miss Lonsdale was not specific about.

"We have been discussing your case for the past hour, Elizabeth," Mrs. Deardorff said. Her eyes, fixed on Beth, were cold and dangerous.

Beth watched her and said nothing. She felt something was going on that was like chess. In chess you did not let on what your next move would be.

"Your behavior has come as a profound shock to all of us. Nothing"—for a moment the muscles at the sides of Deardorff's jaw stood out like steel cables—"*nothing* in the history of the Methuen Home has been so deplorable. It must not happen again."

Mr. Schell spoke up. "We are terribly disappointed—"

"I can't sleep without the pills," Beth said.

There was a startled silence. No one had expected her to speak. Then Mrs. Deardorff said, "All the more reason why you should not have them." But there was something odd in her voice, as though she were frightened.

"You shouldn't have given them to us in the first place," Beth said.

"*I will not have back talk from a child,*" Mrs. Deardorff said. She stood up and leaned across the desk toward Beth. "If you speak to me like that again, you will regret it."

The breath caught in Beth's throat. Mrs. Deardorff's body seemed enormous. Beth drew back as though she had touched something white hot.

Mrs. Deardorff sat down and adjusted her glasses. "Your library and playground privileges have been suspended. You will not attend the Saturday movies and you will be in bed promptly at eight o'clock in the evenings. Do you understand?"

Beth nodded.

"*Answer me.*"

"Yes."

"You will be in chapel thirty minutes early and will be responsible for setting up the chairs. If you are in any way remiss in this, Miss Lonsdale has been instructed to report to me. If you are seen whispering to another child in chapel or in any class, you will automatically be given ten demerits." Mrs. Deardorff paused. "You understand the meaning of ten demerits, Elizabeth?"

Beth nodded.

"Answer me."

"Yes."

"Elizabeth, Miss Lonsdale informs me that you have often left chapel for long periods. That will end. You will remain in chapel for the full ninety minutes on Sundays. You will write a summary of each Sunday's talk and have it on my desk by Monday morning." Mrs. Deardorff leaned back in the wooden desk chair and folded her hands across her lap. "And Elizabeth . . ."

Beth looked at her carefully. "Yes, ma'am."

Mrs. Deardorff smiled grimly. "No more chess."

The next morning Beth went to the Vitamin Line after breakfast. She could see that the hasp had been replaced on the window and that this time there were screws in all four of the holes at each side of the padlock.

When she came up to the window Fergussen looked at her and grinned. "Want to help yourself?" he said.

She shook her head and held her hand out for the vitamin pills. He handed them to her and said, "Take it easy, Harmon." His voice was pleasant; she had never heard him speak that way at vitamin time before.

Miss Lonsdale wasn't too bad. She seemed embarrassed at having Beth report to her at nine-thirty, and she showed her nervously how to unfold and set out the chairs, helping her with the first two rows of them. Beth was able to handle it easily enough, but listening to Miss Lonsdale talk about godless communism and the way it was spreading in the United States was pretty bad. Beth was sleepy, and she hadn't had time to finish breakfast. But she had to pay attention so she could write her report. She listened to Miss Londsdale talk on in her deadly serious way about how we all had to be careful, that communism was like a disease and could infect you. It wasn't clear to Beth what communism was. Something wicked people believed in, in other countries, like being Nazis and torturing Jews by the millions.

If Mrs. Deardorff hadn't told him, Mr. Shaibel would be expecting her. She wanted to be there to play chess, to try the King's Gambit against him. Maybe Mr. Ganz would be back with someone form the chess club for her to play. She let herself think of this only for a moment and her heart seemed to fill. She wanted to run. She felt her eyes smarting.

She blinked and shook her head and went on listening to Miss Lonsdale, who was talking now about Russia, a terrible place to be.

"You should've *saw* yourself," Jolene said. "Up on that stool. Just floating around up there and Deardorff hollering at you."

"It felt funny."

"Shit, I bet. I bet it felt *good.*" Jolene leaned a little closer. "How many of them downers you take, anyhow?"

"Thirty."

Jolene stared at her. "*She-it!*" she said.

It was difficult to sleep without the pills, but not impossible. Beth saved the few she had for emergencies and decided that if she had to stay awake for several hours every night, she would spend the time learning the Sicilian Defense. There were fifty-seven printed pages on the Sicilian in *Modern Chess Openings,* with a hundred and seventy different lines stemming from P-QB4. She would memorize and play through them all in her mind at night. When that was done and she knew all the variations, she could go on to the Pirć and the Nimzovitch and the Ruy Lopez. *Modern Chess Openings* was a thick, dense book. She would be all right.

Leaving Geography class one day, she saw Mr. Shaibel at the end of the long hallway. He had a metal bucket on wheels with him and was mopping. The students were all going the other way, to the door that led to the yard for recess. She walked down to him, stopping where the floor was wet. She stood for about a minute until he looked up at her.

"I'm sorry," she said. "They won't let me play anymore."

He frowned and nodded but said nothing.

"I'm being punished. I . . ." She looked at his face. It registered nothing. "I wish I could play more with you."

He looked for a moment as if he was going to speak. But instead he turned his eyes to the floor, bent his fat body slightly and went back to mopping. Beth could suddenly taste something sour in her mouth. She turned and walked back down the hall.

Jolene said there were always adoptions around Christmas. The year after they stopped Beth from playing chess there were two in early December. Both pretty ones, Beth thought to herself. "Both white," Jolene said aloud.

The two beds stayed empty for a while. Then one morning before breakfast Fergussen came into the Girls' Ward. Some of the girls giggled to see him there with the heavy bunch of keys at his belt. He came up to Beth, who was putting on her socks. It was near her tenth birthday. She got her second sock on and looked up at him.

He frowned. "We got a new place for you, Harmon. Follow me."

She went with him across the ward, over to the far wall. One of the empty beds was there, under the window. It was a bit larger than the others and had more space around it.

"You can put your things in the nightstand," Fergussen said. He looked at her for a minute. "It'll be nicer over here."

She stood there, amazed. It was the best bed in the ward. Fergussen was making a note on a clipboard. She reached out and touched his forearm with her fingertips, where the dark hairs grew, above his wristwatch. "Thank you," she said.

Chapter 3

"I see that you will be thirteen in two months, Elizabeth," Mrs. Deardorff said.

"Yes, ma'am." Beth was seated in the straight-backed chair in front of Mrs. Deardorff 's desk. Fergussen had come and taken her from study hall. It was eleven in the morning. She had not been in this office for over three years.

The lady on the sofa suddenly spoke up, with strained cheerfulness. "Twelve is such a wonderful age!" she said.

The lady wore a blue cardigan over a silky dress. She would have been pretty except for all the rouge and lipstick and for the nervous way she worked her mouth when she talked. The man sitting next to here wore a gray salt-and-pepper tweed suit with a vest.

"Elizabeth has performed well in all her schoolwork," Mrs. Deardorff went on. "She is at the top of her class in Reading and Arithmetic."

"That's so nice!" the lady said. "I was such a scatterbrain at Arithmetic." She smiled at Beth brightly. "I'm Mrs. Wheatley," she added in a confidential tone.

The man cleared his throat and said nothing. He looked as if he wanted to be somewhere else.

Beth nodded at the lady's remark but could think of nothing to say. Why had they brought her here?

Mrs. Deardorff went on about Beth's schoolwork while the lady in the blue cardigan paid rapt attention. Mrs. Deardorff said nothing about the green pills or about Beth's chess playing; her voice seemed filled with a distant approval of Beth. When she had finished there was an embarrassed silence for a while. Then the man cleared his throat again, shifted his weight uneasily and looked toward Beth as though he were looking over the top of her head. "Do they call you Elizabeth?" He sounded as if there were a bubble of air in his throat. "Or is it Betty?"

She looked at him. "Beth," she said. "I'm called Beth."

During the next few weeks she forgot about the visit in Mrs. Deardorff's office and absorbed herself in schoolwork and in reading. She had found a set of girls' books and was reading through them whenever she had a chance—in study halls, at night in bed, on Sunday afternoons. They were about the adventures of the oldest daughter in a big, haphazard family. Six months before, Methuen had gotten a TV set for the lounge, and it was played for an hour every evening. But Beth found that she preferred Ellen Forbes's adventures to *I Love Lucy* and *Gunsmoke*. She would sit up in bed, alone in the dormitory, and read until lights out. No one bothered her.

One evening in mid-September she was alone reading when Fergussen came in. "Shouldn't you be packing?" he asked.

She closed her book, using her thumb to keep her place. "Why?"

"They haven't told you?"

"Told me what?"

"You've been adopted. You're being picked up after breakfast."

She just sat there on the edge of the bed, staring at Fergussen's broad white T-shirt.

"Jolene," she said, "I can't find my book."

"What book?" Jolene said sleepily. It was just before lights out.

"*Modern Chess Openings,* with a red cover. I keep it in my nightstand."

Jolene shook her head. "Beats the shit out of me."

Beth hadn't looked at the book for weeks, but she clearly remembered putting it at the bottom of the second drawer. She had a brown nylon valise beside her on the bed; it was packed with her three dresses and four sets of underwear, her toothbrush, comb, a bar of Dial soap, two barrettes and some plain cotton handkerchiefs. Her nightstand was now completely empty. She had looked in the library for her book, but it wasn't there. There was nowhere else to look. She had not played a game of chess in three years except in her mind, but *Modern Chess Openings* was the only thing she owned that she cared about.

She squinted at Jolene. "You didn't see it, did you?"

Jolene looked angry for a moment. "Watch who you go accusing," she said. "I got no use for a book like that." Then her voice softened. "I hear you're leaving."

"That's right."

Jolene laughed. "What's the matter? Don't want to go?"

"I don't know."

Jolene slipped under the bedsheet and pulled it up over her shoulders. "Just say 'Yes, sir' and 'Yes, ma'am' and you'll do all right. Tell 'em you're grateful to have a Christian home like theirs and maybe they'll give you a TV in your room."

There was something odd about the way Jolene was talking.

"Jolene," Beth said, "I'm sorry."

"Sorry about what?"

"I'm sorry you didn't get adopted."

Jolene snorted. "Shit," she said, "I make out fine right here." She rolled over away from Beth and curled up in bed. Beth started to reach out toward her, but just then Miss Furth stepped in the doorway and said, "Lights out, girls!" Beth went back to her bed, for the last time.

The next day Mrs. Deardorff went with them out to the parking lot and stood by the car while Mr. Wheatley got into the driver's seat and Mrs. Wheatley and Beth got into the back. "Be a good girl, Elizabeth," Mrs. Deardorff said.

Beth nodded and as she did so saw that someone was standing behind Mrs. Deardorff on the porch of the Administration Building. It was Mr. Shaibel. He had his hands stuffed in his coverall pockets and was looking toward the car. She wanted to get out and go over to him, but Mrs. Deardorff was in the way, so she leaned back in her seat. Mrs. Wheatley began talking, and Mr. Wheatley started the car.

As they pulled out, Beth twisted around in her seat and waved out the back window at him, but he made no response. She could not tell for sure if he had seen her or not.

"You should have seen their faces," Mrs. Wheatley said. She was wearing the same blue cardigan, but this time she had a faded gray dress under it, and her nylons were rolled down to her ankles. "They looked in all my closets and even inspected the refrigerator. I could see immediately that they were impressed with my provisions. Have some more of the tuna casserole. I certainly enjoy watching a young child eat."

Beth put a little more on her plate. The problem was that it was too salty, but she hadn't said anything about that. It was her first meal at the Wheatleys'. Mr. Wheatley had already left for Denver on business and would be away for several weeks. A photograph of him sat on the upright piano by the heavily draped dining-room window. In the living room the TV was playing unattended; a deep male voice was declaiming about Anacin.

Mr. Wheatley had driven them to Lexington in silence and then gone immediately upstairs. He came down after a few minutes with a suitcase, kissed Mrs. Wheatley distractedly on the cheek, nodded a goodbye to Beth and left.

"They wanted to know everything about us. How much money Allston makes a month. Why we have no children of our own. They even inquired"—Mrs. Wheatley bent forward over the Pyrex dish and spoke in a stage whisper—"they even inquired if I had been in psychiatric care." She leaned back and let out her breath. "Can you imagine? Can you imagine?"

"No, ma'am," Beth said, filling in the sudden silence. She took another forkful of tuna and followed it with a drink of water.

"They are *thorough,*" Mrs. Wheatley said. "But, you know, I suppose they have to be." She had not touched anything on her plate. During the two hours since they arrived, Mrs. Wheatley had spent the time jumping up from whatever chair she was sitting in and going to check the oven or adjust one of the Rosa Bonheur prints on the walls, or empty her ashtray. She chattered almost constantly while Beth put in an occasional "Yes, ma'am" or "No, ma'am." Beth had not yet been shown her room; her brown nylon bag still sat by the front door next to the overflowing magazine rack where she had left it at ten-thirty that morning.

"God knows," Mrs. Wheatley was saying, "God knows they have to be meticulous about whom they turn their charges over to. You can't have scoundrels taking the responsibility for a growing child."

Beth set her fork down carefully. "May I go to the bathroom, please?"

"Why, certainly." She pointed to the living room with her fork. Mrs. Wheatley had been holding the fork all during lunch, even though she had eaten nothing. "The white door to the left of the sofa."

Beth got up, squeezed past the piano that practically filled the small dining room and went into the living room and through its clutter of coffee table and lamp tables and huge rosewood TV, now showing an afternoon drama. She walked carefully across the Orlon shag carpet and into the bathroom. The bathroom was tiny and completely done in robin's-egg blue—the same shade as Mrs. Wheatley's cardigan. It had a blue carpet and little blue guest towels and a blue toilet seat. Even the toilet paper was blue. Beth lifted the toilet seat, vomited the tunafish into the bowl and flushed it.

*　　　*　　　*

When they got to the top of the stairs Mrs. Wheatley rested for a moment, leaning her hip against the banister and breathing heavily. Then she took a few steps along the carpeted hallway and dramatically pushed a door open. "This," she said, "will be your room." Since it was a small house, Beth had visualized something tiny for herself, but when she walked in she caught her breath. It looked enormous to her. The floor was bare and painted gray, with a pink oval rug at the side of the double bed. She had never had a room of her own before. She stood, holding her valise, and looked around her. There was a dresser, and a desk whose orange-looking wood matched it, with a pink glass lamp on it, and a pink chenille bedspread on the enormous bed. "You have no *idea* how difficult it is to find good maple furniture," Mrs. Wheatley was saying, "but I think I did very well, if I do say so myself." Beth hardly heard her. This room was *hers*. She looked at the heavily painted white door; there was a key in it, under the knob. She could lock the door and no one could come in.

Mrs. Wheatley showed her where the bathroom was down the hall and then left her alone to unpack, closing the door behind her. Beth set down her bag and walked around, stopping only briefly look out each of the windows at the tree-lined street below. There was a closet, bigger than Mother's had been, and a nightstand by the bed, with a little reading lamp. It was a beautiful room. If only Jolene could see it. For a moment she felt like crying for Jolene, she wanted Jolene to be there, going around the room with her while they looked at all the furniture and then hung Beth's clothes in the closet.

In the car Mrs. Wheatley had said how glad they were to have an older child. Then why not adopt Jolene? Beth had thought. But she said nothing. She looked at Mr. Wheatley with his grim-set jaw and his two pale hands on the steering wheel and then at Mrs. Wheatley and she knew they would never have adopted Jolene.

Beth sat on the bed and shook off the memory. It was a wonderfully soft bed, and it smelled clean and fresh. She bent over and pulled off her shoes and lay back, stretching out on its great, comforting expanse, turning her head happily to look over at the tightly closed door that gave her this room entirely to herself.

She lay awake for several hours that night, not wanting to go to sleep right away. There was a streetlight outside her windows, but they had good, heavy shades that she could pull down to block it out. Before saying goodnight, Mrs. Wheatley had shown Beth her own room. It was on the other side of the hall and exactly the same size as Beth's, but it had a television set in it and chairs with slipcovers and a blue coverlet on the bed. "It's really a remodeled attic," Mrs. Wheatley said.

Lying in bed, Beth could hear the distant sound of Mrs. Wheatley coughing and later she heard her bare feet padding down the hallway to the bathroom. But she didn't mind. Her own door was closed and locked. No one could push it open and let the light fall on her face. Mrs. Wheatley was alone in her own room, and there would be no sounds of talking or quarreling—only music and low synthetic voices from the television set. It would be wonderful to have Jolene there, but then she wouldn't have the room to herself, wouldn't be able to lie alone in this huge bed, stretched out in the middle of it, having the cool sheets and now the silence to herself.

On Monday she went to school. Mrs. Wheatley took her in a taxi, even though it was less than a mile. Beth went into seventh grade. It was a lot like the public high school in that other town where she had done the chess exhibition, and she knew her clothes weren't right, but no one paid much attention to her. A few of the other students stared for a minute when the teacher introduced her to the class, but that was it. She was given books and assigned to a home room. From the books and what the teachers said in class she knew it would be easy. She recoiled a bit at the loud noises in the hallways between classes, and felt self-conscious a few times when other students looked at her, but it was not difficult. She felt she could deal with anything that might come up in this sunny, noisy public school.

At lunchtime she tried to sit alone in the cafeteria with her ham sandwich and carton of milk, but another girl came and sat across from her. Neither of them spoke for a while. The other girl was plain, like Beth.

When she had finished half her sandwich Beth looked across the table at her. "Is there a school chess club?" she asked.

The other girl looked up, startled. "What?"

"Do they have a chess club? I want to join."

"Oh," the girl said. "I don't think they have anything like that. You can try out for junior cheerleader."

Beth finished her sandwich.

"You certain spend a lot of time at your studies," Mrs. Wheatley said. "Don't you have any hobbies?" Actually, Beth was not studying; she was reading a novel from the school library. She was sitting in the armchair in her room, by the window. Mrs. Wheatley had knocked and then come in, wearing a pink chenille bathrobe and pink satin slippers. She walked over and sat on the edge of Beth's bed, smiling at her distractedly, as though she were thinking about something else. Beth had lived with her a week now and she noticed that Mrs. Wheatley was often that way.

"I used to play chess," Beth said.

Mrs. Wheatley blinked. "Chess?"

"I like it a lot."

Mrs. Wheatley shook her head as though shaking something out of her hair. "Oh, *chess!*" she said. "The royal game. How nice."

"Do you play?" Beth said.

"Oh, Lord, no!" Mrs. Wheatley said with a self-deprecating laugh. "I haven't the mind for it. But my father used to play. My father was a surgeon and quite refined in his ways; I believe he was a superior chess player in his time."

"Could I play chess with him?"

"Hardly," Mrs. Wheatley said. "My father passed on years ago."

"Is there anyone I could play with?"

"Play chess? I have no idea." Mrs. Wheatley peered at her for a moment. "Isn't it primarily a game for boys?"

"Girls play," she said.

"How nice!" But Mrs. Wheatley was clearly miles away.

Mrs. Wheatley spent two days getting the house cleaned for Miss Farley, and she sent Beth to brush her hair three times on the morning of the visit.

When Miss Farley came in the door she was followed by a tall man wearing a football jacket. Beth was shocked to see it was Fergussen. He looked mildly embarrassed. "Hi there, Harmon," he said. "I invited myself along." He walked into Mrs. Wheatley's living room and stood there with his hands in his pockets.

Miss Farley had a set of forms and a check list. She wanted to know about Beth's diet and her schoolwork and what plans she had for the summer. Mrs. Wheatley did most of the talking. Beth could see her become more expansive with each question. "You can have no idea," Mrs. Wheatley said, "of how marvelously well Beth has adjusted to the school environment. Her teachers have been immensely impressed with her work . . ."

Beth could not remember any conversations between Mrs. Wheatley and the teachers at school, but she said nothing.

"I had hoped to see Mr. Wheatley, too," Miss Farley said. "Will he be here soon?"

Mrs. Wheatley smiled at her. "Allston called earlier to say he was terribly sorry, but he couldn't come. He's really been working so hard." She looked over at Beth, still smiling. "Allston is a marvelous provider."

"Is he able to spend much time with Beth?" Miss Farley said.

"Why, of *course*!" Mrs. Wheatley said. "Allston is a wonderful father to her."

Shocked, Beth looked down at her hands. Not even Jolene could lie so well. For a moment she had believed it herself, had seen an image of a helpful, fatherly Allston Wheatley—an Allston Wheatley who did not exist outside of Mrs. Wheatley's words. But then she remembered the real one, grim, distant and silent. And there had been no call from him.

During the hour they were there, Fergussen said almost nothing. When they got up to leave, he held out his hand to Beth and her heart sank. "Good to see you, Harmon," he said. She took his hand to shake it, wishing that he could stay behind somehow, to be with her.

A few days later Mrs. Wheatley took her downtown to shop for clothes. When the bus stopped at their corner, Beth stepped into it without hesitation, even though it was the first time she'd ever been on a bus. It was a warm fall Saturday, and Beth was uncomfortable in her Methuen wool skirt and could hardly wait to get a new one. She began to count the blocks to downtown.

They got off at the seventeenth corner. Mrs. Wheatley took her hand, although it was hardly necessary, and ushered her across a few yards of busy sidewalks into the revolving doors of Ben Snyder's Department Store. It was ten in the morning and the aisles were full of women carrying big dark purses and shopping bags. Mrs. Wheatley walked through the crowd with the sureness of an expert. Beth followed.

Before they looked at anything to wear, Mrs. Wheatley took her down the broad stairs to the basement, where she spent twenty minutes at a counter with what a card said were "Dinner Napkin Irregulars," putting together six blue ones from the multicolored pile, rejecting dozens in the process. She waited while Mrs. Wheatley assembled her set in a kind of mesmerized trial and error and then decided she didn't really need napkins. They went to another counter with "Book Bargains" on it. Mrs. Wheatley read out the titles of a great many thirty-nine-cent books, picked up several and leafed through them but didn't buy any.

Finally they took the escalator back to the main floor. There they stopped at a perfume counter so Mrs. Wheatley could spray one wrist with Evening in Paris and the other with Emeraude. "All right, dear," Mrs. Wheatley said finally, "we'll go up to four." She smiled at Beth. "Young Ladies' Ready-to-Wear."

Between the third and fourth floors Beth looked back and saw a sign on a counter that said BOOKS AND GAMES, and right near the sign, on a glass-topped counter, were three chess sets. "Chess!" she said, tugging Mrs. Wheatley's sleeve.

"What is it?" Mrs. Wheatley said, clearly annoyed.

"They sell chess sets," Beth said. "Can we go back?"

"Not so *loud,*" Mrs. Wheatley said. "We'll go by on the way back down."

But they didn't. Mrs. Wheatley spent the rest of the morning having Beth try on coats from marked-down racks and turn around to show her the hemline and go over near the window so she could see the fabric by "natural light," and finally buying one and insisting they go down by elevator.

"Aren't we going to look at the chess sets?" Beth said, but Mrs. Wheatley didn't answer. Beth's feet hurt, and she was perspiring. She did not like the coat she was carrying in a cardboard box. It was the same robin's-egg blue as Mrs. Wheatley's omnipresent sweater, and it didn't fit. Beth did not know much about clothes, but she could tell that this store sold cheap ones.

When the elevator stopped at the third floor, Beth started to remind her about the chess sets, but the door closed and they went down to the main floor. Mrs. Wheatley took Beth's hand and led her across the street to the bus stop, complaining about the difficulty of finding anything these days. "But after all," she said philosophically as the bus drew up to the corner, "we got what we came for."

The next week in English class some girls behind Beth were talking before the teacher came in. "Did you get those shoes at Ben Snyder's or something?" one of them said.

"I wouldn't be caught dead in Ben Snyder's," the other girl said, laughing.

Beth walked to school every morning, along shady streets of quiet houses with trees on their lawns. Other students went the same way, and Beth recognized some of them, but she always walked alone. She had enrolled two weeks late in the fall term, and after her fourth week, mid-term exams began. On Tuesday she had no tests in the morning and was supposed to go to her home room. Instead she took the bus downtown, carrying her notebook and the forty cents she had saved from her quarter-a-week allowance. She had her change ready when she got on the bus.

The chess sets were still on the counter, but up close she could see that they weren't very good. When she picked up the white queen she was surprised at how light it was. She turned it over. It was hollow inside and made of plastic. She put it back as the saleswoman came up and said, "May I help you?"

"Do you have *Modern Chess Openings*?"

"We have chess and checkers and backgammon," the woman said, "and a variety of children's games."

"It's a book," Beth said, "about chess."

"The book department is across the aisle."

Beth went to the bookshelves and began looking through them. There was nothing about chess. There was no clerk to ask, either. She went back to the woman at the counter and had to wait a long time to get her attention. "I'm trying to find a book about chess," Beth told her.

"We don't handle books in this department," the woman said and started to turn away again.

"Is there a bookstore near here?" Beth asked quickly.

"Try Morris'." She went over to a stack of boxes and began straightening them.

"Where is it?"

The woman said nothing.

"Where's Morris', ma'am?" Beth said loudly.

The woman turned and looked at her furiously. "On Upper Street," she said.

"Where's Upper Street?"

The woman looked for a moment as if she would scream. Then her face relaxed and she said, "Two blocks up Main."

Beth took the escalators down.

Morris' was on a corner, next to a drugstore. Beth pushed open the door and found herself in a big room full of more books than she had ever seen in her life. There was a bald man sitting on a stool behind a counter, smoking a cigarette and reading. Beth walked up to him and said, "Do you have *Modern Chess Openings*?"

The man turned from his book and peered at her over his glasses. "That's an odd one," he said in a pleasant voice.

"Do you have it?"

"I think so." He got up from the stool and walked to the rear of the store. A minute later he came back to Beth, carrying it in his hand. It was the same fat book with the same red cover. She caught her breath when she saw it.

"Here you go," the man said, handing it to her. She took it and opened it to the art on the Sicilian Defense. It was good to see the names of the variations again; the Levenfish, the Dragon, the Najdorf. They were like incantations in her head, or the names of saints.

After a while she heard the man speaking to her. "Are you that serious about chess?"

"Yes," she said.

He smiled. "I thought that book was only for grandmasters."

Beth hesitated. "What's a grandmaster?"

"A genius player," the man said. "Like Capablanca, except that was a long time ago. There are others nowadays, but I don't know their names."

She had never seen anyone quite like this man before. He was very relaxed, and he talked to her as though she were another adult. Fergussen was the closest thing to him, but Fergussen was sometimes very official. "How much is the book?" Beth asked.

"Pretty much. Five ninety-five."

She had been afraid it would be something like that. After today's two bus fares she would have ten cents left. She held the book out to him and said, "Thank you. I can't afford it."

"Sorry," he said. "Just put it on the counter."

She set it down. "Do you have other books about chess?"

"Sure. Under Games and Sports. Go take a look."

At the back of the store was a whole shelf of them with titles like *Paul Morphy and the Golden Age of Chess; Winning Chess Traps; How to Improve Your Chess; Improved Chess Strategy.* She took down one called *Attack and Counterattack in Chess* and began reading the games, picturing them in her mind without reading the diagrams. She stood there for a long time while a few customers went in and out of the store. No one bothered her. She read through game after game and was surprised in some of them by dazzling moves—queen sacrifices and smothered mates. There were sixty games, and each had a title at the top of the page, like "V. Smyslov–I. Rudakavsky: Moscow 1945" or "A. Rubinstein–O. Duras: Vienna 1908." In that one, White queened a pawn on the thirty-sixth move by threatening a discovered check.

Beth looked at the cover of the book. It was smaller than *Modern Chess Openings* and there was a sticker on it that said $2.95. She began going through it systematically. The clock on the bookstore wall read ten-thirty. She would have to leave in an hour to get to school for the History exam. Up front the clerk was paying no attention to her, absorbed in his own reading. She began concentrating, and by eleven-thirty she had twelve of the games memorized.

On the bus back to school she began playing them over in her head. Behind some of the moves—not the glamorous ones like the queen sacrifices but sometimes only in the one-square advance of a pawn—she could see subtleties that made the small hairs on the back of her neck tingle.

She was five minutes late for the test, but no one seemed to care and she finished before everyone else anyway. In the twenty minutes until the end of the period she played "P. Keres–A. Tarnowski: Helsinki 1952." It was the Ruy Lopez Opening where White brought the bishop out in a way that Beth could see meant an indirect attack on Black's king pawn. On the thirty-fifth move White brought his rook down to the knight seven square in a shocking way that made Beth almost cry out in her seat.

Fairfield Junior High had social clubs that met for an hour after school and sometimes during home-room period on Fridays. There was the Apple Pi Club and the Sub Debs and Girls Around Town. They were like sororities at a college, and you had to be pledged. The girls in Apple Pi were eighth and ninth graders; most of them wore bright cashmere sweaters and fashionably scuffed saddle oxfords with argyle socks. Some of them lived in the country and owned horses. Thoroughbreds. Girls like that never looked at you in the hallways; they were always smiling at someone else. Their sweaters were bright yellow and deep blue and pastel green. Their socks came up to just below the knees and were made of 100 percent virgin wool from England.

Sometimes when Beth saw herself in the mirror of the girls' room between classes, with her straight brown hair and narrow shoulders and round face with dull brown eyes and freckles across the bridge of her nose, she would taste the old taste of vinegar in her mouth. The girls who belonged to the clubs wore lipstick and eye shadow; Beth wore no make-up and her hair still fell over her forehead in bangs. It did not occur to her that she would be pledged to a club, nor did it to anyone else.

"This week," Mrs. MacArthur said, "we will begin to study the binomial theorem. Does anyone know what a binomial is?"

From the back row Beth put up her hand. It was the first time she had done this.

"Yes?" Mrs. MacArthur said.

Beth stood, feeling suddenly awkward. "A binomial is a mathematical expression containing two terms." They had studied this last year at Methuen. "X plus Y is a binomial."

"Very *good,*" Mrs. MacArthur said.

The girl in front of Beth was named Margaret; she had glowing blond hair and wore a cashmere sweater of a pale, expensive lavender. As Beth sat down, the blond head turned slightly back toward her. "*Brain!*" Margaret hissed. "*Goddamn brain!*"

Beth was always alone in the halls; it hardly occurred to her that there was any other way to be. Most girls walked in pairs or in threes, but she walked with no one.

One afternoon when she was coming out of the library she was startled by the sound of distant laughter and looked down the hall to see, haloed by afternoon sunlight, the back of a tall black girl. Two shorter girls were standing near her, by the water fountain, looking up at her face as she laughed. None of their features was distinct, and the light from behind them made Beth squint. The taller girl turned slightly, and Beth's heart almost stopped at the familiar tilt of her head. Beth took a quick dozen steps down the hallway toward them.

But it wasn't Jolene. Beth stopped suddenly and turned away. The three girls left the fountain and pushed noisily out the front door of the building. Beth stood staring after them for a long time.

"Could you go to Bradley's and get me some cigs?" Mrs. Wheatley said. "I think I have a cold."

"Yes, ma'am," Beth said. It was Saturday afternoon and Beth was holding a novel in her lap, but she wasn't reading it. She was playing over a game between P. Morphy and someone called simply "grandmaster." There was something peculiar about Morphy's eighteenth move, of knight to bishop five. It was a good attack, but Beth felt Morphy could have been more destructive with his queen's rook.

"I'll give you a note, since you're a bit youthful for smoking yourself."

"Yes, ma'am," Beth said.

"Three packs of Chesterfields."

"Yes, ma'am."

She had been in Bradley's only once before, with Mrs. Wheatley. Mrs. Wheatley gave her a penciled note and a dollar and twenty cents. Beth handed the note to Mr. Bradley at the counter. There was a long rack of magazines behind her. When she got the cigarettes, she turned and began looking. Senator Kennedy's picture was on the cover of *Time* and *Newsweek:* he was running for President and probably wouldn't make it because he was a Catholic.

There was a row of women's magazines that all had faces on their covers like the faces of Margaret and Sue Ann and the other Apple Pi's. Their hair shone; their lips were full and red.

She had just decided to leave when something caught her eye.

At the lower right-hand corner, where the magazines about photography and sunbathing and do-it-yourself were, was a magazine with a picture of a chess piece on its cover. She walked over and took it from the rack. On the cover was the title, *Chess Review,* and the price. She opened it. It was full of games and photographs of people playing chess. There was an article called "The King's Gambit Reconsidered" and another one called "Morphy's Brilliancies." She had just been going over one of Morphy's games! Her heart began beating faster. She kept going through the pages. There was an article about chess in Russia. And the thing that kept turning up was the word "tournament." There was a whole section called "Tournament Life." She had not known there was such a thing as a chess tournament. She thought chess was just something you did, the way Mrs. Wheatley hooked rugs and put together jigsaw puzzles.

"Young lady," Mr. Bradley said, "you have to buy the magazine or put it back."

She turned, startled. "Can't I just . . . ?"

"Read the sign," Mr. Bradley said.

In front of her was a hand-lettered sign: IF YOU WANT TO READ IT—BUY IT. Beth had fifteen cents and that was all. Mrs. Wheatley had told her a few days before that she would have to do without an allowance for a while; they were rather short and Mr. Wheatley had been delayed out West. Beth put the magazine back and left the store.

Halfway back up the block she stopped, thought a moment and went back. There was a stack of newspapers on the counter, by Mr. Bradley's elbow. She handed him a dime and took one. Mr. Bradley was busy with a lady who was paying for a prescription. Beth went over to the end of the magazine rack with her paper under her arm and waited.

After a few minutes Mr. Bradley said, "We have three sizes." She heard him going to the back of the store with the lady following. Beth took the copy of *Chess Review* and slipped it into her newspaper.

Outside in the sunshine she walked a block with the paper under her arm. At the first corner she stopped, took out the magazine and slipped it under the waistband of her skirt, covering it with her robin's-egg-blue sweater, made of reprocessed wool and bought at Ben Snyder's. She pulled the sweater down loosely over the magazine and dropped the newspaper into the corner trash can.

Walking home with the folded magazine tucked securely against her flat belly she thought again about that rook move Morphy hadn't made. The magazine said Morphy was "perhaps the most brilliant player in the history of the game." The rook could come to bishop seven, and Black had better not take it with his knight because . . . She stopped, halfway down the block. A dog was barking somewhere, and across the street from her on a well-mowed lawn two small boys were loudly playing tag. After the second pawn moved to king knight five, then the remaining rook could slide over, and if the black player took the pawn, the bishop could uncover, and if he didn't . . .

She closed her eyes. If he didn't capture it, Morphy could force a mate in two, starting with the bishop sacrificing itself with a check. If he *did* take it, the white pawn moved again, and then the bishop went the other way and there was nothing Black could do. *There it was.* One of the little boys across the street began crying. *There was nothing Black could do.* The game would be over in twenty-nine moves at least. The way it was in the book, it had taken Paul Morphy thirty-six moves to win. He hadn't seen the move with the rook. *But she had.*

Overhead the sun shone in a blank blue sky. The dog continued barking. The child wailed. Beth walked slowly home and replayed the game. Her mind was as lucid as a perfect, stunning diamond.

"Allston should have returned weeks ago," Mrs. Wheatley was saying. She was sitting up in bed, with a crossword-puzzle magazine beside her and a little TV set on the dresser with the sound turned down. Beth had just brought her a cup of instant coffee from the kitchen. Mrs. Wheatley was wearing her pink robe and her face was covered with powder.

"Will he be back soon?" Beth said. She didn't really want to talk with Mrs. Wheatley; she wanted to get back to *Chess Review*.

"He has been unavoidably detained," Mrs. Wheatley said.

Beth nodded. Then she said, "I'd like to get a job for after school."

Mrs. Wheatley blinked at her. "A job?"

"Maybe I could work in a store, or wash dishes somewhere."

Mrs. Wheatley stared at her for a long time before speaking. "At thirteen years of age?" she said finally. She blew her nose quietly on a tissue and folded it. "I should think you are well provided for."

"I'd like to make some money."

"To buy clothes with, I suspect."

Beth said nothing.

"The only girls of your age who work," Mrs. Wheatley said, "are colored." The way she said "colored" made Beth decide to say nothing further about it.

To join the United States Chess Federation cost six dollars. Another four dollars got you a subscription to the magazine. There was something even more interesting: in the section called "Tournament Life" there were numbered regions; including one for Ohio, Illinois, Tennessee and Kentucky, and in the listing under it was an item that read: "Kentucky State Championship, Thanksgiving weekend, Henry Clay High School Auditorium, Lexington, Fri., Sat. Sun.," and under this it said: "$185 in prizes. Entry fee: $5.00. USCF members only."

It would take six dollars to join and five dollars to get into the tournament. When you took the bus down Main you passed Henry Clay High; it was eleven blocks from Janwell Drive. And it was five weeks until Thanksgiving.

"Can anyone say it verbatim?" Mrs. MacArthur said.

Beth put up her hand.

"Beth?"

She stood. "In any right triangle the square of the hypotenuse is equal to the sum of the squares of the other two sides." She sat down.

Margaret snickered and leaned toward Gordon, who sat beside her and sometimes held her hand. "That's the brain!" she whispered in a soft, girlish voice radiant with contempt. Gordon laughed. Beth looked out the window at the autumn leaves.

"I do not know where the money goes!" Mrs. Wheatley said. "I have bought little more than trifles this month, and yet my hoard has been decimated. Decimated." She plopped into the chintz-covered armchair and stared at the ceiling for a moment, wide-eyed, as if expecting a guillotine to fall. "I have paid electric bills and telephone bills and have bought simple, uncomplicated groceries. I have denied myself cream for my morning coffee, have bought nothing whatever for my person, have attended neither the cinema nor the rummage sales at First Methodist, and yet I have seven dollars left where I should have at least twenty." She laid the crumpled one-dollar bills on the table beside her, having fished them from her purse a few moments before. "We have this for ourselves until the end of October. It will scarcely buy chicken necks and porridge."

"Doesn't Methuen send you a check?" Beth said.

Mrs. Wheatley brought her eyes down from the ceiling and stared at her. "For the first year," she said evenly. "As if the expenses of keeping you didn't exhaust it."

Beth knew that wasn't true. The check was seventy dollars, and Mrs. Wheatley didn't spend that much on her.

"It requires twenty dollars for us to live passably until the first of the month," Mrs. Wheatley said. "I am thirteen dollars short of that." She turned her gaze briefly ceilingward and then back to Beth again. "I shall have to keep better records."

"Maybe it's inflation," Beth said, with some truth. She had taken only six, for the membership.

"Maybe it is," Mrs. Wheatley said, mollified.

The problem was the five dollars for the entry fee. In home room, the day after Mrs. Wheatley's oration about money, Beth took a sheet from her composition book and wrote a letter to Mr. Shaibel, Custodian, Methuen Home, Mount Sterling, Kentucky. It read:

Dear Mr. Shaibel:

There is a chess tournament here with a first prize of one hundred dollars and a second prize of fifty dollars. There are other prizes, too. It costs five dollars to enter it, and I don't have that.

If you will send me the money I will pay you back ten dollars if I win any prize at all.

Very truly yours,
Elizabeth Harmon

The next morning she took an envelope and a stamp from the cluttered desk in the living room while Mrs. Wheatley was still in bed. She put the letter in the mailbox on her way to school.

In November she took another dollar from Mrs. Wheatley's purse. It had been a week since she wrote Mr. Shaibel, and there had been no answer. This time, with part of the money, she bought the new issue of *Chess Review*. She found several games that she could improve upon—one by a young grandmaster named Benny Watts. Benny Watts was the United States Champion.

Mrs. Wheatley seemed to have a good many colds. "I have a proclivity for viruses," she would say. "Or they for me." She handed Beth a prescription to take to Bradley's and a dime to buy herself a Coke.

Mr. Bradley gave her an odd look when she came in, but he said nothing. She gave him the prescription and he went to the back of the store. Beth carefully avoided standing near the magazines. When she took the *Chess Review* a month before, it had been the only copy. He might have noticed it right away.

Mr. Bradley brought back a plastic container with a typed label on it. He put it down on the counter while he got a white paper bag. Beth stared at the container. The pills in it were oblong and bright-green.

*   *   *

"This will be my tranquillity medicine," Mrs. Wheatley said. "McAndrews has decided I need tranquillity."

"Who's McAndrews?" Beth said.

"Dr. McAndrews," Mrs. Wheatley said, unscrewing the lid. "My physician." She took out two of the pills. "Would you get me a glass of water, dear?"

"Yes, ma'am," Beth said. As she was going into the bathroom for the water, Mrs. Wheatley sighed and said, "Why do they only fill these bottles half full?"

In the November issue there were twenty-two games from an invitational tournament in Moscow. The players had names like Botvinnik and Petrosian and Laev; they sounded like people in a fairy tale. There was a photograph showing two of them hunched over a board, dark-haired and grim-lipped. They wore black suits. Out of focus, behind them, sat a huge audience.

In a game between Petrosian and someone named Benkowitz, in the semifinals, Beth saw a bad decision of Petrosian's. He started an attack with pawns but shouldn't have. There was a commentary on the game by an American grandmaster, who thought the pawn moves were good, but Beth saw deeper than that. How could Petrosian have misjudged it? Why hadn't the American seen the weakness? They must have spent a long time studying it, since the magazine said the game took five hours.

Margaret only slipped the shaft into her gym lock and didn't twist the dial afterward. They were in shower stalls side by side now, and Beth could see Margaret's sizable breasts, like solid cones. Beth's chest was still like a boy's and her pubic hair had just started coming in. Margaret ignored Beth and hummed while she soaped herself. Beth stepped out and wrapped herself in a towel. Still wet, she went back into the locker room. There was no one there.

Beth dried her hands quickly and very quietly slipped the shaft out of Margaret's lock, muffling it in her towel. Her hair dripped on her hands, but that didn't matter; there was water all over from the boys' gym. Beth slipped off the lock and opened the locker door, slowly so it wouldn't squeak. Her heart was thumping like some kind of little animal in her chest.

It was a fine brown purse of real leather. Beth dried her hands again and lifted it down from the shelf, listening carefully. There were giggles and shouts from the girls in the shower, but nothing else. she had made a point of being the first in, to get the stall nearest the door, and she had left quickly. No one else would be through yet. She opened the purse.

There were colored postcards and a new-looking lipstick and a tortoise-shell comb and an elegant linen handkerchief. Beth pushed through these with her right hand. At the bottom, in a little silver money clip, were bills. She pulled them out. Two fives. She hesitated for a moment and then took them both, together with the clip. She put the purse back and replaced the lock.

She had left her own door shut but unlocked. She opened it now and slid the clipped fives into her algebra book. Then she locked her door, went back to the shower and stayed there washing herself until all the other girls had left.

When everyone else was gone, Beth was still getting dressed. Margaret had not opened her purse. Beth sighed deeply, like Mrs. Wheatley. Her heart was still pounding. She got the money clip out of her algebra book and pushed it under the locker Margaret had used. It might have just fallen there from Margaret's purse, and anybody could have taken the money. She folded the bills and put them in her shoe. Then she took her own blue plastic purse from the shelf, opened it and reached into the little pocket that held the mirror. She took out two green pills, put them in her mouth, went to the washstand and swallowed them down with a paper cup of water.

Supper that night was spaghetti and meatballs from a can, with Jell-O for dessert. While Beth was doing the dishes and Mrs. Wheatley was in the living room turning the volume up on the TV, Mrs. Wheatley suddenly said, "Oh, I forgot."

Beth went on scrubbing the spaghetti pan and in a minute Mrs. Wheatley appeared with an envelope in her hand. "This came for you," she said and went back to the *Huntley-Brinkley Report.*

It was a smudged enveloped addressed in pencil. She dried her hands and opened it; there were five one-dollar bills inside and no message. She stood at the sink for a long time, holding the bills in her hand.

The green pills were four dollars for a bottle of fifty. The label read: "Three refills." Beth paid with four one-dollar bills. She walked home briskly and put the prescription slip back in Mrs. Wheatley's desk.

Chapter 4

At the entrance to the gym a desk had been set up, and two men in white shirts were sitting behind it. Behind them were rows of long tables with green-and-white chessboards. The room was full of people talking and a few playing; most of them were young men or boys. Beth saw one woman and no colored people. Pinned to the desk near the man on the left was a sign that read ENTRY FEES HERE. Beth walked up to him with her five dollars.

"Do you have a clock?" the man asked.

"No."

"We have a clock-sharing system," he said. "If your opponent doesn't have one, come back to the desk. Play starts in twenty minutes. What's your rating?"

"I don't have a rating."

"Have you ever played in a tournament before?"

"No."

The man pointed to Beth's money. "Are you sure you want to do this?"

"I'm sure."

"We don't have a woman's section," he said.

She just stared at him.

"I'll put you in Beginners," he said.

"No," Beth said, "I'm not a beginner."

The other young man had been watching them. "If you're an unrated player, you go in Beginners with the people under sixteen hundred," he said.

Beth had paid little attention to ratings in *Chess Review*, but she knew that masters had at least 2200. "What's the prize for Beginners?" she said.

"Twenty."

"What about the other section?"

"First prize in the Open is one hundred."

"Is it against any rule for me to be in the Open?"

He shook his head. "Not a rule, exactly, but—"

"Then put me in it." Beth held out the bills.

The man shrugged and gave Beth a card to fill out. "There are three guys out there with ratings over eighteen hundred. Beltik may show up, and he's the state champion. They'll eat you alive."

She took a ball-point pen and began filling in the card with her name and address. Where a blank said "Rating" she put a large zero. She handed the card back.

They started twenty minutes late. It took them a while to get the pairings posted. When they were putting the names on the board Beth asked the man next to her if it was done at random. "Not at all," he said. "They arrange it by ratings on the first round. After that, winners play winners, and losers, losers."

When her card was finally put up it said "Harmon-Unr—Black." It was put under one that said "Packer-Unr—White." The two cards were by the number Twenty-seven. They turned out to be the last two.

She walked over to Board Twenty-seven and seated herself at the black pieces. She was at the last board on the farthest table.

Sitting next to her was a woman of about thirty. After a minute, two more women came walking over. One was about twenty, and the other was Beth's opponent—a tall, heavy high school girl. Beth looked over the expanse of tables, where players were getting settled or, already seated, were beginning games; all of them were male, mostly young. There were four female players at the tournament and they were all clumped together at the far end, playing against one another.

Beth's opponent sat down with some awkwardness, put her two-faced chess clock at the side of the board and held out a hand. "I'm Annette Packer," she said.

Her hand felt large and moist in Beth's. "I'm Beth Harmon," she said. "I don't understand about chess clocks."

Annette seemed relieved to have something to explain. "The clock face nearest you measures your playing time. Each player has ninety minutes. After you move, you press the button on top, and it stops your clock and starts your opponent's. There are little red flags over the number twelve on each clock face; yours will fall down when the ninety minutes are up. If it does that, you've lost." Beth nodded. It seemed like a lot of time to her; she had never put more than twenty minutes into a chess game. There was a ruled sheet of paper by each player, for recording moves.

"You can start my clock now," Annette said.

"Why do they put all the girls together?" Beth said.

Annette raised her eyebrows. "They're not supposed to. But if you win, they move you up."

Beth reached out and pressed down the button and Annette's clock began ticking. Annette took her king's pawn somewhat nervously and moved it to king four. "Oh," she said, "it's touch move, you know."

"What's that?"

"Don't touch a piece unless you're going to move it. If you touch it, you have to move it somewhere."

"Okay," Beth said. "Don't you push your button now?"

"Sorry," Annette said and pressed her button. Beth's clock started ticking. she reached out firmly and moved her queen bishop's pawn to its fourth square. The Sicilian Defense. She pressed the button and then put her elbows on the table, on each side of the board, like the Russians in the photographs.

She began attacking on the eighth move. On the tenth she had one of Annette's bishops, and on the seventeenth her queen. Annette had not even castled yet. She reached out and laid her king on its side when Beth took her queen. "That was quick," she said. She sounded relieved to have lost. Beth looked at the clock faces. Annette had used thirty minutes, and Beth seven. Waiting for Annette to move had been the only problem.

The next round would not be until eleven. Beth had recorded the game with Annette on her score sheet, circled her own name at the top as winner; she went now to the front desk and put the sheet into the basket with the sign reading WINNERS. It was the first one there. A young man who looked like a college student came up as she was walking away and put his sheet in. Beth had already noticed that most of the people here weren't good-looking. A lot of them had greasy hair and bad complexions; some were fat and nervous-looking. But this one was tall and angular and relaxed, and his face was open and handsome. He nodded amiably at Beth, acknowledging her as another fast player, and she nodded back.

She began walking around the room, quietly, looking at some of the games being played. Another couple finished theirs, and the winner went up front to turn in the record. She did not see any positions that looked interesting. On Board Number Seven, near the front of the room, Black had a chance to win a rook by a two-move combination, and she waited for him to move the necessary bishop. But when the time came he simply exchanged pawns in the center. He had not seen the combination.

The tables began with Board Number Three rather than One. She looked around the room, at the rows of heads bowed over the boards, at the Beginners Section far across the gym. Players were getting up from their chairs as games ended. At the far side of the room was a doorway she hadn't noticed before. Above it was a cardboard sign saying "Top Boards." Beth walked over.

It was a smaller room, not much bigger than Mrs. Wheatley's living room. There were two separate tables and a game was going on at each. The tables sat in the center of the floor and a black velvet rope on wooden stanchions kept the watchers from getting too close to the players. There were four or five people silently watching the games, most of them clustered around

Board Number One, on her left. The tall, good-looking player was one of them.

At Board One two men were sitting in what seemed to be utter concentration. The clock between them was different from the others Beth had seen; it was bigger and sturdier. One man was fat and balding with a darkness to his features like the Russians in the pictures, and he wore a dark suit like the Russians'. The other was much younger and wore a gray sweater over a white shirt. He unbuttoned his shirtsleeves and pulled up the sleeves to his elbows, one arm at a time, not taking his eyes from the board. Something in Beth's stomach thrilled. This was the real thing. She held her breath and studied the position on the board. It took a few moments to penetrate it; it was balanced and diffi-cult, like some of the championship games in *Chess Review*. She knew it was Black's move because the indicator on his clock was moving, and just as she saw that knight to bishop five was what was called for, the older man reached out and moved his knight to bishop five.

The good-looking man was leaning against the wall now. Beth went over to him and whispered, "Who are they?"

"Beltik and Cullen. Beltik's the State Champion."

"Which is which?" Beth said.

The tall man held a finger to his lips. Then he said softly, "Bel-tik's the young one."

That was a surprise. The Kentucky State Champion looked to be about the age of Fergussen. "Is he a grandmaster?"

"He's working on it. He's been a master for years."

"Oh," Beth said.

"It takes time. You have to play grandmasters."

"How much time?" Beth said. A man in front of them by the velvet ropes turned and stared at her angrily. The tall man shook his head, pursing his lips for silence. Beth turned back to the ropes and watched the game. Other people came in and the room began to fill up. Beth held her place at the front.

There was a great deal of tension in the middle of the board. Beth studied it for several minutes trying to decide what she would do if it were her move; but she wasn't certain. It was Cullen's move. She waited for what seemed an awfully long time. He sat there with his forehead supported by clenched fists, knees together under the table, motionless. Beltik leaned back in his chair and yawned, looking amusedly at Cullen's bald head in front of him. Beth could see that his teeth were bad, with dark stains and several empty spaces, and that his neck wasn't properly shaved.

Finally Cullen moved. He traded knights in the center. There were several fast moves and the tension lessened, with each player relinquishing a knight and a bishop in trades. When his move came again he looked up at Beltik and said, "Draw?"

"Hell, no," Beltik said. He studied the board impatiently, screwed up his face in a way that looked funny, smacked a fist into a palm, and moved his rook down to the seventh rank. Beth liked the move, and she liked the way Beltik picked up his pieces firmly and set them down with a tiny graceful flourish.

In five more moves Cullen resigned. He was down by two pawns, his remaining bishop was locked into the back rank, and the time on his clock was almost up. He toppled his king with a kind of elegant disdain, reached over and gave a hasty handshake to Beltik, stood up and stepped over the rope, brushing past Beth, and left the room. Beltik stood and stretched. Beth looked at him standing over the board with the toppled king, and something in her swelled with excitement. She felt goose bumps on her arms and legs.

Beth's next game was with a small and bristly man named Cooke; his rating was 1520. She printed it in at the top of the score sheet by Board Thirteen: "Harmon–Unr: Cooke-1520." It was her turn to play white. She moved pawn to queen four and pressed Cooke's clock, and he moved instantly with pawn to queen four. He seemed wound up very tight and his eyes kept glancing around the room. He couldn't sit still in his chair.

Beth played fast too, picking up some of his impatience. In five minutes they had both developed their pieces, and Cooke started an attack on her queenside. She decided to ignore it and advanced a knight. He hastily pushed a pawn up, and she saw with surprise that she could not take the pawn without risking a nasty double attack. She hesitated. Cooke was pretty good. The 1500 rating must mean something, after all. He was better than Mr. Shaibel or Mr. Ganz, and he looked a little scary with his impatience. She slid her rook to the bishop's home square, putting it below the oncoming pawn.

Cooke surprised her. He picked up his queen bishop and took one of the pawns next to her king with it, checking her and sacrificing the piece. She stared at the board, suddenly unsure for a moment. What was he up to? Then she saw it. If she took, he checked again with a knight and picked off a bishop. It would win him the pawn and bring her king out. Her stomach was tight for a moment; she did not like being surprised. It took her a minute to see what to do. She moved the king over but did not take the bishop.

Cooke brought the knight down anyway. Beth traded the pawns over on the other side and opened the file for her rook. Cooke kept nagging her king with complications. She could see now that there was really no danger yet if she didn't let it bluff her. She brought the rook out, and then doubled up with her queen. She liked that arrangement; it looked to her imagination like two cannons, lined up and ready to fire.

In three moves she was able to fire them. Cooke seemed obsessed with the maneuvers he was setting up against her king and blind to what Beth was really doing. His moves were interesting, but she saw they had no solidity because he wasn't taking in the whole board. If she had been playing only to avoid checkmate, he would have had her by the fourth move after his first check with the bishop. But she nailed him on the third. She felt the blood rushing into her face as she saw the way to fire her rook. She took her queen and brought it all the way to the last rank, offering it to the black rook that sat back there, not yet moved. Cooke stopped his squirming for a moment and looked at her face. She looked back at him. Then he studied the position, and studied it. Finally he reached out and took her queen with his rook.

Something in Beth wanted to jump and shout. But she held herself back, reached out, pushed her bishop over one square and quietly said, "Check." Cooke started to move his king and stopped. Suddenly he saw what was going to happen: he was going to lose his queen and that rook he had just captured with, too. He looked at her. She sat there impassively. Cooke turned his attention to the board and studied it for several minutes, squirming in his seat and scowling. Then he looked back to Beth and said, "Draw?"

Beth shook her head.

Cooke scowled again. "You got me. I resign." He stood up and held out his hand. "I didn't see that coming at all." His smile was surprisingly warm.

"Thanks," Beth said, shaking his hand.

They broke for lunch and Beth got a sandwich and milk at a drugstore down the block from the high school; she ate it alone at the counter and left.

Her third game was with an older man in a sleeveless sweater. His name was Kaplan and his rating was 1694. She played Black, used the Nimzo-Indian defense, and beat him in thirty-four moves. She might have done it quicker, but he was skillful at defending—even though with White a player should be on the attack. By the time he resigned she had his king exposed and a bishop about to be captured, and she had two passed pawns. He looked dazed. Some other players had gathered around to watch.

It was three-thirty when they finished. Kaplan had played with maddening slowness, and Beth had gotten up from the table for several moves, to walk off her energy. By the time she brought the score sheet to the desk with her name circled on it, most of the other games were over and the tournament was breaking up for supper. There would be a round at eight o'clock that evening, then three more on Saturday. The final round would be on Sunday morning at eleven.

Beth went to the girls' room and washed her face and hands; it was surprisingly how grubby her skin felt after three games of chess. She looked at herself in the mirror, under the harsh lights, and saw what she had always seen: the round uninterest-ing face and the colorless hair. But there was something different. The cheeks were flushed with color now, and her eyes looked more alive than she had ever seen them. For once in her life she liked what she saw in the mirror.

Back outside by the front table the two young men who had registered her were putting up a notice on the bulletin board. Some players had gathered around it, the handsome one among them. She walked over. The lettering on top, done with a Magic Marker, read UNDEFEATED. There were four names on the list. At the bottom was HARMON: she held her breath for a moment when she saw it. And at the top of the list was the name BELTIK.

"You're Harmon, aren't you?" It was the handsome one.

"Yes."

"Keep it up, kid," he said, smiling.

Just then the young man who had tried to put her in the Beginners Section shouted from the table, "Harmon!"

She turned.

"Looks like you were right, Harmon," he said.

Mrs. Wheatley was eating a potroast TV dinner with whipped potatoes when Beth came in. *Bat Masterson* was on, very loudly. "Yours is in the oven," Mrs. Wheatley said. She was in the chintz chair with the aluminum plate on a tray in her lap. Her stockings were rolled down to the tops of her black pumps.

During the commercial, while Beth was eating the carrots from her TV dinner, Mrs. Wheatley asked, "How did you do, honey?" and Beth said, "I won three games."

"That's nice," Mrs. Wheatley said, not taking her eyes from the elderly gentleman who was telling about the relief he had gotten from Haley's M.O.

That evening Beth was on Board Six opposite a homely young man named Klein. His rating was 1794. Some of the games printed in *Chess Review* were from players with lower ratings than that.

Beth was White, and she played pawn to king four, hoping for the Sicilian. She knew the Sicilian better than anything else. But Klein played pawn to king four and then fianchettoed his king's bishop, setting it over in the corner above his castled king. She wasn't quite sure but thought this was the kind of opening called "Irregular."

In the middle game, things got complex. Beth was unsure what to do and decided to retreat a bishop. She set her index finger on the piece and immediately saw she had better move pawn to queen four. She reached over to the queen pawn.

"Sorry," Klein said. "Touch move."

She looked at him.

"You have to move the bishop," he said.

She could see in his face he was glad to say it. He had probably seen what she could do if she moved the pawn.

She shrugged and tried to act unconcerned, but inside she was feeling something she hadn't felt before in a chess game. She was frightened. She moved the bishop to bishop four, sat back and folded her hands in her lap. Her stomach was in a knot. She should have moved the pawn.

She looked at Klein's face as he studied the board. After a moment she saw a little malicious grin. He pushed his queen's pawn to the fifth square, punched his clock smartly and folded his arms across his chest.

He was going to get one of her bishops. And abruptly her fear was replaced by anger. She leaned over the board and placed her cheeks against her palms, studying intently.

It took her almost ten minutes, but she found it. She moved and sat back.

Klein hardly seemed to notice. He took the bishop as she hoped he would. Beth advanced her queen rook pawn, way over on the other side of the board, and Klein grunted slightly but moved quickly, pushing the queen pawn forward again. Beth brought her knight over, covering the pawn's next step, and more important, attacking Klein's rook. He moved the rook. Inside Beth's stomach something was beginning to uncoil. Her vision seemed extremely sharp, as though she could read the finest print from across the room. She moved the knight, attacking the rook again.

Klein looked at her, annoyed. He studied the board and

moved the rook, to the very square Beth had known, two moves ago, that he would move. She brought her queen out to bishop five, right above Klein's castled king.

Still looking annoyed and sure of himself, Klein brought a knight over to defend. Beth picked up her queen, her face flushing, and took the pawn in front of the king, sacrificing her queen.

He stared and took the queen. There was nothing else he could do to get out of check.

Beth brought her bishop out for another check. Klein interposed the pawn, as he knew he would. "That's mate in two," Beth said quietly.

Klein stared at her, his face furious. "What do you mean?" he said.

Beth's voice was still quiet. "The rook comes over for the next check and then the knight mates."

He scowled. "My queen—"

"Your queen'll be pinned," she said, "after the king moves."

He looked back to the board and stared at the position. Then he said, "Shit!" He did not turn over his king or offer to shake Beth's hand. He got up from the table and walked away, jamming his hands into his pockets.

Beth took her pencil and circled HARMON on her score sheet.

When she left at ten o'clock there were three names on the UNDEFEATED list. HARMON was still at the bottom. BELTIK was still at the top.

In her room that night she could not get to sleep because of the way the games kept playing themselves over and over in her head long after she had stopped enjoying them.

After several hours of this she got out of bed and in her blue pajamas walked over to the dormer windows. She raised a shade and looked out at the newly bare trees by the light of the street lamp, and at the dark houses beyond the trees. The street was silent and empty. There was a sliver of a moon, partly obscured by clouds. The air was chilly.

Beth had learned not to believe in God during her time in Methuen's chapel, and she never prayed. But now she said, under her breath, *Please God let me play Beltik and checkmate him.*

In her desk drawer, in the toothbrush holder, were seventeen green pills, and there were more in a little box on her closet shelf. She had thought earlier about taking two of them to help her doze off. But she did not. She went back to bed, exhausted now and her mind blank, and slept soundly.

On Saturday morning she had hoped to be playing someone with a rating over 1800. The man at registration had said there were three who were that high. But on the pairings she was shown playing Black against someone named Townes with a rating of 1724. That was lower than her last game, the evening before. She went to the desk and asked about it.

"That's the breaks, Harmon," the man in the white shirt said. "Consider yourself lucky."

"I want to play the best," Beth said.

"You have to get a rating before that happens," the young man said.

"How do I get a rating?"

"You play thirty games in USCF tournaments and then wait four months. That's how you get a rating."

"That's too long."

The man leaned toward her. "How old are you, Harmon?"

"Thirteen."

"You're the youngest person in the room. You can wait for a rating."

Beth was furious. "I want to play Beltik."

The other man at the table spoke up. "If you win your next three games, honey. And if Beltik does the same."

"I'll win them," Beth said.

"No, you won't, Harmon," the first young man said. "You'll have to play Sizemore and Goldmann first, and you can't beat both of them."

"Sizemore and Goldmann shit," the other man said. "The guy you're playing now is underrated. He plays first board for the university team and last month he came in fifth in Las Vegas. Don't let the rating fool you."

"What's in Las Vegas?" Beth asked.

"The U.S. Open."

Beth went to Board Four. The man seated behind the white pieces was smiling as she came up. It was the tall, handsome one. Beth felt a bit rattled to see him. He looked like some kind of movie star.

"Hi, Harmon," he said, holding out his hand. "It looks like we've been stalking each other."

She shook his big hand awkwardly and seated herself. There was a pause for a long minute before he said, "Do you want to start my clock?"

"Sorry," she said. She reached out to start it, almost knocked it over but caught it in time. "Sorry," she said again, almost inaudibly. She pressed the button and his clock started ticking. She looked down at the board, her cheeks burning.

He played pawn to king four, and she replied with the Sicilian. He continued with book moves and she followed with the Dragon variation. They traded pawns in the center. Gradually she got her composure back, playing these mechanical moves, and she looked across the board at him. He was attentive to the pieces, scowling. But even with a scowl on his face and his hair slightly mussed he was handsome. Something in Beth's stomach felt strange as she looked at him, with his broad shoulders and clear complexion and his brow wrinkled in concentration.

He surprised her by bringing his queen out. It was a bold move, and she studied it for a while and saw that there wasn't any weakness to it. She brought out her own queen. He moved a knight to the fifth rank, and Beth moved a knight to the fifth rank. He checked with a bishop, and she defended with a pawn. He retreated the bishop. She was feeling light now, and her fingers with the pieces were nimble. Both players began moving fast but easily. She gave a non-threatening check to his king, and he pulled away delicately and began advancing pawns. She stopped that handily with a pin and then feinted on the queenside with a rook. He was undeceived by the feint and, smiling, removed her pin, and on his next move continued the pawn advances. She retreated, hiding her king in a queenside castle. She felt somehow spacious and amused, yet her face remained serious. They continued their dance.

It made her sad in a way when she eventually saw how to beat him. It was after the nineteenth move, and she felt herself resisting it as it opened up in her mind, hating to let go of the pleasant ballet they had danced together. But there it was: four moves and he would have to lose a rook or worse. She hesitated and made the first move of the sequence.

He didn't see what was happening until two moves later, when he frowned suddenly and said, "Jesus Christ, Harmon, I'm going to drop a rook!" She loved his voice; she loved the way he said it. He shook his head in mock bafflement; she loved that.

Some players who had finished their game early had gathered around the board, and a couple were whispering about the maneuver Beth had brought off.

Townes went on playing for five more moves, and Beth felt genuinely sorry for him when he resigned, tipping his king over and saying "Damn!" But he stood up, stretched and smiled down at her. "You're one hell of a chess player, Harmon," he said. "How old are you?"

"Thirteen."

He whistled. "Where do you go to school?"

"Fairfield Junior."

"Yeah," he said. "I know where that is."

He was even better-looking than a movie star.

An hour later she drew Goldmann and Board Three. She walked into the tournament room at exactly eleven, and the people standing stopped talking when she came in. Everyone looked at her. She heard someone whisper, "Thirteen fucking years old," and immediately the thought came into her mind, along with the exultant feeling the whispered voice had given her: *I could have done this at eight.*

Goldmann was tough and silent and slow. He was a short, heavy man, and he played the black pieces like a gruff general trained in defense. For the first hour everything that Beth tried he got out of. Every piece he had was protected; it seemed as

though there were double the usual complement of pawns to protect them.

Beth got fidgety during the long waits for him to move; once
after she had advanced a bishop she got up, and went to the bathroom. Something was hurting in her abdomen, and she felt a bit
faint. She washed her face with cold water and dried it on a paper
towel. As she was leaving, the girl she'd played her first game
with came in. Packer. Packer looked glad to see her. "You're
moving right on up, aren't you?" she said.

"So far," Beth said, feeling another twinge in her belly.

"I heard you're playing Goldmann."

"Yes," Beth said. "I have to get back."

"Sure," Packer said, "sure. Beat his ass, will you? Just beat
his ass."

Suddenly Beth grinned. "Okay," she said.

When she got back she saw that Goldmann had moved, and
her clock was ticking. He sat there in his dark suit looking bored.
She felt refreshed and ready. She seated herself and put everything out of her mind except the sixty-four squares in front of
her. After a minute she saw that if she attacked on both flanks
simultaneously, as Morphy did sometimes, Goldmann would
have difficulty playing it safe. She played pawn to queen rook
four.

It worked. After five moves she had opened his king up a little,
and after three more she was at his throat. She paid no attention
to Goldmann himself or to the crowd or to the feeling in her
lower abdomen or the sweat that had broken out on her brow.
She played against the board only, with lines of force etched for
her into its surface: the small stubborn fields for the pawns, the
enormous one for the queen, the gradations in between. Just before his clock was about to run out she checkmated him.

When she circled her name on the score sheet she looked again
at the number of Goldmann's rating. It was 1997. People were
applauding.

She went directly to the girls' room and discovered that she
had begun to menstruate. For a moment she felt, looking at the
redness in the water below her, as though something cata-

strophic had happened. Had she bled on the chair at Board
Three? Were the people there staring at the stains of her blood?
But she saw with relief that her cotton panties were barely spot-
ted. She thought abruptly of Jolene. If it hadn't been for Jolene,
she would have had no idea what was happening. No one else
had said a word about this—certainly not Mrs. Wheatley. She
felt a sudden warmth for Jolene, remembering that Jolene had
also told her what to do "in an emergency." Beth began pulling
a long sheet from the roll of toilet paper and folding it into a
tightly packed rectangle. The pain in her abdomen had eased.
She was menstruating, and she had just beaten Goldmann: 1997.
She put the folded paper into her panties, pulled them up tight,
straightened her skirt and walked confidently back into the playing area.

Beth had seen Sizemore before; he was a small, ugly, thin-faced
man who smoked cigarettes continuously. Someone had told her
he was State Champion before Beltik. Beth would play him on
Board Two in the room with the sign reading "Top Boards."

Sizemore wasn't there yet, but next to her, at Board One, Beltik was facing in her direction. Beth looked at him and then
looked away. It was a few minutes before three. The lights in
this smaller room—bare bulbs under a metal protection basket—seemed brighter than those in the big room, brighter than
they had been in the morning, and for a moment the shine on
the varnished floor with its painted red lines was blinding.

Sizemore came in, combing his hair in a nervous, quick way.
A cigarette hung from his thin lips. As he pulled his chair back,
Beth felt herself becoming very tight.

"Ready?" Sizemore asked gruffly, slipping the comb into his
shirt pocket.

"Yes," she said and punched his clock.

He played pawn to king four and then pulled out his comb
and started biting on it the way a person bites on the eraser end
of a pencil. Beth played pawn to queen bishop four.

By the middle game Sizemore had begun combing his hair
after each move. He hardly ever looked at Beth but concentrated

on the board, wriggling in his seat sometimes as he combed and parted and reparted his hair. The game was even, and there were no weaknesses on either side. There was nothing to do but find the best squares for her knights and bishops and wait. She would move, write the move down on her score sheet and sit back in her chair. After a while a crowd began to gather at the ropes. She glanced at them from time to time. There were more people watching her play than watching Beltik. She kept looking at the board, waiting for something to open up. Once when she looked up she saw Annette Packer standing at the back. Packer smiled and Beth nodded to her.

Back at the board, Sizemore brought a knight to queen five, posting it in the best place for a knight. Beth frowned; she couldn't dislodge it. The pieces were thick in the middle of the board and for a moment she lost the sense of them. There were occasional twinges in her abdomen. She could feel the thick batch of paper between her thighs. She adjusted herself in her chair and squinted at the board. This wasn't good. Sizemore was creeping up on her. She looked at his face. He had put away his comb and was looking at the pieces in front of him with satisfaction. Beth leaned over the table, digging her fists into her cheeks, and tried to penetrate the position. Some people in the crowd were whispering. With an effort she drove distractions from her mind. It was time to fight back. If she moved the knight on the left . . . No. If she opened the long diagonal for her white bishop . . . That was it. She pushed the pawn up, and the bishop's power was tripled. The picture started to become clearer. She leaned back in her seat and took a deep breath.

During the next five moves Sizemore kept bringing pieces up, but Beth, seeing the limits to what he could do to her, kept her attention focused on the far right-hand corner of the board, on Sizemore's queenside; when the time came she brought her bishop down in the middle of his clustered pieces there, setting it on his knight two square. From where it sat now, two of his pieces could capture it, but if either did, he would be in trouble.

She looked at him. He had taken out his comb again and was running it through his hair. His clock was ticking.

It took him fifteen minutes to make the move, and when he did it was a shock. He took the bishop with his rook. Didn't he know he was a fool to move the rook off the back rank? Couldn't he see that? She looked back at the board, double-checked the position and brought out her queen.

He didn't see it until the move after next, and his game fell apart. He still had his comb in his hand six moves later when she got her queen's pawn, passed, to the sixth rank. He brought his rook under the pawn. She attacked it with her bishop. Sizemore stood up, put his comb in his pocket, reached down to the board and set his king on its side. "You win," he said grimly. The applause was thunderous.

After she had turned in the score sheet she waited while the young man checked it, made a mark on a list in front of him, stood up and walked to the bulletin board. He took the pushpins from the card saying SIZEMORE and threw the card into a green metal wastebasket. Then he pulled the pins out of the bottom card and raised it to where Sizemore's had been. The UNDE-FEATED list now read: BELTIK, HARMON.

When she was walking toward the girls' room Beltik came out of "Top Boards" striding fast and looking very pleased with himself. He was carrying the little score sheet, on his way to the winners' basket. He didn't seem to see Beth.

She went over to the doorway of the "Top Boards" room, and Townes was standing there. There were lines of fatigue in his face; he looked like Rock Hudson, except for the weariness. "Good work, Harmon," he said.

"I'm sorry you lost," she said.

"Yeah," he said. "It's back to the drawing board." And then, nodding to where Beltik was standing at the front table with a small crowd gathered near him, he said, "He's a killer, Harmon. A genuine killer."

She looked at his face. "You need a rest."

He smiled down at her. "What I need, Harmon, is some of your talent."

As she passed the front table, Beltik took a step toward her and said, "Tomorrow."

* * *

When Beth came into the living room just before supper, Mrs. Wheatley looked pale and strange. She was sitting in the chintz armchair and her face was puffy. She was holding a brightly colored postcard in her lap.

"I've started menstruating," Beth said.

Mrs. Wheatley blinked. "That's nice," she said, as though from a great distance.

"I'll need some pads or something," Beth said.

Mrs. Wheatley seemed nonplused for a moment. Then she brightened. "That's certainly a milepost for you. Why don't you just go up to my room and look in the top drawer of my chiffonier? Take all you require."

"Thank you," Beth said, heading for the stairs.

"And, dear," Mrs. Wheatley said, "bring down that little bottle of green pills by my bedside."

When Beth came back she gave the pills to Mrs. Wheatley. Mrs. Wheatley had half a glass of beer sitting beside her; she took out two of the pills and swallowed them with the beer. "My tranquillity needs to be refurbished," she said.

"Is something wrong?" Beth asked.

"I'm not Aristotle," Mrs. Wheatley said, "but it could be construed as wrong. I have received a message from Mr. Wheatley."

"What did he say?"

"Mr. Wheatley has been indefinitely detained in the Southwest. The American Southwest."

"Oh," Beth said.

"Between Denver and Butte."

Beth sat down on the sofa.

"Aristotle was a moral philosopher," Mrs. Wheatley said, "while I am a housewife. Or was a housewife."

"Can't they send me back if you don't have a husband?"

"You put it concretely." Mrs. Wheatley sipped her beer. "They won't if we lie about it."

"That's easy enough," Beth said.

"You're a good soul, Beth," Mrs. Wheatley said, finishing her beer. "Why don't you heat the two chicken dinners in the freezer? Set the oven at four hundred."

Beth had been holding two sanitary napkins in her right hand. "I don't know how to put these on."

Mrs. Wheatley straightened herself up from her slumped position in the chair. "I am no longer a wife," she said, "except by legal fiction. I believe I can learn to be a mother. I'll show you how if you promise me never to go near Denver."

During the night Beth woke to hear rain on the roof over her head and intermittent rattling against the panes of her dormer windows. She had been dreaming of water, of herself swimming easily in a quiet ocean of still water. She put a pillow over her head and curled up on her side, trying to get back to sleep. But she could not. The rain was loud, and as it continued to fall, the sad languor of her dream was replaced by the image of a chessboard filled with pieces demanding her attention, demanding the clarity of her intelligence.

It was two in the morning and she did not get back to sleep for the rest of the night. It was still raining when she went downstairs at seven; the backyard outside the kitchen window looked like a swamp with hillocks of near-dead grass sticking up like islands. She was not certain how to fry eggs but decided she could boil some. She got two from the refrigerator, filled a pan with water and put it on the burner. She would play pawn to king four against him, and hope for the Sicilian. She boiled the eggs five minutes and put them in cold water. She could see Beltik's face, youthful, arrogant and smart. His eyes were small and black. When he stepped toward her yesterday as she was leaving, some part of her had thought he would hit her.

The eggs were perfect; she opened them with a knife, put them in a cup and ate them with salt and butter. Her eyes were grainy under the lids. The final game would begin at eleven; it was seven-twenty now. She wished she had a copy of *Modern Chess Openings*, to look over variations on the Sicilian. Some of the other players at the tournament had carried battered copies of the book under their arms.

It was only drizzling when she left the house at ten, and Mrs. Wheatley was still upstairs asleep. Before she left, Beth went into the bathroom and checked the sanitary belt Mrs. Wheatley had given her to wear, and the thick white pad. It was all right. She put on her galoshes and her blue coat, got Mrs. Wheatley's umbrella from the closet and left.

She had noticed before that the pieces at Board One were different. They were solid wooden ones like Mr. Ganz's and not the hollow plastic pieces that sat on the other boards at the tournament. When she walked by the table in the empty room at ten-thirty she reached out and picked up the white king. It was satisfyingly heavy, with a solid lead weight and green felt on the the bottom. She placed the piece on its home square, stepped back over the velvet rope and walked to the girls' room. She washed her face for the third time that day, tightened her sanitary belt, combed her bangs and went back to the gymnasium. More players had come in. She stuffed her hands into the pockets of her skirt so that no one could see they were trembling.

When eleven o'clock came she was ready behind the white pieces at Board One. Boards Two and Three had already started their games. Sizemore was at Board Two. She didn't recognize the others.

Ten minutes passed, and Beltik did not appear. The tournament director in the white shirt climbed over and stood near Beth for a minute. "Hasn't shown yet?" he said softly.

Beth shook her head.

"Make your move and punch the clock," the director whispered. "You should have done it at eleven."

That annoyed her. No one had told her about that. She moved pawn to king four and started Beltik's clock.

It was ten more minutes before Beltik came in. Beth's stomach hurt and her eyes smarted. Beltik looked casual and relaxed, wearing a bright-red shirt and tan corduroy pants. "Sorry," he said in a normal voice. "Extra cup of coffee." The other players looked over at him with irritation. Beth said nothing.

Beltik, still standing, loosened an extra button on his shirt front and held out his hand. "Harry Beltik," he said. "What's your name?"

He must know what her name was. "I'm Beth Harmon," she said, taking his hand but avoiding his eyes.

He seated himself behind the black pieces, rubbed his hands together briskly and moved his king pawn to the third square. He punched Beth's clock smartly.

The French Defense. She had never played it. She didn't like the look of it. The thing to do was play pawn to queen four. But what happened if he played the same? Did she trade pawns or push one of them forward, or bring out her knight? She squinted and shook her head; it was difficult to picture what the board would look like after the moves. She looked again, rubbed her eyes, and played pawn to queen four. When she reached out to punch the clock she hesitated. Had she made a mistake? But it was too late now. She pressed the button hastily and as it clicked down Beltik immediately picked up his queen pawn, put it on queen four and slapped down the button on his clock.

Although it was difficult to see with her usual clarity, she had not lost her sense of the requirements of an opening. She brought out her knights and involved herself for a while in a struggle for the center squares. But Beltik, moving fast, nipped off one of her pawns and she saw that she couldn't capture the pawn he did it with. She tried to shrug off the advantage she'd allowed and went on playing. She got her pieces off the back rank, and castled. She looked over the board at Beltik. He seemed completely at ease; he was looking at the game going on next to them. Beth felt a knot in her stomach; she could not get comfortable in her seat. The heavy cluster of pieces and pawns in the center of the board seemed for a while to have no pattern, to make no sense.

Her clock was ticking. She inclined her head to look at its face; twenty-five minutes were gone, and she was still down by a pawn. And Beltik had used only twenty-two minutes altogether, even including the time he'd wasted by being late. There was a ringing in her ears, and the bright light in the room hurt her eyes. Beltik was leaning back with his arms outstretched, yawning, showing the black places on the undersides of his teeth.

She found what looked like a good square for her knight, reached out her hand and then stopped. The move would be terrible; something had to be done about his queen before he had it on the rook file and was ready to threaten. She had to protect and attack at the same time, and she couldn't see how. The pieces in front of her just sat there. She should have taken a green pill last night, to make her sleep.

Then she saw a move that looked sensible and quickly made it. She brought a knight back near the king, protecting herself against Beltik's queen.

He raised his eyebrows almost imperceptibly and immediately took a pawn on the other side of the board. There was suddenly a diagonal open for his bishop. The bishop was aimed at the knight she'd wasted time bringing back, and she was down by another pawn. At the corner of Beltik's mouth was a sly little smile. She quickly looked away from his face, frightened.

She had to do something. He would be all over her king in four or five moves. She needed to concentrate, to see it clearly. But when she looked at the board, everything was dense, interlocked, complicated, dangerous. Then she thought of something to do. With her clock still running she stood up, stepped over the rope and walked through the small crowd of silent spectators to the main gym floor and across it to the girls' room. There was no one there. She went to a sink, washed her face with cold water, wet a handful of paper towels and held them for a minute to the back of her neck. After she threw them away she went into one of the little stalls and, sitting, checked her sanitary napkin. It was okay. She sat there relaxing, letting her mind go blank. Her elbows were on her knees, her head was bent down.

With an effort of will she made the chessboard with the game on Board One on it appear in front of her. There it was. She could see immediately that it was difficult, but not as difficult as some of the games she'd memorized from the book at Morris' Book Store. The pieces before her, in her imagination, were crisp and sharply focused.

She stayed where she was, not worrying about time, until she had it penetrated and understood. Then she got up, washed her face again and walked back into the gym. She had found her move.

There were more people gathered in "Top Boards" than before; as games ended they came in to watch the finals. She pushed by them, stepped over the rope and sat down. Her hands were perfectly steady, and her stomach and eyes felt fine. She reached out and moved; she punched the clock firmly.

Beltik studied the move for a few minutes and took her knight with his bishop, as she knew he would. She did not retake; she brought a bishop over to attack one of his rooks. He moved the rook out of the line of fire. He had to. She felt the blood rush into her cheeks as she brought her queen from the back to the center of the board. It now threatened to take the rook, pinned the king's knight pawn and could take the bishop with a check. She looked at Beltik. He was studying the board and rolling up his sleeves. His clock was ticking.

It took him almost fifteen minutes to find the rook move that Beth, in the bathroom, had been certain he would make. She was ready. Her rook came over behind her queen and she heard Beltik take in his breath sharply. Someone in the crowd began to whisper. Beth waited.

After ten more minutes Beltik moved his queen into a defensive position. It wouldn't work. She reached out with her hand steady and her mind crystalline and advanced a pawn, attacking his queen.

Beltik stared at the pawn for a moment as though it were a cockroach on the board. If he took it, he would find his queen pinned, unable to move. If he moved his queen away, Beth would begin a series of threats. If he left it where it was, he would lose it. "Son of a bitch!" he whispered.

By the time he had decided what to do, there were only ten more minutes on his clock. Beth had fifty. He had wasted his time stretching his arms and wriggling in his chair and distorting his face and, every now and then, starting out as if he knew what to do and then stopping, his hand arrested in midair over a piece. Finally he picked up the queen and moved it across the board, out of harm's way.

She brought up a bishop behind her queen: the threat was checkmate, and he was forced to parry it with his queen. She ignored the queen when he brought it over and pushed her rook to the third rank, where it was free to move either right or left. She would get either his queen or a checkmate, whatever he did.

Beltik was bent over the board with his face on his open palms. She could hear his foot tapping. "Son of a bitch," he said. "Son of a bitch."

Beth spoke softly. "I think that's it."

"I can get out of this."

"I don't think so," Beth said.

He had four more minutes on his clock. He kept staring at the board as though he were going to destroy it with the intensity of his desire to find some way out of the trap. Finally, with thirty seconds left, he grabbed his queen and slammed it in front of the rook, interposing and offering to sacrifice the queen for the rook. He slapped the button down on his clock, leaned back in his chair and drew a deep breath.

"It doesn't work," Beth said. "I don't have to take the queen."

"Move," Beltik said.

"I'll check you first with the bishop—"

"*Move!*"

She nodded and checked with the bishop. Beltik, with his clock ticking, quickly moved his king away and pressed the button. Then Beth did what she had planned all along. She brought her queen crashing down next to the king, sacrificing it. Beltik looked at her, stunned. She stared back at him. He shrugged, snatched up the queen and stopped his clock by hitting it with the base of the captured piece.

Beth pushed her other bishop from the back rank out to the middle of the board and said, "Check. Mate next move." Beltik stared at it for a moment, said, "Son of a bitch!" and stood up.

"The rook mates," Beth said.

"Son of a bitch," Beltik said.

The crowd that had now filled the room began applauding. Beltik, still scowling, held out his hand, and Beth shook it.

Chapter 5

They were ready to close by the time she got to the teller. She'd had to wait for the bus after school and wait again transferring down Main. And this was the second bank.

She'd carried the folded check in her blouse pocket all day, under the sweater. It was in her hand when the man in front of her picked up his rolls of nickels and stuffed them in the pocket of his overcoat and left the space at the window for her. She set her hand on the cold marble, holding the check out and standing on tiptoe, to be able to see the face of the teller. "I'd like to open an account," Beth said.

The man glanced at the check. "How old are you, miss?"

"Thirteen."

"I'm sorry," he said. "You'll need a parent or guardian with you."

Beth put the check back in her blouse pocket and left.

At the house, Mrs. Wheatley had four empty Pabst Blue Ribbon beer bottles sitting on the little table by her chair. The TV was off. Beth had picked up the afternoon paper from the front porch; she unfolded it as she came into the living room.

"How was school, dear?" Mrs. Wheatley's voice was dim and far away.

"It was okay." As Beth set the newspaper on the green plastic hassock by the sofa she saw with quiet astonishment that her own picture was printed on the front page, at the bottom. Near the top was the face of Nikita Khrushchev and at the bottom, one column wide, was her face, scowling beneath a headline: LOCAL PRODIGY TAKES CHESS TOURNEY. Under this, in smaller letters, boldface: TWELVE-YEAR-OLD ASTONISHES EXPERTS. She remembered the man taking her picture before they gave her the trophy and the check. She had told him she was thirteen.

Beth bent over, reading the paper:

> The world of Kentucky Chess was astonished this weekend by the playing of a local girl, who triumphed over hardened players to win the Kentucky State Championship. Elizabeth Harmon, a seventh-grade student at Fairfield Junior, showed "a mastery of the game unequaled by any female" according to Harry Beltik, whom Miss Harmon defeated for the state crown.

Beth grimaced; she hated the picture of herself. It showed her freckles and her small nose all too clearly.

"I want to open a bank account," she said.

"A bank account?"

"You'll have to go with me."

"But, my dear," Mrs. Wheatley said, "what would you open a bank account *with*?"

Beth reached into her blouse pocket, took out the check and handed it to her. Mrs. Wheatley sat up in her chair and held the check in her hand as though it were a Dead Sea Scroll. She was silent for a moment, reading it. Then she said softly, "One hundred dollars."

"I need a parent or guardian. At the bank."

"One hundred dollars," Mrs. Wheatley said. "Then you won it?"

"Yes. It says 'First Place' on the check."

"I *see,*" Mrs. Wheatley said. "I hadn't the foggiest idea people made money playing chess."

"Some tournaments have bigger prizes than that."

"Goodness!" Mrs. Wheatley was still staring at the check.

"We can go to the bank after school tomorrow."

"Certainly," Mrs. Wheatley said.

The next day, when they came into the living room after the bank, there was a copy of *Chess Review* on the cobbler's bench in front of the sofa. Mrs. Wheatley hung her coat in the hall closet and picked up the magazine. "While you were at school," she said, "I was leafing through this. I see there's a major tournament in Cincinnati the second week in December. First prize is five hundred dollars."

Beth studied her for a long moment. "I have to be in school then," she said. "And Cincinnati's pretty far from here."

"The Greyhound bus requires only two hours for the trip," Mrs. Wheatley said. "I took the liberty of calling."

"What about school?" Beth said.

"I can write a medical excuse, claiming mono."

"Mono?"

"Mononucleosis. It's quite the thing in your age group, according to the *Ladies' Home Journal.*"

Beth kept looking at her, trying not to let the astonishment show in her face. Mrs. Wheatley's dishonesty seemed in every way to match her own. Then she said, "Where would we stay?"

"At the Gibson Hotel, in a double room at twenty-two dollars a night. The Greyhound tickets will be eleven-eighty apiece, and there will, of course, be the cost of food. I have calculated all of it. Even if you win second or third prize, there will be a profit."

Beth had twenty dollars in cash and a packet of ten checks in her plastic purse. "I need to buy some chess books," she said.

"By all means," Mrs. Wheatley said, smiling. "And if you'll make out a check for twenty-three dollars and sixty cents, I'll get the bus tickets tomorrow."

After buying *Modern Chess Openings* and a book on the endgame at Morris', Beth walked across the street to Purcell's Department Store. She knew from the way girls talked at school that Purcell's was better than Ben Snyder's. She found what she wanted on the fourth floor: a wooden set almost identical to the one Mr. Ganz owned, with hand-carved knights and big, substantial pawns, and rooks that were fat and solid. She was undecided for a while over the board and almost bought a wooden one before settling on a folding linen board with green and beige squares. It would be more portable than the other.

Back home she cleared off her desk, put the board on it and set up the pieces. She piled her new chessbooks on one side and placed the tall silver trophy in the shape of a chess king on the other. She turned on her student lamp and sat at the desk, just looking at the pieces, at the way their curves picked up the light. She sat for what seemed like a long time, her mind quiet. Then she picked up *Modern Chess Openings*. This time she began at the beginning.

She had never seen anything like the Gibson Hotel before. Its size and bustle, the bright chandeliers in its lobby, the heavy red carpeting, the flowers, even the three revolving doors and the uniformed doorman who stood beside them were overwhelming. She and Mrs. Wheatley walked up to the front of the hotel from the bus station, carrying their new luggage. Mrs. Wheatley refused to hand it over to the doorman. She lugged her suitcase up to the front desk and registered for them both, unperturbed by the look the room clerk gave them.

In the room afterward, Beth began to relax. There were two big windows overlooking Fourth Street with its rush hour traffic. It was a crisp, cold day outside. Inside they had this thick-carpeted room with the big white bathroom and fluffy red towels and a huge plate-glass mirror covering one wall. There was a color TV on the dresser and a bright-red bedspread on each of the beds.

Mrs. Wheatley was inspecting the room, checking the dresser drawers, clicking the TV on and off, patting away a wrinkle on the bedspread. "Well," she said, "I asked them for a pleasant room, and I believe they gave it to me." She seated herself in the high-backed Victorian chair by her bed as though she had lived in the Gibson Hotel all her life.

The tournament was on the mezzanine in the Taft Room; all

Beth had to do was take the elevator. Mrs. Wheatley found them a diner down the street where they had bacon and eggs for breakfast, then she went back to bed with a copy of the Cincinnati *Enquirer* and a pack of Chesterfields while Beth went down to the tournament and registered. She still did not have a rating, but this time one of the men at the desk knew who she was; they didn't try to put her in the Beginners Section. There would be two games a day, and the time control would be 120/40, which meant you had two hours to make forty moves.

While she was signing in, she could hear a deep voice coming through one of the double doors that stood open to the Taft Room, where the games would be. She looked that way and saw part of the big ballroom, with a long row of empty tables and a few men walking around.

When she walked in, she saw a strange man slouched on a sofa with black-booted feet resting on a coffee table. ". . . and the rook comes to the seventh rank," he was saying. "Bone in the throat, man, that rook there. He took one look at it and paid up." He leaned his head against the back of the sofa and laughed loudly in a deep baritone. "Twenty bucks."

Since it was early, there were only half a dozen people in the room, and no one was at the long rows of tables with paper chessboards on them. Everyone was listening to the man talking. He was about twenty-five and looked like a pirate. He wore dirty jeans, a black turtleneck and a black wool cap pulled down to his heavy eyebrows. He had a thick black mustache and clearly needed a shave; the backs of his hands were tanned and scraped-looking. "The Caro-Kann *De*fense," he said, laughing. "A genuine bummer."

"What's wrong with the Caro-Kann?" someone asked. A neat young man in a camel's hair sweater.

"All pawns and no hope." He lowered his legs to the floor and sat up. On the table was a soiled old beige-and-green chessboard with battered wooden pieces on it. The head had fallen off the black king at some time or other; it was held on with a piece of gritty adhesive tape. "I'll show you," the man said, sliding the board over. Beth was now standing next to him. She was the only girl in the room. The man reached down to the board and with surprising delicacy picked up the white king pawn with his fingertips and dropped it lightly on king four. Then he picked up the black queen bishop pawn and dropped it on queen's bishop three, put White's queen pawn on the fourth rank and did the same with Black's. He looked up at the people around him, who were by now all paying close attention.

"The Caro-Kann. Right?"

Beth was familiar with these moves, but she had never seen them played. She expected the man to move the white queen's knight next, and he did. Then he had the black pawn capture the white, and took the capturing pawn with the white knight. He played Black's king knight to bishop three and brought White's other knight out. Beth remembered the move. Looking at it now, it seemed tame. She found herself speaking up. "I'd take the knight," she said quietly.

The man looked at her and raised his eyebrows. "Aren't you that kid from Kentucky—the one who wiped out Harry Beltik?"

"Yes," Beth said. "If you take the knight, it doubles his pawns . . ."

"Big deal," the man said. "All pawns and no hope. Here's how to win with Black." He left the knight in the center of the board and played Black's pawn to king four. Then he continued laying out the moves of a game, shuffling the pieces around on the board with casual dexterity, occasionally pointing out a potential trap. The game built to a balanced fugue in the center. It was like time-lapse photography on TV where a pale-green stalk humps itself from dirt, heightens, swells and explodes into a peony or a rose.

Some other people had come into the room and were watching. Beth was feeling a new kind of excitement with this display, with the knowingness, the clarity and nerve of the man in the black cap. He began trading pieces in the center, lifting the captured ones off the board with his fingertips as though they were dead flies, keeping up a soft-voiced patter that pointed out necessities and weaknesses, pitfalls and strengths. Once, when he had to reach across the board to the back rank and move a rook from its home square, she was astonished to see as he stretched his body that he was carrying a knife at his waist. The leather-and-metal handle protruded above his belt. He looked so much like someone out of *Treasure Island* that the knife did not seem out of place. Just then he paused in his moving and said, "Now watch this," and brought the black rook up to its king five square, setting it down with a muted flourish. He folded his arms across his chest. "What does White do here?" he asked, looking around him.

Beth considered the board. There were pitfalls all over for white. One of the men watching spoke up. "Queen takes pawn?"

The man in the cap shook his head, smiling. "Rook to king eight check. And the queen falls."

Beth had seen that. It looked to be all over for the white pieces and she started to say so when another man spoke up. "That's Mieses-Reshevsky. From the thirties."

The man looked up at him. "You've got it," he said. "Margate. Nineteen thirty-five."

"White played rook to queen one," the first man said.

"Right," said the other. "What else has he got?" He made the move and continued. It was clear now that White was losing. There were some fast trades and then an endgame that looked for a moment as though it might be slow, but Black made a striking sacrifice of a passed pawn and abruptly the topology of pawn-queening made it clear that Black would have a queen two moves before White. It was a dazzling game, like some of the best ones Beth had learned from books.

The man stood up, took off his cap and stretched. He looked down at Beth for a moment. "Reshevsky was playing like that when he was your age, little girl. Younger."

Back in the room Mrs. Wheatley was still reading the *Enquirer*. She looked over her reading glasses at Beth as she came in the door. "Finished already?" she said.

"Yes."

"How did you do?"

"I won."

Mrs. Wheatley smiled warmly. "Honey," she said, "you are a treasure."

Mrs. Wheatley had seen an ad about a sale at Shillito's—a department store a few blocks from the Gibson. Since there were four hours before Beth's next game, they went over, through lightly falling snow, and Mrs. Wheatley rummaged in the basement awhile until Beth said, "I'd like to look at their sweaters."

"What kind of sweaters, dear?"

"Cashmere."

Mrs. Wheatley's eyebrows went up. "Cashmere? Are you sure we can afford it?"

"Yes."

Beth found a pale-gray sweater on sale for twenty-four dollars, and it fit her perfectly. Looking in the tall mirror, she tried to imagine herself as a member of the Apple Pi Club, like Margaret; but the face was still Beth's face, round and freckled, with straight brown hair. She shrugged and bought the sweater with a traveler's check. They had passed an elegant little shoe store with saddle oxfords in the window on the way to Shillito's and she took Mrs. Wheatley there and bought herself a pair. Then she bought argyle socks to go with them. The tag said: "100% wool. Made in England." Going back to the hotel through a wind that whipped tiny snowflakes against her, Beth kept looking down at her new shoes and high plaid socks. She liked the way her feet felt, liked the tightness of the warm socks against her calves, and liked the way they looked—bright expensive socks above bright brown-and-white shoes. She kept looking down.

That afternoon she was matched with a middle-aged Ohioan with a rating of 1910. She played the Sicilian and forced him to resign after an hour and a half. Her mind was as clear as it had ever been, and she was able to use some of the things she had learned over the past weeks from studying her new book by the Russian master Boleslavski.

When she turned in her score sheet Sizemore was standing

near the desk. She saw a few other familiar faces from that tournament, and it felt good to see them, but she really wanted to see only one player from before—Townes. She looked several times but didn't find him.

Back in their room that evening, Mrs. Wheatley watched *The Beverly Hillbillies* and *The Dick Van Dyke Show*, while Beth set up and went over her two games, looking for weaknesses in her play. There weren't any. Then she got out the book by Reuben Fine on endgames and began studying. The endgame in chess had its own feeling; it was like an altogether different contest, once you got down to a piece or two on each side and the question became one of queening a pawn. It could be agonizingly subtle; there was no chance for the kind of violent attack Beth loved.

But she was bored with Reuben Fine, and after a while she closed the book and went to bed. She had two of the little green pills in her pajama pocket, and she took them after the lights were off. She didn't want to risk not sleeping.

The second day was as easy as the first, even though Beth was matched against stronger players. It had taken her a while to clear her head from the effect of the pills, but by the time she started playing her mind was sharp. She even handled the pieces themselves with confidence, picking them up and setting them down with aplomb.

There was no "Top Boards" room at this tournament. Board One was merely the first board at the first table. For the second game Beth was at Board Six, and people were gathered around her as she forced the master to resign after taking one of his rooks. When she looked up during the applause, there stood Alma Wheatley at the back of the room smiling broadly.

In her final game, at Board One, Beth was playing a master named Rudolph. He managed to start trading pieces in the center during the middle game, and Beth was alarmed to find herself crowded into an ending with a rook, a knight and three pawns. Rudolph had the same thing, except for a bishop where she had a knight. She didn't like it, and his bishop was a distinct advantage. But she managed to pin it and trade her knight for it and then play with great care for an hour and a half until Rudolph made a blunder and she zeroed in on it. She checked with a pawn, traded rooks and got one of her pawns passed with the king protecting. Rudolph looked furious at himself and resigned.

There was strong applause. Beth looked at the crowd around the table. Near the back, in her blue dress, was Mrs. Wheatley, clapping her hands enthusiastically.

Going back to the room, Mrs. Wheatley carried the heavy trophy and Beth had the check in her blouse pocket. Mrs. Wheatley had written it all out on a sheet of hotel stationery that sat on top of the TV: sixty-six dollars for three days at the Gibson, plus three-thirty tax; twenty-three sixty for the bus, and the price of each meal, including tip. "I've allowed twelve dollars for our celebration supper tonight and two dollars for a small breakfast tomorrow. That makes our total expenses equal one seventy-two thirty."

"It leaves over three hundred dollars," Beth said.

There was a silence for a while. Beth looked at the sheet of paper, although she understood it perfectly well. She was wondering if she should offer to split the money with Mrs. Wheatley. She did not want to do that. She had won it herself.

Mrs. Wheatley broke the silence. "Perhaps you could give me ten percent," she said pleasantly. "As an agent's commission."

"Thirty-two dollars," Beth said, "and seventy-seven cents."

"They told me at Methuen that you were marvelous at math."

Beth nodded. "Okay," she said.

They had something with veal in it at an Italian restaurant. Mrs. Wheatley ordered herself a carafe of red wine and drank it and smoked Chesterfields throughout the meal. Beth liked the bread and the cold, pale butter. She liked the little tree with oranges on it that sat on the bar, not far from their table.

Mrs. Wheatley wiped her chin with her napkin when she finished the wine and lit a final cigarette. "Beth, dear," she said, "there's a tournament in Houston over the holidays, starting the twenty-sixth. I understand it's very easy to travel on Christmas Day, since most people are eating plum pudding or whatever."

"I saw," Beth said. She had read the ad in *Chess Review* and wanted very much to go. But Houston had seemed awfully far away for a six-hundred-dollar prize.

"I believe we could fly to Houston," Mrs. Wheatley said brightly. "We could have a pleasant winter vacation in the sun."

Beth was finishing her spumoni. "Okay," she said and then, looking down at the ice cream, "Okay, Mother."

Their Christmas dinner was microwave turkey served on an airplane, with a complimentary glass of champagne for Mrs. Wheatley and canned orange juice for Beth. It was the best Christmas she had ever had. The plane flew over a snow-covered Kentucky and, at the end of the trip, circled out above the Gulf of Mexico. They landed in warm air and sunshine. Driving in from the airport, they passed one construction site after the other, the big yellow cranes and bulldozers standing idle near stacks of girders. Someone had hung a Christmas wreath on one of them.

A week before they left Lexington a new copy of *Chess Review* had come in the mail. When Beth opened it she found a small picture of herself and Beltik at the back, and a banner headline: SCHOOLGIRL TAKES KENTUCKY CHAMPIONSHIP FROM MASTER. Their game was printed and the commentary said: "Onlookers were amazed at her youthful mastery of the fine points of strategy. She shows the assurance of players twice her age." She read it twice before showing it to Mrs. Wheatley. Mrs. Wheatley was ecstatic; she had read the article in the Lexington paper aloud and then said "Wonderful!" This time she read in silence before saying, "This is *national* recognition, dear," in a hushed voice.

Mrs. Wheatley had brought the magazine with her, and they spent part of the time on the plane marking the tournaments Beth would play over the next several months. They settled on one a month; Mrs. Wheatley was afraid they would run out of diseases and, as she said, "credibility" if she wrote more excuses than that. Beth wondered to herself if they shouldn't just ask for permission in a straightforward way—after all, boys were allowed to miss classes for basketball and football—but she was wise enough to say nothing. Mrs. Wheatley seemed to take immense enjoyment in doing it this way. It was like a conspiracy.

She won in Houston without any trouble. She was, as Mrs. Wheatley said, really "getting the hang of it." She was forced to draw her third game but took the final one by a dazzling combination, beating the forty-year-old Southwest Champion as though he were a beginner. They stayed over two days "for the sun" and visited the Museum of Fine Arts and the Zoological Gardens. On the day after the tournament Beth's picture was in the paper, and this time it made her feel good to see it. The article called her a *"Wunderkind."* Mrs. Wheatley bought three copies, saying, "I just might start a scrapbook."

In January, Mrs. Wheatley called the school to say that Beth had a relapse of mono, and they went to Charleston. In February it was Atlanta and a cold; in March, Miami and the flu. Sometimes Mrs. Wheatley talked to the Assistant Principal and sometimes to the Dean of Girls. No one questioned the excuses. It seemed likely that some of the students knew about her from out-of-town papers or something, but no one in authority said anything. Beth worked on her chess for three hours every evening between tournaments. She lost one game in Atlanta but still came in first, and she stayed undefeated in the other two cities. She enjoyed flying with Mrs. Wheatley, who sometimes became comfortably buzzed by martinis on the planes. They talked and giggled together. Mrs. Wheatley said funny things about the stewardesses and their beautifully pressed jackets and bright, artificial make-up, or talked about how silly some of her neighbors in Lexington were. She was high-spirited and confidential and amusing, and Beth would laugh a long time and look out the window at the clouds below them and feel better than she had ever felt, even during those times at Methuen when she had saved up her green pills and taken five or six at once.

She grew to love hotels and restaurants and the excitement of being in a tournament and winning it, moving up gradually game by game and having the crowd around her table increase with each win. People at tournaments knew who she was now.

She was always the youngest there, and sometimes the only female. Back at school afterward things seemed more and more drab. Some of the other students talked about going to college after high school, and some had professions in mind. Two girls she knew wanted to be nurses. Beth never participated in these conversations; she already was what she wanted to be. But she talked to no one about her traveling or about the reputation she was building in tournament chess.

When they came back from Miami in March, there was an envelope from the Chess Federation in the mail. In it was a new membership card with her rating: 1881. She had been told it would take time for the rating to reflect her real strength; she was satisfied for now to be, finally, a rated player. She would push the figure up soon enough. The next big step was Master, at 2200. After 2000 they called you an Expert, but that didn't mean much. The one she liked was International Grandmaster; that had weight to it.

That summer they went to New York to play at the Henry Hudson Hotel. They had developed a taste for fine food, though at home it was mostly TV dinners, and in New York they ate at French restaurants, taking buses crosstown to Le Bistro and Café Argenteuil. Mrs. Wheatley had gone to a gas station in Lexington and bought a *Mobil Travel Guide;* she picked places with three or more stars, and then they found them with the little map. It was terribly expensive, but neither of them said a word about the cost. Beth would eat smoked trout but never fresh fish; she remembered the fish she'd had to eat on Fridays at Methuen. She decided that next year at school she would take French.

The only problem was that, on the road, she took the pills from Mrs. Wheatley's prescription to help her sleep at night, and sometimes it required an hour or so to get her head clear in the morning. But tournament games never started before nine, and she made a point of getting up in time to have several cups of coffee from room service. Mrs. Wheatley did not know about the pills and showed no concern over Beth's appetite for coffee;

she treated her in every way like an adult. Sometimes it seemed as though Beth were the older of the two.

Beth loved New York. She liked riding on the bus, and she liked taking the IRT subway with its grit and rattle. She liked window shopping when she had a chance, and she enjoyed hearing people on the street talking Yiddish or Spanish. She did not mind the sense of danger in the city or the arrogant way the taxis drove or the dirty glitter of Times Square. They went to Radio City Music Hall on their last night and saw *West Side Story* and the Rockettes. Sitting high in the cavernous theater in a velvet seat, Beth was thrilled.

She had expected a reporter from *Life* to be someone who chain-smoked and looked like Lloyd Nolan, but the person who came to the door of the house was a small woman with steel-gray hair and a dark dress. The man with her was carrying a camera. She introduced herself as Jean Balke. She looked older than Mrs. Wheatley, and she walked around the living room with quick little movements, hastily checking out the books in the bookcase and studying some of the prints on the walls. Then she began asking questions. Her manner was pleasant and direct. "I've really been impressed," she said, "even though I don't play chess myself." She smiled. "They say you're the real thing."

Beth was a little embarrassed.

"How does it feel? Being a girl among all those men?"

"I don't mind it."

"Isn't it frightening?" They were sitting facing each other. Miss Balke leaned forward, looking intently at Beth.

Beth shook her head. The photographer came over to the sofa and began taking readings with a meter.

"When I was a girl," the reporter said, "I was never allowed to be competitive. I used to play with dolls."

The photographer backed off and began to study Beth through his camera. She remembered the doll Mr. Ganz had given her. "Chess isn't always 'competitive,' " she said.

"But you play to win."

Beth wanted to say something about how beautiful chess was

sometimes, but she looked at Miss Balke's sharp, inquiring face and couldn't find the words for it.

"Do you have a boyfriend?"

"No. I'm fourteen." The photographer began snapping pictures.

Miss Balke had lighted a cigarette. She leaned forward now and tapped the ashes into one of Mrs. Wheatley's ashtrays. "Are you interested in boys?" she asked.

Beth was feeling more and more uneasy. She wanted to talk about learning chess and about the tournaments she had won and about people like Morphy and Capablanca. She did not like this woman and did not like her questions. "I'm interested in chess mostly."

Miss Balke smiled brightly. "Tell me about it," she said. "Tell me how you learned to play and how old you were."

Beth told her and Miss Balke took notes, but Beth felt that she wasn't really interested in any of it. She found as she went on talking that she really had very little to say.

The next week at school, during algebra class, Beth saw the boy in front of her pass a copy of *Life* to the girl next to him, and they both turned and looked back at her as though they had never seen her before. After class the boy, who had never spoken to her before, stopped her and asked if she would autograph the magazine. Beth was stunned. She took it from him and there it was, filling a full page. There was a picture of her looking serious at her chessboard, and there was another picture of the main building at Methuen. Across the top of the page a headline read: A GIRL MOZART STARTLES THE WORLD OF CHESS. She signed her name with the boy's ball-point pen, setting the magazine on an empty desk.

When she got home, Mrs. Wheatley had the magazine in her lap. She began reading aloud:

" 'With some people chess is a pastime, with others it is a compulsion, even an addiction. And every now and then a person comes along for whom it is a birthright. Now and then a small boy appears and dazzles us with his precocity at what may be the world's most difficult game. But what if that boy were a girl—a young, unsmiling girl with brown eyes, brown hair and a dark-blue dress?

" 'It has never happened before, but it happened recently. In Lexington, Kentucky, and in Cincinnati. In Charleston, Atlanta, Miami, and lately in New York City. Into the male-dominated world of the nation's top chess tournaments strolls a fourteen-year-old with bright, intense eyes, from eighth grade at Fairfield Junior High in Lexington, Kentucky. She is quiet and well-mannered. And she is out for blood . . .' It's *marvelous*!" Mrs. Wheatley said. "Shall I read on?"

"It talks about the orphanage." Beth had bought her own copy. "And it gives one of my games. But it's mostly about my being a girl."

"Well, you are one."

"It shouldn't be that important," Beth said. "They didn't print half the things I told them. They didn't tell about Mr. Shaibel. They didn't say anything about how I play the Sicilian."

"But, Beth," Mrs. Wheatley said, "it makes you a *celebrity*!"

Beth looked at her thoughtfully. "For being a girl, mostly," she said.

The next day Margaret stopped her in the hall. Margaret was wearing a camel's-hair coat and her blond hair fell just to her shoulders; she was even more beautiful than she had been a year before, when Beth had taken the ten dollars from her purse. "The other Apple Pi's asked me to invite you," Margaret said respectfully. "We're having a pledge party Friday night at my house."

The Apple Pi's. It was very strange. When Beth accepted and asked for the address she realized it was the first time she had ever actually spoken to Margaret.

She spent over an hour that afternoon trying on dresses at Purcell's before picking a navy-blue with a simple white collar from the store's most expensive line. When she showed it to Mrs. Wheatley that evening and told her she was going to the Apple Pi Club, Mrs. Wheatley was clearly pleased. "You look just like a debutante!" she said when Beth tried on the dress for her.

* * *

The white woodwork of Margaret's living room glistened beautifully and the pictures on the walls were oil paintings—mostly of horses. Even though it was a mild evening in March, a big fire burned under the white mantel. Fourteen girls were sitting on the white sofas and colored wingback chairs when Beth arrived in her new dress. Most of the others were wearing sweaters and skirts. "It was really something," one of them said, "to find a face from Fairfield Junior High in *Life*. I nearly flipped!" but when Beth started to talk about the tournaments, the girls interrupted her to ask about the boys at them. Were they good-looking? Did she date any of them? When Beth said, "There's not much time for that," the girls changed the subject.

For an hour or more they talked about boys and dating and clothes, veering erratically from cool sophistication to giggles, while Beth sat uneasily at one end of a sofa holding a crystal glass of Coca-Cola, unable to think of anything to say. Then, at nine o'clock, Margaret turned on the huge television set by the fireplace and they were all quiet, except for an occasional giggle, while the "Movie of the Week" came on.

Beth sat through it, not participating in the gossip and laughter during the commercials, until it ended at eleven. She was astounded at the dullness of the evening. This was the elite Apple Pi Club that had seemed so important when she first went to school in Lexington, and this was what they did at their sophisticated parties: they watched a Charles Bronson movie. The only break in the dullness was when a girl named Felicia said, "I wonder if he's as well-hung as he looks." Beth laughed at that, but it was the only thing she laughed at.

When she left after eleven no one urged her to stay, and no one said anything about her joining. She was relieved to get into the taxi and go home, and when she got there she spent an hour in her room with *The Middle Game in Chess*, translated from the Russian of D. Luchenko.

The school knew about her, well enough, by the next tournament, and this time she hadn't claimed illness as an excuse. Mrs. Wheatley talked to the principal, and Beth was excused from her classes. Nothing was said about the illnesses she had lied about. They wrote her up in the school paper, and people pointed her out in the hallways. The tournament was in Kansas City, and after she won it the director took her and Mrs. Wheatley to a steakhouse for dinner and told her they were honored to have her participate. He was a serious young man, and he treated both of them politely.

"I'd like to play in the U.S. Open," Beth said over dessert and coffee.

"Sure," he said. "You might win it."

"Would that lead to playing abroad?" Mrs. Wheatley asked. "In Europe, I mean?"

"No reason why not," the young man said. His name was Nobile. He wore thick glasses and kept drinking ice water. "They have to know about you before they invite you."

"Would winning the Open make them know about me?"

"Sure. Benny Watts plays in Europe all the time, now that he's got his international title."

"How's the prize money?" Mrs. Wheatley asked, lighting a cigarette.

"Pretty good, I think."

"What about Russia?" Beth said.

Nobile stared at her a minute, as though she had suggested something illicit. "Russia's murder," he said finally. "They eat Americans for breakfast over there."

"Now, *really* . . ." Mrs. Wheatley said.

"They really do," Nobile said. "I don't think there's been an American with a prayer against the Russians for twenty years. It's like ballet. They *pay* people to play chess."

Beth thought of those pictures in *Chess Review,* of the men with grim faces, bending over chessboards—Borgov and Tal, Laev and Shapkin, scowling, wearing dark suits. Chess in Russia was a different thing than chess in America. Finally she asked, "How do I get in the U.S. Open?"

"Just send in an entry fee," Nobile said. "It's like any other tournament, except the competition's stiffer."

*   *   *

She sent in her entry fee, but she did not play in the U.S. Open that year. Mrs. Wheatley developed a virus that kept her in bed for two weeks, and Beth, who had just passed her fifteenth birthday, was unwilling to go alone. She did her best to hide it, but she was furious at Alma Wheatley for being sick, and at herself for being afraid to make the trip to Los Angeles. The Open was not as important as the U.S. Championship, but it was time she started playing in something other than events chosen solely on the basis of the prize money. There was a tight little world of tournaments like the United States Championship and the Merriwether Invitational that she knew of through overheard conversations and from articles in *Chess Review;* it was time she got into it, and then into international chess. Sometimes she would visualize herself as what she wanted to become; a truly professional woman and the finest chessplayer in the world, traveling confidently by herself in the first-class cabins of airplanes, tall, perfectly dressed, good-looking and poised—a kind of white Jolene. She often told herself that she would send Jolene a card or a letter, but she never did. Instead she would study herself in the bathroom mirror, looking for signs of that poised and beautiful woman she wanted to become.

At sixteen she had grown taller and better-looking, had learned to have her hair cut in a way that showed her eyes to some advantage, but she still looked like a schoolgirl. She played tournaments about every six weeks now—in states like Illinois and Tennessee, and sometimes in New York. They still chose ones that would pay enough to show a profit after the expenses for the two of them. Her bank account grew, and that was a considerable pleasure, but somehow her career seemed to be on a plateau. And she was too old to be called a prodigy anymore.

Chapter 6

Although the U.S. Open was being held in Las Vegas, the other people at the Mariposa Hotel seemed oblivious to it. In the main room the players at the craps tables, at roulette and at the black-jack tables wore brightly colored double-knits and shirts; they went about their business in silence. On the other side of the casino was the hotel coffee shop. The day before the tournament Beth walked down an aisle between crapshooters where the main sound was the tapping of clay chips and of dice on felt. In the coffee shop she slid onto a stool at the counter, turned around to look at the mostly empty booths and saw a handsome young man sitting hunched over a cup of coffee, alone. It was Townes, from Lexington.

She stood up and went over to the booth. "Hello," she said.

He looked up and blinked, not recognizing her at first. Then he said, "Harmon! For Christ's sake!"

"Can I sit down?"

"Sure," he said. "I should have known you. You were on the list."

"The list?"

"The tournament list. I'm not playing. *Chess Review* sent me to write it up." He looked at her. "I could write you up. For the *Herald-Leader.*"

"Lexington?"

"You got it. You've grown a lot, Harmon. I saw the piece in *Life*." He looked at her closely. "You've even gotten good-looking."

She felt flustered and did not know what to say. Everything about Las Vegas was strange. On the table in each booth was a lamp with a glass base filled with purple liquid that bubbled and swirled below its bright pink shade. The waitress who handed her a menu was dressed in a black miniskirt and fishnet hose, but she had the face of a geometry teacher. Townes was handsome, smiling, dressed in a dark sweater with a striped shirt open at the throat. She chose the Mariposa Special: hot cakes, scrambled eggs and chili peppers with the Bottomless Cup of coffee.

"I could do half a page on you for the Sunday paper," Townes was saying.

The hot cakes and eggs came, and Beth ate them and drank two cups of coffee.

"I've got a camera in my room," Townes said. He hesitated. "I've got chessboards, too. Do you want to play?"

She shrugged. "Okay. Let's go up."

"Terrific!" His smile was dazzling.

The drapes were open, with a view of a parking lot. The bed was huge and unmade. It seemed to fill the room. There were three chessboards set up: one on a table by the window, one on the bureau, and the third in the bathroom next to the basin. He posed her by the window and shot a roll of film while she sat at the board and moved the pieces. It was difficult not to look at him as he walked around. When he came close to her and held a little light meter near her face, she found herself catching her breath at the sensation of warmth from his body. Her heart was beating fast, and when she reached out to move a rook she saw that her fingers were trembling.

He clicked off the last shot and began rewinding the film. "One of those should do it," he said. He set the camera on the night-stand by the bed. "Let's play chess."

She looked at him. "I don't know what your first name is."

"Everyone calls me Townes," he said. "Maybe that's why I call you Harmon. Instead of Elizabeth."

She began setting up the pieces on the board. "It's Beth."

"I'd rather call you Harmon."

"Let's play skittles," she said. "You can play White."

Skittles was speed chess, and there wasn't time for much complexity. He got his chess clock from the bureau and set it to give them each five minutes. "I should give you three," he said.

"Go ahead," Beth said, not looking at him. She wished he would just come over and touch her—on the arm maybe, or put his hand on her cheek. He seemed terribly sophisticated, and his smile was easy. He couldn't be thinking about her the way she was thinking about him. But Jolene had said, "They all think about it, honey. That's just what they think about." And they were alone in his room, with the king-sized bed. In Las Vegas.

When he set the clock at the side of the board, she saw they both had the same amount of time. She did not want to play this game with him. She wanted to make love with him. She punched the button on her side, and his clock started ticking. He moved pawn to king four and pushed his button. She held her breath for a moment and began to play chess.

When Beth came back to their room Mrs. Wheatley was sitting in bed, smoking a cigarette and looking mournful. "Where've you been, honey?" she said. Her voice was quiet and had some of the strain it had when she spoke of Mr. Wheatley.

"Playing chess," Beth said. "Practicing."

There was a copy of *Chess Review* on the television set. Beth got it and opened it to the masthead page. His name wasn't among the editors, but down below, under "Correspondents," were three names; the third was D. L. Townes. She still didn't know his first name.

After a moment Mrs. Wheatley said, "Would you hand me a can of beer? On the dresser."

Beth stood up. Five cans of Pabst were on one of the brown trays room service used, and a half-eaten bag of potato chips. "Why don't you have one yourself?" Mrs. Wheatley said.

Beth picked up two cans; they felt metallic and cold. "Okay." She handed them to Mrs. Wheatley and got herself a clean glass from the bathroom.

When Beth gave her the glass, Mrs. Wheatley said, "I guess you've never had a beer before."

"I'm sixteen."

"Well . . ." Mrs. Wheatley frowned. She lifted the tab with a little *pop* and poured expertly into Beth's glass until the white collar stood above the rim. "Here," she said, as though offering medicine.

Beth sipped the beer. She had never had it before but it tasted much as she had expected, as though she had always known what beer would taste like. She tried not to make a face and finished almost half the glass. Mrs. Wheatley reached out from the bed and poured the rest of it in. Beth drank another mouthful. It stung her throat slightly, but then she felt a sensation of warmth in her stomach. Her face was flushed—as though she were blushing. She finished off the glassful. "Goodness," Mrs. Wheatley said, "you shouldn't drink so fast."

"I'd like another," Beth said. She was thinking of Townes, how he had looked after they finished playing and she stood up to leave. He had smiled and taken her hand. Just holding his hand for that short time made her cheeks feel the way the beer had. She had won seven fast games from him. She held her glass tightly and for a moment wanted to throw it on the floor as hard as she could and watch it shatter. Instead she walked over, picked up another can of beer, put her finger in the ring and opened it.

"You really shouldn't . . ." Mrs. Wheatley said. Beth filled her glass. "Well," Mrs. Wheatley said, resigned, "if you're going to do that, let me have one too. I just don't want you to be sick . . ."

Beth banged her shoulder against the door frame going into the bathroom and barely got to the toilet in time. It stung her nose horribly as she threw up. After she finished, she stood by the toilet for a while and began to cry. Yet, even while she was crying, she knew that she had made a discovery with the three cans of beer, a discovery as important as the one she had made when she was eight years old and saved up her green pills and then took them all at one time. With the pills there was a long wait before the swooning came into her stomach and loosened the tightness. The beer gave her the same feeling with almost no wait.

"No more beer, honey," Mrs. Wheatley said when Beth came back into the bedroom. "Not until you're eighteen."

The ballroom was set up for seventy chess players, and Beth's first game was at Board Nine, against a small man from Oklahoma. She beat him as if in a dream, in two dozen moves. That afternoon, at Board Four, she crushed the defenses of a serious young man from New York, playing the King's Gambit and sacrificing the bishop the way Paul Morphy had done.

Benny Watts was in his twenties, but he looked nearly as young as Beth. He was not much taller, either. Beth saw him from time to time during the tournament. He started at Board One and stayed there; people said he was the best American player since Morphy. Beth stood near him once at the Coke machine, but they did not speak. He was talking to another male player and smiling a lot; they were amiably debating the virtues of the Semi-Slav defense. Beth had made a study of the Semi-Slav a few days before, and she had a good deal to say about it, but she remained silent, got her Coke and walked away. Listening to the two of them, she had felt something unpleasant and familiar: the sense that chess was a thing between men, and she was an outsider. She hated the feeling.

Watts was wearing a white shirt open at the collar, with the sleeves rolled up. His face was both cheerful and sly. With his flat straw-colored hair he looked as American as Huckleberry Finn, yet there was something untrustworthy about his eyes. He, too, had been a child prodigy and that, besides the fact that he was Champion, made Beth uneasy. She remembered a Watts game book with a draw against Borstmann and a caption reading "Copenhagen: 1948." The meant Benny had been eight years old—the age Beth was when she was playing Mr. Shaibel in the basement. In the middle of that book was a photograph of him at thirteen, standing solemnly at a long table facing a group of uniformed midshipmen seated at chessboards; he had played against the twenty-three-man team at Annapolis without losing a game.

When she came back with her empty Coke bottle, he was still standing by the machine. He looked at her. "Hey," he said pleasantly, "you're Beth Harmon."

She put the bottle in the case. "Yes."

"I saw the piece in *Life,*" he said. "The game they printed was a pretty one." It was the game she'd won against Beltik.

"Thanks," she said.

"I'm Benny Watts."

"I know."

"You shouldn't have castled, though," he said smiling.

She stared at him. "I needed to get the rook out."

"You could have lost your king pawn."

She wasn't sure what he was talking about. She remembered the game well and had gone over it in her head a few times but found nothing wrong with it. Was it possible he had memorized the moves from *Life* and found a weakness? Or was he just showing off? Standing there, she pictured the position after the castle; the king pawn looked all right to her.

"I don't think so."

"He plays bishop to B-5, and you've got to break the pin."

"Wait a minute," she said.

"I can't," Benny said. "I've got to play an adjournment. Set it up and think it out. Your problem is his queen knight."

Suddenly she was angry. "I don't have to set it up to think it out."

"Goodness!" he said and left.

When he was gone, she stood by the Coke machine for several minutes going over the game, and then she saw it. There was an empty tournament board on a table near her; she set up the position before castling against Beltik, just to be certain, but she felt a knot in her stomach doing it. Beltik could have made the pin, and then his queen knight became a threat. She had to break the pin and then protect against a fork with that damned knight, and after that he had a rook threat and, bingo, there went her pawn. It could have been crucial. But what was worse, she hadn't seen it. And Benny Watts, just reading *Life* magazine, reading about a player he knew nothing about, had picked it up. She was standing at the board; she bit her lip, reached down and toppled the king. She had been so proud of finding an error in a Morphy game when she was in seventh grade. Now she'd had something like that done to her, and she did not like it. Not at all.

She was sitting behind the white pieces at Board One when Watts came in. When he shook her hand, he said in a low voice, "Knight to knight five. Right?"

"Yes," she said, between her teeth. A flash bulb popped. Beth pushed her queen's pawn to queen four.

She played the Queen's Gambit against him and by midgame felt with dismay that it had been a mistake. The Queen's Gambit could lead to complicated positions, and this one was Byzantine. There were half a dozen threats on each side, and the thing that made her nervous, that made her reach out for a piece several times and then stop her hand before touching it and draw back, was that she didn't trust herself. She did not trust herself to see everything Benny Watts could see. He played with a calm, pleasant precision, picking up his pieces lightly and setting them down noiselessly, sometimes smiling to himself as he did so. Every move he made looked solid as a rock. Beth's great strength was in fast attack, and she could find no way to attack. By the sixteenth move she was furious with herself for playing the gambit in the first place.

There must have been forty people clustered around the especially large wooden table. There was a brown velvet curtain behind them with the names HARMON and WATTS pinned to it. The horrible feeling, at the bottom of the anger and fear, was that she was the weaker player—that Benny Watts knew more about chess than she did and could play it better. It was a new feeling for her, and it seemed to bind and restrict her as she had not been bound and restricted since the last time she sat in Mrs. Deardorff's office. For a moment she looked over the crowd around the table, trying to find Mrs. Wheatley, but she was not there. Beth turned back to the board and looked briefly at Benny. He smiled at her serenely, as though he were offering her a drink rather than a head-splitting chess position. Beth set her elbows on the table, leaned her cheeks against her clenched fists and began to concentrate.

After a moment a simple thought came to her: I'm not playing Benny Watts; I'm playing chess. She looked at him again. His eyes were studying the board now. He can't move until I do. He can only move one piece at a time. She looked back to the board and began to consider the effects of trading, to picture where the pawns would be if the pieces that clogged the center were exchanged. If she took his king knight with her bishop and he retook with the queen pawn . . . No good. She could advance the knight and force a trade. That was better. She blinked and began to relax, forming and reforming the relationships of pawns in her mind, searching for a way of forcing an advantage. There was nothing in front of her now but the sixty-four squares and the shifting architecture of pawns—a jagged skyline of imaginary pawns, black and white, that flowed and shifted as she tried variation after variation, branch after branch of the game tree that grew from each set of moves. One branch began to look better than the others. She followed it for several half-moves to the possibilities that grew from it, holding in her mind the whole set of imaginary positions until she found one that had what she wanted to find.

She sighed and sat upright. When she pulled her face away from her fists, her cheeks were sore and her shoulders stiff. She looked at her clock. Forty minutes had passed. Watts was yawning. She reached out and made the move, advancing a knight in a way that would force the first trade. It looked innocuous enough. Then she punched the clock.

Watts studied the board for half a minute and started the trade. For a moment she felt panic in her stomach: Could he see what she was planning? That quickly? She tried to shake off the idea and took the offered piece. He took another, just as she had planned. She took. Watts reached out to take again, but hesitated. *Do it!* she commanded silently. But he pulled his hand back. If he saw through what she was planning, there was still time to get out of it. She bit her lip. He was studying the board intently. He would see it. The ticking of the clock seemed very loud. Beth's heart was beating so strongly that for a moment she feared Watts would hear it and know she was panicked and—

But he didn't. He took the trade just as she had planned it. She looked at his face almost in disbelief. It was too late for him now. He pressed the button that stopped his clock and started hers.

She pushed the pawn up to rook five. Immediately he stiffened in his chair—almost imperceptibly, but Beth saw it. He began studying the position intently. But he must have seen he was going to be stuck with doubled pawns; after two or three minutes he shrugged and made the necessary move, and Beth did her continuation, and then on the next move the pawn was doubled and the nervousness and anger had left her. She was out to win now. She would hammer at his weakness. She loved it. She loved attack.

Benny looked at her impassively for a moment. Then he reached out his hand, picked up his queen, and did something astonishing. He quietly captured her center pawn. Her protected pawn. The pawn that had been holding the queen to her corner for most of the game. He was sacrificing his queen. She could not believe it.

And then she saw what it meant, and her stomach twisted sharply. How had she missed it? With the pawn gone, she was open to a rook-bishop mate because of the bishop on the opened diagonal. She could protect by retreating her knight and moving one of her rooks over, but the protection wouldn't last, because—she saw now with horror—his innocent-looking knight would block her king's escape. It was terrible. It was the kind of thing she did to other people. It was the kind of thing Paul Morphy had done. And she had been thinking about doubled pawns.

She didn't have to take the queen. What would happen if she didn't? She would lose the pawn he had just taken. His queen would sit there in the center of the board. Worse, it could come over to her king rook file and press down on her castled king. The more she looked, the worse it became. And it had caught her completely off-guard. She put her elbows on the table and stared at the position. She needed a counterthreat, a move that would stop him in his tracks.

There wasn't any. She spent a half-hour studying the board and found only that Benny's move was even sounder than she had thought.

Maybe she could trade her way out of it if he attacked too quickly. She found a rook move and made it. If he would just bring the queen over now, there would be a chance to trade.

He didn't. He developed his other bishop. She brought the rook up to the second rank. Then he swung the queen over, threatening mate in three. She had to respond by retreating her knight into the corner. He kept attacking, and with impotent dismay, she saw a lost game gradually become manifest. When he took her king bishop pawn with his bishop, sacrificing it, it was over, and she knew it was over. There was nothing to do. She wanted to scream, but instead set her king on its side and got up from the table. Her legs and back were stiff and painful. Her stomach was knotted. All she had really needed was a draw, and she hadn't been able to get even that. Benny had drawn twice already in the tournament. She had gone into the game with a perfect score, and a draw would have given her the title. But she had gone for a win.

"Tough game," Benny was saying. He was holding out his hand. She forced herself to take it. People were applauding. Not applauding her but Benny Watts.

By evening she could still feel it, but it had lessened. Mrs. Wheatley tried to console her. The prize money would be split. She and Benny would be co-champions, each with a small trophy. "It happens all the time," Mrs. Wheatley said. "I have made inquiries, and the Open Championship is often shared."

"I didn't see what he was doing," Beth said, picturing the move where his queen took her pawn. It was like putting your tongue against an aching tooth.

"You can't finesse everything, dear," Mrs. Wheatley said. "Nobody can."

Beth looked at her. "You don't know anything about chess," she said.

"I know what it feels like to lose."

"I bet you do," Beth said, as viciously as she could. "I just bet you do."

Mrs. Wheatley peered at her meditatively for a moment. "And now you do too," she said softly.

Sometimes on the street that winter in Lexington people would look back over their shoulders at her. She was on the *Morning Show* on WLEX. The interviewer, a woman with heavily lacquered hair and harlequin glasses, asked Beth if she played bridge; Beth said no. Did she like being the U.S. Open Champion at chess? Beth said she was co-champion. Beth sat in a director's chair with bright lights shining on her face. She was willing to talk about chess, but the woman's manner, her false appearance of interest, made it difficult. Finally she was asked how she felt about the idea that chess was a waste of time, and she looked at the woman in the other chair and said, "No more than basketball." But before she could go on about that, the show was over. She had been on for six minutes.

The one-page article Townes had written about her appeared in the Sunday supplement of the *Herald-Leader* with one of the pictures he had taken at the window of his room in Las Vegas. She liked herself in the picture, with her right hand on the white queen and her face looking clear, serious and intelligent. Mrs. Wheatley bought five copies of the paper for her scrapbook.

Beth was in high school now, and there was a chess club, but she did not belong. The boys in it were nonplused to have a Master walking the hallways, and they would stare at her in a kind of embarrassed awe when she passed. Once a boy from twelfth grade stopped her to ask nervously if she would give a simultaneous in Chess Club sometime. She would play about thirty students at once. She remembered that other high school, near Methuen, and the way she was stared at afterward. "I'm sorry," she said, "I don't have time." The boy was unattractive and creepy-looking; it made her feel unattractive and creepy just to be talking with him.

She spent about an hour a night on her homework and made As. But homework meant nothing to her. It was the five or six hours of studying chess that was at the center of her life. She was enrolled as a special student at the university for a class in Russian that met one night a week. It was the only schoolwork that she paid serious attention to.

Chapter 7

Beth puffed, inhaled and held the smoke in. There was nothing to it. She handed the joint to the young man on her right, and he said, "Thank you." He had been talking about Donald Duck with Eileen. They were in Eileen and Barbara's apartment, a block off Main Street. It was Eileen who had invited Beth to the party, after the night class.

"It's got to be Mel Blanc," Eileen was saying now. "They're all Mel Blanc." Beth was still holding the smoke in, hoping that it would loosen her up. She had been sitting on the floor with these college students for half an hour and had said nothing.

"Blanc does Sylvester, but he doesn't do Donald Duck," the young man said with finality. He turned around to face Beth. "I'm Tim," he said. "You're the chess player."

Beth let the smoke out. "That's right."

"You're the U.S. Women's Champion."

"I'm the U.S. Open Co-Champion," Beth said.

"Sorry. It must be a trip." He was red-haired and thin. She had seen him sitting in the middle of the classroom and could remember his soft voice when they recited Russian phrases in unison.

"Do you play?" Beth did not like the strain in her voice. She felt out of place. She should either go home or call Mrs. Wheatley.

He shook his head. "Too cerebral. You want a beer?"

She hadn't had a beer since Las Vegas, a year before. "Okay," she said. She started to get up from the floor.

"I'll get it." He pushed himself up from where they were sitting on the carpet. He came back with two cans and handed her one. She took a long drink. During the first hour the music had been so loud that conversation was impossible, but when the last record ended no one replaced it. The disk on the hi-fi against the far wall was still turning, and she could see the little red lights on the amplifier. She hoped no one would notice and play another record.

Tim eased himself back down next to her with a sigh. "I used to play Monopoly a lot."

"I've never played that."

"It makes you a slave of capitalism. I still dream about big bucks."

Beth laughed. The joint had come back her way, and she held it between her fingertips and got what she could from it before passing it to Tim. "Why are you taking Russian," she said, "if you're a slave of capitalism?" She took another swallow of beer.

"You've got nice boobs," he said and took a drag. "We need another joint," he announced to the group at large. He turned back to Beth. "I wanted to read Dostoevsky in the original."

She finished her beer. Somebody produced another joint and began sending it around. There were a dozen people in the room. They'd had their first exam in the evening class, and Beth had been invited to the party afterward. With the beer and marijuana and talking to Tim, who seemed very easy to talk to, she felt better. When the joint came up again, she took a long drag on it, and then another. Someone put on a record. The music sounded much better, and the loudness didn't bother her now.

Suddenly she stood up. "I ought to call home," she said.

"In the bedroom, through the kitchen."

In the kitchen she opened another beer. She took a long swallow, pushed open the bedroom door and felt for a light switch.

She could not find it. A box of wooden matches sat on the stove by the frying pan, and she took it into the bedroom. She still could not find a switch, but on the dresser was a collection of candles in different shapes. She lit one and shook out the match. She stared for a moment at the candle. It was a lavender upright wax penis with a pair of glossy testicles at its base. The wick came from the glans, and most of the glans had already melted away. Something in her was shocked.

The telephone was on a table by the unmade bed. She carried the candle with her, sat on the edge of the bed, and dialed.

Mrs. Wheatley was a bit confused at first; she was dazed from either TV or beer. "You go on to bed," Beth said. "I've got a key."

"Did you say you were partying with college students?" Mrs. Wheatley said. "From the university?"

"Yes."

"Well, be careful what you smoke, honey."

There was a marvelous feeling across Beth's shoulders and on the back of her neck. For a moment she wanted to rush home and embrace Mrs. Wheatley and hold her tight. But all she said was, "Okay."

"See you in the morning," Mrs. Wheatley said.

Beth sat on the edge of the bed, listening to the music from the living room, and finished her beer. She hardly ever listened to music and had never been to a school dance. If you didn't count the Apple Pi's, this was the first party she had ever been to. In the living room the song ended. A moment later, Tim sat on the bed beside her. It seemed perfectly natural, like the response to a request she had made. "Have another beer," he said.

She took it and drank. Her movements felt slow and certain. "Jesus!" Tim whispered in mock alarm. "What's that purple thing burning there?"

"You tell me," Beth said.

She panicked for a moment as he pushed himself into her. It seemed frighteningly big, and she felt helpless, as if she were in a dentist's chair. But that didn't last. He was careful, and it didn't hurt badly. She put her arms around his back, feeling the roughness of his bulky sweater. He began moving. He began to squeeze her breasts under her blouse. "Don't do that," she said, and he said, "Whatever you say," and kept moving in and out. She could barely feel his penis now, but it was all right. She was seventeen, and it was about time. He was wearing a condom. The best part had been watching him put it on, joking about it. What they were doing was really all right and nothing like books or movies. Fucking. Well, now. If only he were Townes.

Afterward she fell asleep on the bed. Not in a lovers' embrace, not even touching the man she had just made love with, but sprawled out on the bed with her clothes on. She saw Tim blow out the candle and heard the door close quietly after him.

When she awoke, she saw by the electric alarm clock that it was nearly ten in the morning. Sunlight came around the edges of the bedroom window blinds. The air smelled stale. Her legs were prickly from her wool skirt, and the neck of her sweater had been pressed against her throat, which felt sweaty. She was ferociously hungry. She sat on the edge of the bed a minute, blinking. She got up and pushed open the kitchen door. Empty bottles and beer cans were everywhere. The air was foul with dead smoke. A note was fastened to the refrigerator door with a magnet in the shape of Mickey Mouse's head. It read: "Everybody went to Cincinnati to see a movie. Stay as long as you like."

The bathroom was off the living room. When she had finished showering and had dried herself, she wrapped a towel around her hair, went back to the kitchen and opened the refrigerator. There were eggs in a carton, two cans of Budweiser and some pickles. On the door shelf was a Baggie. She picked it up. Inside was a single, tightly rolled joint. She took it out, put it in her mouth and lit it with a wooden match. She inhaled deeply. Then she took out four eggs and put them on to boil. She had never felt so hungry in her life. She cleaned up the apartment in an organized way, as if she were playing chess, getting four large grocery bags to put all the bottles and butts in and stacking these on the back porch. She found a half-full bottle of Ripple and four unopened beer cans in the debris. She opened a beer and began vacuuming the living-room carpet.

Hanging over a chair in the bedroom was a pair of jeans. When she had finished cleaning she changed into them. They fit her perfectly. She found a white T-shirt in a drawer and put it on. Then she drank the rest of her beer and opened another. Someone had left a lipstick on the back of the toilet. She went to the bathroom and studying herself in the mirror, reddened her lips carefully. She had never worn lipstick before. She was beginning to feel very good.

Mrs. Wheatley's voice sounded faint and anxious. "You might have *called.*"

"I'm sorry," Beth said. "I didn't want to wake you up."

"I wouldn't have minded . . ."

"Anyway, I'm all right. And I'm going to Cincinnati to see a movie. I won't be home tonight either."

There was a silence at the other end of the line.

"I'll be back after school Monday."

Finally, Mrs. Wheatley spoke. "Are you with a boy?"

"I was last night."

"Oh." Mrs. Wheatley's voice sounded distant. "*Beth* . . ."

Beth laughed. "Come on," she said. "I'm all right."

"Well . . ." She still sounded grave, then her voice became lighter. "I suppose it's all right. It's just that—"

Beth smiled. "I won't get pregnant," she said.

At noon she put the rest of the eggs in a pot to boil and turned on the hi-fi. She had never really listened to music before, but she listened now. She danced a few steps in the middle of the living room, waiting for the eggs. She would not let herself get sick. She would eat frequently and drink one beer—or one glass of wine—every hour. She had made love the night before, and now it was time to learn about being drunk. She was alone, and she liked it. It was the way she had learned everything important in her life.

At four in the afternoon she walked into Larry's Package Store, a block from the apartment, and bought a fifth of Ripple.

When the man was putting it in the bag, she said, "Do you have a wine like Ripple that's not so sweet?"

"These soda-pop wines are all the same," the man said.

"What about burgundy?" Sometimes Mrs. Wheatley ordered burgundy with her dinner when they ate out.

"I've got Gallo, Italian Swiss Colony, Paul Masson . . ."

"Paul Masson," Beth said. "Two bottles."

That night at eleven she was able to get undressed by being careful. She had found a pair of pajamas earlier and she managed to get them on and to pile her clothes on a chair before getting into bed and passing out.

No one had come back by morning. She made scrambled eggs and ate them with two pieces of toast before having her first glass of wine. It was another sunny day. In the living room she found Vivaldi's "The Four Seasons." She put it on. Then she began drinking in earnest.

On Monday morning Beth took a taxi to Henry Clay High School and arrived ten minutes before her first class. She had left the apartment empty and clean; the owners had not yet returned from Cincinnati. Most of the wrinkles had hung out of her sweater and skirt, and she had washed her argyle socks. She had drunk the second bottle of burgundy Sunday night and slept soundly for ten hours. Now, in the taxi, there was a dim ache at the back of her head and her hands trembled slightly, but outside the window the May morning was exquisite, and the green of the young leaves on trees was delicate and fresh. By the time she paid and got out she felt light and springy, ready to go ahead and finish high school and devote her energy to chess. She had three thousand dollars in her savings account; she was no longer a virgin; and she knew how to drink.

There was an embarrassed silence when she came home after school. Mrs. Wheatley, wearing a blue housedress, was mopping the kitchen floor. Beth settled herself on the sofa and picked up Reuben Fine's book on the endgame. It was a book she hated. She had seen a can of Pabst on the side of the sink, but she did not want any. It would be better not to drink anything for a long while. She had had enough.

When Mrs. Wheatley finished, she set the mop against the refrigerator and came into the living room. "I see you're back," she began. Her voice was carefully neutral.

Beth looked at her. "I had a good time," she said.

Mrs. Wheatley seemed uncertain what attitude to take. Finally she allowed herself a small smile. It was surprisingly shy, like a girl's smile. "Well," she said, "chess isn't the only thing in life."

Beth graduated from high school in June, and Mrs. Wheatley gave her a Bulova watch. The back of the case read *With love from Mother.* She liked that, but what she liked better was the rating that came in the mail: 2243. At the school party, several other graduates offered Beth surreptitious drinks, but she refused. She had fruit punch and went home early. She needed to study; she would be playing her first international tournament, in Mexico City, in two weeks, and after that came the United States Championship. She had been invited to the Remy-Vallon in Paris, at the end of the summer. Things were beginning to happen.

Chapter 8

_____

An hour after the plane crossed the border, Beth was absorbed in pawn-structure analysis and Mrs. Wheatley was drinking her third bottle of Cerveza Corona. "Beth," Mrs. Wheatley said, "I have a confession to make."

Beth put the book down, reluctantly.

Mrs. Wheatley seemed nervous. "Do you know what a pen pal is, dear?"

"Someone you trade letters with."

"Exactly! When I was in high school, our Spanish class was given a list of boys in Mexico who were studying English. I picked one and sent him a letter about myself." Mrs. Wheatley gave a little laugh. "His name was Manuel. We corresponded for a long time—even while I was married to Allston. We exchanged photographs." Mrs. Wheatley opened her purse, rummaged through it and produced a bent snapshot which she handed to Beth. It was a picture of a thin-faced man, surprisingly pale-looking, with a pencil-thin mustache. Mrs. Wheatley hesitated and said, "Manuel will be meeting us at the airport."

Beth had no objection to this; it might even be a good thing to have a Mexican friend. But she was put off by Mrs. Wheatley's manner. "Have you met him before?"

"Never." She leaned over in her seat and squeezed Beth's forearm. "You know, I'm really quite thrilled."

Beth could see that she was a little drunk. "Is that why you
wanted to come down early?"

Mrs. Wheatley pulled back and straightened the sleeves of her
blue cardigan. "I suppose so," she said.

"Si como no?" Mrs. Wheatley said. "And he dresses so well, and
opens doors for me and orders dinner beautifully." She was pulling up her pantyhose as she talked, tugging fiercely to get them
over her broad hips.

They were probably fucking—Mrs. Wheatley and Manuel
Córdoba y Serano. Beth did not let herself visualize it. Mrs.
Wheatley had come back to the hotel at about three that morn-
ing, and at two-thirty the night before. Beth, pretending to be
asleep, had smelled the ripe mix of perfume and gin while Mrs.
Wheatley fumbled around the room, undressing and sighing.

"I thought at first it was the altitude," Mrs. Wheatley said.
"Seven thousand three hundred and fifty feet." Sitting down at
the little brass vanity bench, she leaned forward on one elbow
and began rouging her cheeks. "It makes a person positively
giddy. But I think now it's the culture." She stopped and turned
to Beth. "There is no hint of a Protestant ethic in Mexico. They
are all Latin Catholics, and they all live in the here and now."
Mrs. Wheatley had been reading Alan Watts. "I think I'll have
just one margarita before I go out. Would you call for one,
honey?"

Back in Lexington, Mrs. Wheatley's voice would sometimes
have a distance to it, as though she were speaking from some
lonely reach of an interior childhood. Here in Mexico City the
voice was distant but the tone was theatrically gay, as though
Alma Wheatley were savoring an incommunicable private
mirth. It made Beth uneasy. For a moment she wanted to say
something about the expensiveness of room service, even measured in pesos, but she didn't. She picked up the phone and dialed six. The man answered in English. She told him to send a
margarita and a large Coke to 713.

"You could come to the Folklórico," Mrs. Wheatley said, "I understand the costumes alone are worth the price of admission."

"The tournament starts tomorrow. I need to work on endgames."

Mrs. Wheatley was sitting on the edge of the bed, admiring her feet. "Beth, honey," she said dreamily, "perhaps you need to work on *yourself.* Chess certainly isn't all there is."

"It's what I know."

Mrs. Wheatley gave a long sigh. "My experience has taught me that what you know isn't always important."

"What is important?"

"Living and growing," Mrs. Wheatley said with finality. "Living your life."

With a sleazy Mexican salesman? Beth wanted to say. But she kept silent. She did not like the jealousy she felt.

"Beth," Mrs. Wheatley went on in a voice rich with plausibility. "You haven't visited Bellas Artes or even Chapultepec Park. The zoo there is delightful. You've taken your meals in this room and spent your time with your nose in chess books. Shouldn't you just relax on the day before the tournament and think about something other than chess?"

Beth wanted to hit her. If she had gone to those places, she would have had to go with Manuel and listen to his endless stories. He was forever touching Mrs. Wheatley's shoulder or her back, standing too close to her, smiling too eagerly. "Mother," she said, "tomorrow at ten I play the black pieces against Octavio Marenco, the champion of Brazil. That means he has the first move. He is thirty-four years old and an International Grandmaster. If I lose, we will be paying for this trip—this adventure—out of capital. If I win, I will be playing someone the next day who is even better than Marenco. I need to work on my endgames."

"Honey, you are what is called an 'intuitive' player, aren't you?" Mrs. Wheatley had never discussed chess playing with her before.

"I've been called that. Moves come to me sometimes."

"I've noticed the moves they applaud the loudest are the ones you make quickly. And there's a certain look on your face."

Beth was startled. "I suppose you're right," she said.

"Intuition doesn't come from books. I think it's because you don't like Manuel."

"Manuel's all right," Beth said, "but he doesn't come by to see *me.*"

"That's irrelevant," Mrs. Wheatley said. "You need to *relax.* There's not another player in the world as gifted as you are. I haven't the remotest idea what faculties a person uses in order to play chess well, but I am convinced that relaxation can only improve them."

Beth said nothing. She had been furious for several days. She did not like Mexico City or this enormous concrete hotel with its cracked tiles and leaky faucets. She did not like the food in the hotel, but she did not want to eat alone in restaurants. Mrs. Wheatley had gone out for lunch and dinner every day with Manuel, who owned a green Dodge and seemed to be always at her disposal.

"Why don't you have lunch with us?" Mrs. Wheatley said. "We can drop you off afterward and you can study then."

Beth started to answer, when there was a knock at the door. It was room service with Mrs. Wheatley's margarita. Beth signed for it while Mrs. Wheatley took a few thoughtful sips and stared out the window at the sunlight. "I really haven't been well lately," Mrs. Wheatley said, squinting.

Beth looked at her coolly. Mrs. Wheatley was pale and clearly overweight. She held the glass by the stem in one hand while her other hand fluttered at her thick waist. There was something deeply pathetic about her, and Beth's heart softened. "I don't want lunch," Beth said, "but you can drop me off at the zoo. I'll take a cab back."

Mrs. Wheatley hardly seemed to hear, but after a moment she turned to Beth, still holding the glass in the same way, and smiled vaguely. "That'll be nice, dear," she said.

*　　　*　　　*

Beth spent a long time looking at the Galápagos turtles—big, lumbering creatures in permanent slow motion. One of the keepers had dumped a bushel of wet-looking lettuce and overripe tomatoes into their pen and the five of them pushed through the pile as a group, munching and trampling, their feet like the dusty feet of elephants and their stupid innocent faces intent on something beyond vision or food.

While she was standing by the fence a vendor came by with a cart of iced beer and, hardly thinking, she said, *"Cerveza Corona, por favor,"* and held out a five-peso note. The man flipped off the bottle top and poured the drink into a paper cup with an Aztec Eagle logo. *"Muchisimas gracias,"* she said. It was her first beer since high school; in the hot Mexican sun, it tasted wonderful. She drank it quickly. A few minutes later she saw another vendor standing by a circle of red flowers; she bought another beer. She knew she should not be doing this; the tournament started tomorrow. She did not need liquor. Nor tranquilizers. She had not had a green pill for several months now. But she drank the beer. It was three in the afternoon, and the sun was ferocious. The zoo was full of women, most of them in dark rebozos, with small dark-eyed children. What few men there were gave Beth significant looks, but she ignored them, and none of them tried to speak to her. Despite the Mexican reputation for gaiety and abandon, it was a quiet place, and the crowd seemed more like the crowd at a museum. There were flowers everywhere.

She finished her beer, bought another and continued walking. She was beginning to feel high. She passed more trees, more flowers, cages with sleeping chimpanzees. Around a corner she came face to face with a family of gorillas. Inside the cage the huge male and the baby were asleep head to head with their black bodies pressed against the bars in front. In the middle of the cage the female leaned philosophically against an enormous truck tire, scowling and biting a fingertip. Standing on the asphalt outside the cage was a human family, also a mother, father and child, watching the gorillas attentively. They were not Mexicans.

It was the man who caught Beth's attention. She recognized his face.

He was a short, heavy man, not unlike a gorilla himself, with jutting brow ridges, bushy eyebrows, coarse black hair and an impassive look. Beth stiffened, holding her paper cup of beer. She felt her cheeks flushing. The man was Vasily Borgov, Chess Champion of the World. There was no mistaking the grim Russian face, the authoritarian scowl. She had seen it on the cover of *Chess Review* several times, once with the same black suit and splashy green-and-gold tie.

Beth stared for a full minute. She had not known Borgov would be at this tournament. She had already received her board assignment by mail: it was Board Nine. Borgov would be Board One. She felt a sudden chill at the back of her neck and looked down at the beer in her hand. She raised it to her mouth and finished it, resolving it would be her last until after the tournament. Looking at the Russian again, she panicked; would he recognize her? He must not see her drinking. He was looking into the cage as though waiting for the gorilla to move a pawn. The gorilla was clearly lost in her own thoughts, ignoring everyone. Beth envied her.

Beth had no more beer that day and went to bed early, but she was awakened by Mrs. Wheatley's arrival, sometime in the middle of the night. Mrs. Wheatley coughed a good deal while she was undressing in the darkened room. "Go ahead and turn the light on," Beth said. "I'm awake."

"I'm sorry," Mrs. Wheatley gasped between coughs. "I seem to have a virus." She turned the bathroom light on and partially closed the door. Beth looked at the little Japanese clock on the nightstand. It was ten after four. The sounds she made undressing—the rustling and partly suppressed coughing—were infuriating. Beth's first chess game would begin in six hours. She lay in bed furious and tense, waiting for Mrs. Wheatley to be quiet.

Marenco was a somber little dark-skinned man in a dazzling canary-colored shirt. He spoke almost no English and Beth no Portuguese; they began playing without preliminary conversation.

Beth did not feel like talking, anyway. Her eyes were scratchy, and her body was uncomfortable all over. She had felt generally unpleasant from the time their plane landed in Mexico, as though she were on the verge of developing an illness that she never quite got, and she had not gone back to sleep the night before. Mrs. Wheatley had coughed in her sleep and muttered and rasped, while Beth tried to force herself to relax, to ignore the distractions. She did not have any green pills with her. There were three left, but they were in Kentucky. She lay on her back with her arms straight at her sides as she had as an eight-year-old trying to sleep by the hallway door at Methuen. Now, sitting on a straight wooden chair in front of a long tableful of chessboards in the ballroom of a Mexican hotel, she felt irritated and a bit dizzy. Marenco had just opened with pawn to king four. Her clock was ticking. She shrugged and played pawn to queen's bishop four, trusting the formal maneuvers of the Sicilian to keep her steady until she got into the game. Marenco brought the king's knight out with civil orthodoxy. She pushed the queen pawn to the fourth rank; he exchanged pawns. She began to relax as her mind moved away from her body and onto the tableau of forces in front of her.

By eleven-thirty she had him down by two pawns, and just after noon he resigned. They had got nowhere close to an endgame; when Marenco stood up and offered her his hand, the board was still massed with uncaptured pieces.

The top three boards were in a separate room across the hallway from the main ballroom. Beth had glanced at it that morning while rushing, five minutes late, to the place where she was to play, but she had not stopped to look in. She walked toward it now, across the carpeted room with its rows of players bent over boards—players from the Philippines and West Germany and Iceland and Norway and Chile, most of them young, almost all of them male. There were two other women: a Mexican official's niece, at Board Twenty-two, and an intense young housewife from Buenos Aires; she was at Board Seventeen. Beth did not stop to look at any of the positions.

Several people were standing in the hallway outside the smaller game room. She pushed past them into the doorway, and there across the room from her at Board One, wearing the same dark suit, the same grim scowl, was Vasily Borgov, his expressionless eyes on the game in front of him. A respectfully silent crowd stood between her and him, but the players sat on a kind of wooden stage a few feet above floor level, and she could see him clearly. Behind him on the wall was a display chessboard with cardboard pieces; a Mexican was just moving one of the white knights into its new position as Beth came in. She studied the board for a moment. Everything was very tight, but Borgov seemed to have an edge.

She looked at Borgov and quickly looked away. His face was alarming in its concentration. She turned and left, walking slowly along the hall.

Mrs. Wheatley was in bed but awake. She blinked at Beth from the bed, pulling the covers up to her chin. "Hi, sweetie."

"I thought we could have lunch," Beth said. "I don't play again until tomorrow."

"Lunch," Mrs. Wheatley said. "Oh my." And then: "How did you do?"

"He resigned after thirty moves."

"You're a wonder," Mrs. Wheatley said. She pushed herself carefully up in bed until she was sitting. "I'm feeling wonky, but I probably need something in my stomach. Manuel and I had *cabrito* for dinner. It may yet be the end of me." She looked very pale. She got out of bed slowly and walked to the bathroom. "I suppose I could have a sandwich, or one of those less inflamed tacos."

The competition at the tournament was more consistent, vigorous and professional than anything Beth had seen before, yet its effect on her, once she had got through the first game after a near-sleepless night, was not disturbing. It was a smoothly run affair, with all announcements made in both Spanish and English. Everything was hushed. In her game the next day she played the Queen's Gambit Declined against an Austrian named Diedrich, a pale, esthetic young man in a sleeveless sweater, and she forced him to resign in midgame with a relentless pressure in the center of the board. She did it mostly with pawns and was herself quietly amazed at the intricacies that seemed to flow from her fingertips as she took the center of the board and began to crush his position as one might crush an egg. He had played well, made no blunders or anything that could properly be called a mistake, but Beth moved with such deadly accuracy, such measured control, that his position was hopeless by the twenty-third move.

Mrs. Wheatley had invited her to have dinner with her and Manuel; Beth had refused. Although you didn't eat dinner in Mexico until ten o'clock, she did not expect to find Mrs. Wheatley in the room when she came back from shopping at seven.

She was dressed but in bed with her head propped up against a pillow. A half-finished drink sat on the nightstand beside her. Mrs. Wheatley was in her mid-forties, but the paleness of her face and the lines of worry in her forehead made her look much older. "Hello, dear," she said in a faint voice.

"Are you sick?"

"A bit under the weather."

"I could get a doctor."

The word "doctor" seemed to hang in the air between them until Mrs. Wheatley said, "It's not that bad. I just need rest."

Beth nodded and went into the bathroom to wash up. Mrs. Wheatley's appearance and behavior were disturbing. But when Beth came back into the room, she was out of bed and looking lively enough, smoothing the covers. She smiled wryly. "Manuel won't be coming."

Beth looked inquiringly at her.

"He had business in Oaxaca."

Beth hesitated for a moment. "How long will he be away?"

Mrs. Wheatley sighed. "At least until we leave."

"I'm sorry."

"Well," Mrs. Wheatley said, "I've never been to Oaxaca, but I suspect it resembles Denver."

Beth stared at her a moment and then laughed. "We can have

dinner together," she said. "You can take me to one of the places you know about."

"Of course," Mrs. Wheatley said. She smiled ruefully. "It was fun while it lasted. He really had a pleasant sense of humor."

"That's good," Beth said. "Mr. Wheatley didn't seem very amusing."

"My God," Mrs. Wheatley said, "Allston never thought anything was funny, except maybe Eleanor Roosevelt."

In this tournament each player played one game a day. It would go on for six days. Beth's first two games were simple enough for her, but the third came as a shock.

She arrived five minutes early and was at the board when her opponent came walking up, a bit awkwardly. He looked about twelve years old. Beth had seen him around the ballroom, had passed boards where he was playing, but she had been distracted, and his youth hadn't really registered. He had curly black hair and wore an old-fashioned white sport shirt, so neatly ironed that its creases stood out from his thin arms. It was very strange, and she felt uncomfortable. *She* was supposed to be the prodigy. He looked so damned *serious*.

She held out her hand. "I'm Beth Harmon."

He stood, bowed slightly, took her hand firmly and shook it once. "I am Georgi Petrovitch Girev," he said. Then he smiled shyly, a small furtive smile. "I am honored."

She felt flustered. "Thanks." They both sat, and he pressed the button down on her clock. She played pawn to queen four, glad to have the first move against this unnerving child.

It started out as a routine Queen's Gambit Accepted; he took the offered bishop pawn, and they both developed toward the center. But as they got into the midgame it became more complex than usual, and she realized that he was playing a very sophisticated defense. He moved fast—maddeningly fast—and he seemed to know exactly what he was going to do. She tried a few threats, but he was unperturbed by them. An hour passed, then another. The move numbers were now in the thirties, and the board was dense with men. She looked at him as he was moving a piece—at the skinny little arm stuck out from the absurd shirt—and she hated him. He could have been a machine. You little creep, she thought, suddenly realizing that the adults she had played as a child must have thought the same thing about her.

It was afternoon now, and most of the games were finished. They were on move thirty-four. She wanted to get this over with and get back to Mrs. Wheatley. She was worried about Mrs. Wheatley. She felt old and weary playing this tireless child with his bright dark eyes and quick little movements; she knew that if she made even a small blunder, he would be at her throat. She looked at her clock. Twenty-five minutes left. She would have to speed up and get forty moves in before her flag dropped. If she didn't watch it, he would have her in serious time pressure. That was something she was in the habit of putting other people in; it made her uneasy. She had never been behind on the clock before.

For the last several moves she had been considering a series of trades in the center—knight and bishop for knight and bishop, and a rook exchange a few moves later. It would simplify a good deal, but the problem was that it made for an endgame and she tried to avoid endgames. Now, seeing that she was forty-five minutes behind him on the clock, she felt uncomfortable. She would have to get rid of this log jam. She picked up her knight and took his king's bishop with it. He responded immediately, not even looking up at her. He took her queen's bishop. They continued with the moves as though they had been predetermined, and when it was over, the board was full of empty spaces. Each player had a rook, a knight, four pawns and the king. She brought her king out from the back rank, and so did he. At this stage the king's power as an attacker became abruptly manifest; it was no longer necessary to hide it. The question now was one of getting a pawn to the eighth rank and promoting it. They were in the endgame.

She drew in her breath, shook her head to clear it and began to concentrate on the position. The important thing was to have a plan.

"We should perhaps adjourn now." It was Girev's voice, almost a whisper. She looked at his face, pale and serious, and then looked back at the clock. Both flags had fallen. That had never happened to her before. She was startled and sat stupidly in her chair for a moment. "You must seal the move," Girev said. Suddenly he looked uncomfortable and held up his hand for the tournament director.

One of the directors came over, walking softly. It was a middle-aged man with thick glasses. "Miss Harmon must seal her move," Girev said.

The director looked at the clock. "I'll get an envelope."

She looked at the board again. It seemed clear enough. She should advance the rook pawn that she had decided on already, putting it on the fourth rank. The director handed her an envelope and stepped discreetly back a few steps. Girev rose and turned away politely. Beth wrote "P-QR4" on her score sheet, folded it, put it in the envelope and handed it to the tournament director.

She stood up stiffly and looked around her. There were no more games in progress, although a few players were still there, some seated and some standing, looking over positions on the boards. A few were huddled over boards, analyzing games that had ended.

Girev had come back to the table. His face was very serious. "May I ask something?" he said.

"Yes."

"In America," he said, "I am told that one sees films in cars. Is this true?"

"Drive-ins?" she said. "You mean drive-in movies?"

"Yes. Elvis Presley movies that you watch from inside a car. Debbie Reynolds and Elizabeth Taylor. That happens?"

"It sure does."

He looked at her, and suddenly his earnest face broke into a broad smile. "I would dig that," he said. "I would certainly dig that."

*   *   *

Mrs. Wheatley slept soundly through the night and was still sleeping when Beth got up. Beth felt refreshed and alert; she had gone to sleep worried about the adjourned game with Girev, but she felt all right about it in the morning. The pawn move had been strong enough. She walked barefoot from the sofa where she had been sleeping to the bed where Mrs. Wheatley lay and felt her forehead. It was cool. Beth kissed her lightly on the cheek and went into the bathroom and showered. When she left for breakfast, Mrs. Wheatley was still asleep.

Her morning game was with a Mexican in his early twenties. Beth had the black pieces, played the Sicilian and caught him off-guard on the nineteenth move. Then she began wearing him down. Her head was very clear, and she was able to keep him so busy trying to answer her threats that she was able eventually to pick off a bishop in exchange for two pawns and drive his king into an exposed position with a knight check. When she brought her queen out, the Mexican stood up, smiled at her coldly and said, "Enough. Enough." He shook his head angrily. "I resign the game."

For a moment she was furious, wanting to finish, to drive his king across the board and checkmate it. "You play a game that is . . . awesome," the Mexican said. "You make a man feel helpless." He bowed slightly, turned and left the table.

Playing out the Girev game that afternoon, she found herself moving with astonishing speed and force. Girev was wearing a light-blue shirt this time, and it stuck out from his elbows like the edges of a child's kite. She sat at the board impatiently while the tournament director opened the envelope and made the pawn move she had sealed the day before. She got up and paced across the nearly empty ballroom where two other adjournments were being played out, waiting for Girev to move. She looked back across the room toward him several times and saw him hunched over the board, his little fists jammed into his pale cheeks, the blue shirt seeming to glow under the lights. She hated him—hated his seriousness and hated his youth. She wanted to crush him.

She could hear the click of the clock button from halfway across the room and made a beeline back to the table. She did not take her seat but stood looking at the position. He had put his rook on the queen bishop file, as she had thought he might. She was ready for that and pushed her pawn again, turned and walked back across the room. There was a table there with a water pitcher and a few paper cups. She poured herself a cup, surprised to see that her hand trembled as she did so. By the time she got back to the board, Girev had moved again. She moved immediately, not bringing the rook to defend but abandoning the pawn and instead advancing her king. She picked the piece up lightly with her fingertips the way she had seen that piratical-looking man in Cincinnati do years before and dropped it on the queen four square, turned and walked away again.

She kept it up that way, not sitting down at all. Within three quarters of an hour she had him. It was really simple—almost too easy. It was only a matter of trading rooks at the right time. The trade pulled his king back a square on the recapture, just enough to let her pawn get by and queen. But Girev did not wait for that; he resigned immediately after the rook check and the trade which followed. He stepped toward her as if to say something, but seeing her face, stopped. For a moment she softened, remembering the child she had been only a few years before and how it devastated her to lose a chess game.

She held out her hand, and when he shook it she forced a smile and said, "I've never been to a drive-in either."

He shook his head. "I should not have let you do that. With the rook."

"Yes," she said. And then: "How old were you when you started playing chess?"

"Four. I was district champion at seven. I hope to be World Champion one day."

"When?"

"In three years."

"You'll be sixteen in three years."

He nodded grimly.

"If you win, what will you do afterward?"

He looked puzzled. "I don't understand."

"If you're World Champion at sixteen, what will you do with the rest of your life?"

He still looked puzzled. "I don't understand," he said.

Mrs. Wheatley went to bed early and seemed better the next morning. She was up before Beth, and when they went downstairs together for breakfast in the Cámara de Toreros, Mrs. Wheatley ordered a Spanish omelet and two cups of coffee and finished it all. Beth felt relieved.

On the bulletin board near the registration desk was a list of players; Beth had not looked at it for several days. Coming into the room now ten minutes before game time, she stopped and checked the scores. They were listed in order of their international ratings, and Borgov was at the top with 2715. Harmon was seventeenth with 2370. After each player's name was a series of boxes showing his score for the rounds. "0" meant a loss, "½" a draw, and "1" a win. There were a great many "½'s." Three names had an uninterrupted string of "1's" after them; Borgov and Harmon were two of these.

The pairings were a few feet to the right. At the top of the list was BORGOV–RAND, and below that HARMON–SOLOMON. If she and Borgov both won today, they would not necessarily play each other in the final game tomorrow. She was not sure whether she wanted to play him or not. Playing Girev had rattled her. She felt a dim unsureness about Mrs. Wheatley, despite her apparent resurgence; the image of her white skin, rouged cheeks and forced smiles made Beth uneasy. A buzz of voices had begun in the room as players found their boards, set up their clocks, settled into preparations for play. Beth shook off her unease as well as she could and found Board Four—the first board in the big room—an waited for Solomon.

Solomon was by no means easy, and the game lasted four hours before he was forced to resign. Yet at no point during all of that time did she ever lose her edge—the tiny advantage that the opening move gives to the player of the white pieces. Solomon did not say anything, but she could tell from the way he stalked off afterward that he was furious to be beaten by a woman. She had seen it often enough before to recognize it. Usually it made her angry, but it didn't matter right now. She had something else on her mind.

When he had gone she went to look in the smaller room where Borgov played, but it was empty. The winning position—Borgov's—was still displayed on the big board on the wall; it was as devastating as Beth's win over Solomon had been.

In the ballroom she looked at the bulletin board. Some of tomorrow's pairings were already up. That was a surprise. She stepped closer to look, and her heart caught in her throat; at the top of the finals list in black printed letters was BORGOV–HARMON. She blinked and read it again, holding her breath.

Beth had brought three books with her to Mexico City. She and Mrs. Wheatley ate dinner in their room, and afterward Beth took out *Grandmaster Games;* in it were five of Borgov's. She opened it to the first one and began to play through it, using her board and pieces. She seldom did this, generally relying on her ability to visualize a game when going over it, but she wanted to have Borgov in front of her as palpably as possible. Mrs. Wheatley lay in bed reading while Beth played through the games, looking for weaknesses. She found none. She played through them again, stopping in certain positions where the possibilities seemed nearly infinite, and working them all out. She sat staring at the board with everything in her present life obliterated from her attention while the combinations played themselves out in her head. Every now and then a sound from Mrs. Wheatley or a tension in the air of the room brought her out of it for a moment, and she looked around dazedly, feeling the pained tightness of her muscles and the thin, intrusive edge of fear in her stomach.

There had been a few times over the past year when she felt like this, with her mind not only dizzied but nearly terrified by the endlessness of chess. By midnight Mrs. Wheatley had put her book aside and gone quietly to sleep. Beth sat in the green armchair for hours, not hearing Mrs. Wheatley's gentle snores, not sensing the strange smell of a Mexican hotel in her nostrils, feeling somehow that she might fall from a precipice, that sitting over the chessboard she had bought at Purcell's in Kentucky, she was actually poised over an abyss, sustained there only by the bizarre mental equipment that had fitted her for this elegant and deadly game. On the board there was danger everywhere. A person could not rest.

She did not go to bed until after four and, asleep, she dreamed of drowning.

A few people had gathered in the ballroom. She recognized Marenco, dressed in a suit and tie now; he waved at her as she came in, and she forced herself to smile in his direction. It was frightening to see even this player she had already beaten. She was jumpy, knew she was jumpy, and did not know what to do about it.

She had showered at seven that morning, unable to rid herself of the tension she had awakened with. She was barely able to get down her morning coffee in the near-empty coffee shop and had washed her face afterward, carefully, trying to focus herself. Now she crossed the ballroom's red carpet and went to the ladies' room and washed her face again. She dried carefully with paper towels and combed her hair, watching herself in the big mirror. Her movements seemed forced, and her body looked impossibly frail. The expensive blouse and skirt did not fit right. Her fear was as sharp as a toothache.

As she came down the hallway, she saw him. He was standing there solidly with two men she did not recognize. All of them wore dark suits. They were close together, talking softly, confidentially. She lowered her eyes and walked past them into the small room. Some men were waiting there with cameras. Reporters. She slipped behind the black pieces at Board One. She stared at the board for a moment, heard the tournament director's voice saying, "Play will begin in three minutes," and looked up.

Borgov was walking across the room toward her. His suit fit him well, with the trouser legs draping neatly above the tops of his shined black shoes. Beth turned her eyes back to the board, embarrassed, feeling awkward. Borgov had seated himself. She heard the director's voice as if from a great distance, "You may start your opponent's clock," and she reached out, pressed the button on the clock and looked up. He was sitting there solid, dark and heavy, looking fixedly at the board, and she watched as if in a dream as he reached out a stubby-fingered hand, picked up the king pawn and set it on the fourth rank. Pawn to king four.

She stared at it for a moment. She always played the Sicilian to that opening—the most common opening for White in the game of chess. But she hesitated. Borgov had been called "Master of the Sicilian" somewhere in a journal. Almost impulsively she played pawn to king four herself, hoping to play him on ground that was fresh for both of them, that would not give him the advantage of superior knowledge. He brought out his king's knight to bishop three, and she brought hers to queen bishop three, protecting the pawn. And then without hesitation he played his bishop to knight five and her heart sank. The Ruy Lopez. She had played it often enough, but in this game it frightened her. It was as complex, as thoroughly analyzed, as the Sicilian, and there were dozens of lines she hardly knew, except for memorizing them from books.

Someone flashed another bulb for a picture and she heard the tournament director's angry whisper not to disturb the players. She pushed her pawn up to rook three, attacking the bishop. Borgov pulled it back to rook four. She forced herself to concentrate, brought out her other knight, and Borgov castled. All this was familiar, but it was no relief. She now had to decide to play either the open variation or the closed. She glanced up at Borgov's face and then back at the board. She took his pawn with her knight, starting the open. He played pawn to queen four, as she knew he would, and she played pawn to queen knight four because she had to, so she would be ready when he moved the rook. The chandelier overhead was too bright. And now she began to feel dismay, as though the rest of the game were inevitable—as though she were locked into some choreography of feints and counterthreats in which it was a fixed necessity that she lose, like a game from one of the books where you knew the outcome and played it only to see how it happened.

She shook her head to clear it. The game had not gone that far. They were still playing out tired old moves and the only advantage White had was the advantage White always had—the first move. Someone had said that when computers really learned to play chess and played against one another, White would always win because of the first move. Like tick-tack-toe. But it hadn't come to that. She was not playing a perfect machine.

Borgov brought his bishop back to knight three, retreating. She played pawn to queen four, and he took the pawn and she brought her bishop to king three. She had known this much back at Methuen from the lines she memorized in class from *Modern Chess Openings*. But the game was ready now to enter a wide-open phase, where it could take unexpected turns. She looked up just as Borgov, his face smooth and impassive, picked up his queen and set it in front of the king, on king two. She blinked at it for a moment. What was he doing? Going after the knight on her king five? He could pin the pawn that protected the knight easily enough with a rook. But the move looked somehow suspicious. She felt the tightness in her stomach again, a touch of dizziness.

She folded her arms across her chest and began to study the position. Out of the corner of her eye she could see the young man who moved the pieces on the display board placing the big cardboard white queen on the king two square. She glanced out into the room. There were about a dozen people standing there watching. She turned back to the board. She would have to get rid of his bishop. Knight to rook four looked good for that. There was also knight to bishop four or bishop to king two, but that was very complicated. She studied the possibilities for a moment and discarded the idea. She did not trust herself against Borgov with those complications. To put a knight on the rook file cut its range in half; but she did it. She had to get rid of the bishop. The bishop was up to no good.

Borgov reached down without hesitation and played knight

to queen four. She stared at it; she had expected him to move his rook. Still there seemed to be no harm in it. Pushing her queen bishop pawn up to the fourth square looked good. It would force Borgov's knight to take her bishop, and after that she could take his bishop with her knight and stop the annoying pressure on her other knight, the one that sat a bit too far down the board on king five and didn't have enough flight squares for comfort. Against Borgov, the loss of a knight would be lethal. She played the queen bishop pawn, holding the piece for a moment between her fingers before letting it go. Then she sat a bit farther back in her chair and drew a deep breath. The position looked good.

Without hesitation Borgov took the bishop with his knight, and Beth retook with her pawn. Then he played his queen bishop pawn to the third rank, as she thought he might, creating a place for the nuisance bishop to hide. She took the bishop with relief, getting rid of it and getting her knight off the embarrassing rook file. Borgov remained impassive, taking the knight with his pawn. His eyes flicked up to hers and back to the position.

She looked down nervously. It had looked good a few moves before; it did not look so good now. The problem was her knight on king five. He could move his queen to knight four, threatening to take her king's pawn with check, and when she protected against this, he could attack the knight with his king bishop pawn, and it would have no place to go. Borgov's queen would be there to take it. There was another annoyance on her queen side: he could play rook takes pawn, giving up the rook to hers only to get it back with a queen check, coming out a pawn ahead and with an improved position. No. Two pawns ahead. She would have to put her queen on knight three. Queen to queen two was no good because of his damned bishop pawn that could attack her knight. She did not like this defensiveness and studied the board for a long time before moving, trying to find something that would counterattack. There was nothing. She had to move the queen and protect the knight. She felt her cheeks burning and studied the position again. Nothing. She brought her queen to knight three and did not look at Borgov.

With no hesitation whatever Borgov brought his bishop to king three, protecting his king. *Why hadn't she seen that?* She had looked long enough. Now if she pushed the pawn she had planned to push, she would lose her queen. *How could she have missed it?* She had planned the threat of discovered check with the new position of her queen, and he had parried it instantly with a move that was chillingly obvious. She glanced at him, at his well-shaven, imperturbable Russian face with the tie so finely knotted beneath his heavy chin, and the fear she felt almost froze her muscles.

She studied the board with all the intensity she could muster, sitting rigidly for twenty minutes staring at the position. Her stomach sank even farther as she tried and rejected a dozen continuations. She could not save the knight. Finally she played her bishop to king two, and Borgov predictably put his queen on knight four, threatening again to win the knight by pushing up his king bishop pawn. Now she had the choice of king to queen two or of castling. Either way the knight was lost. She castled.

Borgov immediately moved the bishop pawn to attack her knight. She could have screamed. Everything he was doing was obvious, unimaginative, bureaucratic. She felt stifled and played pawn to queen five, attacking his bishop, and then watched his inevitable moving of the bishop to rook six, threatening to mate. She would have to bring her rook up to protect. He would take the knight with his queen, and if she took the bishop, the queen would pick off the rook in the corner with a check, and the whole thing would blow apart. She would have to bring the rook over to protect it. And meanwhile she was down a knight. Against a world's champion, whose shirt was impeccably white, whose tie was beautifully tied, whose dark-jowled Russian face admitted no doubt or weakness.

She saw her hand reach out, and taking the black king by its head, topple it onto the board.

She sat there for a moment and heard the applause. Then, looking at no one, she left the room.

Chapter 9

"Give me a tequila sunrise," she said. The clock over the bar pointed to twelve-thirty, and there was a group of four American women at one of the tables at the far end of the room eating lunch. Beth had not eaten breakfast, but she did not want lunch.

"Con mucho gusto," the bartender said.

The awards ceremony was at two-thirty. She drank through it in the bar. She would be fourth place, or maybe fifth. The two who had done a grandmaster draw together would be ahead of her with five and a half points each. Borgov had six. Her score was five. She had three tequila sunrises, ate two hard-boiled eggs and shifted to beer. Dos Equis. It took four of them to make the pain in her stomach go away, to blur the fury and shame. Even when it began to ease, she could still see Borgov's dark, heavy face and could feel the frustration she had felt during their match. She had played like a novice, like a passive, embarrassed fool.

She drank a lot, but she did not get dizzy, and her speech did not slur when she ordered. There seemed to be a kind of insulation around her that kept everything at a distance. She sat at a table at one end of the cocktail lounge with her glass of beer, and she did not get drunk.

At three o'clock two players from the tournament came into

the bar, talking quietly. Beth got up and went straight to her room.

Mrs. Wheatley was lying in bed. She had a hand on her head with the fingers dug into her hair as though she had a headache. Beth walked over to the bed. Mrs. Wheatley did not look right. Beth reached out and took her by the arm. Mrs. Wheatley was dead.

It seemed as though she felt nothing, but five minutes passed before Beth was able to let go of Mrs. Wheatley's cold arm and pick up the telephone.

The manager knew exactly what to do. Beth sat in the armchair drinking *café con leche* from room service while two men with a stretcher came and the manager instructed them. She heard him, but she did not watch. She kept her eyes on the window. Sometime later she turned to see a middle-aged woman in a gray suit, using a stethoscope on Mrs. Wheatley. Mrs. Wheatley was on the bed and the stretcher was under her. The two men in green uniform were standing at the edge of the bed, looking embarrassed. The woman took off her stethoscope, nodded to the manager and came over to Beth. Her face was strained. "I'm sorry," she said.

Beth looked away from her. "What was it?"

"Hepatitis, possibly. We'll know tomorrow."

"Tomorrow," Beth said. "Could you give me a tranquilizer?"

"I have a sedative . . ."

"I don't want a sedative," Beth said. "Can you give me a prescription for Librium?"

The doctor stared at her for a moment and shrugged. "You don't need a prescription to buy Librium in Mexico. I suggest meprobamate. There's a *farmacia* in the hotel."

Using a map in the front of Mrs. Wheatley's *Mobil Travel Guide,* Beth wrote down the names of the cities between Denver, Colorado, and Butte, Montana. The manager had told her his assistant would be of whatever help she needed in phoning, signing papers, dealing with the authorities. Ten minutes after they had taken Mrs. Wheatley away, Beth called the assistant and read him the list of towns and gave him the name. He said he would call her back. She ordered a Coca-Cola *grande* and more coffee from room service. Then she undressed quickly and took a shower. There was a phone in the bathroom, but the call did not come through. She still felt nothing.

She dressed in fresh jeans and a white T-shirt. On the little table by the bed was Mrs. Wheatley's pack of Chesterfields, empty, crumpled by Mrs. Wheatley's hands. The ashtray beside it was full of butts. One cigarette, the last one Mrs. Wheatley had ever smoked, sat on the edge of the little tray, with a long cold ash. Beth stared at it a minute; then she went into the bathroom and dried her hair.

The boy who brought the big bottle of Coke and the carafe of coffee was very respectful and waved away her attempt to sign the bill. The telephone rang. It was the manager. "I have your call," he said. "From Denver."

There was a series of clicks in the receiver and then a male voice, surprisingly loud and clear. "This is Allston Wheatley."

"It's Beth, Mr. Wheatley."

There was a pause. "Beth?"

"Your daughter. Elizabeth Harmon."

"You're in *Mexico*? You're calling from Mexico?"

"It's about Mrs. Wheatley." She was looking at the cigarette, never really smoked, on the ashtray.

"How's Alma?" the voice said. "Is she there with you? In Mexico?" The interest sounded forced. She could picture him as she had seen him at Methuen, wishing he were somewhere else, everything about him saying that he wanted to make no connections, wanted always to be somewhere else.

"She's dead, Mr. Wheatley. She died this morning."

There was silence at the other end of the line. Finally she said, "Mr. Wheatley . . ."

"Can't you handle this for me?" he said. "I can't be going off to Mexico."

"They're going to do an autopsy tomorrow, and I've got to get new plane tickets. I mean, get a new plane ticket for myself . . ." Her voice had suddenly gone weak and aimless. She picked up the coffee cup and took a drink from it. "I don't know where to bury her."

Mr. Wheatley's voice came back with surprising crispness. "Call Durgin Brothers, in Lexington. There's a family plot in her maiden name. Benson."

"What about the house?"

"Look"—the voice was louder now—"I don't want any part of this. I've got problems enough here in Denver. Get her up to Kentucky and bury her and the house is yours. Just make the mortgage payments. Do you need money?"

"I don't know. I don't know what it will cost."

"I heard you were doing all right. The child prodigy thing. Can't you charge it or something?"

"I can talk to the hotel manager."

"Good. You do that. I'm strapped for cash right now, but you can have the house and the equity. Call the Second National Bank and ask for Mr. Erlich. That's E-r-l-i-c-h. Tell him I want you to have the house. He knows how to reach me."

There was silence again. Then she said, as strongly as she could, "Don't you want to know what she died of?"

"What was it?"

"Hepatitis, I think. They'll know tomorrow."

"Oh," Mr. Wheatley said. "She was sick a lot."

The manager and the doctor took care of everything—even the refund on Mrs. Wheatley's plane ticket. Beth had to sign some official papers, had to absolve the hotel of responsibility and fill out government forms. One had the title "U.S. Customs—Transfer of Remains." The manager got Durgin Brothers in Lexington. The assistant manager drove Beth to the airport the following day, with the hearse discreetly trailing them through the streets of Mexico City and along the highway. She saw the metal coffin only once, looking out the window from the TWA waiting room. The hearse had driven up to the 707 at the gate and some men were unloading it in brilliant sunlight. They set it on a forklift, and she could hear the dim whine of the engine through the glass as it was raised to the level of the cargo hold.

For a moment it trembled in the sunshine and she had a sudden horrific vision of it falling off the lift and crashing to the tarmac, spilling out the embalmed middle-aged corpse of Mrs. Wheatley on the hot gray asphalt. But that did not happen. The casket was pulled handily into the cargo hold.

On board Beth declined a drink from the stewardess. When she had gone back down the aisle, Beth opened her purse and took out one of her new bottles of green pills. She had spent three hours the day before, after signing the papers, going from *farmacia* to *farmacia*, buying the limit of one hundred pills in each.

The funeral was simple and brief. A half-hour before it began, Beth took four green pills. She sat in the church alone, in a quiet daze, while the minister said the things ministers say. There were flowers at the altar, and she was mildly surprised to see a pair of men from the funeral home step up and carry them out as soon as the minister had finished. Six other people were there, but Beth knew none of them. One old lady hugged her afterward and said, "You poor dear."

She finished unpacking that afternoon and came down from the bedroom to fix coffee. While the water was coming to a boil she went into the little downstairs bathroom to wash her face and suddenly, standing there surrounded by blue, by Mrs. Wheatley's blue bathroom rug and blue towels and blue soap and blue washcloths, something hot exploded in her belly and her face was drenched with tears. She took a towel from the rack and held it against her face and said "Oh Jesus Christ" and leaned against the washbasin and cried for a long time.

She was still drying her face when the phone rang.

The voice was male. "Beth Harmon?"

"Yes."

"This is Harry Beltik. From the State Tournament."

"I remember."

"Yeah. I hear you dropped one to Borgov. Wanted to give condolences."

As she laid the towel on the back of the overstuffed sofa she noticed a half-finished pack of Mrs. Wheatley's cigarettes on its arm. "Thanks," she said, picking up the package and holding on to it tightly.

"What were you playing? White?"

"Black."

"Yeah." There was a pause. "Is something wrong?"

"No."

"It's better that way."

"What's better?"

"It's better to be Black if you're going to lose it."

"I suppose so."

"What'd you play? Sicilian?"

She gently set the package of cigarettes back on the chair arm. "Ruy Lopez. I let him do it to me."

"Mistake," Beltik said. "Look, I'm in Lexington for the summer. Would you like some training?"

"Training?"

"I know. You're better than me. But if you're going to play Russians, you'll need help."

"Where are you?"

"At the Phoenix Hotel. I'm moving to an apartment Thursday."

She looked around the room for a moment, at the stack of Mrs. Wheatley's women's magazines on the cobbler's bench, the pale-blue drapes on the windows, the oversized ceramic lamps with the cellophane still wrapped around their yellowing shades. She took in a long breath and let it out silently. "Come on over," she said.

He drove up twenty minutes later in a 1955 Chevrolet with red-and-black flames painted on the fenders and a broken headlamp, pulling up to the curb at the end of the patterned-brick walk. She had been watching for him from the window and was on the front porch when he got out of the car. He waved at her and went to the trunk. He was wearing a bright-red shirt and gray corduroy pants with a pair of sneakers that matched the shirt. There was something dark and quick about him, and Beth, remembering his bad teeth and his fierce way of playing chess, felt herself stiffen a little at the sight of him.

He bent over the trunk and lifted out a cardboard box, clearly heavy, tossed the hair out of his eyes and came up the walk. The box said HEINZ TOMATO KETCHUP in red letters; it was open at the top and filled with books.

He set it on the living-room rug and unceremoniously took Mrs. Wheatley's magazines from the coffee table and slipped them into the magazine rack. He began taking books out of the box one at a time, reading off the titles and piling them on the table. "A. L. Deinkopf, *Middle Game Strategy;* J. R. Capablanca, *My Chess Career;* Fornaut, *Alekhine's Games 1938–1945;* Meyer, *Rook and Pawn Endings."*

Some of them were books she had seen before; a few of them she owned. But most were new to her, heavy-looking and depressing to see. She knew there were a great many things she needed to know. But Capablanca had almost never studied, had played on intuition and his natural gifts, while inferior players like Bogolubov and Grünfeld memorized lines of play like German pedants. She had seen players at tournament after their games had ended, sitting motionless in uncomfortable chairs oblivious to the world, studying opening variations or middle-game strategy or endgame theory. It was endless. Seeing Beltik methodically removing one heavy book after another, she felt weary and disoriented. She glanced over at the TV: a part of her wanted to turn it on and forget chess forever.

"My summer's reading," Beltik said.

She shook her head irritably. "I study books. But I've always tried to play it by ear."

He stopped, holding three copies of *Shakhmatni Byulleten* in his hands, their covers worn with use, frowning at her. "Like Morphy," he said, "or Capablanca?"

She was embarrassed. "Yes."

He nodded grimly and set the stack of bulletins on the floor by the coffee table. "Capablanca would have beaten Borgov."

"Not every game."

"Every game that counted," Beltik said.

She studied his face. He was younger than she remembered him. But she was older now. He was an uncompromising young man; every part of him was uncompromising. "You think I'm a prima donna, don't you?"

He permitted himself a small smile. "We're all prima donnas," he said. "That's chess for you."

When she put the TV dinners in the oven that night, they had two boards set up with endgame positions: his set with its green and cream squares, its heavy plastic pieces; her wooden board with its rosewood and maple men. Both sets were the Staunton pattern that all serious players used; both had four-inch kings. She hadn't invited him to stay for lunch and dinner; it had been understood. He went to the grocery store a few blocks away for the food while she sat musing over a group of possible rook moves, trying to avoid a draw in a theoretical game. While she made lunch he lectured her about keeping in good physical shape and getting enough sleep. He had also bought the two frozen dinners for supper.

"You've got to stay *open,*" Beltik said. "If you get locked into one idea—like this king knight pawn, say—it's death. Look at this . . ." She turned to his board on the kitchen table. He was holding a cup of coffee and standing, frowning down at the board, holding his chin with the other hand.

"Look at what?" she said, irritated.

He reached down, picked up the white rook, moved it across the board to king rook one—the lower right-hand corner. "Now his rook pawn's pinned."

"So what?"

"He's got to move the king now or he gets stuck later."

"I see that," she said, her voice a little softer now. "But I don't see—"

"Look at the queenside pawns, way over here." He pointed to the other side of the board, at the three white pawns interlinked. She walked over to the table to get a better look. "He can do this," she said, and moved the black rook over two squares.

Beltik looked up at her. "Try it."

"Okay." She sat down behind the pieces.

In half a dozen moves Beltik had gotten his queen bishop

pawn to the seventh rank and queening it was inevitable. It would cost the rook and the game to stop it. He had been right; it was necessary to move the king when the rook had come across the board. "You were right," she said. "Did you figure it out?"

"It's from Alekhine somewhere," he said. "I got it from a book."

Beltik went back to his hotel after midnight, and Beth stayed up for several hours reading the middle-game book, not setting up the positions on a board but reviewing them in her imagination. One thing bothered her, but she did not let herself dwell on it. She could not picture the pieces as easily as she had when she was eight and nine years old. She could still do it, but it was more of an effort and sometimes she was uncertain about where a pawn or a bishop belonged and had to retrace the moves in her mind to make sure. She played on doggedly into the night, using her mind and the book only, sitting in Mrs. Wheatley's old television-watching armchair in T-shirt and blue jeans. Every now and then she would blink and look around her, half expecting to see Mrs. Wheatley sitting nearby with her stockings rolled down and her black pumps on the floor beside her chair.

Beltik was back at nine the next morning, with half a dozen more books. They had coffee and played a few five-minute games on the kitchen table. Beth won all of them, decisively, and when they had finished the fifth game Beltik looked at her and shook his head. "Harmon," he said, "you have really got it. But it's improvisation."

She stared at him. "What the hell," she said. "I wiped you out five times."

He looked back across the table at her coolly and took a sip from his coffee cup. "I'm a master," he said, "and I've never played better in my life. But I'm not what you're going to be up against if you go to Paris."

"I can beat Borgov with a little more work."

"You can beat Borgov with a lot more work. Years more work. What in hell do you think he is? Another Kentucky ex-champion like me?"

"He's World Champion. But—"

"Oh, shut up!" Beltik said. "Borgov could have beaten both of us when he was ten. Do you know his career?"

Beth looked at him. "No, I don't."

Beltik got up from the table and walked purposively into the living room. He pulled a green-jacketed book from the stack next to Beth's chessboard and brought it to the kitchen, tossing it on the table in front of her. *Vasily Borgov: My Life in Chess.* "Read it tonight," he said. "Read the games from Leningrad 1962 and look at the way he plays rook-pawn endings. Look at the games with Luchenko and with Spassky." He picked up his near-empty coffee cup. "You might learn something."

It was the first week in June and japonica blazed in bright coral outside the kitchen window. Mrs. Wheatley's azaleas had begun to bloom and the grass needed mowing. There were birds. It was a beautiful week of the best kind of Kentucky spring. Sometimes late at night after Beltik had left, Beth would go out to the back-yard to feel the warmth on her cheeks and to take a few deep breaths of warm clean air, but the rest of the time she ignored the world outside. She had become caught up in chess in a new way. Her bottles of Mexican tranquilizers remained unused in the nightstand; the cans of beer in the refrigerator stayed in the refrigerator. After standing in the backyard for five minutes, she would go back into the house and read Beltik's chess books for hours and then go upstairs and fall into bed exhausted.

On Thursday afternoon Beltik said, "I'm supposed to move into an apartment tomorrow. The hotel bill is killing me."

They were in the middle of the Benoni Defense. She had just played the P-K5 he had taught her, on move eight—a move Beltik said came from a player named Mikenas. She looked up from the position. "Where is it? The apartment."

"New Circle Road. I won't be coming by so much."

"It's not that far."

"Maybe not. But I'll be taking classes. I ought to get a part-time job."

"You could move in here," she said. "Free."

He looked at her for a moment and smiled. His teeth weren't really so bad. "I thought you'd never ask," he said.

She had not been so immersed in chess since she was a little girl. Beltik was in class three afternoons a week and two mornings, and she spent that time studying his books. She played mentally through game after game, learning new variations, seeing stylistic differences in offense and defense, biting her lip sometimes in excitement over a dazzling move or a subtlety of position, and at other times wearied by a sense of the hopeless depth of chess, of its endlessness, move after move, threat after threat, complication after complication. She had heard of the genetic code that could shape an eye or hand from passing proteins. Deoxyribonucleic acid. It contained the entire set of instructions for constructing a respiratory system and a digestive one, as well as the grip of an infant's hand. Chess was like that. The geometry of a position could be read and reread and not exhausted of possibility. You saw deeply into this layer of it, but there was another layer beyond that, and another.

Sex, with its reputation for complexity, was refreshingly simple. At least for Beth and Harry. They were in bed together on his second night in the house. It took ten minutes and was punctuated by a few sharp intakes of breath. She had no orgasm, and his was restrained. Afterward he went to his bed in her old room and she slept easily, falling asleep to images not of love but of wooden counters on a wooden board. The next morning she played him at breakfast and the combinations arose from her fingertips and spread themselves on the board as prettily as flowers. She beat him four quick games, letting him play the white pieces each time and hardly looking at the board.

While he was washing the dishes he talked about Philidor, one of his heroes. Philidor was a French musician who had played blindfolded in Paris and London.

"I read about those old players sometimes, and it all seems strange," she said. "I can't believe it was really chess."

"Don't knock it," Beltik said. "Bent Larsen plays Philidor's Defense."

"It's too cramped. The king's bishop gets locked in."

"It's solid," he said. "What I wanted to tell you about Philidor was that Diderot wrote him a letter. You know Diderot?"

"The French Revolution?"

"Yeah. Philidor was doing blindfold exhibitions and burning out his brain, or whatever it was they thought you did in the eighteenth century. Diderot wrote him: 'It is foolish to run the risk of going mad for vanity's sake.' I think of that sometimes when I'm analyzing my ass off over a chessboard." He looked at her quietly for a moment. "Last night was nice," he said.

She sensed that for him it was a concession to talk about it, and her feelings were mixed. "Doesn't Koltanowski play blindfolded all the time?" she said. "He's not crazy."

"I know. It was Morphy who went crazy. And Steinitz. Morphy thought people were trying to steal his shoes."

"Maybe he thought shoes were bishops."

"Yeah," he said. "Let's play chess."

By the end of the third week she had gone through his four *Shakhmatni* bulletins and most of the other game books. One day after he had been in an engineering class all morning they were studying a position together. She was trying to show him why a particular knight move was stronger than it looked.

"Look here," she said and began moving the pieces around fast. "Knight takes and then this pawn comes up. If he doesn't bring it up, the bishop is locked in. When he does, the other pawn falls. *Zip.*" She took the pawn off.

"What about the other bishop? Over here?"

"Oh, for Christ's sake," she said. "It'll have the check once the pawn is moved and the knight's traded. Can't you see that?"

Suddenly he froze and glared at her. "No, I can't," he said. "I can't find it that fast."

She looked back at him. "I wish you could," she said levelly. "You're too sharp for me."

She could see the hurt underneath his anger, and she softened. "I miss them too, sometimes," she said.

He shook his head. "No, you don't," he said. "Not anymore."

*   *   *

On Saturday she started playing him with odds of a knight. He tried to act casual about it, but she could see that he hated it. There was no other way for them to have a real game. Even with the odds and with his playing the white pieces she beat him the first two and drew the third.

That night he did not come to her bed, nor did he the next. She did not miss the sex, which meant very little to her, but she missed something. On the second night she had some difficulty going to sleep and found herself getting up at two in the morning. She went to the refrigerator and got out one of Mrs. Wheatley's cans of beer. Then she sat down at the chessboard and began idly moving the pieces around, sipping from the can. She played over some Queen's Gambit games: Alekhine–Yates; Tarrasch–von Scheve; Lasker–Tarrasch. The first of these was one she had memorized years before at Morris' Book Store; the other two she had analyzed with Beltik during their first week together. In the last there was a beautiful pawn to queen's rook four on the fifteenth move, as sweetly deadly as a pawn move could be. She left it on the board for the time it took to drink two beers, just looking at it. It was a warm night and the kitchen window was open; moths battered at the screen and somewhere far away a dog was barking. She sat at the table wearing Mrs. Wheatley's pink chenille robe and drinking Mrs. Wheatley's beer, feeling relaxed and easy in herself. She was glad to be alone. There were three more beers in the refrigerator, and she finished all of them. Then she went back up to bed and slept soundly until nine in the morning.

On Monday at breakfast he said, "Look, I've taught you everything I know."

She started to say something but kept silent.

"I've got to start studying. I'm supposed to be an electrical engineer, not a chess bum."

"Okay," she said. "You've taught me a lot."

They were quiet for a few minutes. She finished her eggs and took her plate to the sink. "I'm moving to that apartment," Beltik said. "It's closer to the university."

"Okay," Beth said, not turning from the sink.

He was gone by noon. She took a TV dinner from the freezer for her lunch but didn't turn on the oven. She was alone in the house, her stomach was in a knot, and she did not know any place to go. There were no movies she wanted to see or people she wanted to call; there was nothing she wanted to read. She walked up the stairs and through the two bedrooms. Mrs. Wheatley's dresses still hung in the closets and a half bottle of her tranquilizers was still on the nightstand by the unmade bed. The tension she felt would not go away. Mrs. Wheatley was gone, her body buried in a cemetery at the edge of town, and Harry Beltik had driven off with his chessboard and books, not even waving goodbye as he left. For a moment she had wanted to shout at him to stay with her, but she said nothing as he went down the steps and into his car. She took the bottle from the nightstand and shook three of the green pills into her hand, and then a fourth. She hated being alone. She swallowed the four pills without water, the way she had as a child.

In the afternoon she bought herself a steak and a large baking potato at Kroger's. Before pushing her cart to the checkout, she went to the wine-and-beer case and took out a fifth of burgundy. That night she watched television and got drunk. She went to sleep on the couch, only barely able to get to the set to turn it off.

Sometime during the night she awoke to a sense that the room was reeling. She had to vomit. Afterward, when she went upstairs to bed, she found that she was fully awake and very clear in her mind. There was a burning sensation in her stomach, and her eyes were wide open in the dark room as though looking for light. There was a powerful ache at the back of her neck. She reached over, found the bottle and took more tranquilizers. Eventually she went to sleep again.

She awoke the next morning with a crushing headache and a determination to get on with her career. Mrs. Wheatley was dead. Harry Beltik was gone. The U.S. Championship was in three weeks; she had been invited to it before going to Mexico, and if she was going to win it, she was going to have to beat

Benny Watts. While her coffee was percolating in the kitchen, she poured out the leftover burgundy from the night before, threw away the empty bottle and found two books she had ordered from Morris' the day the invitation had come. One was the game record from the last U.S. Championship and the other was called *Benny Watts: My Fifty Best Games of Chess.* On its dustjacket was a blowup of Benny's Huckleberry Finn face. Seeing it now, she winced at the memory of losing, at her damnfool attempt to double his pawns. She got herself a cup of coffee and opened the book, forgetting her hangover.

By noon she had analyzed six of the games and was getting hungry. There was a little restaurant two blocks away, the kind of place that has liver and onions on the menu and display cards of cigarette lighters at the cashier's stand. She brought the book with her and went over two more games while eating her hamburger and home fries. When the lemon custard came and was too thick and sweet to eat, she felt a sudden pang of longing for Mrs. Wheatley and the French desserts they had shared in places like Cincinnati and Houston. She shook it off, ordered a last cup of coffee and finished the game she was going over: the King's Indian Defense, with the black bishop fianchettoed in the upper right-hand corner of the board, looking down the long diagonal for a chance to pounce. Black worked the king's side while White worked the queen's side after the bishop went into the corner. Very civilized. Benny, playing Black, won it handily.

She paid her check and left. For the rest of the day and night until one in the morning she played over all of the games in the book. When she had finished, she knew a great deal more about Benny Watts and about precision chess than she had known before. She took two of her Mexican tranquilizers and went to bed, falling asleep instantly. She awoke pleasantly at nine-thirty the next morning. While her breakfast eggs were boiling, she chose a book for morning study: *Paul Morphy and the Golden Age of Chess.* It was an old book, in some ways outdated. The diagrams were grayish and cluttered, and it was hard to tell the black pieces from the white. But something in her could still thrill at the name Paul Morphy and at the idea of that strange New Orleans prodigy, well-bred, a lawyer, son of a high court judge, who when young dazzled the world with his chess and then quit playing altogether and lapsed into muttering paranoia and an early death. When Morphy played the King's Gambit he sacrificed knights and bishops with abandon and then moved in on the black king with dizzying speed. There had never been anything like him before or since. It made her spine tingle just to open the book and see the games list: Morphy–Lowenthal; Morphy–Harrwitz; Morphy–Anderssen, followed by dates in the eighteen-fifties. Morphy would stay up all night in Paris before his games, drinking in cafés and talking with strangers, and then would play the next day like a shark—well-mannered, well-dressed, smiling, moving the big pieces with small, ladylike, blue-veined hands, crushing one European master after another. Someone had called him "the pride and the sorrow of chess." If only he and Capablanca had lived at the same time and played each other! She began going over a game between Morphy and someone named Paulsen, played in 1857. The U.S. Championship would be in three weeks; it was time it was won by a woman. It was time she won it.

Chapter 10

When she came into the room, she saw a thin young man wearing faded blue jeans and a matching denim shirt seated at one of the tables. His blond hair came almost to his shoulders. It was only when he rose and said, "Hello, Beth," that she saw it was Benny Watts. The hair had been long in the cover photograph of *Chess Review* a few months before, but not that long. He looked pale and thin and very calm. Still, Benny had always been calm.

"Hello," she said.

"I read about the game with Borgov." Benny smiled. "It must have felt terrible."

She looked at him suspiciously, but his face was open and sympathetic. And she did not hate him anymore for beating her; there was only one player she hated now, and he was in Russia.

"I felt like a fool," she said.

"I know." He shook his head. "Helpless. It all goes, and you just push wood."

She stared at him. Chess players did not talk so easily about humiliations, did not admit weakness. She started to say something, when the tournament director spoke up loudly. "Play will begin in five minutes." She nodded to Benny, attempted a smile, and found her table.

There wasn't a face over a chessboard that she didn't know from hotel ballrooms where tournaments were played or from photographs in *Chess Review*. She herself had been on the cover six months after Townes took her picture in Las Vegas. Half the other players here on this campus in the small Ohio town had been on the cover themselves at one time or another. The man she was playing now in her first game, a middle-aged master named Phillip Resnais, was on the cover of the current issue. There were fourteen players, many of them grandmasters. She was the only woman.

They played in some kind of lecture room with dark-green blackboards along the wall at one end and fluorescent lights recessed into the ceiling. There was a row of large institutional windows along one blue wall, with bushes, trees and a wide stretch of the campus visible through them. At one end of the room were five rows of folding chairs, and out in the hallway a sign announced a visitor's fee of four dollars per session. During her first game there were about twenty-five people watching. A display board hung above each of the seven game tables, and two directors moved silently between the tables, changing the pieces after moves had been made on the real boards. The spectators' seats were on a wooden platform to give them a view of the playing surfaces.

But it was all second-rate, even the university they were playing at. They were the highest-ranked players in the country, assembled here in a single room, but it had the feel of a high school tournament. If it were golf or tennis, Benny Watts and she would be surrounded by reporters, would be playing under something other than these fluorescent lights and on plastic boards with cheap plastic pieces, watched by a few polite middle-aged people with nothing better to do.

Phillip Resnais seemed to take it all seriously, but she felt like walking out. She did not, however. When he played pawn to king four, she pushed up her queen bishop pawn and started the Sicilian Defense. Now she was in the middle of the Rossolimo-Nimzovitch Attack, getting equality on the eleventh move with pawn to queen three. It was a move she had gone over with Beltik, and it worked the way Beltik said it would work.

By the fourteenth move she had him on the run, and by the twentieth it was decisive. He resigned on the twenty-sixth. She looked around her at the other games, all of them still in progress, and felt better about the whole thing. It would be good to be U.S. Champion. If she could beat Benny Watts.

She had a small private room in a dormitory with the bathroom down the hall. It was austerely furnished, but there was no sense of anyone else's having lived in it, and she liked that. For the first several days she took her meals alone in the cafeteria and spent the evenings either at the desk in her room or in bed, studying. She had brought a suitcase full of chess books with her. They were lined up neatly at the back of the desk. She had also brought tranquilizers, just in case, but she did not even open the bottle during the first week. Her one game a day went smoothly, and although some of them lasted three or four hours and were grueling, she was never in danger of losing. As time went on, the other players looked at her with more and more respect. She felt serious, professional, sufficient.

Benny Watts was doing as well as she. The games were printed up every night from a Xerox in the college library, and copies were given to the players and spectators. She went over them in the evenings and mornings, playing some out on her board but going through most of them in her head. She always took the trouble to set up the game Benny had played and actually move the pieces, carefully studying the way he had played it. In a round robin each player met each of the others one time; she would meet Benny in the eleventh game.

Since there were thirteen games and the tournament lasted two weeks, there was one day off—the first Sunday. She slept late that morning, stayed a long time in the shower, and then took a long walk around the campus. It was very tranquil, with well-mowed lawns and elm trees and an occasional patch of flowers—a serene Midwestern Sunday morning, but she missed the competition of the match. She momentarily considered walking into the town, where she had heard there were a dozen places to drink beer, but thought better of it. She did not want to erode any more brain cells. She looked at her watch; it was eleven o'clock. She headed for the Student Union Building, where the cafeteria was. She would get some coffee.

There was a pleasant wood-paneled lounge on the main floor. When she came in, Benny Watts was sitting on a beige corduroy sofa at the far end of it with a chessboard and clock on the table in front of him. Two other players were standing nearby, and he was smiling at them, explaining something about the game in front of him.

She had started downstairs for the cafeteria when Benny's voice called to her. "Come on over." She hesitated, turned and walked over. She recognized the other two players at once; one of them she had beaten two days before with the Queen's Gambit.

"Look at this, Beth," Benny said, pointing to the board. "White's move. What would you do?"

She looked at it a moment. "The Lopez?"

"That's right."

She was a little irritated. She wanted a cup of coffee. The position was delicate, and it took concentration. The other players remained silent. Finally she saw what was needed. She bent over wordlessly, picked up the knight at king three and set it down on queen five.

"*See!*" Benny said to the others, laughing.

"Maybe you're right," one of them said.

"I know I'm right. And Beth here thinks the same way I do. The pawn move's too weak."

"The pawn works only if he plays his bishop," Beth said, feeling better.

"Exactly!" Benny said. He was wearing jeans and some kind of loose white blouse. "How about some skittles, Beth?"

"I was on my way for coffee," she said.

"Barnes'll get you coffee. Won't you, Barnes?" A big, soft-looking young man, a grandmaster, nodded assent. "Sugar and cream?"

"Yes."

Benny was pulling a dollar bill out of his jeans pocket. He handed it to Barnes. "Get me some apple juice. But not in one of those plastic cups. Get a milk glass."

Benny set the clock by the board. He held out two pawns concealed in his hands, and the hand Beth tapped had the white one. After they set up the pieces Benny said, "Would you like to bet?"

"Bet?"

"We could play for five dollars a game."

"I haven't had my coffee yet."

"Here it comes." Beth saw Barnes hurrying across the room with a glass of juice and a white Styrofoam cup.

"Okay," she said. "Five dollars."

"Have some coffee," Benny said, "and I'll punch your clock."

She took it from Barnes, had a long drink and set the half-empty cup on the coffee table. "Go ahead," she said to Benny. She felt very good. The spring morning outdoors was all right, but this was what she loved.

He beat her with only three minutes on his clock. She played well but he played brilliantly, moving almost immediately each time, seeing through whatever she tried doing to him. She handed him a five-dollar bill from the billfold in her pocket and set up the pieces again, this time taking the black ones for herself. There were four other players standing nearby now, watching them.

She tried the Sicilian against his pawn to king four, but he wiped it away with a pawn gambit and got her into an irregular opening. He was incredibly fast. She had him in trouble at midgame with doubled rooks on an open file, but he ignored them and attacked down the center, letting her check him twice with the rooks, exposing his king. But when she tried to bring a knight into it for mate, he sprang loose and was at her queen and then her king, catching her finally in a mating net. She resigned before he could move in for the kill. She gave him a ten this time and he gave her the five back. She had sixty dollars in her pocket and more money back at the room.

By noon there were forty or more people watching. Most of

the players from the tournament were there along with some of
the spectators who regularly attended the games, college students and a group of men who might have been professors. She
and Benny kept playing, not even talking now between games.
Beth won the third one with a beautiful save just before her flag
dropped, but she lost the next four and drew the fifth. Some of
the positions were brilliantly complex, but there was no time for
analysis. It was thrilling but frustrating. She had never in her
life been beaten so consistently, and although it was only
five-minute chess and not serious, it was an immersion in quiet
humiliation. She had never felt like this before. She played beautifully, followed the game with precision and responded accu-
rately to every threat, mounted powerful threats of her own, but
it meant nothing. Benny seemed to have some resource beyond
her understanding, and he won game after game from her. She
felt helpless, and inside her there grew a quiet sense of outrage.

Finally she gave him her last five dollars. It was five-thirty in
the afternoon. A row of empty Styrofoam cups sat by the board.
When she got up to leave, there was applause and Benny shook
her hand. She wanted to hit him but said nothing. There was
random applause from the crowd in the room.

As she was leaving, the man she had played the first of the
week, Phillip Resnais, stopped her. "I wouldn't worry about it,"
he said. "Benny plays speed chess as well as anyone in the world.
It doesn't really mean a lot."

She nodded curtly and thanked him. When she went outside
into the late-afternoon sunlight, she felt like a fool.

That night she stayed in her room and took tranquilizers. Four
of them.

She felt rested in the morning, but stupid. Mrs. Wheatley had
once described things as looking askew; that was how they
looked to Beth when she awoke from her deep, tranquilized
sleep. But she no longer felt the humiliation she had felt after
being beaten by Benny. She took her pill bottle from the bed-
stand drawer and squeezed the top on it tight. It would not do
to take any more. Not until the tournament was over. She
thought suddenly of Thursday, the day she would play Benny,

and she tensed. But she put the pills back in the drawer and got dressed. She ate breakfast early and drank three cups of strong coffee with it. Then she took a brisk walk around the main part of the campus, playing through one of the games from Benny Watts's book. He was brilliant, she told herself, but not unbeatable. Anyway, she wouldn't play him for three more days.

The games started at one and went on until four or five in the afternoon. Adjournments were finished either in the evening or the morning of the next day. By noon her head was clear and when she started her one o'clock game against a tall, silent Californian in a Black Power T-shirt, she was ready for him. Although he wore his hair in a kind of Afro, he was white—as all of them were. She answered his English Opening with both knights, making it a four-knights game, and decided against her normal practice to trade him down to an endgame. It worked beautifully, and she was pleased with her handling of the pawns; she had one on the sixth and one on the seventh rank when he resigned. It was easier than she had expected; her endgame study with Beltik had paid off.

That evening Benny Watts joined her at the cafeteria table while she was eating her dessert. "Beth," he said, "it's going to be you or me."

She looked up from her rice pudding. "Are you trying to psych me out?"

He laughed. "No. I can beat you without that."

She went on eating and said nothing.

"Look," he said, "I'm sorry about yesterday. I wasn't trying to hustle you."

She took a sip of coffee. "You weren't?"

"I just wanted some action."

"And money," Beth said. Although that wasn't the point.

"You're the best player here," he said. "I've been reading your games. You attack like Alekhine."

"You held me off well enough yesterday."

"That doesn't count. I know speed chess better than you. I play a lot of it in New York."

"You beat me in Las Vegas."

"That was a long time ago. You were too wrapped up in doubling my pawns. I couldn't get away with that again."

She finished her coffee in silence while he ate his dinner and drank his milk. When he had finished, she said, "Do you go over games in your head when you're alone? I mean, play all the way through them?"

He smiled. "Doesn't everybody?"

She permitted herself to watch television in the lounge of the Student Union Building that evening. Benny wasn't there, although a few of the other players were. She went back to her room afterward, feeling lonely. It was her first tournament since Mrs. Wheatley died, and she missed her now. She took the endgame book from the collection on the desk and began studying. Benny was all right. It had been nice of him to talk to her that way. And she had gotten used to his hair by now; she liked it long, the way it was. He had really very good-looking hair.

She won Tuesday's game, and Wednesday's. Benny was still playing when she finished on Wednesday and she walked over to his table and saw in a moment that he had it all but won. He looked up at her and smiled. Then he made the word silently with his mouth: "Tomorrow."

There was a children's playground at the edge of the campus. She walked to it by moonlight and sat on one of the swings. What she really wanted was a drink, but that was out of the question. A bottle of red wine, with a little cheese. Then a few pills and off to bed. But she couldn't. She had to be clear in the morning, had to be ready for the game against Benny Watts at one o'clock. Maybe she could take one pill and go to bed. Or two. She would take two. She swung herself back and forth a few times, listening to the squeaking of the chain that held the swing, before heading purposively back to the dormitory. She took the two pills, but it still was over an hour before she could sleep.

Something in the deferential manner of the tournament directors and the way the other players looked at her told her that the attention of the tournament had focused on this game. She and

Benny were the only players who had come this far without even a draw. In a round robin there was no precedence of boards; they would play at the third table in the row that began at the classroom door. But attention was centered on that table, and the spectators, who had already filled the seats and now included a dozen people standing, all became quiet as she seated herself. Benny came in a minute after she did; there was whispering when he arrived at the table and sat down. She looked over at the crowd, and a thought that had been present in her mind suddenly solidified itself: the two of them were the best players in America.

Benny was wearing his faded denim shirt with a silver medallion on a chain. His sleeves were rolled up like a laborer's. He was not smiling, and he looked a good deal older than twenty-four. He glanced briefly at the crowd, nodded almost imperceptibly to Beth, and stared at the board as the tournament director signaled for the games to begin. Benny was playing the white pieces. Beth punched his clock.

He played pawn to king four, and she did not hesitate; she replied with pawn to queen bishop four: the Sicilian. He brought out the king knight, and she played pawn to king three. There was no point in using an obscure opening against Benny. He knew openings better than she. The place to get him would be in the middle game, if she could mount an attack before he did. But first she would have to get equality.

She felt a sensation she had felt only once before, in Mexico City playing Borgov: she felt like a child trying to outsmart an adult. When she made her second move, she looked across the board at Benny and saw the quiet seriousness of his face and felt unready for this game with him. But it wasn't so. She knew in part of herself that it wasn't, that in Mexico City she had overwhelmed a string of professionals before wilting in the game with Borgov, that she had beaten grandmaster after grandmaster in this tournament, that even when she had been playing the janitor at Methuen Home as an eight-year-old she had played with a solidity that was altogether remarkable, altogether professional. Yet she felt now, however illogically, inexperienced.

Benny thought for several minutes and made an unusual move. Instead of playing the queen pawn, he pushed the queen bishop pawn to the fourth rank. It sat there, facing her queen bishop pawn, unsupported. She looked at it for a minute, wondering what he had in mind. He might be going for the Maróczy Bind, but doing it out of the normal sequence. It was new—something probably planned especially for this game. She suddenly felt embarrassed, aware that although she had gone through Benny's game book, she had prepared nothing special for today and had approached it as she always approached chess, ready to play by intuition and attack.

And then she began to see that there was nothing sinister about Benny's move, nothing she could not handle. It became clear to her that she did not have to play into it. She could decline the invitation. If she played her knight to queen bishop three, his move might be wasted. Maybe he was only fishing for a quick advantage—as though playing speed chess. She brought her knight out. What the hell, as Alma Wheatley would say.

Benny played pawn to queen four; she took the pawn, and he retook with his knight. She brought out the other knight and waited for him to bring out his. She would pin it when he did and then take it, getting doubled pawns. That queen bishop pawn move of his was costing him, and although the advantage wasn't much, it was certain.

But he did not bring out the knight. Instead he took hers. Clearly he didn't want the doubled pawn. She let that sink in a moment before retaking. It was astounding; he was already on the defensive. A few minutes before, she had felt like an amateur, and here Benny Watts had tried to confuse her on the third move and had put himself in trouble.

The obvious thing was to take his knight with her knight pawn, capturing toward the center. If she took the other way, with her queen pawn, he would trade queens. That would prevent her from castling and would deny her the queen she loved for quick attack. She reached her hand out to take the knight with the knight pawn and then brought it back. Somehow the idea of opening the queen file, shocking though it was, looked attractive. She began to study it. And gradually it began to make sense. With an early queen trade, castling would be irrelevant. She could bring the king out the way you did in the endgame. She looked across at Benny again and saw that he was wondering why she was taking so long with this routine recapture. Somehow he looked smaller to her. What the hell, she thought again and took with the queen pawn, exposing her queen.

Benny did not hesitate; he took her queen with his and punched the clock smartly. He did not even say "Check." She took with her king as she had to, and he pushed up the other bishop pawn to protect his king pawn. It was a simple defensive move, but something in her exulted when he did it. She felt naked with no queen this early in the game, yet she was beginning to feel strong without it. She already had the initiative, and she knew it. She pushed her pawn to king four. It was not an obvious move at this stage, and the soundness of it warmed her. It opened up the diagonal for her queen bishop and held his king pawn to the fourth rank. She looked up from the board and around her. All the other games were intently in progress; the spectators were hushed, watching. There were more people standing, and they were standing where they could see the game she was playing with Benny. The director came by and made the move on the display board in front of their table, pushing the king pawn to king four. The spectators began to take that in. She looked to the other side of the room and out the window. It was a beautiful day, with fresh leaves on the trees and an impeccably blue sky. She felt herself expand, relax, open up. She was going to beat him. She was going to beat him soundly.

The continuation she found on the nineteenth move was a beautiful and subtle wonder. It sprang to her mind full-blown, with half a dozen moves as clear as if they were projected on a screen in front of her, her rook, bishop and knight dancing together down in his king's corner of the board. Yet there was no checkmate in it or even an advantage in material. After her knight came to queen five on the twenty-fifth move and Benny was forced merely to push a pawn because he could do nothing to defend, she traded rook and knight for rook and knight and brought her king to queen three. Although the pieces and pawns were equal, it was only a matter of counting moves. It would take twelve for him to get a pawn to the eighth rank and queen it, while she could do it in ten.

Benny made a few moves, bringing his king out in the hopeless attempt to take off her pawns before she took away his, but even his arm as it moved the king was listless. And when she took his queen bishop pawn, he reached out and toppled his king. There was silence and then quiet applause. She had won in thirty moves.

As they were leaving the room Benny said to her, "I never thought you'd let me trade queens."

"I didn't either," she said.

Chapter 11

After the ceremony Saturday evening, Benny took her to a bar in town. They sat in a back booth and Beth drank her first beer and ordered another. They both tasted delicious. "Easy," Benny said. "Easy." He had not finished his first.

"You're right," she said and slowed down. She felt high enough already. No losses. No draws. Her last two opponents had offered draws in midgame, and she had refused.

"A perfect score," Benny said.

"It feels good," she said, meaning the victory, but the beer felt good too. She looked at him more closely. "I appreciate the way you're taking it."

"A mask," he said. "I'm raging inwardly."

"It doesn't show."

"I should not have played that goddamned bishop pawn."

They sat silently for a while. He took a thoughtful sip of beer and asked, "What are you going to do about Borgov?"

"When I go to Paris? I don't even have a passport."

"When you go to Moscow."

"I don't know what you're talking about."

"Don't they deliver the mail in Kentucky?"

"Of course they do."

"The Moscow Invitational. The U.S. winner is invited."

"I want another beer," she said.

"You didn't know that?" Benny looked shocked.

"I'll get the beer myself."

"Go ahead."

She went up to the bar and ordered another bottle. She had heard of the Moscow Invitational but knew nothing about it. The bartender brought her the beer, and she told him to get another. When she came back to the table, Benny said, "That's too much beer."

"Probably." She waited for the foam to settle and took a swallow. "How do I get to Moscow if I go?"

"When I went, the Federation bought my ticket and a church group put up the rest."

"Did you have a second?"

"Barnes."

Barnes?" She stared at him.

"It would be tough to be in Russia alone." He frowned. "You shouldn't drink beer like that. You'll be washed up at twenty-one."

She set down the glass. "Who else will be playing in Moscow?"

"Four other countries and the four top Russians."

That would mean Luchenko and Borgov. Possibly Shapkin. She did not want to think about it. She looked at him quietly for a minute. "Benny, I like the way your hair looks."

He stared at her. "Sure you do," he said. "What about Russia?"

She took another drink of beer. She *did* like Benny's hair and his blue eyes. She had never thought of him sexually before, but she was thinking that way now. "Four Russian chess players," she said, "is a lot of Russian chess players."

"Murderous." He raised his glass and finished off his beer. He had drunk only the one. "Beth," he said, "you're the only American I know who might do it."

"I went to pieces with Borgov in Mexico City . . ."

"When do you go to Paris?" Benny said.

"In five weeks."

"Then get your life organized around that and study. Get a trainer."

"What about you?"

He thought a moment. "Can you come to New York?"

"I don't know."

"You can sleep in my living room, and leave for Paris from there."

The idea shocked her. "I've got a house to take care of, in Kentucky."

"Let the fucking house fall down."

"I'm not ready . . ."

"When will you be? Next year? Ten years?"

"I don't know."

He leaned forward and said slowly, "If you don't do it, you'll drink your talent away. It'll go down the drain."

"Borgov made me look like a fool."

"*You weren't ready.*"

"I don't know how good I really am."

"*I* know," he said. "You're the best there is."

She took a deep breath. "All right. I'll come to New York."

"You can come with me from here," he said. "I'll drive us."

"When?" This was happening too fast. She felt frightened.

"Tomorrow afternoon, when everything here's finished. Whenever we can get away." He stood up. "And about sex . . ."

She looked up at him.

"Forget it," he said.

"Spring," Benny said, "is first class. Absolutely first class."

"How can you tell?" Beth asked. They were driving along a gray asphalt section of the Pennsylvania Turnpike, pounding along the gritty road with semis and dusty passenger cars.

"It's out there somewhere. Up in the hills. It's even in New York."

"Ohio was pleasant," Beth said. But she didn't like this discussion. Weather did not interest her. She had made no arrangements for the house in Lexington, had not been able to get the lawyer on the telephone and did not know what to expect in New York. She did not like Benny's insouciance in the face of her uncertainty, the kind of sunny blankness that suffused his face from time to time. He had looked that way during the awards ceremony and during the time she did her interviews and signed autographs and thanked the officials and the USCF people who had come down from upstate New York to talk about the importance of chess. His face was blank now. She turned her eyes to the road.

After a while he spoke up. "When you go to Russia I want to go with you."

That was a surprise. They hadn't talked about Russia, or chess, since getting in the car. "As my second?"

"Whatever. I can't afford to pay expenses."

"You want me to pay them?"

"Something will turn up. While you were interviewed by that magazine, I talked to Johanssen. He said there wouldn't be any Federation money for seconds."

"I'm only thinking about Paris," she said. "I haven't decided to go to Moscow yet."

"You'll go."

"I don't even know if I'm going to stay more than a few days with you. I have to get a passport."

"We can do that in New York."

She started to say something but didn't. She looked at Benny. Now that blankness had left his face, she felt warmer toward him. She had made love to two men in her life, and it was hardly making love; if she and Benny went to bed together, there would be more to it. She would see there was more to it. They would be in his apartment by midnight; maybe something would happen there. Maybe he would feel differently at home.

"Let's play chess," Benny said. "I'll be White. Pawn to king four."

She shrugged. "Pawn to queen bishop four."

"N," he said, using the letter for "knight." "K-B3."

"Pawn to queen three." She wasn't sure she liked this. She had never shared her interior chessboard before, and there was a sense of violation in opening it to Benny's moves.

"P to Q four," Benny said.

"Pawn takes pawn."

"Knight takes."

"Knight. King bishop three." Actually it was easy. She could look at the road ahead and at the same time see the imaginary chessboard and the pieces on it without difficulty.

"N to Q-B3," Benny said.

"Pawn to king's knight three."

"P to B four."

"P to B four."

"The Levenfish," Benny said dryly. "I never liked it."

"Play your knight."

Suddenly his voice was like ice. "Don't tell me what to move," he said. She pulled back as if stung.

They drove in silence for a few miles. Beth watched the gray steel divider that separated them from the oncoming lanes. Then, as they were coming to a tunnel, Benny said, "You were right about the knight on B-3. I'll put it there."

She hesitated a moment before speaking. "Okay. I'll take the knight."

"Pawn takes," Benny said.

"Pawn to king five."

"Pawn takes again," Benny said. "Do you know what Scharz says about that one? The footnote?"

"I don't read footnotes," Beth said.

"It's time you started."

"I don't like Scharz."

"I don't either," Benny said. "But I read him. What's your move?"

"Queen takes queen. Check." She could hear the sullenness in her voice.

"King takes," Benny said, relaxing now at the wheel. Pennsylvania rolled by. Beth forced him to resign on the twenty-seventh move and felt somewhat better for it. She had always liked the Sicilian.

*　　　*　　　*

There were plastic bags full of garbage in the entryway to Benny's apartment and the light overhead was only a dirty bare bulb. It was a white tile hallway and as depressing at midnight as the toilet in a bus station. There were three locks on Benny's front door, which was painted red and had some impenetrable word like *"Bezbo"* written on it in black spray paint.

Inside was a small and cluttered living room with books piled everywhere. But the lighting was pleasant when he got the lamps on. One end of the room was a kitchen, and near it was a door going off to the bedroom. There was a grass rug and no sofa and chairs—just black pillows to sit on with lamps beside them.

The bathroom was orthodox enough, with a floor made of black-and-white tile and a broken handle on the hot-water tap. There was a tub and shower with a black plastic curtain. She washed her hands and face and came back into the living room. Benny had gone into the bedroom to unpack. Her bag was still on the living-room floor next to a bookcase. She walked over to it and looked wearily at the books. They were all on chess—all five shelves of them. Some were in Russian and German, but they were all on chess. She walked across the hard little rug to the other side of the room where there was another bookcase, this one made of boards resting on bricks. More chess. One whole shelf was *Shakhmatni Byulleten* going back to the nineteen-fifties.

"There's room in this closet," Benny shouted from the bedroom. "You can hang up when you want to."

"Okay," she said. Back on the turnpike she had thought they might make love when they got here. Now she wanted only to sleep. And what was she supposed to sleep on? "I thought I was going to get a sofa," she said.

He came into the doorway. "I said 'living room.'" He went back to the bedroom and returned with a bulky-looking thing and some kind of pump. He flipped it out in the middle of the floor and began pedaling the pump with his foot, and after a while it puffed up and became an air mattress. "I'll get sheets," Benny said. He brought them out of the bedroom.

"I'll do it," she said and took them from him. She didn't like the looks of the mattress, but she knew where her pills were. She could get them out after he fell asleep, if she needed to. There would be nothing to drink in this apartment. Benny had not said so, but she knew.

She must have fallen asleep before Benny did, since she forgot about the pills in her luggage. She awoke to the sound of a klaxon outside—an ambulance or fire truck. When she tried to sit up she could not; there was no edge of the bed to hang her legs over. She pushed herself up and stood, wearing pajamas, and looked around. Benny was standing at the sink counter with his back to her. She knew where she was, but it looked different by daylight. The siren faded and was replaced by the general traffic sounds of New York. One blind was open and she could see the cab of a big truck as close as Benny was, and beyond it taxis weaving past. A dog barked intermittently.

Benny turned and came over to her. He was holding out a big cardboard cup to her.

"Chock Full O' Nuts," the cup read. Something seemed very strange about this. No one had ever given her anything in the morning—certainly not Mrs. Wheatley, who was never up before Beth had eaten her breakfast. She took the plastic top off and tasted the coffee. "Thanks," she said.

"Dress in the bedroom," Benny said.

"I need a shower."

"It's all yours."

Benny had set up a folding card table with a green and beige chessboard on it. He was arranging the pieces when she came into the living room. "Okay," he said, "we'll start with these." He handed her a roll of pamphlets and magazines wrapped with a rubber band. On top was a small pamphlet with a cheap paper cover reading "The Hastings Christmas Chess Congress—Falaise Hall, White Rock Gardens," and under this, "A Record of Games." The pages inside were dense with type, smudgily printed. There were two chess games on a page, with boldface captions: Luchenko–Uhlmann; Borgov–Penrose. He handed her another, titled simply *Grandmaster Chess*. It was much like the Hastings booklet. Three of the magazines were from Germany, and one was from Russia.

"We'll play through the Hastings games," Benny said. He went into the bedroom and came back with two plain wooden chairs, setting one on each side of the card table near the front window. The truck was still parked outside and the street was full of slow-moving cars. "You play the white pieces and I'll play Black."

"I haven't had breakfast . . ."

"Eggs in the fridge," Benny said. "We'll play the Borgov games first."

"All of them?"

"He'll be in Paris when you go."

She looked at the magazine in her hand and then over at the table by the window again, then at her watch. It was ten after eight. "I'll have the eggs first," she said.

They got sandwiches from a deli for lunch and ate them over the board. Supper came from a Chinese take-out on First Avenue. Benny would not let her play quickly through the openings; he stopped her whenever a move was at all obscure and asked her why she did it. He made her analyze everything out of the ordinary. Sometimes he would physically stop her hand from moving a piece to ask questions. "Why not advance the knight?" or "Why isn't he defending against the rook?" or "What's going to become of the backward pawn?" It was rigorous and intense, and he did not let up. She had been aware of such questions for years but had never allowed herself to pursue them with this kind of rigor. Often her mind would be racing with the attack possibilities inherent in the positions that developed in front of her, wanting to push Luchenko or Mecking or Czerniak into lightning attacks against Borgov, when Benny stopped her with a question about defense or opening the light or dark squares or contesting a file with a rook. It infuriated her sometimes, yet she could see the rightness of his questions. She had been playing grandmaster games in her head from the time she first discovered *Chess Review,* but she had not been disciplined about it. She played them to exult in the win—to feel the stab of excitement at a sacrifice or a forced mate, especially in the games that were printed in books precisely because they incorporated drama of that kind—like the game books by Fred Reinfeld that were full of queen sacrifices and melodrama. She knew from her tournament experience that you couldn't rely on your opponent setting himself up for a queen sacrifice or a surprise mate with knight and rook; still, she treasured the thrill of games like that. It was what she loved in Morphy, not his routine games and certainly not his lost ones—and Morphy like everyone else had lost games. But she had always been bored by ordinary chess even when it was played by grandmasters, bored in the way that she was bored by Reuben Fine's endgame analyses and the counteranalyses in places like *Chess Review* that pointed out errors in Reuben Fine. She had never done anything like what Benny was making her do now.

The games she was playing were serious, workmanlike chess played by the best players in the world, and the amount of mental energy latent in each move was staggering. Yet the results were often monumentally dull and inconclusive. An enormous power of thought might be implicit in a single white pawn move, say, opening up a long-range threat that could become manifest only in half a dozen moves; but Black would foresee the threat and find the move that canceled it out, and the brilliancy would be aborted. It was frustrating and anticlimactic, yet—because Benny forced her to stop and see what was going on—fascinating. They kept it up for six days, leaving the apartment only when necessary and once, on Wednesday night, going to a movie. Benny did not own a TV, or a stereo; his apartment was for eating, sleeping and chess. They played through the Hastings booklet and the Russian one, not missing a game except for the grandmaster draws.

On Tuesday she got her lawyer in Kentucky on the phone and asked him to see if everything was all right at the house. She went to Benny's branch of Chemical Bank and opened an account with the winner's check from Ohio. It would take five days for it to clear. She had enough traveler's checks to pay her share of the expenses until then.

They did remarkably little talking during the first week. Nothing sexual happened. Beth had not forgotten about it, but she was too busy going over chess games. When they finished, sometimes at midnight, she would sit for a while on a pillow on the floor or take a walk to Second or Third Avenue and get an ice cream or a Hershey bar at a deli. She went into none of the bars, and she seldom stayed out long. New York could be grim and dangerous-looking at night, but that wasn't the reason. She was too tired to do more than go back to the apartment, pump up her mattress and go to sleep.

Sometimes being with Benny was like being with no one at all. For hours at a time he would be completely impersonal. Something in her responded to that, and she became impersonal and cool herself, communicating nothing but chess.

But sometimes it would change. Once when she was studying an especially complex position between two Russians, a position that ended in a draw, she saw something, followed it, and cried out, "Look at this, Benny!" and started moving the pieces around. "He missed one. Black has this with the knight . . ." and she showed a way for the black player to win. And Benny, smiling broadly, came over to where she was sitting at the board and hugged her around the shoulders.

Most of the time, chess was the only language between them. One afternoon when they had spent three or four hours on end-game analysis she said wearily, "Don't you get bored sometimes?" and he looked at her blankly. "What else is there?" he said.

They were doing rook and pawn endings when there was a knock at the door. Benny got up and opened it, and there were three people. One was a woman. Beth recognized one man from a *Chess Review* piece about him a few months before and the other looked familiar, although she couldn't place him. The woman was striking. She was about twenty-five, with black hair and a pale complexion, and she was wearing a very short gray skirt and some kind of military shirt with epaulets.

"This is Beth Harmon," Benny said. "Hilton Wexler, Grandmaster Arthur Levertov, and Jenny Baynes."

"Our new champ," Levertov said, giving her a little bow. He was in his thirties and balding.

"Hi," Beth said. She stood up from the table.

"Congratulations!" Wexler said. "Benny needed a lesson in humility."

"I'm already tops in humility," Benny said.

The woman held out her hand. "Nice to meet you."

It felt strange to Beth to have all these people in Benny's small living room. It seemed as though she had lived half her life in this apartment with him, studying chess games, and it was outrageous for anyone else to be there. She had been in New York nine days. Not knowing exactly what to do, she sat down at the board again. Wexler came over and stood at the other side. "Do you do problems?"

"No." She had tried a few as a child, but they did not interest her. The positions did not look natural. *White to move and mate in two.* It was as, as Mrs. Wheatley would have said, irrelevant.

"Let me show you one," Wexler said. His voice was friendly and easy. "Can I mess this up?"

"Go ahead."

"Hilton," Jenny said, coming over to them, "she's not one of your problem freaks. She's the U.S. Champion."

"It's okay," Beth said. But she was glad of what Jenny had said.

Wexler put pieces on the board until there was a weird-looking position with both queens in corners and all four rooks on the same file. The kings were nearly centered, which would be unlikely in a real game. When he finished, he folded his arms across his chest. "This is my favorite," he said. "White wins it in three."

Beth looked at it, annoyed. It seemed silly to deal with something like this. It could never come up in a game. Advance the pawn, check with the knight, and the king moved to the corner. But then the pawn queened, and it was stalemate. Maybe the pawn knighted, to make the next check. That worked. Then if the king didn't move there after the first check . . . She went back to that for a moment and saw what to do. It was like a problem in algebra, and she had always been good at algebra. She looked up at Wexler. "Pawn to queen seven."

He looked astonished. "Jesus," he said. "That's fast."

Jenny was smiling. "See, Hilton," she said.

Benny had been watching all this silently. "Let's do a simultaneous," he said suddenly to Beth. "Play us all."

"Not me," Jenny said. "I don't even know the rules."

"Do we have enough boards and pieces?" Beth asked.

"On the shelf in the closet." Benny went into the bedroom and returned with a cardboard box. "We'll set these up on the floor."

"Time control?" Levertov said.

Beth suddenly thought of something. "Let's do speed chess."

"It gives us an edge," Benny said. "We can think on your time."

"I want to try it."

"No good." Benny's tone was severe. "You're not very good at speed chess anyway. Remember?"

Something in her responded strongly to what he was not saying. "I'll bet you ten I beat you."

"What if you throw the other games and use all your time against me?"

She could have kicked him. "I'll bet you ten on each of them, too." She was surprised at the firmness in her own voice. She sounded like Mrs. Deardorff.

Benny shrugged. "Okay. It's your money."

"Let's put all three boards on the floor. I'll sit in the middle."

They did it, using three clocks. Beth had been very sharp for the past several days, and she played with unhesitating precision, attacking on all the boards at once. She beat the three of them with time to spare.

When it was over, Benny didn't say anything. He went to the bedroom, got his billfold, took three tens out of it and handed them to Beth.

"Let's do it again," Beth said. There was a bitterness in her voice; hearing the words, she knew it could have meant sex: *Let's do it again.* If this was what Benny wanted, this was what he would get. She began setting up the pieces.

They got into position on the floor, and Beth played the whites on all three again. The boards were fanned out in front of her so that she didn't have to spin around to play them, but she found herself hardly consulting them, anyway, except to make the moves. She played from chessboards in her head. Even the mechanical business of making the moves and punching the clocks was effortless. Benny's position was hopeless when his clock flag fell; she had time left over. He gave her another thirty, and when she suggested trying again he said, "No."

There was tension in the room, and no one knew how to deal with it. Jenny tried to laugh about it, saying, "It's just male chauvinism," but it didn't help. Beth was furious with Benny—furious at him for being easy to beat and furious with the way he was taking it, trying to look unmoved, as though nothing affected him.

Then Benny did something surprising. He had been sitting with his back straight. Suddenly he leaned against the wall, pushing his legs out on the floor, relaxing. "Well, kid," he said, "I think you've got it." And everybody laughed. Beth looked at Jenny, who was sitting on the floor next to Wexler. Jenny, who was beautiful and intelligent, was looking at her with admiration.

Beth and Benny spent the next few days studying *Shakhmatni Byulleten*s, going back to the nineteen-fifties. Every now and then they would play a game, and Beth always won it. She could feel herself moving past Benny in a way that was almost physical. It was astounding to them both. In one game she uncovered an attack on his queen on the thirteenth move and had him laying down his king on the sixteenth. "Well," he said softly, "nobody's done that to me in fifteen years."

"Not even Borgov?"

"Not even Borgov."

Sometimes chess would keep her awake at night for hours. It was like Methuen, except that she was more relaxed and not afraid of sleeplessness. She would lie on her mattress on the living-room floor after midnight with New York street noises coming in through the open bay window and study positions in her mind. They were as clear as they had ever been. She did not take tranquilizers, and that helped the clarity. It was not whole games now but particular situations—positions called "theoretically important" and "warranting close study." She lay there hearing the shouts of drunks in the street outside and mastered the intricacies of chess positions that were classic in their difficulty. Once during a lovers' quarrel where the woman kept shouting, "I'm at my fucking wit's end. At my wit's fucking *end!*" and the man kept saying, "Like your fucking sister," Beth lay on her cot and came to see a way of queening a pawn that she had never seen before. It was beautiful. It would work. She could use it. "Up your ass," the woman shouted, and Beth lay back exulting and then fell pleasantly asleep.

They spent their third week repeating the Borgov games and finished the last of them after midnight on Thursday. When Beth had done her analysis of the resignation, pointing out how Borgov could avoid a draw, she looked up to see Benny yawning. It was a hot night and the windows were open.

"Shapkin went wrong in midgame," Beth said. "He should have protected his queenside."

Benny looked at her sleepily. "Even I get tired of chess sometimes."

She stood up from the board. "It's time for bed."

"Not so fast," Benny said. He looked at her for a moment and smiled. "Do you still like my hair?"

"I've been trying to learn how to beat Vasily Borgov," Beth said. "Your hair doesn't enter into it."

"I'd like you to come to bed with me."

They had been together three weeks and she had almost forgotten sex. "I'm *tired,*" she said, exasperated.

"So am I. But I'd like you to sleep with me."

He looked very relaxed and pleasant. Suddenly she felt warm toward him. "All right," she said.

She was startled to wake up in the morning with someone beside her in bed. Benny had rolled over to his side and all she could see of him was his pale, bare back and some of his hair. She felt self-conscious at first and afraid of waking him; she sat up carefully, leaning her back against the wall. Being in bed with a man was really all right. Making love had been all right too, although not as exciting as she had hoped. Benny hadn't said much. He was gentle and easy with her, but there was still that distance of his. She remembered a phrase from the first man she had made love with: "Too cerebral." She turned toward Benny. His skin did look good in the light; it seemed almost luminous. For a moment she felt like putting her arms around him and hugging him with her naked body, but she restrained herself.

Eventually Benny woke, rolled over on his back and blinked at her. She had the sheet up, covering her breasts. After a moment she said, "Good morning."

He blinked again. "You shouldn't try the Sicilian against Borgov," he said. "He's just too good at it."

They spent the morning with two Luchenko games; Benny put the emphasis on strategy rather than tactics. He was in a cheerful mood, but Beth felt somehow resentful. She wanted something more in the way of lovemaking, or at least in intimacy, and Benny was lecturing her. "You're a born tactician," he said, "but your planning is jerry-built." She said nothing and dealt with her annoyance as well as she could. What he was saying was true enough, but the pleasure he took in pointing it out was irritating.

At noon he said, "I've got to get to a poker game."

She looked up from the position she had just analyzed. "A poker game?"

"I have to pay the rent."

That was astonishing. She had not thought of him as a gambler. When she asked about it, he said he made more money from poker and backgammon than from chess. "You ought to learn," he said, smiling. "You're good at games."

"Then take me with you."

"This one's all men."

She frowned. "I've heard that said about chess."

"I bet you have. You can come along and watch if you want to. But you'll have to keep quiet."

"How long will it last?"

"All night, maybe."

She started to ask him how long he had known about this game, but didn't. Clearly he had known it before last night. She rode the Fifth Avenue bus with him down to Forty-fourth Street and walked with him over to the Algonquin Hotel. Benny seemed to have his mind on something he wasn't interested in talking about, and they walked in silence. She was beginning to feel angry again; she hadn't come to New York for this, and she was annoyed at Benny's way of offering no explanations and no advance notice. His behavior was like his chess game: smooth and easy on the surface but tricky and infuriating beneath. She did not like tagging along, but she did not want to go back to the apartment and study alone.

The game was in a small suite on the sixth floor and it was, as he had said, all male. Four men were seated around a table with coffee cups and chips and cards. An air conditioner whirred noisily. There were two other men who seemed merely to be hanging around. The players looked up when Benny came in and greeted him jokingly. Benny was cool and pleasant. "Beth Harmon," he said, and the men nodded without recognition. He had gotten out his billfold, and now he slipped a pile of bills from it, set them in front of an empty place at the table and sat down, ignoring Beth. Not knowing what her role in all this was, Beth went into the bedroom, where she had seen a coffee pitcher and cups. She got a cup of coffee and went back into the other room. Benny had a stack of chips in front of him and was holding cards in his hand. The man on his left said, "I'll bump that," flatly, and threw a blue chip into the center of the table. The others followed suit, with Benny last.

She stood at a distance from the table watching. She remembered standing in the basement watching Mr. Shaibel, and the intensity of her interest in what he was doing, but she felt nothing like that now. She did not care how poker was played, even though she knew she would be good at it. She was furious with

Benny. He went on playing without looking at her. He handled the cards with dexterity and tossed chips into the center of the table with quiet aplomb, sometimes saying things like "I'll stay" or "Back to you." Finally, while one of the men was dealing, she tapped Benny on the shoulder and said softly, "I'm leaving." He nodded and said "Okay" and turned his attention back to his cards. Going down in the elevator, she felt she could have beaten him over the head with a two-by-four. The cool son of a bitch. It was quick sex with her, and then off to the boys. He had probably planned it that way for a week. Tactics and strategy. She could have killed him.

But the walk across town eased her anger, and by the time she got on the Third Avenue bus to go back up to the apartment on Seventy-eighth Street, she was calm. She was even pleased to be alone for a while. She spent the time with Benny's *Chess Informants,* a new series of books from Yugoslavia, playing out games in her head.

He came in sometime during the middle of the night; she woke when he got into bed. She was glad he was back, but she didn't want to make love with him. Fortunately he wasn't interested either. She asked him how he had done. "Nearly six hundred," he said, pleased with himself. She rolled over and went back to sleep.

They made love in the morning, and she did not enjoy it much. She knew she was still angry with him for the poker game—not for the game itself but for the way he had used it just when they had become lovers. When they were finished, he sat up in bed and looked at her for a minute. "You're pissed at me, aren't you?"

"Yes."

"The poker game?"

"The way you didn't tell me about it."

He nodded. "I'm sorry. I do keep my distance."

She was relieved that he had said it. "I suppose I do too," she said.

"I've noticed."

After breakfast she suggested a game between the two of them, and he agreed reluctantly. They set the clock for a half-hour each, to keep it brief, and she proceeded to beat him handily with her Sicilian Levenfish, brushing aside his threats with ease and hounding his king mercilessly. When it was over he shook his head wryly and said, "I needed that six hundred."

"Maybe so," she said, "but your timing was bad."

"It doesn't pay to cross you, does it?"

"Do you want to play another?"

Benny shrugged and turned away. "Save it for Borgov." But she could see he would have played her if he had thought he could win. She felt a whole lot better.

They continued as lovers and did not play any more games, except from the books. He went out a few days later for another poker game and came back with two hundred in winnings and they had one of their best times in bed together, with the money beside them on the night table. She was fond of him, but that was all. And by the last week before Paris, she was beginning to feel that he had little left to teach her.

Chapter 12

Mrs. Wheatley had always carried Beth's adoption papers and birth certificate with her when they traveled, and Beth had continued the practice, though up to now they had never been needed. During her first week in New York, Benny took her to Rockefeller Center, and she used them in applying for her passport. Mexico had required only a tourist card, and Mrs. Wheatley had taken care of that. The little booklet with the green cover and her tight-lipped picture inside came two weeks later. Even though she wasn't sure of going, she had sent the Paris acceptance in a few days before leaving Kentucky for Ohio.

When the time came, Benny drove her to Kennedy Airport and dropped her off at the Air France terminal. "He's not impossible," Benny said. "You can beat him."

"We'll see," she said. "Thanks for the help." She had gotten her suitcase out of the car and was standing by the driver's window. They were in a no-parking zone, and he could not leave the car to see her off.

"See you next week," Benny said.

For a moment she wanted to lean in the open window and kiss him, but she restrained herself. "See you then." She picked up her suitcase and went into the terminal.

*　　　*　　　*

This time she was expecting to feel the dark hostility that even seeing him across a room could make her feel, but being prepared for it did not stop her from a sharp intake of breath. He was standing with his back to her, talking to reporters. She looked away nervously, as she had looked away the first time at the zoo in Mexico City. He was just another man in a dark suit, another Russian who played chess, she told herself. One of the men was taking his picture while the other was talking to him. Beth watched the three of them for a while, and her tension eased. She could beat him. She turned and went to the desk to register. Play would start in twenty minutes.

It was the smallest tournament she had ever seen, in this elegant old building near the École Militaire. There were six players and five rounds—one round a day for five days. If she or Borgov lost an early round, they would still have to play each other. The competition was strong. Yet, strong as it was, she did not feel either of them would be beaten by anyone else. She walked through the doorway into the tournament room proper, feeling no anxiety about the game she would be playing this morning or about the ones over the next few days. She would not play Borgov until one of the final rounds. She would meet a Dutch grandmaster in ten minutes and play Black against him, but she felt no apprehension.

France was not known for its chess, but the room they played in was beautiful. Two crystal chandeliers hung from its high blue ceiling, and the blue flowered carpet on the floor was thick and rich. There were three tables of polished walnut, each with a pink carnation in a small vase at the side of the board. The antique chairs were upholstered in blue velvet that matched the floor and ceiling. It was like an expensive restaurant, and the tournament directors were like well-trained waiters in tuxedos. Everything was quiet and smooth. She had flown in from New York the night before, had seen almost nothing yet of Paris, but she felt at ease here. She had slept well on the plane and then slept again in her hotel; before that she had put in five solid weeks of practice. She had never felt more prepared.

The Dutchman played the Réti Opening, and she treated it

the way she did when Benny played it, getting equality by the ninth move. She began attacking before he had a chance to castle, at first with a bishop sacrifice and then by forcing him to give up a knight and two pawns to defend his king. By the sixteenth move she was threatening combinations all over the board and although she was never able to bring one off, the threat was enough. He was forced to yield to her a bit at a time until, bottled up and irrecoverably behind, he gave up. She was walking happily along the Rue de Rivoli by noon, enjoying the sunshine. She looked at blouses and shoes in the shop windows, and while she bought nothing, it was a pleasure. Paris was a bit like New York but more civilized. The streets were clean and the shop windows bright; there were real sidewalk cafés and people sitting in them enjoying themselves, talking in French. She had been so wrapped up in chess that only now did she realize: she was actually in Paris! This was Paris, this avenue she was walking on; those beautifully dressed women walking toward her were Frenchwomen, *Parisiennes,* and she herself was eighteen years old and the United States Champion at chess. She felt for a moment a joyful pressure in her chest and slowed her walking. Two men were passing her, heads bent in conversation, and she heard one saying ". . . *avec deux parties seulement.* " Frenchmen, and she understood the words! She stopped walking and stood where she was for a moment, taking in the fine gray buildings across the avenue, the light on the trees, the odd smells of this humane city. She might have an apartment here someday, on the Boulevard Raspail or the Rue des Capucines. By the time she was in her twenties she could be World's Champion and live wherever she wanted to live. She could have a *pied à terre* in Paris and go to concerts and plays, eat lunch every day in a different café, and dress like these women who walked by her, so sure of themselves, so smart in their well-made clothes, with their heads high and their hair impeccably cut and combed and shaped. She had something that none of them had, and it could give her a life that anyone might envy. Benny had been right to urge her to play here and then, next summer, in Moscow. There was nothing to hold her in Kentucky, in her house; she had possibilities that were endless.

She wandered the boulevards for hours, not stopping to buy anything, just looking at people and buildings and shops and restaurants and trees and flowers. Once she accidentally bumped into an old lady while crossing the Rue de la Paix and found herself saying *"Excusez-moi, madame"* as easily as if she had been speaking French all her life.

There was to be a reception at the building the tournament was in at four-thirty; she had difficulty finding her way back and was ten minutes late and out of breath when she arrived. The playing tables had all been pushed to one side of the room, and the chairs placed around the walls. She was ushered to a seat near the door and handed a small cup of *café filtre.* A pastry cart was wheeled by with the most beautiful pastries she had ever seen. She felt a momentary sadness, wishing that Alma Wheatley could be there to see them. Just as she was taking a napoleon from the cart she heard loud laughter from across the room and looked up. There was Vasily Borgov, holding a coffee cup. The people on each side of him were bent toward him expectantly, taking in his amusement. His face was distorted with ponderous mirth. Beth felt her stomach turn to ice.

She walked back to her hotel that evening and grimly played a dozen of Borgov's games—games that she already knew thoroughly from studying them with Benny—and went to bed at eleven; she took no pills and slept beautifully. Borgov had been an International Grandmaster for eleven years and World Champion for five, but she would not go passive against him this time. Whatever happened she would not be humiliated by him. And she would have one distinct advantage: he would not be as prepared for her as she was for him.

She went on winning, beating a Frenchman the next day and an Englishman on the day after. Borgov won his games also. On the next to the last day when she was playing another Dutchman—an older and more experienced one—she found herself at the table next to Borgov. Seeing him so close distracted her for a few moments, but she was able to shrug it off. The Dutchman was a strong player, and she concentrated on the game. When she finished, forcing a resignation after nearly four hours, she looked up and saw that the pieces were gone from the next table and Borgov had left.

Leaving, she stopped at the desk and asked whom she would be playing in the morning. The director shuffled through his papers and smiled faintly. "Grandmaster Borgov, mademoiselle."

She had expected it, but her breath caught when he said it.

That night she took three tranquilizers and went to bed early, uncertain if she could relax enough to sleep. But she slept beautifully and awoke refreshed at eight, feeling confident, smart and ready.

When she came in and saw him sitting at the table, he did not seem so formidable. He was wearing his usual dark suit, and his coarse black hair was combed neatly back from his forehead. His face was, as always, impassive, but it did not look threatening. He stood up politely, and when she offered her hand he shook it, but he did not smile. She would be playing the white pieces; when they seated themselves he pressed the button on her clock.

She had already decided what to do. Despite Benny's advice, she would play pawn to king four and hope for the Sicilian. She had gone through all of Borgov's published Sicilian games. She did it, picking up the pawn and setting it on the fourth rank, and when he played his queen bishop pawn she felt a pleasant thrill. She was ready for him. She played her knight to king bishop three; he brought his to queen bishop three, and by the sixth move they were in the Boleslavski. She knew, move by move, eight games in which Borgov had played this variation, had gone over each of them with Benny, analyzing each remorselessly. He started the variation with pawn to king four on the sixth move; she played knight to knight three with the certainty that came from knowing she was right, and then looked across the board at him. He was leaning a cheek against a fist, looking down at the board like any other chess player. Borgov was strong, imperturbable and wily, but there was no sorcery in his play. He put his bishop on king two without looking at her. She castled. He castled. She looked around herself at the bright, beautifully furnished room she was in with its two other games of chess quietly in progress.

By the fifteenth move she began to see combinations opening up on both sides, and by the twentieth she was startled by her own clarity. Her mind moved with ease, picking its way delicately among the combination of moves. She began to pressure him along the queen bishop file, threatening a double attack. He side-stepped this, and she strengthened her center pawns. Her position opened more and more, and the possibilities for attack increased, although Borgov seemed to side-step them just in time. She knew this might happen and it did not dismay her; she felt in herself an inexhaustible ability to find strong, threatening moves. She had never played better. She would force him by a series of threats to compromise his position, and then she would mount threats that were double and triple and that he would not be able to avoid. Already his queen bishop was locked in by moves she had forced, and his queen was tied down protecting a rook. Her pieces were freeing themselves more with every move. There seemed to be no end to her ability to find threats.

She looked around again. The other games were finished. That was a surprise. She looked at her watch. It was after one o'clock. They had been playing for over three hours. She turned her attention back to the board, studied it a few minutes and brought her queen to the center. It was time to apply more pressure. She looked across the table at Borgov.

He was an unruffled as ever. He did not meet her eyes but kept his on the board, studying her queen move. Then he shrugged almost imperceptibly and attacked the queen with a rook. She had known he might do that, and she had her response ready. She interposed a knight, threatening a check that would take the rook. He would have to move the king now and she would bring the queen over to the rook file. She could see half a dozen ways of threatening him from there, with threats more urgent than the ones she had been making.

Borgov moved immediately, and he did not move his king. He

merely advanced a rook pawn. She had to study it for five minutes before seeing what he was up to. If she checked him, he would let her take the rook and then station his bishop ahead of the pawn he had just pushed, and she would have to move her queen. She held her breath, alarmed. Her rook on the back rank would fall, and with it two pawns. That would be disastrous. She had to back her queen off to a place where it could escape. She gritted her teeth and moved it.

Borgov brought the bishop out, anyway, where the pawn protected it. She stared at it a moment before the meaning of it dawned on her; any of the several moves she could make to dislodge it would cost her in some way, and if she left it there, it strengthened everything about his position. She looked up at his face. He was regarding her now with a hint of a smile. She looked quickly back at the board.

She tried countering with one of her own bishops, but he neutralized it with a pawn move that blocked the diagonal. She had played beautifully, was still playing beautifully, but he was outplaying her. She would have to bear down harder.

She did bear down harder and found excellent moves, as good as any she had ever found, but they were not enough. By the thirty-fifth her throat was dry, and what she saw in front of her on the board was the disarray of her position and the growing strength of Borgov's. It was incredible. She was playing her best chess, and he was beating her.

On the thirty-eighth move he brought his rook crisply down to her second rank for the first threat of mate. She could see clearly enough how to parry that, but behind it were more and more threats that would either mate her or take her queen or give him a second queen. She felt sick. For a moment it dizzied her just to look at the board, at the visible manifestation of her own powerlessness.

She did not topple her king. She stood up, and looking at his emotionless face, said, "I resign." Borgov nodded. She turned and walked out of the room, feeling physically ill.

*　　*　　*

The plane back to New York was like a trap; she sat in her window seat and could not escape the memory of the game, could not stop playing through it in her mind. Several times the stewardess offered her a drink, but she forced herself to decline. She wanted one only too badly; it was frightening. She took tranquilizers, but the knot would not leave her stomach. She had made no mistakes. She had played extraordinarily well. And at the end of it her position was a shambles, and Borgov looked as though it had been nothing.

She did not want to see Benny. She was supposed to call him to pick her up, but she did not want to go back to his apartment. It had been eight weeks since she left her house in Lexington; she would go back and lick her wounds for a while. Her third-prize money from Paris had been surprisingly good; she could afford a quick round trip to Lexington. And there were still papers to sign with her lawyer. She would stay a week and then come back and go on studying with Benny. But what else had she to learn from him? Remembering for a moment all the work she had done readying herself for Paris, she felt sick again. With an effort she shook it off. The main thing was to get ready for Moscow. There was still time.

She called Benny from Kennedy Airport and told him she had lost the final game, that Borgov had outplayed her. Benny was sympathetic but a little distant, and when she told him she was going to Kentucky for a while he sounded irritated.

"Don't quit," he said. "One lost game doesn't prove anything."

"I'm not quitting," she said.

In the pile of mail waiting for her at home were several letters from Michael Chennault, the lawyer who had arranged for the deed to the house. It seemed there was some kind of problem; she did not yet have clear title or something. Allston Wheatley was creating difficulty. Without opening the rest of the mail she went to the phone and called Chennault's office.

The first thing he said when he came on the line was "I tried to get you three times yesterday. Where've you been?"

"In Paris," Beth said, "playing chess."

"How sweet it must be." He paused. "It's Wheatley. He doesn't want to sign."

"Sign what?"

"Title," Chennault said. "Can you get over here? We've got to work it out."

"I don't see why you need me," Beth said. "You're the lawyer. He told me he'd sign what was necessary."

"He's changed his mind. Maybe you could talk to him."

"Is he *there*?"

"Not in the office. But he's in town. I think if you could look him in the eye and remind him you're his legal daughter . . ."

"Why won't he sign?"

"Money," the lawyer said. "He wants to sell the house."

"Can the two of you come here tomorrow?"

"I'll see what I can do," the lawyer said.

She looked around the living room after hanging up. The house still belonged to Wheatley. That was a shock. She had barely seen him in it, and yet it was in fact *his*. She did not want him to have it.

Although it was a hot July afternoon, Allston Wheatley was wearing a suit, a dark-gray salt-and-pepper tweed, and when he seated himself on the sofa he pulled up the creases in the pants legs, showing the whiteness of his thin shanks above the tops of his maroon socks. He had lived in the house for sixteen years, but he showed no interest in anything in it. He entered it like a stranger, with a look that could have been anger or apology, sat down at one end of the sofa, pulled his pants legs up an inch and said nothing.

Something about him made Beth feel sick. He looked exactly the way he had looked when she first saw him, when he came to Mrs. Deardorff's office with Mrs. Wheatley to look her over.

"Mr. Wheatley has a proposal, Beth," the lawyer was saying. She looked at Wheatley's face, which was turned slightly away from them. "You can live here," the lawyer said, "while you are finding something permanent." *Why wasn't Wheatley telling her this?*

Wheatley's embarrassment made her somehow squirm for him, as though she were embarrassed herself. "I thought I could keep the house if I made the payments," she said.

"Mr. Wheatley says you misconstrued him."

Why was *her* lawyer speaking for him? Why couldn't he get his own lawyer, for Christ's sake? She looked over at him and saw he was lighting a cigarette, his face still inclined away from her, a pained look on his features. "He claims he was only permitting you to stay in the house until you got settled."

"That's not true," Beth said. "He said I could *have* it . . ." Suddenly something hit her with full force and she turned to Wheatley. "I'm your *daughter,*" she said. "You adopted me. Why don't you talk to me?"

He looked at her like a startled rabbit. "Alma," he said, "Alma wanted a child . . ."

"You signed the papers," Beth said. "You took on a responsibility. Can't you even look at me?"

Allston Wheatley stood up and walked across the room to the window. When he turned around, he had somehow pulled himself together, and he looked furious. "Alma wanted to adopt you. Not me. You're not entitled to everything I own just because I signed some damned papers to shut Alma up." He turned back to the window. "Not that it worked."

"You adopted me," Beth said. "I didn't ask you to do it." She felt a choking sensation in her throat. "You're my legal father."

When he turned and looked at her, she was shocked to see how contorted his face was. "The money in this house is mine, and no smart-assed orphan is going to take it away from me."

"I'm not an orphan," Beth said. "I'm your daughter."

"Not in my book you aren't. I don't give a shit what your goddamned lawyer says. I don't give a shit what Alma said either. That woman could not keep her mouth *shut.*"

No one spoke for a while. Finally Chennault asked quietly, "What do you want from Beth, Mr. Wheatley?"

"I want her out of here. I'm selling the house."

Beth looked at him for a moment before speaking. "Then sell it to me," she said.

"What are you talking about?" Wheatley said.

"I'll buy it. I'll pay you whatever your equity is."

"It's worth more than that now."

"How much more?"

"I'd need seven thousand."

She knew his equity was less than five. "All right," she said.

"You have that much?"

"Yes," she said. "But I'm subtracting what I paid for burying my mother. I'll show you the receipts."

Allston Wheatley sighed like a martyr. "All right," he said. "You two can draw up the papers. I'm going back to the hotel." He walked over to the door. "It's too hot in here."

"You could have taken off your coat," Beth said.

It left her two thousand in the bank. She didn't like having so little, but it was all right. In the mail there had been invitations to play in two strong tournaments, with good prize money. Fifteen hundred for one and two thousand for the other. And there was the heavy envelope from Russia, inviting her to Moscow in July.

When she got back with her copy of the signed papers she walked around the living room several times, passing her hand lightly over pieces of furniture. Wheatley hadn't said anything about the furniture, but it was hers. She had asked the lawyer. Wheatley hadn't even shown up, and Chennault took the papers over to the Phoenix Hotel for him to sign while she waited in the office and read a *National Geographic*. The house felt different, now that it was hers. She would get some new pieces—a good, low sofa and two small modern armchairs. She could visualize them, with pale-blue linen upholstery and darker blue piping. Not Mrs. Wheatley blue, but her own. Beth blue. She wanted things brighter in the living room, more cheerful. She wanted to erase Mrs. Wheatley's half-real presence from the place. She would get a bright rug for the floor and have the windows washed. She would get a stereo and some records, a new bedspread and pillowcases for the bed upstairs. From Purcell's.

Mrs. Wheatley had been a good mother; she had not intended to die and leave her.

Beth slept well and awoke feeling angry. She put on the chenille robe and padded downstairs in slippers—Mrs. Wheatley's slippers—and found herself thinking furiously of the seven thousand dollars she had paid Allston Wheatley. She loved her money; she and Mrs. Wheatley had both taken great pleasure in accumulating it from tournament to tournament, watching it gather interest. They had always opened Beth's bank statements together to see how much new interest had been credited to the account. And after Mrs. Wheatley's death it had consoled her to know that she could go on living in the house, buying her groceries at the supermarket and going to movies when she wanted to without feeling pinched for money or having to think about getting work or going to college or finding tournaments to win.

She had brought three of Benny's chess pamphlets with her from New York; while her eggs were boiling she set up her board on the kitchen table and got out the booklet with games from the last Moscow Invitational. The Russian booklets were printed on expensive paper with good, clear type. She had not really mastered Russian from the night course at the university, but she could read the names and the notations easily enough. Yet the Cyrillic characters were irritating. It angered her that the Soviet government put so much money into chess, and that they even used a different alphabet from hers. When the eggs were done, she peeled them into a bowl with butter and began playing a game between Petrosian and Tal. Grünfeld Defense. Semi-Slav Variation. She got it to the black king knight on queen two for the eighth move and then became bored with it. She had been moving the pieces too fast for analysis, not stopping herself as Benny would have made her do to trace out everything that was going on. She finished the last spoonful of egg and went out the back door into the garden.

It was a hot morning. The grass in the yard was overgrown, it nearly covered the little brick pathway that went to where some shabby tea roses stood. She went back into the house and played the white rook to queen one and then stared at it. She did not want to study chess. That was frightening; a vast amount of study lay ahead of her if she wanted to avoid humiliation in Moscow. She pushed down the fear and went upstairs for a shower. As she dried her hair, she saw with a kind of relief that she needed to have it cut. That would be something to do today. Afterward she could go to Purcell's and look at sofas for the living room. But it wouldn't be wise to buy—not until she had more money. And how could she get the lawn mowed? A boy had done it for Mrs. Wheatley, but she didn't know his telephone number or address.

She needed to clean up the place. There were cobwebs and messy-looking sheets and pillowcases. She could use some new ones. Some new clothes, too. Harry Beltik had left his razor in the bathroom; should she mail it back? The milk had gone sour and the butter was old. The freezer was full of ice crystals with a stack of old frozen chicken dinners stuck in the back. The bedroom rug was dusty, and the windows had fingerprints on the glass and grit on the sills.

Beth shook the confusion out of her head as well as she could and made an appointment with Roberta for a haircut at two. She would ask where to find a cleaning woman for a few weeks. She would go to Morris', order some chess books, and have lunch at Toby's.

But her usual clerk wasn't at Morris' that day, and the woman who had replaced him knew nothing about ordering chess books. Beth managed to get her to find a catalogue and ordered three on the Sicilian Defense. She needed game books from grandmaster matches and *Chess Informants*. But she didn't know which Yugoslav press published *Chess Informant*, and neither did the new clerk. It was infuriating. She needed a library as good as Benny's. Better. Thinking of this, she finally realized angrily that she could go back to New York and forget all this confusion and continue with Benny from where she had left off. But what could Benny teach her now? What could any American teach her? She had moved past them all. She was on her own. She would have to bridge the gap herself that separated American chess from Russian.

At Toby's the headwaiter knew her and put her at a good table near the front. She ordered *asperges vinaigrette* for an appetizer and told the waiter she would have that before ordering a main course. "Would you care for a cocktail?" he asked pleasantly. She looked around her at the quiet restaurant, at the people eating lunch, at the table with desserts near the velvet rope at the entrance to the dining room. "A Gibson," she said. "On the rocks."

It came almost immediately. It was wonderful to look at. The tumbler was clear and clean; the gin inside was crystalline; the white onions were like two pearls. When she tasted it, it stung her upper lip, then stung her throat with a sweet tease as it went down. The effect on her tense stomach was remarkable; everything about it was rewarding. She finished it slowly, and the deep fury in her began to subside. She ordered another. Back in the shadows at the far end of the room someone was playing a piano. Beth looked at her watch. It was a quarter to twelve. It was good to be alive.

She never got around to ordering the main course. She came out of Toby's at two, squinting into the sunshine, and jaywalked across Main to David Manly's Wine Shop. Using two of her traveler's checks from Ohio she bought a case of Paul Masson burgundy, four bottles of Gordon's gin and a bottle of Martini & Rossi vermouth and had Mr. Manly call her a taxi. Her speech was clear and sharp; her gait was steady. She had eaten six stalks of asparagus and drunk four Gibsons. She had flirted with alcohol for years. It was time to consummate the relationship.

The phone was ringing when she came in, but she did not answer it. The driver helped her with the case of wine, and she tipped him a dollar. When he had left, she got the bottles out one at a time and put them neatly into the cabinet over the toaster, in front of Mrs. Wheatley's old cans of spaghetti and chili. Then she opened a bottle of gin and twisted the cap off the vermouth. She had never made a cocktail before. She poured gin into the tumbler and added a little vermouth, stirring it with one of Mrs. Wheatley's spoons. She carried the drink carefully into the living room, sat down and took a long swallow.

The mornings were horrible, but she managed them. She went to Kroger's on the third day and bought three dozen eggs and a supply of TV dinners. After that she always had two eggs before her first glass of wine. By noon she had usually passed out. She would awake on the sofa or in a chair with her limbs stiff and the back of her neck damp with hot sweat. Sometimes, her head reeling, she would feel in the depth of her stomach an anger as intense as the pain of a burst abscess in the jaw—a toothache so potent that nothing but drink could alleviate it. Sometimes the drink had to be forced against a rejection of it by her body, but she did it. She would get it down and wait and the feelings would subside a bit. It was like turning down the volume.

On Saturday morning she spilled wine on her kitchen chessboard, and on Monday she bumped into the table by accident and sent some of the pieces falling to the floor. She left them there, picking them up only on Thursday, when finally the young man came by to mow the lawn. She lay on the sofa drinking from the last bottle in her case and listened to the roaring of his power mower, smelling the grass cuttings. When she had paid him, she went outside into the grass smell and looked at the lawn with its clumps of cuttings. It touched her to see it so altered, so changed from what it had been. She went back in, got her purse and called a cab. The law did not permit deliveries of wine or liquor. She would have to get another case on her own. Two would be smarter. And she would try Almadén. Someone had said Almadén burgundy was better than Paul Masson. She would try it. Maybe a few bottles of white wine, too. And she needed food.

Lunches came from a can. The chili was pretty good if you added pepper and ate it with a glass of burgundy. Almadén was better than Paul Masson, less astringent on the tongue. The Gibsons, though, could hit her like a club, and she became wary of them, saving them until just before passing out or, sometimes, for the first drink in the morning. By the third week she was taking a Gibson up to bed with her on the nights she made it upstairs to bed. She put it on the nightstand with a *Chess Informant* over it to keep the alcohol from evaporating, and drank it when she woke up in the middle of the night. Or if not then, in the morning, before going downstairs.

Sometimes the phone rang, but she answered it only when her head and voice were clear. She always spoke aloud to check her level of sobriety before picking up the receiver. She would say "Peter Piper picked a peck of pickled peppers," and if it came out all right, she would take up the phone. A woman called from New York, wanting her on the *Tonight Show*. She refused.

It wasn't until her third week of drinking that she went through the pile of magazines that had come while she was in New York and found the *Newsweek* with her picture in it. They had given her a full page under "Sport." The picture showed her playing Benny, and she remembered the moment it was taken, during the game's opening. The position of the pieces on the display board was visible in the photograph, and she saw that her memory was right, she had just made her fourth move. Benny looked thoughtful and distant, as usual. The piece said she was the most talented woman since Vera Menchik. Beth, reading it half-drunk, was annoyed at the space given to Menchik, going on about her death in a 1944 bombing in London before pointing out that Beth was the better player. And what did being women have to do with it? She was better than any male player in America. She remembered the *Life* interviewer and the questions about her being a woman in a man's world. To hell with her; it wouldn't *be* a man's world when she finished with it. It was noontime, and she put a pan of canned spaghetti on to heat before reading the rest of the article. The last paragraph was the strongest.

At eighteen, Beth Harmon has established herself as the queen of American chess. She may be the most gifted player since Morphy or Capablanca; no one knows just how gifted she is—how great a potential she holds in that young girl's body with its dazzling brain. To find out, to show the world if America has outgrown its inferior status in world chess, she will have to go where the big boys are. She will have to go to the Soviet Union.

Beth closed the magazine and poured a glass of Almadén Mountain Chablis to drink with her spaghetti. It was three in the afternoon and hot as fury. And the wine was getting low; only two more bottles stood on the shelf above the toaster.

A week after reading the *Newsweek* article she awoke on a Thursday morning too sick to get out of bed. When she tried to sit up, she couldn't. Her head and stomach were throbbing. She was still wearing her jeans and T-shirt from the night before, and she felt suffocated by them. But she could not get them off. The shirt was stuck to her upper body, and she was too weak to pull it over her head. There was a Gibson on the nightstand. She managed to roll over and take it with both hands, and she got half of it down before beginning to retch. For a moment she thought she was choking, but her breath came back eventually and she finished the drink.

She was terrified. She was alone in that furnace of a room and frightened of dying. Her stomach was raw and all of her organs hurt. Had she poisoned herself on wine and gin? She tried sitting up again, and with the gin in her she managed it. She sat there for a few moments calming herself before she went unsteadily into the bathroom and vomited. It seemed to cleanse her. She managed to get her clothes off, and afraid of slipping in the shower and breaking her hip the way unsteady old women did, she filled the tub with lukewarm water and took a bath. She should call McAndrews, Mrs. Wheatley's old doctor, and make an appointment for sometime around noon. If she could make it to his office. This was more than a hangover; she was ill.

But downstairs, after her bath, she was steadier and got down two eggs with no difficulty. The thought of picking up the phone and calling someone seemed distant now. There was a barrier between herself and whatever world the phone would attach her to; she could not penetrate the barrier. She would be all right.

She would drink less, taper off. Maybe she would feel like calling McAndrews after a drink. She poured herself a glass of Chablis and began sipping it, and it healed her like the magic medicine it was.

The next morning while she was eating breakfast the phone rang and she picked it up without thinking. Someone named Ed Spencer was at the other end; it took a moment to remember that he was the local tournament director. "It's about tomorrow," he said.

"Tomorrow?"

"The tournament. We wondered if you could come an hour early. The Louisville paper is sending a photographer and we think WLEX will have somebody. Could you come in at nine?"

Her heart sank. He was talking about the Kentucky State Championship, she had completely forgotten it. She was supposed to defend her title. She was supposed to go to Henry Clay High School tomorrow morning and begin a two-day tournament as defending champion. Her head was throbbing and her hand that held her coffee cup was unsteady. "I don't know," she said. "Can you call back in an hour?"

"Sure, Miss Harmon."

"Thank you. I'll tell you in an hour."

She felt frightened, and she did not want to play chess. She had not looked at a chess book or touched her pieces since buying the house from Allston Wheatley. She did not want even to think about chess. Last night's bottle was still sitting on the counter next to the toaster. She poured half a glass, but when she drank it, it stung her mouth and tasted foul. She set the unfinished glass in the sink and got orange juice from the refrigerator. If she didn't clear her head and play the tournament, she would just be drunker tomorrow and sicker. She finished the orange juice and went upstairs, thinking of all the wine she had been drinking, remembering it in the pit of her stomach. Her insides felt fouled and abused. She needed a hot shower and fresh clothes.

It would be a waste. Beltik wouldn't be in it, and there was no one else as good as he. Kentucky was nothing in chess. Standing naked in the bathroom, she started going through the Levenfish Variation of the Sicilian, squinting her eyes and picturing the pieces on an imaginary board. She did the first dozen moves without a mistake, although the pieces didn't stand out as clearly as they had a year before. She hesitated after move eighteen, where Black played pawn to knight four and got equality. Smyslov–Botvinnik, 1958. She tried to play out the rest of it, but her head was aching, and after stopping to take two aspirin, she wasn't sure where the pawns were supposed to be. But she had gotten the first eighteen moves right. She would stay sober today and play tomorrow. When she won the state championship for the second time two years before, it had been simple. After herself and maybe Harry, there weren't any really strong players in Kentucky. Goldmann and Sizemore were no problem.

When the phone rang again she told Ed Spencer she'd be there at nine-thirty. A half-hour would be plenty of time for pictures.

In the back of her mind she had hoped Townes might show up with a camera, but there was no sign of him. The man from Louisville wasn't there either. She posed at Board One for a woman photographer from the *Herald-Leader,* did a three-minute interview with a man from a local television station, and excused herself to go out for a walk around the block before the tournament began. She had managed to get through the day before without drinking and had slept soundly enough with the help of three green pills, but her stomach felt queasy. It was still morning but the sun was too bright; she found herself beginning to sweat after one turn around the block. Her feet hurt. Eighteen years old, and she felt like forty. She would have to stop drinking. Her first opponent was somebody named Foster with a rating in the 1800s. She would be playing Black, but it should be easy—especially if he tried pawn to king four and let her get into the Sicilian.

Foster seemed calm enough, considering that he was playing the U.S. Champion in his first round. He had the good sense not to open with the king pawn against her. He played pawn to queen four, and she decided to avoid the Queen's Gambit and try to lead him into unfamiliar territory with the Dutch Defense. That meant pawn to king bishop four. They went through the book moves for a while until, somehow, she found herself getting into the Stonewall Formation. It was a position she did not particularly like, and after she started considering the way the board looked she began to feel annoyed with herself. The thing to do was break it open and go for Foster's throat. She had just been diddling with him, and she wanted to get this over with. Her head was still aching, and she felt uncomfortable even in the good swivel chair. There were too many spectators in the room. Foster was a pale blond in his twenties; he made his moves with a prissy carefulness that was maddening. After the twelfth she looked at the tight position on the board and quickly pushed a center pawn up for sacrifice; she would open up the game and start threatening. She must have a good 600 rating points on this creep; she would wipe him out, get a good lunch and some coffee, and be ready for Goldmann or Sizemore in the afternoon.

Somehow the pawn sacrifice had been hasty. After Foster took with a knight instead of the pawn she had planned on, she found she had either to defend or to drop another pawn. She bit her lip, annoyed, and looked for something to terrorize him with. But she could find nothing. And her mind was working with damnable slowness. She retreated a bishop to protect the pawn.

Foster raised his eyebrows slightly at that and brought a rook over to the queen file, the one she had opened with her pawn sacrifice. She blinked. She did not like the way this was going. Her headache was getting worse. She got up from the board, went to the director and asked him for aspirin. He found some somewhere, and she took three, chasing them with water from a paper cup, before she went back to Foster. As she walked through the main tournament room people looked up from their games to stare at her. She was suddenly angry that she had agreed to play in this third-rate tournament, and angry that she had to go back and contend with Foster. She hated the situation: if she beat him, it was meaningless to her, and if he beat her, she would look terrible. But he wouldn't beat her. Benny Watts couldn't beat her, and some prissy graduate student from Louisville wasn't about to drive her into a corner. She would find a combination somewhere and tear him apart with it.

But there was no combination to be found. She kept staring at the position as it changed gradually from move to move, and it did not open up for her. Foster was good—clearly better than his rating showed—but he wasn't that good. The people who filled the little room watched in silence as she went more and more on the defensive, trying to keep her face from showing the alarm that was beginning to dominate her moves. And what was wrong with her *mind*? She hadn't had a drink for a day and two nights. What was *wrong*? In the pit of her stomach she was beginning to feel terrified. If she had somehow damaged her talent . . .

And then, on the twenty-third move, Foster began a series of trades in the center of the board, and she found herself unable to stop it, watching her pieces disappear with a sick feeling in her stomach, watching her position become more and more stark in its deterioration. She found herself playing out a lost game, overwhelmed by the two-pawn advantage of a player with a rating of 1800. There was nothing she could do about it. He would queen a pawn and humiliate her with it.

She lifted her king from the board before he could do it and left the room without looking at him, pushing her way through a crowd of people, avoiding their eyes, almost holding her breath, going out into the main room and up to the desk.

"I'm feeling ill," she told the director. "I'm going to have to drop out."

She walked up Main, heavy-footed and in turmoil, trying not to think about the game. It was horrible. She had allowed this tournament to be a test for her—the kind of rigged test an alcoholic makes for himself—and still she had failed it. She must not drink when she got home. She must read and play chess and get herself together. But the thought of going to the empty house was frightening. What else could she do? There was nothing she wanted to do and no one to call. The game she had lost was inconsequential and the tournament was nothing, but the humiliation was overwhelming. She did not want to hear discussions about how she had lost to Foster, did not want to see Foster himself again. *She must not drink.* She had a real tournament coming up in California in five months. *What if she had already done it to herself?* What if she had shaved away from the surface of her brain whatever synaptic interlacings had formed her gift? She remembered reading somewhere that some pop artist once bought an original drawing by Michelangelo—and had taken a piece of art gum and *erased* it, leaving blank paper. The waste had shocked her. Now she felt a similar shock as she imagined the surface of her own brain with the talent for chess wiped away.

At home she tried a Russian game book, but she couldn't concentrate. She started going through her game with Foster, setting the board up in the kitchen, but the moves of it were too painful. That damned Stonewall, and the hastily pushed pawn. A *patzer*'s move. Bad chess. Hungover chess. The telephone rang, but she didn't answer. She sat at the board and wished for a moment, painfully, that she had someone to call. Harry Beltik would be back in Louisville. And she didn't want to tell him about the game with Foster. He would find out soon enough. She could call Benny. But Benny had been icy after Paris, and she did not want to talk to him. There was no one else. She got up wearily and opened the cabinet next to the refrigerator, took down a bottle of white wine and poured herself a glassful. A voice inside her cried out at the outrage, but she ignored it. She drank half of it in one long swallow and stood waiting until she could feel it. Then she finished the glass and poured another. A person could live without chess. Most people did.

When she awoke on the sofa the next morning, still wearing the Paris clothes she had worn when losing the game to Foster, she was frightened in a new way. She could sense her brain being physically blurred by alcohol, its positional grasp gone clumsy, its penetration clouded. But after breakfast she showered and changed and then poured herself a glass of wine. It was almost mechanical; she had learned to cut off thought as she did it. The main thing was to eat some toast first, so the wine wouldn't burn her stomach.

She kept drinking for days, but the memory of the game she had lost and the fear of what she was doing to the sharp edge of her gift would not go away, except when she was so drunk that she could not even think. There was a piece in the Sunday paper about her, with one of the pictures taken that morning at the high school, and a headline reading CHESS CHAMP DROPS FROM TOURNEY. She threw the paper away without reading the article.

Then one morning after a night of dark and confusing dreams she awoke with an unaccustomed clarity: if she did not stop drinking immediately she would ruin what she had. She had allowed herself to sink into this frightening murk. She had to find a foothold somewhere to push herself free of it. She would have to get help. With a great sense of relief, she suddenly knew who it was she wanted to get help from.

Chapter 13

Jolene was not in the Lexington directory. Beth tried Information in Louisville and Frankfort. No Jolene DeWitt. She could have married and changed her name. She could be in Chicago or the Klondike for that matter; Beth had not seen or heard from her since the day she left Methuen. And there was only one thing to do if she was to go through with this. Her adoption papers were in a drawer in Mrs. Wheatley's desk. She got the folder out and found a letter with the Methuen name and slogan at the top of it in red. The phone number was there. She held the paper nervously for several moments. At the bottom it was signed in a small, neat hand: Helen Deardorff, Superintendent.

It was almost noon, and she had not had a drink yet. For a moment she thought of steadying herself with a Gibson, but she could not hide the stupidity of that idea from herself. A Gibson would be the end of her resolve. She might be alcoholic, but she was not a fool. She went upstairs and got her bottle of Mexican Librium and took two. Waiting for the tension to ease, she walked into the yard which the boy had mowed the day before. The tea roses had finally bloomed. The petals had fallen from most of them, and at the end of some of the stems were spherical, pregnant-looking hips where the flowers had been. She had never noticed them when they were blooming in June and July.

Back in the kitchen, she felt steadier. The tranquilizers were working. How many brain cells did *they* kill with each milligram? It couldn't be as bad as liquor. She walked into the living room and dialed the Methuen Home.

The operator at Methuen put her on hold. Beth reached over to the bottle, shook out a green pill and swallowed it. Finally the voice came, shockingly crisp, from the receiver. "Helen Deardorff speaking."

For a moment she couldn't speak and wanted to hang up, but she sucked in her breath and said, "Mrs. Deardorff, this is Beth Harmon."

"Really?" The voice sounded surprised.

"Yes."

"*Well.*" During the pause that followed it occurred to Beth that Mrs. Deardorff might have nothing to say. She might find it as difficult talking to Beth as Beth did talking to her. "Well," Mrs. Deardorff said, "we've been reading about you."

"How's Mr. Shaibel?" Beth asked.

"Mr. Shaibel is still with us. Is that what you called about?"

"I called about Jolene DeWitt. I need to get in touch with her."

"I'm sorry," Mrs. Deardorff said. "Methuen cannot give out the addresses or phone numbers of its charges."

"Mrs. Deardorff," Beth said, her voice suddenly breaking through into feeling, "Mrs. Deardorff, do this for me. I have to talk to Jolene."

"There are laws—"

"Mrs. Deardorff," Beth said, "*please.*"

Mrs. Deardorff's voice took on a different tone. "All right, Elizabeth. DeWitt lives in Lexington. Here's her phone number."

"Jesus fucking Christ!" Jolene said on the phone. "Jesus fucking Christ!"

"How are you, Jolene?" Beth felt like crying, but she kept the quaver out of her voice.

"Oh my God, child," Jolene said, laughing. "It is so good to hear your voice. Are you still ugly?"

"Are you still black?"

"I am one black lady," Jolene said. "And you've lost your ugly. I saw you in more magazines than Barbra Streisand. My famous friend."

"Why didn't you call?"

"Jealous."

"Jolene," Beth said, "did you ever get adopted?"

"Shit, no. I *graduated* from that place. Why in hell didn't you mail me a card or a box of cookies?"

"I'll buy you dinner tonight. Can you get to Toby's on Main Street at seven?"

"I'll cut a class," Jolene said. "Son of a bitch! U.S. Champion at the historic game of chess. A genuine winner."

"That's what I want to talk about," Beth said.

When they met at Toby's the spontaneity was gone. Beth had spent the day without a drink, had her hair cut at Roberta's and cleaned up the kitchen, almost overcome with the excitement of talking to Jolene again. She arrived at Toby's a quarter of an hour early and nervously turned down the waiter's offer to bring her a drink. She had a Coke in front of her when Jolene arrived.

At first Beth didn't recognize her. The woman who came toward her table in what looked like a Coco Chanel suit and a full, bushy Afro was so tall that Beth could not believe it was Jolene. She looked like a movie star, or a rock-and-roll princess—fuller in the figure than Diana Ross and as cool as Lena Horne. But when Beth saw that it was in fact Jolene, that the smile and the eyes were the Jolene she remembered, she stood up awkwardly, and they embraced. Jolene's perfume was strong. Beth felt self-conscious. Jolene patted her back while they hugged, and said, "Beth Harmon. Old Beth."

They sat down and looked at each other awkwardly. Beth decided she had to have a drink to see her though this. But when the waiter came, blessedly breaking the silence, Jolene ordered a club soda and Beth had him bring her another Coke.

Jolene was carrying something in a manila envelope, which

she set on the table in front of Beth. Beth picked it up. It was a book, and she knew immediately what it was. She slipped off the envelope. *Modern Chess Openings.* Her old, nearly worn-out copy.

"Me all the time," Jolene said. "Pissed at you for being adopted."

Beth grimaced, opening the book to the title page where the childish handwriting read "Elizabeth Harmon, Methuen Home." "What about for being white?"

"Who could forget?" Jolene said.

Beth looked at Jolene's good, beautiful face with all the remarkable hair and the long black eyelashes and the full lips, and the self-consciousness dropped away from her with a relief that was physical in its simplicity. She smiled broadly. "It's good to see you." What she wanted to say was, "I love you."

During the first half of the meal Jolene talked about Methuen—about sleeping through chapel and hating the food and about Mr. Schell, Miss Graham and the Saturday Christian movies. She was hilarious on the subject of Mrs. Deardorff, imitating her tight voice and her way of tossing her head. She ate slowly and laughed a lot, and Beth found herself laughing with her. It had been a long time since Beth had laughed, and she had never felt so easy with anyone—not even with Mrs. Wheatley. Jolene ordered a glass of white wine with her veal and Beth hesitated before asking the waiter for ice water.

"You not old enough?" Jolene said.

"That's not it. I'm eighteen."

Jolene raised her eyebrows and went back to her veal. After a few moments she started talking again. "When you went off to your happy home, I started doing serious volleyball. I graduated when I was eighteen and the University gave me a scholarship in Phys. Ed."

"How do you like it?"

"It's all right," Jolene said, a bit fast. And then, "No, it isn't. It's a shuck is what it is. I don't want to be a gym coach."

"You could do something else."

Jolene shook her head. "It wasn't till I got my bachelor's last year that I really caught on." She had been talking with her mouth full. Now she swallowed and leaned forward with her elbows on the table. "I should have been in law or government. These are the right days for what I've got, and I blew it on learning the side straddle hop and the major muscles of the abdomen." Her voice got lower and stronger. "I'm a black woman. I'm an *orphan*. I ought to be at Harvard. I ought to be getting my picture in *Time* magazine like you."

"You'd look great with Barbara Walters," Beth said. "You could talk about the emotional deprivation of orphans."

"Could I ever," Jolene said. "I'd like to tell about Helen Deardorff and her goddamn tranquilizers."

Beth hesitated a moment. Then she said, "Do you still take tranquilizers?"

"No," Jolene said. "Hell, no." She laughed. "Never forget you ripping off that whole jarful. Right there in the Multi-Purpose Room in front of the whole fucking *orphanage*, with Old Helen ready to turn into a pillar of salt and the rest of us with our jaws hanging slack." She laughed again. "Made you a hero, it did. I told the new ones about it after you was gone." Jolene had finished her meal; she sat back from the table now and pushed the plate toward the center. Then she leaned back, took a package of Kents from her jacket pocket and looked at it for a moment. "When your picture came out in *Life*, I was the one put it on the bulletin board in the library. Still there as far as I know." She lit a cigarette, using a little black lighter, and inhaled deeply. " 'A Girl Mozart Startles the World of Chess.' My, my."

"I still take tranquilizers," Beth said. "Too many of them."

"Oh, you poor thing," Jolene said wryly, looking at her cigarette.

Beth was quiet for a while. The silence between them was palpable. Then she said, "Let's have dessert."

"Chocolate mousse," Jolene said. During dessert she stopped eating and looked across the table. "You don't look *good*, Beth," she said. "You're puffy." Beth nodded and finished her mousse.

Jolene drove her home in her silver VW. When they got to

Janwell, Beth said, "I'd like you to come in for a while, Jolene. I want you to see my house."

"Sure," Jolene said. Beth showed her where to pull over, and when they got out of the car Jolene said, "That whole house belong to you?" and Beth said, "Yes."

Jolene laughed. "You're no orphan," she said. "Not anymore."

But when they came into the little entryway inside the front door, the stale, fruity smell was a shock. Beth had not noticed it before. There was an embarrassed silence while she turned on the lamps in the living room and looked around. She had not seen the dust on the TV screen or the stains on the cobbler's bench. At the corner of the living-room ceiling near the staircase was a dense cobweb. The whole place was dark and musty.

Jolene walked around the room, looking. "You been doing more than pills, honey," she said.

"I've been drinking wine."

"I believe it."

Beth made them coffee in the kitchen. At least the floor in there was clean. She opened the window out into the garden to let fresh air in.

Her chessboard was still set up on the table and Jolene picked up the white queen and held it for a moment. "I get tired of games," she said. "Never did learn this one."

"Want me to teach you?"

Jolene laughed. "It'd be something to tell about." She set the queen back on the board. "They've instructed me in handball, racquetball and paddleball. I play tennis, golf, dodgeball, and I wrestle. Don't need chess. What I want to hear about is all this wine."

Beth handed her a mug of coffee.

Jolene set it down and got out a cigarette. Sitting in the drab kitchen with her bright-navy suit and her Afro, she was like a new center in the room.

"It start with the pills?" Jolene asked.

"I used to love them," Beth said. "Really love them."

Jolene shook her head twice, from side to side.

"I haven't had anything to drink today," Beth said abruptly. "I'm supposed to play in Russia next year."

"Luchenko," Jolene said. "Borgov."

Beth was surprised that she knew the names. "I'm scared of it."

"Then don't go."

"If I don't, there's nothing else for me to do. I'll just drink."

"Looks like you do that, anyway."

"I just need to quit drinking and quit those pills and fix this place up. Look at the grease on that stove." She pointed to it. "I've got to study chess eight hours a day, and I've got to do some tournaments. They want me to play in San Francisco, and they want me on the *Tonight Show*. I should do all that."

Jolene studied her.

"What I want is a drink," Beth said. "If you weren't here, I'd have a bottle of wine."

Jolene frowned. "You sound like Susan Hayward in those movies," she said.

"It's no movie," Beth said.

"Then quit talking like one. Let me tell you what to do. You come over to the Alumni Gymnasium on Euclid Avenue tomorrow morning at ten. That's when I work out. Bring your gym shoes and a pair of shorts. You need to get that puffy look out of you before you make any more plans."

Beth stared at her. "I always hated gym . . ."

"I remember," Jolene said.

Beth thought about it. There were bottles of red wine and white in the cabinet behind her, and for a moment she became impatient for Jolene to leave so that she could get one out and twist the cork off and pour herself a full glass. She could feel the sensation of it at the back of her throat.

"It's not that bad," Jolene said. "I'll get you a couple of fresh towels and you can use my hair dryer."

"I don't know how to get there."

"Take a cab. Hell, *walk.*"

Beth looked at her, dismayed.

"You've got to get your ass moving, girl," Jolene said. "You got to quit sitting in your own funk."

"Okay," Beth said. "I'll be there."

When Jolene left, Beth had one class of wine but not a second. She opened up all the windows in the house and drank the wine out in the backyard, with the moon, nearly full, directly above the little shed at the back. There was a cool breeze. She took a long time over the drink, letting the breeze blow into the kitchen window, fluttering the curtains, blowing through the kitchen and living room, clearing out the air inside.

The gym was a high-ceilinged room with white walls. Light came in from enormous windows along the side where a row of strange-looking machines sat. Jolene was wearing yellow tights and gym shoes. The morning was warm, and Beth had worn her white shorts in the taxi. At the far end of the exercise room a doleful-looking young man in gray trunks lay on his back on a bench, pushing up weights and groaning. Otherwise they were alone.

They started with a pair of stationary bicycles. Jolene set the drag on Beth's at ten, and sixty for her own. By the time they had pedaled ten minutes Beth was covered with sweat and her calves were aching.

"It gets worse," Jolene said.

Beth gritted her teeth and kept pedaling.

She could not get the rhythm right on the hip-and-back machine, and her ass slid on the imitation-leather bench she had to lie on while she pushed the weights down with her legs. Jolene had set it for forty pounds, but even that seemed too much. Then there was the machine where she raised the weights with her ankles, making the tendons in her upper legs stand out and hurt. After that she had to sit upright in what reminded her of an electric chair and pull in weights with her elbows. "Firm up your pectorals," Jolene said.

"I thought that was a kind of fish," Beth said.

Jolene laughed. "Trust me, honey. This is what you need."

Beth did them all—furious and terribly out of breath. It made her fury worse to see that Jolene used far heavier weights than she did. But then, Jolene's figure was perfect.

The shower afterward was exquisite. There were strong water jets, and Beth sprayed herself hard, getting the sweat off. She soaped herself thoroughly and watched the foam swirl on the white tiles at her feet as she rinsed it off with a stinging hot spray.

The woman at the cafeteria was handing Beth a plate with salisbury steak on it when Jolene pushed her tray up next to Beth's. "None of that," Jolene said. She took the plate and handed it back. "No gravy," she said, "and no potatoes."

"I'm not overweight," Beth said. "It won't hurt me to eat potatoes."

Jolene said nothing. When they pushed their trays past the Jell-O and Bavarian cream pie, Jolene shook her head. "You ate chocolate mousse last night," Beth said.

"Last night was special," Jolene said. "This is today."

They had lunch at eleven-thirty because Jolene had a twelve o'clock class. When Beth asked her what it was, Jolene said, "Eastern Europe in the Twentieth Century."

"Is that part of Phys. Ed.?" Beth asked.

"I didn't tell all of it yesterday. I'm getting an M.S. in political science." Beth stared at her. *"Honi soit qui mal y pense,"* Jolene said.

When Beth got up the next morning, her back and calves were sore, and she decided not to go to the gym. But when she opened the refrigerator to find something for breakfast, she saw stacks of TV dinners and suddenly thought of the way Mrs. Wheatley's pale legs had looked when she rolled down her stockings. She shook her head in revulsion and started prying the boxes loose. The thought of frozen fried chicken and roast beef and turkey made her ill; she dumped them all in a plastic shopping bag. When she opened the cabinet to look over the canned foods, there were three bottles of Almadén Mountain Rhine sitting in front of the cans. She hesitated and closed the door. She would think about that later. She had toast and black coffee for breakfast. On her way to the gym, she dropped the sack of frozen dinners into the garbage.

At lunch Jolene told her about a bulletin board in the Student Union that listed students who would do unskilled work at two dollars an hour. Jolene walked her over on the way to class, and Beth took down two numbers. By three o'clock that afternoon she had a Business Administration major beating the carpets in the backyard and an Art History major scrubbing the refrigerator and kitchen cabinets; Beth did not supervise them; she spent the time working out variations on the Nimzo-Indian Defense.

By the next Monday, she was using all seven of the Nautilus machines and doing sit-ups afterward. On Wednesday, Jolene added ten pounds to each of them for her and had her hold a five-pound weight on her chest when she did the sit-ups. The week after that, they started playing handball. Beth was awkward at it and got out of breath quickly. Jolene beat her badly. Beth kept at it doggedly, panting and sweating and sometimes bruising the palm of her hand on the little black ball. It took her ten days and a few lucky bounces before she won her first game.

"I knew you'd start winning soon enough," Jolene said. They stood in the center of the court, sweating.

"I hate losing," Beth said.

That day there was a letter waiting for her from something called Christian Crusade. The stationery had about twenty names down the side, under an embossed cross. The letter read:

Dear Miss Harmon:

As we have been unable to reach you by telephone we are writing to determine your interest in the support of Christian Crusade in your forthcoming competition in the U.S.S.R.

Christian Crusade is a non-profit organization dedicated to the opening of Closed Doors to the Message of Christ. We have found your career as a Trainee of a Christian Institution, the Methuen Home, noteworthy. We would like to help in your forthcoming struggle since we share your Christian ideals and aspirations. If you are interested in our support, please contact us at our offices in Houston.

Yours in Christ,
Crawford Walker
Director
Christian Crusade
Foreign Division

She almost threw the letter away until she remembered Benny's saying that he had been given money for his Russian trip by a church group. She had Benny's phone number on a folded piece of paper in her chess clock box; she got it out and dialed. Benny answered after the third ring.

"Hi," she said, "It's Beth."

Benny was a bit cool, but when she told him about the letter, he said at once, "Take it. They're loaded."

"Would they pay for my ticket to Russia?"

"More than that. If you ask them, they'll send me over with you. Separate rooms, considering their views."

"Why would they pay so much money?"

"They want us to beat the Communists for Jesus. They're the ones who paid part of my way two years ago." He paused. "Are you coming back to New York?" His voice was carefully neutral.

"I need to stay in Kentucky a while longer. I'm working out in a gym, and I've entered a tournament in California."

"Sure," Benny said. "It sounds all right to me."

She wrote Christian Crusade that afternoon to say that she was very much interested in their offer and would like to take Benjamin Watts with her as a second. She used the pale-blue stationery, crossing out "Mrs. Allston Wheatley" at the top and writing in "Elizabeth Harmon." When she walked to the corner to mail the letter, she decided to go on downtown and buy new sheets and pillowcases for the bed and a new tablecloth for the kitchen.

The winter light in San Francisco was remarkable; she had never seen anything quite like it before. It gave the buildings a preternatural clarity of line, and when she climbed to the top of Telegraph Hill and looked back, she caught her breath at the sharp focus of the houses and hotels that lined the long steep street and below them the perfect blue of the bay. There was a flower stand at the corner, and she bought a bunch of marigolds. Looking back at the bay, she saw a young couple a block away climbing toward her. They were clearly out of breath and stopped to rest. Beth realized with surprise that the climb had been easy for her. She decided to take long walks during her week there. Maybe she could find a gym somewhere.

When she walked up the hill to the tournament in the morning, the air was still splendid and the colors bright, but she was tense. The elevator in the big hotel was crowded. Several people in it stared at her, and she looked away nervously. The man at the desk stopped what he was doing the minute she walked up.

"Do I register here?" she asked.

"No need, Miss Harmon. Just go on in."

"Which board?"

He raised his eyebrows. "Board One."

Board One was in a room by itself. The table was on a three-foot-high platform, and a display board as big as a home-movie screen stood behind it. On each side of the table was a big swivel chair of brown leather and chrome. It was five minutes before starting time, and the room was jammed with people; she had to push her way through them to the playing space. As she did so, the buzz of talk died down. Everyone looked at her. When she climbed the steps to the platform, they began to applaud. She tried not to let her face show anything, but she was frightened. The last game of chess she had played was five months before, and she had lost it.

She didn't even know who her opponent was; she hadn't thought to ask. She sat there for a moment with her mind nearly empty, and then an arrogant-looking young man came briskly through the crowd and up the steps. He had long black hair and a broad, drooping mustache. She recognized him from somewhere, and when he introduced himself as Andy Levitt, she remembered the name from *Chess Review*. He seated himself stiffly. A tournament director came up to the table and spoke quietly to Levitt. "You can start her clock now." Levitt reached out, looking unconcerned, and pressed the button on Beth's clock. She held herself steady and played her queen's pawn, keeping her eyes on the board.

By the time they had got into the middle game, there were people jammed in the doorway and someone was shushing the crowd and trying to maintain order. She had never seen so many spectators at a match. She turned her attention back to the board and carefully brought a rook to an open file. If Levitt didn't find a way to prevent it, she could try attacking in three moves. If she wasn't missing something in the position. She started moving in on him cautiously, prying the pawns loose from his castled king. Then she took a deep breath and brought a rook to the seventh rank. She could hear at the back of her mind the voice of the chess bum in Cincinnati years before: "Bone in the throat, a rook on the seventh rank." She looked across the board at Levitt. He looked as if it were indeed a chicken bone and deeply imbedded. Something in her exulted, seeing him try to hide his confusion. And when she followed the rook with her queen, looking brutal on the seventh rank, he resigned immediately. The applause in the room was loud and enthusiastic. When she came down from the platform she was smiling. There were people waiting with old copies of *Chess Review*, wanting her to autograph her picture on the cover. Others wanted her to sign their programs or just sheets of paper.

While she was signing one of the magazines, she looked for a moment at the black-and-white photograph of herself holding the big trophy in Ohio, with Benny and Barnes and a few others out of focus in the background. Her face looked tired and plain, and she recalled with a sudden remembered shame that the magazine had sat with its tan mailing cover in a stack on the cobbler's bench for a month before she had opened it and found her picture. Someone thrust another copy at her to sign, and she shook off the memory. She autographed her way out of the crowded room and through yet another crowd that was waiting outside the door, filling the space between her playing area and the ballroom where the rest of the tournament was still in progress. Two directors were trying to hush the crowd to avoid disturbing the other games as she came through. Some of the players looked up from their boards angrily and frowned in her direction. It was exhilarating and frightening, having all these people pressed near her, pushing up to her with admiration. One of the women who had got her autograph said, "I don't know a thing about chess, dear, but I'm thrilled for you," and a middle-aged man insisted on shaking her hand, saying, "You're the best thing for the game since Capablanca." "Thanks," she said. "I wish it were as easy for me." Maybe it is, she thought. Her brain seemed to be all right. Maybe she hadn't ruined it.

She walked confidently down the street to her hotel in bright sunshine. She would be going to Russia in six months. Christian Crusade had agreed to buy tickets on Aeroflot for her and Benny and a woman from the USCF and would pay their hotel bills. The Moscow tournament would provide the meals. She had been studying chess for six hours a day, and she could keep it up. She stopped to buy more flowers—carnations this time. The woman at the desk had asked for her autograph last night when she came in from dinner; she would be glad to get her another vase. Before leaving for California, Beth had mailed off checks for subscriptions to all the magazines Benny took. She would be getting *Deutsche Schachzeitung,* the oldest chess magazine, and *British Chess Magazine* and, from Russia, *Shakhmatni v USSR*. There would be *Échecs Europe* and *American Chess Bulletin.* She planned to play through every grandmaster game in them, and when she found games that were important she would memorize them and analyze every move that had consequence or developed any idea that she was not familiar with. In early spring she might go to New York and play the U.S. Open and get in a few weeks with Benny. The flowers in her hand glowed crimson, her new jeans and cotton sweater felt fresh on her skin in the cool San Francisco air, at the bottom of the street the blue ocean lay like a dream of possibility. Her soul sang silently with it, reaching out toward the Pacific.

When she came home with her trophy and the first-prize check, she found in the pile of mail two business envelopes: one was from the USCF and contained a check for four hundred dollars and a brief apology that they couldn't send more. The second was from Christian Crusade. It had a three-page letter that spoke of the need to promote international understanding through Christian principles and to annihilate Communism for the advancement of those same principles. The word "His" was capitalized in a way that made Beth uneasy. The letter was signed "Yours in Christ" by four people. Folded up in it was a check for four thousand dollars. She held the check in her hand for a long time. Her prize money at San Francisco was two thousand, and she had to take her travel expenses out of it. Her bank account had been dwindling for the past six months. She had hoped to get at most two thousand dollars from the people in Texas. Whatever crazy ideas they might have, the money was a gift from heaven. She called Benny to tell him the good news.

When she came in from her Wednesday morning squash game the phone was ringing. She got her raincoat off in a hurry, threw it on the sofa and picked up the phone. It was a woman's voice. "Is this Elizabeth Harmon?"

"Yes."

"This is Helen Deardorff, at Methuen." She was too astonished to speak. "I have something to tell you, Elizabeth. Mr. Shaibel died last night. I thought you might want to know."

She had a sudden image of the fat old janitor bent over his chess set in the basement, with the bare light bulb over his head, and herself standing by him, watching the deliberateness, the *oddness* of him there alone by the furnace.

"Last night?" she said.

"A heart attack. He was in his sixties."

What Beth said next surprised her. It came out almost without conscious thought. "I'd like to come to the funeral."

"The funeral?" Mrs. Deardorff said. "I'm not sure when— There's an unmarried sister, Hilda Shaibel. You could call her."

When the Wheatleys drove her to Lexington six years before, they had gone on narrow asphalt roads through towns where she had stared out the car windows at stoplights while brightly dressed people crossed the streets and walked on crowded sidewalks in front of shops. Now, driving back with Jolene, it was four-lane concrete most of the way and the towns were visible only as names printed on green signs.

"He looked like a mean son of a bitch," Jolene said.

"He wasn't easy to play chess with, either. I think I was terrified of him."

"I was scared of all of 'em," Jolene said. "Motherfuckers."

That surprised Beth. She had imagined Jolene as fearless. "What about Fergussen?"

"Fergussen was an oasis in the desert," Jolene said, "but he frightened me when he first came. He turned out to be okay." She smiled. "Old Fergussen."

Beth hesitated a moment. "Was there ever anything between you two?" She remembered those extra green pills.

Jolene laughed. "Wishful thinking."

"How old were you when you came?"

"Six."

"Do you know anything about your parents?"

"Just my grandmother, and she's dead. Somewhere near Louisville. I don't want to know anything about them. I don't care whether I'm a bastard or why it was they wanted to put me with my grandmother or why she wanted to shove me off on Methuen. I'm just glad to be free of it all. I'll have my master's in August, and I'm leaving this state for good."

"I still remember my mother," Beth said. "Daddy's not so clear."

"Best to forget it," Jolene said. "If you can."

She pulled into the left lane and passed a coal truck and two campers. Up ahead a green sign gave the mileage to Mount Sterling. It was spring, almost exactly a year since Beth's last trip in a car, with Benny. She thought of the griminess of the Pennsylvania Turnpike. This white concrete road was fresh and new, with Kentucky fields and white fences and farmhouses on either side of it.

After a while Jolene lit up a cigarette, and Beth said, "Where will you go when you graduate?"

She was beginning to think that Jolene hadn't heard her when Jolene spoke. "I've got an offer from a white law firm in Atlanta that looks promising." She fell silent again. "What they want is an imported nigger to stay even with the times."

Beth looked at her. "I don't think I'd go any farther south if I was black."

"Well, you sure ain't," Jolene said. "These people in Atlanta will pay me twice what I could get in New York. I'd be doing public relations, which is the kind of shuck I understand right to my fingertips, and they'll start me out with two windows in my office and a white girl to type my letters."

"But you haven't studied law."

Jolene laughed. "I expect they like it that way. Fine, Slocum and Livingston don't want any black female reviewing torts. What they want is a clean black woman with a nice ass and a good vocabulary. When I did the interview I dropped a lot of words like 'reprehensible' and 'dichotomy,' and they picked right up."

"Jolene," Beth said, "you're too smart for that. You could teach at the University. And you're a fine athlete . . ."

"I know what I'm doing," Jolene said. "I play good tennis and golf and I'm ambitious." She took a deep drag on her cigarette. "You may have no idea just how ambitious I am. I worked hard at sports, and I had coaches promising I'd be a pro if I kept at it."

"That doesn't sound bad."

Jolene let the smoke out slowly. "Beth," she said, "what I want is what *you've* got. I don't want to work on my backhand for two years so I can be a bush league pro. You've been the best at what you do for so long you don't know what it's like for the rest of us."

"I'd like to be half as good-looking as you are . . ."

"Quit giving me that," Jolene said. "Can't spend your life in front of a mirror. You ain't ugly anymore anyhow. What I'm talking about is your talent. I'd give my ass to play tennis the way you play chess."

The conviction in Jolene's voice was overwhelming. Beth looked at her face in profile, with its Afro grazing at the top of the car interior, at her smooth brown arms out to where her steady hands held the wheel, at the anger clouding her face, and said nothing.

A minute later Jolene said, "Well, now. There it is."

About a mile ahead to the right of the road stood three dark brick buildings with black roofs and black window shutters. The Methuen Home for Orphaned Children.

A yellow-painted wooden stairway at the end of a concrete path led to the building. Once the steps had looked broad and imposing to her, and the tarnished brass plaque had seemed a stern warning. Now it looked like only the entrance to a shabby provincial institution. The paint on the steps was peeling. The bushes that flanked them were grubby, and their leaves were covered with dust. Jolene was in the playground, looking over the rusty swings and the old slide that they had not been allowed to use except when Fergussen was there to supervise. Beth stood on the path in the sunlight, studying the wooden doors. Inside was Mrs. Deardorff's big office and the other offices and, filling one whole wing, the library and the chapel. There were two classrooms in the other wing, and past them was the door at the end of the hallway that led to the basement.

She had come to accept the Sunday-morning chess games as her prerogative. Until that day. It still constricted her throat to remember the silent tableau following Mrs. Deardorff's voice shouting "Elizabeth!" and the cascade of pills and fragmented glass. Then no more chess. Instead it had been the full hour and a half of chapel and Beth helping Miss Lonsdale with the chairs and listening to her give her Talks. It took another hour after putting the chairs away to write the précis Mrs. Deardorff had assigned. She did it every Sunday for a year, and Mrs. Deardorff returned it every Monday with red marks and some grim exhortation like "Rewrite. Faulty organization." She'd had to look up

"Communism" in the library for the first précis. Beth had felt somewhere in her that Christianity ought to have something more to it.

Jolene had come over and was standing beside her, squinting in the sunlight. "That's where you learned to play?"

"In the basement."

"Shit," Jolene said. "They should have encouraged you. Sent you on more exhibitions after that one. They like publicity, just like anybody else."

"Publicity?" She was feeling dazed.

"It brings in money."

She had never thought of anyone there encouraging her. It began to enter her mind now, standing in front of the building. She could have played in tournaments at nine or ten, like Benny. She had been bright and eager, and her mind was voracious in its appetite for chess. She could have been playing grandmasters and learning things that people like Shaibel and Ganz could never teach her. Girev was planning at thirteen to be World Champion. If she had had half his chances, she would have been as good at ten. For a moment the whole autocratic institution of Russian chess merged in her mind with the autocracy of the place where she was now standing. Institutions. There was no violation of Christianity in chess, any more than there was a violation of Marxism. It was nonideological. It wouldn't have hurt Deardorff to let her play—to *encourage* her to play. It would have been something for Methuen to boast about. She could see Deardorff's face in her mind—the thin, rouged cheeks, the tight, reproving smile, the little sadistic glint in her eyes. It had pleased her to cut Beth off from the game she loved. It had *pleased* her.

"You want to go in?" Jolene asked.

"No. Let's find that motel."

The motel had a small pool only a few yards from the road, with some weary-looking maples beside it. The evening was warm enough for a quick swim after dinner. Jolene turned out to be a superb swimmer, going back and forth the length of the pool with hardly a ripple, while Beth treaded water under the diving board. Jolene pulled up near her. "We were chicken," she said. "We should have gone in the Administration Building. We should have gone in her office."

The funeral was in the morning at the Lutheran Church. There were a dozen people and a closed casket. It was an ordinary-sized coffin, and Beth wondered briefly how they could fit a man of Shaibel's girth into it. Although the church was smaller, it was much like Mrs. Wheatley's funeral in Lexington. After the first five minutes of it, she was bored and restless, and Jolene was dozing. After the ceremony they followed the small procession to the grave. "I remember," Jolene said, "he scared shit out of me once, hollering to keep off the library floor. He just mopped it, and Mr. Schell sent me in to get a book. Son of a bitch hated kids."

"Mrs. Deardorff wasn't at the church."

"None of them were."

The graveside service was an anticlimax. They lowered the coffin, and the minister said a prayer. Nobody cried. They looked like people waiting in line at a teller's window at the bank. Beth and Jolene were the only young ones there, and none of the others spoke to them. They left immediately after it was over, walking along a narrow path in the old cemetery, past faded gravestones and patches of dandelions. Beth felt no grief for the dead man, no sadness that he was gone. The only thing she felt was guilt that she had never sent him his ten dollars—she should have mailed him a check years ago.

They had to pass Methuen on the way back to Lexington. Just before the turnoff, Beth said, "Let's go in. There's something I want to see," and Jolene turned the car down the drive to the orphanage.

Jolene stayed in the car. Beth got out and pushed her way into the side door of the Administration Building. It was dark and cool inside. Straight in front of her was a door that read HELEN DEARDORFF—SUPERINTENDENT. She walked down the empty hallway to the doorway at the end. When she pushed it open, there was a light on below. She went slowly down the steps.

The chessboard and pieces weren't there, but the table he had played on still sat by the furnace, and his unpainted chair was still in position. The bare bulb over it was on. She stood looking down at the table. Then she seated herself thoughtfully in Mr. Shaibel's chair and looked up and saw something she had not seen before.

Behind the place where she used to sit to play was a kind of rough partition made of unplaned wooden boards nailed to two-by-fours. A calendar used to hang there, with scenes from Bavaria above the sheets for the months. Now the calendar was gone and the entire partition was covered with photographs and clippings and covers from *Chess Review*, each of them neatly taped to the wood and covered with clear plastic to keep it clean and free of dust—the only thing in this dingy basement that was. They were pictures of her. There were printed games from *Chess Review*, and newspaper pieces from the Lexington *Herald-Leader* and the New York *Times* and from some magazines in German. The old *Life* piece was there, and next to it was the cover of *Chess Review* with her holding the U.S. Championship trophy. Filling in the smaller spaces were newspaper pictures, some of them duplicates. There must have been twenty photographs.

"You find what you were looking for?" Jolene asked when she got back to the car.

"More," Beth said. She started to say something else but didn't. Jolene backed the car up, drove out of the lot and turned back onto the road that led to the highway.

When they drove up the ramp and pulled onto the interstate, Jolene gunned the VW and it shot ahead. Neither of them looked back. Beth had stopped crying by then and was wiping her face with a handkerchief.

"Didn't bite off more than you could chew, did you?" Jolene said.

"No." Beth blew her nose. "I'm fine."

The taller of the two women looked like Helen Deardorff. Or didn't exactly look like her as much as display all indications of spiritual sisterhood. She wore a beige suit and pumps and smiled a good deal in a way totally devoid of feeling. Her name was Mrs. Blocker. The other was plump and slightly embarrassed and wore a dark floral print and no-nonsense shoes. She was Miss Dodge. They were on their way from Houston to Cincinnati and had stopped by for a chat. They sat side by side on Beth's sofa and talked about the ballet in Houston and the way the city was growing in culture. Clearly they wanted Beth to know Christian Crusade was not merely a narrow, fundamentalist organization. And just as clearly they had come to look her over. They had written ahead.

Beth listened politely while they talked about Houston and about the agency they were helping to set up in Cincinnati—an agency that had something to do with protecting the Christian environment. The conversation faltered for a moment, and Miss Dodge spoke. "What we would really like, Elizabeth, would be some kind of a statement."

"A statement?" Beth was sitting in Mrs. Wheatley's armchair facing them on the sofa.

Mrs. Blocker picked it up. "Christian Crusade would like you to make your position public. In a world where so many keep silent . . ." She didn't finish.

"What position?" Beth asked.

"As we know," Mrs. Dodge said, "the spread of Communism is also the spread of atheism."

"I suppose so," Beth said.

"It's not a matter of supposing," Mrs. Blocker said quickly. "It's a matter of fact. Of Marxist-Leninist fact. The Holy Word is anathema to the Kremlin, and it is one of the major purposes of Christian Crusade to contest the Kremlin and the atheists who sit there."

"I have no quarrel with that," Beth said.

"Good. What we want is a statement." The way Mrs. Blocker said it echoed something that Beth had recognized years before in Mrs. Deardorff's voice. It was the tone of the practiced bully. She felt the way she did when a player brought out his queen too soon against her. "You want me to make a statement for the press?"

"Exactly!" Mrs. Blocker said. "If Christian Crusade is going to—" She stood and felt the manila envelope in her lap as though estimating its weight. "We had something prepared."

Beth looked at her, hating her and saying nothing.

Mrs. Blocker opened the clasp on the envelope and pulled out a sheet of paper filled with typing. She gave it to Beth.

It was the same stationery the original letter had come on, with its list of names running down the side. Beth glanced down the list and saw "Telsa R. Blocker, Executive Secretary," just above half a dozen men's names with the abbreviation "Rev." in front of them. Then she read the statement quickly. Some phrases in it were underlined, like *the atheist-communist nexus* and *a militant Christian Endeavor.* She looked up from the paper at Mrs. Blocker, who was sitting with her knees pressing together, looking around the room with a subdued dislike. "I'm a chess player," Beth said quietly.

"Of course you are, my dear," Mrs. Blocker said. "And you're a Christian."

"I'm not sure of that."

Mrs. Blocker stared at her.

"Look," Beth said, "I have no intention of saying things like this."

Mrs. Blocker leaned forward and took the statement. "Christian Crusade has already invested a good deal of money . . ." There was a glint in her eye that Beth had seen before.

Beth stood up. "I'll give it back." She walked to the desk and found her checkbook. For a moment she felt like a prig and a fool. It was money for her air fare and Benny's and for the woman from the Federation as an escort. It would pay her hotel bill and incidental expenses on the trip. But at the bottom of the check they had sent her a month ago, in the place where you normally wrote "rent" or "light bill" to say what the money was for, someone—probably Mrs. Blocker—had written "For Christian Service." Beth made out a check for four thousand dollars to Christian Crusade, and in the space at the bottom she wrote "Full refund."

Miss Dodge's voice was surprisingly gentle. "I hope you know what you're doing, dear." She looked genuinely concerned.

"I hope so too," Beth said. Her plane for Moscow left in five weeks.

She got Benny on the phone at the first try. "You're crazy," he said when she told him.

"Anyway, I did it," Beth said. "It's too late to undo it."

"Are the tickets paid for?"

"No," Beth said. "Nothing's paid for."

"You have to pay Intourist for the hotel in advance."

"I know that." Beth did not like Benny's tone. "I've got two thousand in my bank account. It would be more, but I've been keeping up this house. It's going to take three thousand more to do it. At least that."

"I don't have it," Benny said.

"What do you mean? You've got money."

"*I don't have it.*" There was a long silence. "You can call the Federation. Or the State Department."

"The Federation doesn't like me," Beth said. "They think I haven't done as much for chess as I could have."

"You should have gone on *Tonight* and *Phil Donahue.*"

"God damn it, Benny," Beth said. "Come off it."

"You're crazy," Benny said. "What do you care what those dummies believe? What are you trying to prove?"

"*Benny.* I don't want to go to Russia alone."

Benny's voice suddenly became loud. "You *asshole,*" he shouted. "You crazy fucking asshole!"

"Benny . . ."

"First you don't come back to New York and then you pull this crap. You can fucking well go alone."

"Maybe I shouldn't have done it." She was beginning to feel a chill inside. "Maybe I didn't have to give them back the check."

" 'Maybe' is a loser's word." Benny's voice was like ice.

"Benny, I'm sorry."

"I'm hanging up," Benny said. "You were a pain in the ass

when I first met you, and you're a pain in the ass right now. I don't want to talk to you anymore." The phone in her hand went *click*. She put it back in the cradle. She had blown it. She had lost Benny.

She called the Federation and had to wait on hold for ten minutes before the director came on the line. He was pleasant with her and sympathetic and wished her well in Moscow but said there was no money to be had. "What we have comes mostly from the magazine. The four hundred dollars is all we can possibly spare."

It wasn't until the next morning that she got her call returned from Washington. It was somebody named O'Malley, from Cultural Affairs. When she told him the problem, he went on about how excited they were, there at State, over her "giving the Russians a jolt at their own game." He asked her how he could help.

"I need three thousand dollars right away."

"I'll see what I can do," O'Malley said. "I'll get back to you in an hour."

But it was four hours later that he called back. She paced around the kitchen and the garden and made a quick call to Anne Reardon, who was to be the chaperone required by Christian Crusade. Anne Reardon had a woman's rating of 1900 or so and at least knew the game. Beth had wiped her out once somewhere out West, practically blasting her pieces off the board. No one answered the phone. Beth made herself coffee and leafed through some copies of *Deutsche Schachzeitung,* waiting for the call. She felt almost nauseated at the way she had let the Christian Crusade money go. Four thousand dollars—for a gesture. Finally the phone rang.

It was O'Malley again. No dice. He was terribly sorry, but there was no way government funds could be handed out to her without more time and approval. "We'll be sending one of our men with you, though."

"Don't you have petty cash or something?" Beth asked. "I don't need funds to undermine the government in Moscow. I just need to take some people to help me."

"I'm sorry," O'Malley said. "I'm really sorry."

After hanging up, she went back out into the garden. She would send the check to the Washington office of Intourist in the morning. She would go alone, or with whomever the State Department found to send with her. She had studied Russian, and she would not be totally at a loss. The Russian players would speak English, anyway. She could do her own training. She had been training alone for months. She finished off the last of her coffee. She had been training alone for most of her life.

Chapter 14

They had to sit in a waiting room at Orly Airport for seven hours, and when the time came to board the Aeroflot plane, a young women in an olive-drab uniform had to stamp everybody's ticket and study everybody's passport while Beth and Mr. Booth waited at the back of the line for another hour. But it cheered her a bit when she finally got to the head of the line and the woman said, "The chess champion!" and smiled broadly at her with a surprising lightening of her features. When Beth smiled back at her, the woman said, "Good luck!" as though she really meant it. The woman was, of course, Russian. No official in America would have recognized Beth's name.

Her seat was by a window near the back; it had heavy brown plastic upholstery and a little white antimacassar on each arm. She got in with Mr. Booth beside her. She looked out the window at the gray Paris sky with the water in broad sheets on the runways and the planes gleaming darkly in the evening wetness. It felt as if she were already in Moscow. After a few minutes a steward started handing out glasses of water. Mr. Booth drank about half of his and then fished in his jacket pocket. After some fumbling he produced a little silver flask and pulled the cap off with his teeth. He filled the glass with whiskey, put the cap back on and slipped the flask into his pocket. Then he held the glass toward Beth in a perfunctory way, and she shook her head. It wasn't easy to do. She could have used a drink. She did not like this strange-looking airplane, and she didn't like the man sitting beside her.

She had disliked Mr. Booth from the moment he met her at Kennedy and introduced himself. Assistant to the Undersecretary. Cultural Affairs. He would show her the ropes in Moscow. She did not want to be shown any ropes—especially not by this gravelly voiced old man with his dark suit, arched eyebrows and frequent theatrical laughter. When he volunteered the information that he had played chess at Yale in the forties, she said nothing; he had spoken of it as though it were a shared perversion. What she wanted was to be traveling with Benny Watts. She hadn't even been able to get hold of Benny the night before; his line was busy the first two times she dialed and then there was no answer. She had a letter from the director of the USCF wishing her well and that was all.

She leaned back against the seat, closed her eyes and tried to relax, tuning out the voices, Russian, German and French, that surrounded her. In a pocket of her hand luggage was a bottle with thirty green pills; she had not taken one for over six months, but she would have one on this airplane if necessary. It would certainly be better than drinking. She needed to rest. The long wait at the airport had left her nerves jagged. She had tried twice to get Jolene on the phone, but there was no answer.

What she really needed was Benny Watts here with her. If she hadn't been such a fool, giving back that money, taking a stand on something she hadn't really cared about. That wasn't so. It wasn't being an asshole to refuse to be bullied, to call that woman's bluff. But she needed Benny. For a moment she let herself imagine traveling with D. L. Townes, the two of them staying together in Moscow. But that was no good. She missed Benny, not Townes. She missed Benny's quick and sober mind, his judgment and tenacity, his knowledge of chess and his knowledge of her. He would be in the seat beside her, and they could talk chess, and in Moscow after her games they would analyze the play and then plan for the next opponent. They would eat their meals together in the hotel, the way she had done with Mrs. Wheatley. They could see Moscow, and whenever they wanted to they could make love at their hotel. But Benny was in New York, and she was in a dark airplane flying toward Eastern Europe.

By the time they came down through the heavy clouds and she had her first sight of Russia, which looked from above as much like Kentucky as anything else, she had taken three of the pills, slept fitfully for a few hours and was feeling the glassy-eyed numbness that she used to feel after a long trip on a Greyhound bus. She remembered taking the pills in the middle of the night. She had walked down an aisle full of sleeping people to the rest room and got water in a funny-looking little plastic glass.

Mr. Booth did turn out to be a help in customs. His Russian was good, and he got her into the right booth for the inspection. What was surprising was the ease of it all; a pleasant old man in uniform went casually through her luggage, opened her two bags, poked around a bit and closed them. That was it.

When they came through the gate, a limousine from the embassy was waiting. They drove through fields where men and women were working in early-morning sunlight, and at one place along the road she saw three enormous tractors, far bigger than anything she had seen in America, driving slowly across a field that stretched as far as she could see. There was very little other traffic on the road. The car started moving through rows of six- and eight-story buildings with tiny windows and, since it was a warm June morning even under the gray sky, people sitting on the doorsteps. Then the road began to broaden, and they drove past a small green park and another large one and past some enormous, newer buildings that looked as if they had been built to last forever. The traffic had become heavier and there were people on bicycles at one side of the road now and a great many pedestrians on the sidewalks.

Mr. Booth was leaning back in his rumpled suit with his eyes half closed. Beth sat stiffly in the back of the long car, looking out the window on her side. There was nothing threatening about the way Moscow looked; she could have been entering any large city. But she could not loosen up inside. The tournament would start the next morning. She felt totally alone, and frightened.

Her teacher at the University had talked abut how Russians drank tea from glasses, straining it through a lump of sugar held between the teeth, but the tea served in this big dark parlor of a room was in thin china cups with a Greek key design in gold. She sat in her high-backed Victorian chair with her knees pressed together, holding the saucer with the cup and a hard little roll on it and tried to listen attentively to the director. He spoke a few sentences first in English and then in French. Then English again: the visitors were welcome in the Soviet Union; games would begin promptly at ten o'clock each morning; a referee would be assigned to each board and should be consulted in the event of any irregularity. There would be no smoking or eating during play. An attendant would accompany players to the rest rooms should the need arise. It would be proper to raise one's right hand in such an event.

The chairs were in a circle, and the director was on Beth's right. Across from her sat Dimitri Luchenko, Viktor Laev and Leonid Shapkin, all dressed in well-tailored suits and wearing white shirts and dark ties. Mr. Booth had said Russian men dressed as though their clothes came from a nineteen-thirties Montgomery Ward catalogue, but these men were soberly dapper in expensive gray gaberdine and worsted. Those three alone—Luchenko, Laev and Shapkin—were a small pantheon next to which the entire establishment of American chess would stammer in humiliation. And on her left was Vasily Borgov. She could not bring herself to look at him, but she could smell his cologne. Between him and the other three Russians was an only slightly lesser pantheon—Jorge Flento from Brazil, Bernt Hellström from Finland and Jean-Paul Duhamel from Belgium, also wearing conservative suits. She sipped her tea and tried to appear calm. There were heavy maroon draperies at the tall windows, and the chairs were upholstered in maroon velvet trimmed with gold. It was nine-thirty in the morning and the summer day outside was splendid, but the draperies here were tightly closed. The Oriental carpet on the floor looked as if it had come from a museum. The walls were paneled in rosewood.

An escort of two women had brought her here from the hotel; she had shaken hands with the other players, and they had been seated like this for a half hour. In her huge, strange hotel room the night before a water tap was dripping somewhere, and she had barely slept. She had been dressed in her expensive navy-blue tailored dress since seven-thirty, and she could feel herself perspiring; her nylons encased her legs in a warm grip. She could hardly have felt more out of place. Every time she glanced at the men around her, they smiled faintly. She felt like a child at an adult social function. Her head ached. She would have to ask the director for aspirin.

And then quite suddenly the director finished his speech, and the men stood up. Beth jumped to her feet, rattling her cup on its saucer. The waiter in a white cossack blouse who had served the tea came running up to take it from her. Borgov, who had ignored her except for a perfunctory handshake at the beginning, ignored her now as he crossed in front of her and walked out the door the director had opened. The others followed, with Beth behind Shapkin and in front of Hellström. As they filed out the door into a carpeted hallway, Luchenko stopped for a moment and turned to her. "I'm delighted you are here," he said. "I look forward keenly to playing you." He had long white hair like an orchestra conductor's and wore an impeccable silvery necktie, beautifully knotted under a starched white collar. The warmth in his face was unquestionable. "Thank you," she said. She had read of Luchenko in Junior High; *Chess Review* wrote of him with the kind of awe that Beth felt now. He had been World Champion then, losing to Borgov in a long match several years ago.

They walked down the hall a good distance before the director stopped at another door and opened it. Borgov went in first, and the others followed.

They were in some kind of anteroom with a closed door on the far side. Beth could hear a distant wave of sound, and when the director walked over and opened the door the sound became louder. Nothing was visible except a dark curtain, but when she could see around it, she sucked in her breath. She was facing a vast auditorium filled with people. It was like the view from the stage of Radio City Music Hall might be with every seat filled. The crowd stretched back for hundreds of yards, and the aisles had folding chairs set up in them with small groups clustered together talking. As the players came across the wide carpeted stage, the sound died. Everyone stared at them. Up above the main floor was a broad balcony, with a huge red banner draped across it, and above this was row after row of more faces.

On the stage were four large tables, each the size of a desk, each clearly new and inlaid with a large chessboard on which the pieces were already set up. To the right of each position for Black sat an oversized, wooden-cased chess clock, and to White's right, a large pitcher of water and two glasses. The high-backed swivel chairs were set up so the players would be visible in profile from the audience. Behind each of them stood a male referee in a white shirt and black bow tie, and behind each referee was a display board with the pieces in their opening position. The lighting was bright but indirect, coming from a luminous ceiling above the playing area.

The director smiled at Beth, took her by the hand and led her out to the center of the stage. There was no sound at all in the auditorium. The director spoke into an old-fashioned microphone on a stand at center stage. Although he was speaking in Russian, Beth understood the words "chess" and "the United States" and finally her name: Elizabeth Harmon. The applause was sudden, warm and thunderous; she felt it as a physical thing. The director escorted her to the chair at the far end and seated her at the black pieces. She watched as he brought out each of the other foreign players for a short introduction and applause. Then came the Russians, beginning with Laev. The applause became deafening, and when he got to the last of them, Vasily Borgov, it went on and on.

Her opponent for the first game was Laev. He was seated across from her during the ovation for Borgov, and she glanced at him while it was going on. Laev was in his twenties. There was a tight smile on his lean and youthful face, his brow was heavy with annoyance and with the fingers of one slim hand he was drumming inaudibly on the table.

When the applause died down, the director, flushed with the excitement, went to the table where Borgov was playing the white pieces and smartly punched the clock. Then he walked to the next table and did the same thing, and to the next. At Beth's he smiled importantly at the two of them and crisply pushed the button on Beth's side, starting Laev's clock.

Laev sighed quietly and moved his king pawn to the fourth rank. Beth without hesitation moved her queen bishop pawn, relieved to be just playing chess. The pieces were large and solid; they stood out with a comforting clarity on the board, each of them exactly centered in its home square, each sharply outlined, cleanly turned, finely burnished. The board had a matte finish with a brass inlay around its outer perimeter. Her chair was substantial and soft, yet firm; she adjusted herself in it now, feeling its comfort, and watched Laev play the king's knight to bishop three. She picked up her queen's knight, enjoying the heaviness of the piece, and set it on queen bishop three. Laev played pawn to queen four; she took with her pawn, setting his to the right of the clock. The referee, his back to them, repeated each move on the big board. There was still a tightness in her shoulders, but she began to relax. It was Russia and it was strange, but it was still chess.

She knew Laev's style from the bulletins she had been studying, and she felt certain that if she played pawn to king four on the sixth move, he would follow the Boleslavski Variation with his knight to bishop three and then castle on the kingside. He had done that against both Petrosian and Tal, in 1965. Players sometimes broke into strange new lines at important tournaments, lines that might have been prepared for weeks in advance, but she felt the Russians would not have taken that trouble with her. As far as they knew, her level of play was roughly that of Benny Watts, and men like Laev would not devote much time to preparation for playing Benny. She was not an important player by their standards; the only unusual thing about her was her sex, and even that wasn't unique in Russia. There was Nona Gaprindashvili, not up to the level of this tournament, but a player who had met all these Russian grandmasters many times before. Laev would be expecting an easy win. He brought the knight out and castled as she had expected. She felt sanguine about the reading she had done over the past six months; it was nice to know what to expect. She castled.

The game gradually began to slow as they moved past the opening without any errors and into a poised middle game with each of them now minus one knight and one bishop, and with the kings well protected and no holes in either position. By the eighteenth move the board had a dangerous equilibrium. This was not the attack chess she had made her American reputation with; it was chamber-music chess, subtle and intricate.

Playing white, Laev still had the advantage. He made moves that contained cunningly deceptive threats, but she parried them without losing tempo or position. On the twenty-fourth, she found an opportunity for a finesse, opening a file for her queen rook while forcing him to retreat a bishop, and when she made it, Laev studied it for a long while and then looked at her in a new way, as though he were seeing her for the first time. A quiver of pleasure went through her. He studied the board again before retreating the bishop. She brought the rook over. Now she had equality.

Five moves later she found a way of adding to it. She pushed a pawn to the fifth rank, offering it in sacrifice. With the move, as quietly pretty as any she had ever made, Laev was on the defensive. He did not take the pawn but was forced to bring the knight it attacked back to the square in front of his queen. She brought her rook to the third rank, and he had to respond to that. She was not pushing him so much as pressing gently. And gradually he began to yield, trying to look unconcerned about it. But he must have been astonished. Russian grandmasters were not supposed to have this done to them by American girls. She kept after him, and finally the point was reached where she could safely post her remaining knight on queen five, where he could not dislodge it. She put it there and, two moves later, brought her rook over to the knight file, directly above his king. He studied it for a long time while his clock ticked loudly and then did what she had fervently hoped he might do; he pushed the king bishop pawn up to attack the rook. When he punched his clock, he did not look at her.

Without hesitation she picked up her bishop and took his pawn with it, offering it as sacrifice. When the referee posted the move she heard an audible response from the spectators and whispering. Laev would have to do something; he could not ignore the bishop. He began running his fingers through his hair with one hand, drumming the tips of the others on the table. Beth leaned back in the chair and stretched. She had him.

He studied the move for twenty minutes on the clock before he suddenly stood up from the table and held out his hand. Beth rose and took it. The audience was silent. The tournament director came over and shook her hand too, and she walked off the stage with him to sudden, shocking applause.

She was supposed to have lunch with Mr. Booth and some people who were coming over from the embassy, but when she walked into the vast lobby of the hotel, which felt like a carpeted gymnasium with Victorian armchairs lining its walls, he was not there. The lady at the desk had a message for her on a sheet of paper: "I'm really awfully sorry, but some work has come up over here and we won't be able to get away. I'll be in touch." The note was typed, with Mr. Booth's name, also typed, at the bottom. Beth found one of the hotel restaurants—another carpeted gymnasium of a room—and managed enough Russian to order *blinchiki* and tea with blackberry jam. Her waiter was a serious-faced boy of about fourteen, and he served the little buckwheat cakes onto her plate and spread the melted butter and caviar and sour cream for her with a little silver spoon. Except for a group of older men in army officers' uniforms and two authoritative-looking men in three-piece suits, there was no one else in the restaurant. After a moment another young waiter came by with a pitcher of what looked like water on a silver tray, and a little shot glass beside it. He smiled at her pleasantly. *"Vodka?"*

She shook her head quickly. *"Nyet"* and poured herself a glass of water from the cut-glass pitcher in the center of the table.

Her afternoon was free, and she could take a tour of Sverdlov Square and the Bely Gorod and the museum at St. Basil's, but even though it was a beautiful summer day, she didn't feel like it. Maybe in a day or two. She was tired, and she needed a nap. She had won her first game with a Russian grandmaster, and that was more important to her than anything she might see outside in the huge city that surrounded her. She would be here eight days. She could see Moscow another time. It was two in the afternoon when she finished lunch. She would take the elevator up to her room and try for a nap.

She found she was too high from beating Laev to sleep. She lay on the huge soft bed staring at the ceiling for nearly an hour and played the game with him over and over, sometimes looking for weakness in the way she had played it, sometimes luxuriating over one or another of her moves. When she came to the place where she had offered him her bishop she would say *zap!* aloud, or *pow!* It was wonderful. She had made no mistakes—or could find none. There were no weaknesses. He'd had that nervous way of drumming his fingers on the table and scowling, but when he resigned he looked only distant and tired.

Finally, rested a bit, she got out of bed, put on jeans and her white T-shirt, and opened the heavy draperies at the window. Eight floors below was some kind of convergence of boulevards with a few cars dotting their emptiness, and beyond the boulevards was a park dense with trees. She decided to take a walk.

But when she was putting on her socks and shoes, she began to think about Duhamel, whom she would be playing White against tomorrow. She knew only two of his games, and they went back a few years. There were more recent ones in the magazines she had brought; she should go over them now. Then there was his game with Luchenko that was still in progress when she left. It would be printed up along with the other three and handed out tonight when the players met for an official dinner here in the hotel. She had better do a few sit-ups and knee bends now and take a walk some other time.

The dinner was a bore, but more than that, it was infuriating. Beth was seated at one end of the long table with Duhamel, Flento and Hellström; the Russian players were at the other end with their wives. Borgov sat at the head of the table with the woman Beth had seen him with at the Mexico City Zoo. The Russians laughed throughout the meal, drinking enormous quantities of tea and gesturing broadly, while their wives looked at them in adoring silence. Even Laev, who had been so withdrawn at the tournament that morning, was ebullient. All of them seemed to be pointedly ignoring Beth's end of the table. She tried for a while to converse with Flento, but his English was poor and his fixed smile made her uncomfortable. After a few minutes of trying, she concentrated on her meal and did what she could to tune out the noise from the other end of the table.

After dinner the tournament director handed out printed sheets with the day's games. In the elevator she started going through them, beginning with Borgov's. The other two were draws, but Borgov had won his. Decisively.

The driver brought her to the hall by a different route the next morning, and this time she could see the huge crowd in the street outside waiting to get in, some of them with dark umbrellas against the morning drizzle. He took her to the same side entrance she had used the day before. There were about twenty people standing there. When she got out and hurried past them into the building they applauded her. Someone shouted "Lisabeta Harmon!" just before the doorman closed the door behind her.

On the ninth move Duhamel made an error in judgment, and Beth pounced on it, pinning his knight in front of a rook. It would cramp him for a moment while she got out her other bishop. She knew from studying his games that he was cautious and strong at defense; she had decided the night before to wait until she got a chance and then overwhelm him. By the fourteenth move she had both bishops aimed at his king, and on the eighteenth she had their diagonals opened. He hid from it, using his knights cleverly to hold her off, but she brought out her queen, and it became too much for him. His twentieth move was a hopeless try at warding her off. On the twenty-second he resigned. The game had taken barely an hour.

They had played at the far end of the stage; Borgov, playing Flento, was at the near end. As she walked past him to the subdued applause the audience gave while games were in progress, he glanced up at her briefly. It was the first time since Mexico City that he had actually looked directly at her, and the look frightened her.

On an impulse she waited for a moment just out of sight of the playing area and then came back to the edge of the curtain and looked across. Borgov's seat was empty. Over at the other end he was standing, looking at the display board with the game Beth had just finished. He had one broad hand cupped over his jaw and the other in his coat pocket. He frowned as he studied the position. Beth turned quickly and left.

After lunch, she walked across the boulevard and went down a narrow street to the park. The boulevard turned out to be Sokolniki Street, and there was a good deal of traffic on it when she crossed in a large crowd of pedestrians. Some of the people looked at her and a few smiled, but no one spoke. The rain had ended and it was a pleasant day with the sun high in the sky and the enormous buildings that lined the street looking a little less prisonlike in the sunshine.

The park was partly forested and had along its lanes a great many cast-iron benches with old people sitting on them. She walked along, ignoring the stares as best she could, going through some places that were dark with trees, and abruptly found herself in a large square with flowers growing in little triangles dotted here and there. Under a kind of roofed pavilion in the center, people were seated in rows. They were playing chess. There must have been forty boards going. She had seen old men playing in Central Park and Washington Square in New York, but only a few at any one time. Here it was a large crowd of men filling the barn-sized pavilion and spilling out onto the steps of it.

She hesitated a moment at the worn marble stairs leading up to the pavilion. Two old men were playing on a battered cloth board on the steps. The older, toothless and bald, was playing King's Gambit. The other was using the Falkbeer Counter Gambit against it. It looked old-fashioned to Beth, but it was clearly a sophisticated game. The men ignored her, and she walked up the steps and into the shade of the pavilion itself.

There were four rows of concrete tables with painted boards on their surfaces, and a pair of chess players, all men, at each. Some kibitzers stood over the boards. There was very little talk. From behind her came the occasional shouts of children, which sounded exactly the same in Russian as in any other language. She walked slowly between two rows of games, smelling the strong tobacco smoke from the players' pipes. Some of them looked up at her as she passed, and in a few faces she sensed recognition, but no one spoke to her. They were all old—very old. Many of them must have seen the Revolution as boys. Generally their clothes were dark, even the cotton shirts they were wearing in the warm weather were gray; they looked like old men anywhere, like a multitude of incarnations of Mr. Shaibel, playing out games that no one would ever pay attention to. On several tables lay copies of *Shakhmatni v USSR*.

At one table where the position looked interesting, she stopped for a moment. It was the Richter-Rauzer, from the Sicilian. She had written a small piece on it for *Chess Review* a few years before, when she was sixteen. The men were playing it right, and Black had a slight variation in his pawns that she had never seen before, but it was clearly sound. It was good chess. First-class chess, being played by two old men in cheap working clothes. The man playing White moved his king's bishop, looked up at her and scowled. For a moment she felt powerfully self-conscious among all these old Russian men with her nylons and pale-blue skirt and gray cashmere sweater, her hair cut and shaped in the proper way for a young American girl, her feet in pumps that probably cost as much money as these men used to earn in a month.

Then the wrinkled face of the man who was staring at her broke into a broad, gap-toothed smile, and said, "Harmon? Elisabeta Harmon?" and, surprised, she said *"Da."* Before she could react further, he stood up and threw his arms around her and hugged her and laughed, repeating "Harmon! Harmon!" over and over. And then there was a crowd of old men in gray clothes around her smiling and eagerly holding out their hands for her to shake, eight or ten of them talking to her at once, in Russian.

Her games with Hellström and Shapkin were rigorous, grim and exhausting, but she was never in any real danger. The work she had done over the past six months gave a solidity to her opening moves that she was able to maintain through the middle game and on to the point at which each of them resigned. Hellström clearly took it hard and did not speak to her afterward, but Shapkin was a very civilized, very decent man, and he resigned gracefully even though her win over him was decisive and merciless.

There would be seven games in all. The players had been given schedules during the long orientation speech on the first day; Beth kept hers in the nightstand by the bed, in the drawer with her bottle of green pills. On the last day she would be playing the whites against Borgov. Today it was Luchenko, with black.

Luchenko was the oldest player there; he had been World Champion before Beth was born, and played and defeated the great Alekhine in an exhibition when he was a boy, had drawn with Botvinnik and crushed Bronstein in Havana. He was no longer the tiger he had once been, but Beth knew him to be a dangerous player when allowed to attack. She had gone through dozens of his games from *Chess Informant,* some of them during the month with Benny in New York, and the power of his attack had been shocking, even to her. He was a formidable player and a formidable man. She would have to be very careful.

They were at the first table—the one Borgov had played at the day before. Luchenko made a short bow, standing by his chair while she took her seat. His suit today was a silky gray, and when he walked up to the table she had noticed his shoes—shiny black and soft-looking, probably imported from Italy.

Beth was wearing a dark-green cotton dress with white piping at the throat and sleeves. She had slept soundly the night before. She was ready for him.

But on the twelfth move he began to attack—very subtly at first, with pawn to queen rook three. A half-hour later he was mounting a pawn storm down the queenside, and she had to delay what she was preparing to deal with it. She studied the board for a long time before bringing a knight over to defend. She wasn't happy about doing it, but it had to be done. She looked across the board at Luchenko. He gave a little shake of his head—a theatrical shake—and a tiny smile appeared on his lips. Then he reached out and continued the advance of his knight's pawn as if heedless of where she now had her knight. *What was he doing?* She studied the position again and then, shocked, she saw it. If she didn't find a way out, she would have to take the rook pawn with her knight, and four moves down from that he would be able to bring his innocent-looking bishop from the back rank out to knight five, there on her fractured queenside, and pick off her queen rook in exchange for it. It was seven moves away, and she hadn't seen it.

She leaned her elbows on the table and rested her cheeks against clenched fists. She had to work this out. She put Luchenko and the crowded auditorium and the ticking of her clock and everything else out of her mind and studied, going through dozens of continuations carefully. But there was nothing. The best she could do was give up the exchange and get his rook pawn as consolation. And he would still have his queenside attack going. She hated it, but it had to be done. *She should have seen it coming.* She pushed up her queen rook pawn as she had to and watched the moves play themselves out. Seven moves later he got the rook for his bishop, and her stomach knotted when she saw him take up the piece in his hand and set it down at the side of the board. When she took the rook pawn two moves later it was no real help. She was behind in the game, and her whole body was tense.

Just stopping the advance of his pawns down the queenside was grim work. She had to return the pawn she had taken from him to manage it, and that done, he was doubling his rooks on the king file. He wouldn't let up. She made a threat toward his king as a cover and managed to trade off one of his rooks for her remaining one. It did no good to trade when you were down, because it increased his advantage, but she had to do it. Luchenko gave up the traded piece casually, and she looked at his snow-white hair as he took hers in exchange, hating him for it. Hating him for his theatrical hair and hating him for being ahead of her by the exchange. If they went on trading, she would be ground down to nothing. She had to find a way to stop him.

The middle game was Byzantine. They were both entrenched with every piece supported at least once and many of them twice. She fought to avoid trades and to find a wedge that could bring her back to even; he countered everything she attempted, moving his pieces surely with his beautifully manicured hand. The intervals between moves were long. Every now and then she would see a glimmer of a possibility way down the line, eight or ten moves away, but she was never able to make it materialize. He had brought his rook to the third rank and put it above his castled king; its movement was limited there to three squares. If she could only find a way to trap it before he lifted the knight that held it back. She concentrated on it as strongly as she knew how, feeling for a moment as though the intensity of her concentration might burn the rook off the board like a laser beam. She attacked it mentally with knights, pawns, the queen, even with her king. She mentally forced him to raise a pawn so that it cut off two of the rook's flight squares, but she could find nothing.

Feeling dizzy from the effort, she pulled her elbows off the able, put her arms in her lap, shook her head and looked at her clock. She had less than fifteen minutes. Alarmed, she looked down at her score sheet. She had to make three more moves before her flag fell or she would forfeit. Luchenko had forty minutes left on his clock. There was nothing to do but move. She had already considered knight to knight five and knew it was sound, although of no particular help. She moved it. His reply was what she expected, forcing her to bring the knight back to king four, where she had planned for it to be in the first place. She had seven minutes left. She studied carefully and put her bishop on the diagonal that his rook sat on. He moved the rook, as she knew he would. She signaled the tournament director, wrote her next move on the score sheet, holding her other hand over it to hide it from Luchenko, and folded the sheet to seal it. When the director came over, she said, "Adjournment," and waited for him to get the envelope. She was exhausted. There was no applause when she got up and walked wearily off the stage.

It was a hot night and she had the window open in her room while she sat at the ornate writing desk with her chessboard on it, studying the adjourned position, looking for ways to embarrass Luchenko's rook, or to use the rook's vulnerability as a cover for attacking him somewhere else. After two hours of it, the heat in the room had become unbearable. She decided to go down to the lobby and then take a walk around the block—if that was safe and legal. She felt dizzy from too much chess and too little food. It would be nice to have a cheeseburger. She laughed wryly at herself; a cheeseburger was what an American of a type she thought she would never be craved when traveling abroad. God, was she tired! She would take a brief walk and come back to bed. She wouldn't be playing the adjournment out until tomorrow night; there would be more time for studying it after her game with Flento.

The elevator was at the far end of the hall. Because of the heat, several rooms were open, and as she approached one of them she could hear deep male voices in some kind of discussion. When she was even with the doorway she looked inside. It must have been part of a suite because what she saw was a grand parlor with a crystal chandelier hanging from an elaborately molded ceiling, a pair of green overstuffed sofas and large, dark oil paintings on the far wall, where an open door led to a bedroom. There were three men in shirtsleeves standing around a table that sat between the couches. On the table was a crystal decanter and three shot glasses. In the center of the table was a chessboard; two of the men were watching and commenting while the third moved pieces around speculatively with his fingertips. The two men watching were Tigran Petrosian and Mikhail Tal. The one moving the pieces was Vasily Borgov. They were three of the best chess players in the world, and they were analyzing what must have been Borgov's adjourned position from his game with Duhamel.

Once as a child she had been on her way down the hall in the Administration Building and had stopped for a moment by the door to Mrs. Deardorff's office, which was uncharacteristically open. Looking furtively inside, she had seen Mrs. Deardorff standing there in the outer office with an older man and a woman, involved in conversation, their heads together in an intimacy she would never have expected Mrs. Deardorff to be capable of. It had been a shock to peer into this adult world. Mrs. Deardorff held her index finger out and was tapping the lapel of the man with it as she talked, eye to eye, with him. Beth never saw the couple again and had no idea what they had been talking about, but she never forgot the scene. Seeing Borgov in the parlor of his suite, planning his next move with the help of Tal and Petrosian, she felt the same thing she had felt then. She felt inconsequential—a child peering into the adult world. Who was she to presume? She needed help. She hurried past the room and to the elevator, feeling awkward and terribly alone.

The crowd waiting by the side door had gotten bigger. When she stepped out of the limousine in the morning they began shouting "Harmon! Harmon!" in unison and waving and smiling. A few reached out to touch her as she went by, and she pushed past them nervously, trying to smile back. She had slept only fitfully the night before, getting up from time to time to study the position of her adjourned game with Luchenko or to pace around the room barefoot, thinking of Borgov and the other two, neckties loosened and in shirtsleeves, studying the board as though they were Roosevelt, Churchill and Stalin with a chart of the final campaign of World War II. No matter how often she told herself she was as good as any of them, she felt with dismay that those men with their heavy black shoes knew something she did not know and never would know. She tried to concentrate on her own career, her quick rise to the top of American chess and beyond it, the way she had become a more powerful player than Benny Watts, the way she had beaten Laev without a moment of doubt in her moves, the way that, even as a child, she had found an error in the play of the great Morphy. But all of it was meaningless and trivial beside her glimpse into the establishment of Russian chess, into the room where the men conferred in deep voices and studied the board with an assurance that seemed wholly beyond her.

The one good thing was that her opponent was Flento, the weakest player in the tournament. He was already out of the running, with a clear loss and two draws. Only Beth, Borgov and Luchenko had neither lost nor drawn a game. She had a cup of tea before playing began, and it helped her a little. More important, just being in this room with the other players dispelled some of what she had been feeling during the night. Borgov was drinking tea when she came in. He ignored her as usual, and she ignored him, but he was not as frightening with a teacup in his hand and a quietly dull look on his heavy face as he had been in her imagination the night before. When the director came to escort them to the stage, Borgov glanced at her just before he left the room and raised his eyebrows slightly as if to say, "Here we go again!" and she found herself smiling faintly at him. She set down her cup and followed.

She knew Flento's erratic career very well and had memorized a dozen of his games. She had decided even before leaving Lexington that the thing to play against him, if she had the white pieces, would be the English Opening. She started it now, pushing the queen bishop pawn to the fourth rank. It was like the Sicilian in reverse. She felt comfortable with it.

She won, but it took four and a half hours and was far more grueling than she had expected. He put up a fight along the two

main diagonals and played the four-knights variation with a sophistication that was, for a while, far beyond her own. But when
they got into the middle game, she saw an opportunity to trade
her way out of the position and took it. She wound up doing a
thing she had seldom done: nursing a pawn across the board
until it arrived at the seventh rank. It would cost Flento his only
remaining piece to remove it. He resigned. The applause this
time was louder than ever before. It was two-thirty. She had
missed breakfast and was exhausted. She needed lunch and a
nap. She needed to rest before the adjournment tonight.

She ate a fast lunch of spinach quiche and a kind of Slavic
pommes frites in the restaurant. But when she went up to her
room at three-thirty and got into bed, she found sleeping out of
the question. There was an intermittent hammering going on
above her head, as though workmen were installing a new carpet.
She could hear the clumping of boots, and every now and then
it sounded as if someone had dropped a bowling ball from waist
level. She lay in bed for twenty minutes, but it was no good.

By the time she finished supper and arrived at the playing hall
she was more tired than she ever remembered being. Her head
ached and her body was sore from being hunched over a chessboard. She wished fervently that she could have been given a shot
to knock her out for the afternoon, that she could face Luchenko
with a few solid hours of dreamless sleep behind her. She wished
she had risked taking a Librium. A little fuzz in her mind would
be better than this.

When Luchenko came into the parlor room where the adjournment was to be played, he looked calm and rested. His suit,
a dark worsted this time, was impeccably pressed and fit him
beautifully across the shoulders. It occurred to her that he must
buy all his clothes abroad. He smiled at her with restrained po-
liteness; she managed to nod and say "Good evening."

There were two tables set up for adjourned games. A classic
rook-pawn ending was in place on one of them, waiting for Borgov and Duhamel. Her position with Luchenko had been laid
out on the other. As she sat down at her end of it, Borgov and
Duhamel came in together and walked to the board at the other

side of the room in grim silence. There was a referee for each game, and the clocks were already set up. Beth had her ninety minutes of overtime, and Luchenko had the same, along with an extra thirty-five minutes left from yesterday. She had forgotten about his extra time. That put three things against her: his having the white pieces, his still unstopped attack, and his extra allotment of time.

Their referee brought over the envelope, opened it, showed the score sheet to both players and made Beth's move himself. He pressed the button that started Luchenko's clock, and without hesitation Luchenko advanced the pawn that Beth had expected. There was a certain relief in seeing him make the move. She had been forced to consider several other replies; now the lines from them could be dropped from her mind. Across the room she heard Borgov cough loudly and blow his nose. She tried to put Borgov out of her mind. She would be playing him tomorrow, but it was time now to get to work on this game, to put everything she had into it. Borgov would almost certainly beat Duhamel and begin tomorrow undefeated. If she wanted to win this tournament she had to rescue the game in front of her. Luchenko was ahead by the exchange, and that was bad. But he had that ineffective rook to contend with, and after several hours of study she had found three ways of using it against him. If she could bring it off, she could exchange a bishop for it and even the score.

She forgot about how tired she was and went to work. It was uphill and intricate. And Luchenko had that extra time. She decided on a plan developed in the middle of the night and began retreating her queenside knight, taking it on a virtual knight's tour to get it up to king five. Clearly he was ready for that—had analyzed it himself sometime since yesterday morning. Probably with assistance. But there was something he might not have analyzed, good as he was, and that he might not see now. She pulled her bishop away from the diagonal his rook was on and hoped he wouldn't see what she was planning. It would appear that she was attacking his pawn formation, forcing him to make an unstable advance. But she wasn't concerned with his pawn position. She wanted that rook off the board badly enough to kill for it.

Luchenko merely pushed up the pawn. He could have thought longer about it—*should* have thought longer—but he didn't. He moved the pawn. Beth felt a tiny thrill. She took the knight off the diagonal and put it not on king five, but on queen bishop five, offering it to his queen. If his queen took it, she would take the rook for her bishop. That in itself would be no good for her—paying for the rook with the knight and the bishop—but what Luchenko hadn't seen was that she would get his knight in return because of the queen move. It was sweet. It was very sweet. She looked up hesitantly at him.

She had not looked at him in almost an hour, and his appearance was a surprise. He had loosened his tie, and it was twisted to one side of his collar. His hair was mussed. He was biting his thumb and his face was shockingly drawn.

He gave it a half-hour and found nothing. Finally he took the knight. She took the rook, wanting to shout with joy as it came off the board, and he took her bishop. Then she checked, he interposed, and she pushed the pawn up to the knight. She looked at him again. The game would be even now. The elegant look was gone. He had become a rumpled old man in an expensive suit, and it suddenly occurred to her that she wasn't the only one exhausted by the games of the past six days. Luchenko was fifty-seven. She was nineteen. And she had worked out with Jolene for five months in Lexington.

From that point on, the resistance left him. There was no clear positional reason why she should be able to hurry him to a resignation after taking his knight; it was a theoretically even game. His queenside pawns were strongly placed. But now she whittled away at the pawns, throwing subtle threats at them while attacking his remaining bishop and forcing him to protect the key pawn with his queen. When he did that, brought up his queen to hold his pawns together, she knew she had him. She focused her mind on his king, giving full attention to attack.

There were twenty-five minutes left on her clock and Luchenko still had nearly an hour, but she gave twenty of her min-

utes to working it out and then struck, bringing her king rook
pawn up to the fourth rank. It was a clear announcement of her
intentions, and he gave it long, hard thought before moving. She
used the time his clock was ticking to work it all out—every variation on each of the moves he might make. She found an answer
to anything he might do, and when he finally made his move,
bringing his queen, wastefully, over to protect, she ignored the
chance to grab one of his attacking pawns and advanced her king
rook pawn another square. It was a splendid move, and she knew
it. Her heart exulted with it. She looked across the board at him.

He seemed lost in thought, as though he had been reading phi-
losophy and had just set down the book to contemplate a difficult
proposition. His face was gray now, with tiny wrinkles reticulat-
ing the dry skin. He bit his thumb again, and she saw, shocked,
that his beautiful manicure of yesterday had been chewed
ragged. He glanced over at her with a brief, weary glance—a
glance with great weight of experience and a whole long career
of chess in it—and back one final time at her rook pawn, now
on the fifth rank. Then he stood up.

"Excellent!" he said, in English. "A beautiful recovery!"

His words were so conciliatory that she was astonished. She
was unsure what to say.

"Excellent!" he said again. He reached down and picked up
his king, held it thoughtfully for a moment and set it on its side
on the board. He smiled wearily. "I resign with relief."

His naturalness and lack of rancor made her suddenly
ashamed. She held out her hand to him, and he shook it warmly.
"I've played games of yours ever since I was a small girl," she
said. "I've always admired you."

He looked at her thoughtfully for a moment. "You are nineteen?"

"Yes."

"I have gone over your games at this tournament." He paused.
"You are a marvel, my dear. I may have just played the best
chess player of my life."

She was unable to speak. She stared at him in disbelief.

He smiled at her. "You will get used to it," he said.

The game between Borgov and Duhamel had finished some-time earlier, and both men were gone. After Luchenko left she went over to the other board and looked at the pieces, which were still in position. The Blacks were huddled around their king in a vain attempt to protect, and the White artillery was coming at its corner from all over the board. The black king lay on its side. Borgov had been playing White.

Back at the lobby of the hotel a man jumped up from one of the chairs along the wall and came smiling toward her. It was Mr. Booth. "Congratulations!" he said.

"What became of you?" she asked.

He shook his head apologetically. "Washington."

She started to say something but let it pass. She was glad he hadn't been bothering her.

He had a folded newspaper under his arm. He pulled it out and handed it to her. It was *Pravda*. She couldn't penetrate the boldface Cyrillic of the headlines, but when she flipped it over, the bottom of page one had her picture on it, playing Flento. It filled three columns. She studied the caption for a moment and managed to translate it: "Surprising strength from the U.S."

"Nice, isn't it?" Booth said.

"Wait till this time tomorrow," she said.

Luchenko was fifty-seven, but Borgov was thirty-eight. Borgov was also known as an amateur soccer player and once held a collegiate record for the javelin throw. He was said to exercise with weights during a tournament, using a gym that the government kept open late especially for him. He did not smoke or drink. He had been a master since the age of eleven. The alarming thing about playing over his games from *Chess Informant* and *Shakh-matni v USSR* was that he lost so few of them.

But she had the white pieces. She must hang on to that advantage for dear life. She would play the Queen's Gambit. Benny and she had discussed that for hours, months before, and finally agreed that that was the way to go if she should get White against him. She did not want to play against Borgov's Sicilian, much as she knew about the Sicilian, and the Queen's Gambit was the best way to avoid it. She could hold him off if she kept her head. The problem was that he didn't make mistakes.

When she came across the stage to an auditorium more crowded than she believed possible, with every inch of the aisles filled and standees packed behind the back row of seats, and a hush fell over the enormous crowd of people and she looked over to see Borgov, already seated, waiting for her, she realized that it wasn't only his remorseless chess that she had to contend with. She was terrified of the man. She had been terrified of him ever since she saw him at the gorilla cage in Mexico City. He was merely looking down at the untouched black pieces now, but her heart and breath stopped at the sight of him. There was no sign of weakness in that figure, motionless at the board, oblivious of her or of the thousands of other people who must be staring at him. He was like some menacing icon. He could have been painted on the wall of a cave. She walked slowly over and sat at the whites. A soft, hushed applause broke out in the audience.

The referee pressed the button, and Beth heard her clock begin ticking. She moved pawn to queen four, looking down at the pieces. She was not ready to look at his face. Along the stage the other three games had started. She heard the movements of players behind her settling in for the morning's work, the click of clock buttons being pushed. Then everything was silent. Watching the board, she saw only the back of his hand, its stubby fingers with their coarse, black hair above the knuckles, as he moved his pawn to queen four. She played pawn to queen bishop four, offering the gambit pawn. The hand declined it, moving pawn to king four. The Albin Counter Gambit. He was resurrecting an old response, but she knew the Albin. She took the pawn, glanced briefly at his face and glanced away. He played pawn to queen five. His face had been impassive and not quite as frightening as she had feared. She played her king's knight and he played his queen's. The dance was in progress. She felt small and lightweight. She felt like a little girl. But her mind was clear, and she knew the moves.

His seventh move came as a surprise, and it was clear immediately that it was something he had saved to spring on her. She gave it twenty minutes, penetrated it as well as she could, and responded with a complete deviation from the Albin. She was glad to get out of it and into the open. They would fight it out from here with their wits.

Borgov's wits, it turned out, were formidable. By the fourteenth move he had equality and possibly an edge. She steeled herself, kept her eyes from his face, and played the best chess she knew, developing her pieces, defending everywhere, watching every opportunity for an opened file, a clear diagonal, a doubled pawn, a potential fork or pin or hurdle or skewer. This time she saw the whole board in her mind and caught every change of balance in the power that shifted over its surface. Each particle of it was neutralized by its counterparticle, but each was ready to discharge itself if allowed and break the structure open. If she let his rook out, it would tear her apart. If he allowed her queen to move to the bishop file, his king's protection would topple. She must not permit his bishop to check. He could not allow her to raise the rook pawn. For hours she did not look at him or the audience or even the referee. In the whole of her mind, in the whole of her attention she saw only those embodiments of danger—knight, bishop, rook, pawn, king and queen.

It was Borgov who spoke the word "Adjourn." He said it in English. She looked at her clock uncomprehendingly before she realized that neither flag had fallen and that Borgov's was closer to it than hers. He had seven minutes left. She had fifteen. She looked at her score sheet. The last move was number forty. Borgov wanted to adjourn the game. She looked behind her; the rest of the stage was empty, the other games were over.

Then she looked at Borgov. He had not loosened his tie or taken off his coat or rumpled his hair. He did not look tired. She turned away. The moment she saw that blank, quietly hostile face, she was terrified.

Booth was in the lobby. This time he was with half a dozen reporters. There was the man from the New York *Times* and the woman from the *Daily Observer* and the Reuters man and the

UPI. There were two new faces among them as they came up to her in the lobby.

"I'm tired as hell," she told Booth.

"I bet you are," he said. "But I promised these people . . ." He introduced the new ones. The first was from *Paris-Match* and the second from *Time*. She looked at the latter and said, "Will I be on the cover?" and he replied, "Are you going to beat him?" and she did not know how to answer. She was frightened. Yet she was even on the board and somewhat ahead on time. She had not made any errors. But neither had Borgov.

There were two photographers and she posed for pictures with them, and when one of them asked if he could shoot her in front of a chess set she took them up to her room, where her board was still set up with the position from the Luchenko game. That already seemed a long time ago. She sat at the board for them, not really minding it—welcoming it, in fact—while they shot rolls of film from all over the room. It was like a party. While the photographers studied her and adjusted their cameras and switched lenses around, the reporters asked her questions. She knew she should be setting up the position of her adjourned game and concentrating on it to find a strategy for tomorrow, but she welcomed this noisy distraction.

Borgov would be in that suite of his now, probably with Petrosian and Tal—and maybe with Luchenko and Laev and the rest of the Russian establishment. Their expensive coats would be off and their sleeves rolled up and they would be exploring her position, looking for weaknesses already there or ten moves down the line, probing at the arrangement of white pieces as though it were her body and they were surgeons ready to dissect. There was something obscene in the image of them doing it. They would go on with it far into the night, eating supper over the board on that huge table in Borgov's parlor, preparing him for the next morning. But she liked what she was doing right now. She did not want to think about the position. And she knew, too, that the position wasn't the problem. She could exhaust its possibilities in a few good hours after dinner. The problem was the way she felt about Borgov. It was good to forget that for a while.

They asked about Methuen, and as always she was restrained. But one of them pressed it a bit, and she found herself saying, "They stopped me from playing. It was a punishment," and he picked up on that immediately. It sounded Dickensian, he said. "Why would they punish you like that?" Beth said, "I think they were cruel on principle. At least the director was. Mrs. Helen Deardorff. Will you print that?" She was talking to the man from *Time.* He shrugged. "That's for the legal department. If you win tomorrow, they might."

"They weren't all cruel," she said. "There was a man named Fergussen, some kind of attendant. He loved us, I think."

The man from UPI who had interviewed her on her first day in Moscow spoke up. "Who taught you to play if they didn't want you doing it?"

"His name was Shaibel," she said, thinking of that wall of pictures in the basement. "William Shaibel. He was the janitor."

"Tell us about it," the woman from the *Observer* said.

"We played chess in the basement, after he taught me how."

Clearly they loved it. The man from *Paris-Match* shook his head, smiling. "The *janitor* taught you to play chess?"

"That's right," Beth said, with an involuntary tremor in her voice. "Mr. William Shaibel. He was a damn good player. He spent a lot of time at it, and he was good."

After they left she took a warm bath, stretching out in the enormous cast-iron tub. Then she put on her jeans and began setting up the pieces. But the minute she had it on the board and began to examine it, all the tightness came back. In Paris her position at this point had looked stronger than this, and she had lost. She turned from the desk and went to the window, opening the draperies and looking out on Moscow. The sun was still high, and the city below looked far lighter and more cheerful than Moscow was supposed to look. The distant park where the old men played chess was bright with green, but she was frightened. She did not think she had the strength to go on and beat Vasily Borgov. She did not want to think about chess. If there had been a television set in her room, she would have turned it on. If she had had a bottle of anything, she would have drunk it. She thought briefly of calling room service and stopped herself just in time.

She sighed and went back to the chessboard. It had to be studied. She had to have a plan for tomorrow morning at ten.

She awoke before dawn and lay in bed for a while before looking at her watch. It was five-thirty. Two hours and a half. She had slept two hours and a half. She closed her eyes grimly and tried to get back to sleep. But it didn't work. The position of the adjourned game forced itself back into her mind. There were her pawns, and there was her queen. There was Borgov's. She saw it, she could not stop seeing it, but it made no sense. She had stared at it for hours the night before, trying to get some kind of plan together for the rest of the game, moving the pieces around, sometimes on the real board and sometimes in her head, but it was no good. She could push the queen bishop pawn or bring the knight over to the kingside or put the queen on bishop two. Or on king two. If Borgov's sealed move was knight to bishop five. If he had moved his queen, the responses were different. If he was trying to make her analysis a waste, he might have played the king bishop. Five-thirty. Four and a half hours until game time. Borgov would have his moves ready now and a game plan arrived at by consultation; he would be sleeping like a rock. From outside the window came a sudden noise like a distant alarm, and she jumped. It was just some Russian fire drill or something, but her hands shook for a moment.

She had kasha and eggs for breakfast and sat down behind the board again. It was seven forty-five. But even with three cups of tea, she somehow could not penetrate it. She tried doggedly to get her mind to open, to let her imagination work for her the way it so often worked over a chessboard, but nothing came. She could see nothing but her responses to Borgov's future threats. It was passive, and she knew it was passive. It had beaten her in Mexico City and it could beat her again. She got up to open the draperies, and as she turned back to the board, the telephone rang.

She stared at it. During her week in this room, it had not rung once. Not even Mr. Booth had called her. Now it was ringing in short bursts, very loudly. She went over and picked it up. A woman's voice said something in Russian. She couldn't make out a word of it.

"This is Beth Harmon," she said.

The voice said something else in Russian. There was a clicking in the receiver, and a male voice came through as clearly as if it were calling from the next room: "If he moves the knight, hit him with the king rook pawn. If he goes for the king bishop, do the same. Then open up your queen file. This is costing me a bundle."

"*Benny!*" she said. "Benny! How can you know . . ."

"It's in the *Times.* It's afternoon here, and we've been working on it for three hours. Levertov's with me, and Wexler."

"Benny," she said, "it's good to hear your voice."

"*You've got to get that file open.* There are four ways, depending on what he does. Do you have it handy?"

She glanced toward the desk. "Yes."

"Let's start with his knight to B-5 where you push the king rook pawn. You got that?"

"Yes."

"All right. There are three things he might do now. B to B four is first. If he does it, your queen pops right up to king four. He'll expect that but may not expect this: pawn to queen five."

"I don't see . . ."

"Look at his queen rook."

She closed her eyes and saw it. Only one of her pawns stood between her bishop and the rook. And if he tried to block the pawn, it made a hole for her knight. But Borgov and the others could not miss that.

"He's got Tal and Petrosian helping him."

Benny whistled. "I suppose he would," he said. "But look further. If he moves the rook before your queen comes out, where's he going to put it?"

"On the bishop file."

"You play pawn to queen bishop five and your file is almost open."

He was right. It was beginning to look possible. "What if he doesn't play B to B four?"

"I'll put Levertov on."

Levertov's voice came over the receiver. "He may play knight to B five. That gets very tricky. I've got it worked out to where you pull ahead by a tempo."

She had not cared for Levertov the one time she met him, but now she could have hugged him. "Give me the moves."

He began reciting them. It was complicated, but she had no difficulty seeing the way it worked.

"That's beautiful," she said.

"I'll put Benny back on," Levertov said.

They went on together, exploring possibilities, following out line after line, for almost an hour. Benny was amazing. He had worked out everything; she began to see ways of crowding Borgov, finessing Borgov, deceiving him, tying up his pieces, forcing him to compromise and retreat.

Finally she looked at her watch and said, "Benny, it's nine-fifteen here."

"Okay," he said. "Go beat him."

There was a crowd outside the building. A display board had been erected above the front entrance for those who couldn't get into the auditorium; she recognized the position immediately from the car as it drove past. There in morning sunshine was the pawn she was going to advance, the file she was going to force open.

The crowd by the side entrance was twice as big as yesterday's. They began chanting "Harmon! Harmon!" before she opened the limousine door. Most of them were older people; several reached out smiling, fingers outspread to touch her as she hurried past.

There was only one table now, on center stage. Borgov was sitting at it when she came in. The referee walked with her to her chair, and when she was seated he opened the envelope and reached down to the board. He picked up Borgov's knight and moved it to bishop five. It was the move she had wanted. She pushed her rook pawn one square forward.

The next five moves followed a line that she and Benny had gone over on the telephone, and she got the file open. But on the sixth, Borgov brought his remaining rook to the center of the board and as she stared at it, sitting on his queen five, occupying a square that analysis had not foreseen, she felt her stomach sink and knew that the call from Benny had only covered over the fear. She had been lucky for it to carry her this many moves. Borgov had started a line of play for which she had no continuation ready. She was alone again.

She took her eyes from the board with an effort and looked out over the audience. She had been playing here for days and still the mere size of it was shocking. She turned uncertainly back to the board, to the rook in the center. She had to do something about that rook. She closed her eyes. Immediately the game was visible to her imagination with the lucidity she had possessed as a child in bed at the orphanage. She kept her eyes closed and examined the position minutely. It was as complicated as anything she had ever played out from a book, and there was no printed analysis to show what the next move was or who would win. There were no backward pawns, no other weaknesses, no clear-cut line of attack for either player. The material was even, but his rook could dominate the board like a tank on a field of cavalry. It sat on a black square, and her black bishop was gone. Her pawns could not attack it. It would take three moves to get a knight near enough. Her own rook was stuck in its home corner. She had one thing to meet it with: her queen. But where could she safely put her queen?

She was leaning her cheeks on her fists now, and her eyes remained shut. The queen sat harmlessly on the back rank, on the queen bishop square, where it had sat since the ninth move. It could only go out by the diagonal, and it had three squares. Each looked weak. She ignored the weakness and examined the squares separately, ending with king knight five. If the queen was there, he could swing his rook under it and occupy the file with a tempo. That would be catastrophic, unless she had a countermove—a check or an attack on the black queen. But no check was possible except with her bishop, and that would be a sacrifice. His queen would merely take the bishop. But after that she could attack the queen with her knight. And where would he put it? It would have to go on one of those two dark squares. She began to see something. She could drive the queen into a king-queen fork with the knight. He would take her queen afterward, and she would still be down by that bishop. But her knight would now be poised for another fork. She would win his bishop. It would be no sacrifice. They would be equal again, and her knight could go on to threaten the rook.

She opened her eyes, blinked, and moved the queen. He brought the rook under it. Without hesitation she picked up her bishop, brought it out for the check, and waited for his queen to take it. He looked at it and did not move. For a moment she held her breath. *Had she missed something?* She closed her eyes again, frightened, and looked at the position. He could move his king, instead of taking the bishop. He could interpose—

Suddenly she heard his voice from across the table saying the astonishing word "Draw." It was like a statement and not a question. *He was offering her a draw.* She opened her eyes and looked at his face. Borgov never offered draws, but he was offering her one. She could accept it and the tournament would be over. They would stand up to be applauded and she would leave the stage in a tie with the champion of the world. Something went slack inside her, and she heard her own silent voice saying, *Take it!*

She looked back at the board, at the real board that sat between them. He had taken the bishop. She could see the endgame that was about to emerge when the dust settled. Borgov was death on endgames; he was famous for it. She had always hated them—hated even reading Reuben Fine's book on endgames. She should accept the draw. People would call it a solid achievement.

A draw, however, was not a win. And the one thing in her life that she was sure she loved was a win. She looked at Borgov's face again and saw with mild surprise that he was tired. She shook her head. *No.*

She turned back to the board. For a brief moment she felt like knight leaving her own *en prise*. He moved his queen where he had to and she brought the knight up for the fork. He moved the king and she lifted his heavy queen from the board. He took hers. She attacked the rook and he moved it back by a square. That had been the whole point of the sequence beginning with the bishop—cutting down the scope of the rook by forcing it to a less threatening rank—but now that it was there she was unsure what to do next. She had to be careful. They were headed toward a rook and pawn ending; there was no room for imprecision. For a moment she felt stuck, without imagination or purpose and afraid of error. She closed her eyes again. There was an hour and a half on her clock; she had the time to do it and do it right.

She did not open her eyes even to see the time remaining on her clock or to look across the table at Borgov or to see the enormous crowd who had come to this auditorium to watch her play. She let all of that go from her mind and allowed herself only the chessboard of her imagination with its intricate deadlock. It did not really matter who was playing the black pieces or whether the material board sat in Moscow or New York or in the basement of an orphanage; this eidetic image was her proper domain.

She did not even hear the ticking of the clock. She held her mind in silence and let it move over the surface of the imagined board, combining and recombining the arrangements of pieces so the black ones could not stop the advance of the pawn she would choose. She saw now that it would be her king knight pawn, on the fourth rank. She moved it mentally to the fifth and surveyed the way the black king would advance to block it. The white knight would halt the king by threatening a key black pawn. If the white pawn stepped forward to the sixth rank its move must be prepared for. It took a very long time to find the way, but she kept at it remorselessly. Her rook was the key, with a threatened hurdle—four moves in all—but the pawn could make the step. Now it had to move forward again. This was inch-meal, but the only way to do it.

For a moment her mind became numb with weariness and the

board unclear. She heard herself sigh as she forced it back to clarity. First the pawn must be supported by the rook pawn, and to get the rook pawn up meant a diversion by sacrificing a pawn on the other side of the board. That would give Black a queen in three and cost White the rook to remove it. *Then* the white pawn, safe for a moment, slipped forward to the seventh rank, and when the black king sidled up to it, the white rook pawn came up to hold it in place. And now the final move, the advance to the eighth rank for promotion.

She had come this far—these twelve moves from the position on the board that Borgov saw—by following hints and guesses and making them concrete in her mind. There was no question it could be done. But she saw no way to move the pawn that final square without having the black king snip it off just before queening, like an unbloomed flower. The pawn looked heavy and impossible to move. She could not budge it. She had got it this far and there was no way to go further. It was hopeless. She had made the strongest mental effort of her life, and it was a waste. The pawn could not queen.

She leaned wearily back in her chair with her eyes still closed and let the screen of her mind go dark for a moment. Then she brought it back for a final look. And this time with a start she saw it. He had used his bishop for taking her rook and now it could not stop her knight. *The knight would force the king aside.* The white pawn would queen, and mate would follow in four moves. Mate in nineteen.

She opened her eyes and squinted for a moment at the brightness of the stage before looking at her clock. She had twelve minutes left. Her eyes had been closed for over an hour. If she had made an error, there would be no time for a new strategy. She reached forward and moved the king knight pawn to the fifth rank. There was a stab of pain in her shoulder as she set it down; her muscles felt rigid.

Borgov advanced his king to stop the pawn. She advanced the knight, forcing him to protect. It was going the way she had seen it would go. The tightness of her body began to loosen, and over the next moves there began to spread through her a fine sense of calm. She moved the pieces with deliberate speed, punching the clock firmly after each, and gradually Borgov's responses began to slow. He was taking more time between moves now. She could see uncertainty in the hand that picked up the pieces. When the threatened hurdle was done with and she inched the pawn to the sixth rank, she watched his face. His expression did not change but he reached up and ran his fingers through his hair, ruffling it. A thrill passed through her body.

When she advanced the pawn to the seventh rank, she heard a soft grunt from him as though she had punched him in the stomach. It took him a long time to bring the king over to block it.

She waited just a moment before letting her hand move out over the board. When she picked up the knight the sense of its power in her fingertips was exquisite. She did not look at Borgov.

When she set the knight down, there was complete silence. After a moment she heard a letting-out of breath from across the table and looked up. Borgov's hair was rumpled and there was a grim smile on his face. He spoke in English. "It's your game." He pushed back his chair, stood up, and then reached down and picked up his king. Instead of setting it on its side he held it across the board to her. She stared at it. "Take it," he said.

The applause began. She took the black king in her hand and turned to face the auditorium, letting the whole massive weight of the ovation wash over her. People in the audience were standing, applauding louder and louder. She received it with her whole body, feeling her cheeks redden with it and then go hot and wet as the thunderous sound washed away thought.

And then Vasily Borgov was standing beside her, and a moment later to her complete astonishment he had his arms spread and then was embracing her, hugging her to him warmly.

During the party at the embassy, a waiter came by with a tray of champagne. She shook her head. Everyone else was drinking and sometimes toasting her. During the five minutes the ambassador himself had been there, he offered her champagne and she took club soda. She ate some black bread with caviar and answered questions. There were over a dozen reporters and several Russians. Luchenko was there, looking beautiful again, but she was disappointed Borgov hadn't come.

It was still midafternoon, and she had not had lunch. She felt weightless and tired, somehow disembodied. She had never liked parties and even though she was the star of this one, she felt out of place. Some of the people from the embassy looked at her strangely, as though she were an oddity. They kept telling her that they weren't clever enough to play chess or that they had played chess when they were kids. She didn't want to hear any more of that. She wanted to do something else. She wasn't sure what it was, but she wanted to be away from these people.

She pushed through the crowd and thanked the woman from Texas who was acting as hostess. Then she told Mr. Booth she needed a ride back to the hotel.

"I'll get a car and driver," he said.

Before leaving, she found Luchenko again. He was standing with the other Russians, dressed impeccably and looking at ease. She held out her hand. "It was an honor to play you," she said.

He took the hand and bowed slightly. For a moment she thought he might kiss it, but he did not. He pressed her hand with both of his. "All this," he said. "It's not like chess at all."

She smiled. "That's right."

The embassy was on Ulitsa Tchaikovskogo, and it was a half-hour drive, some of it through dense traffic, to her hotel. She had seen almost nothing of Moscow, and she would be leaving in the morning, but she did not feel like looking out the windows. They had given her the trophy and the money after the game. She had done her interviews, had received her congratulations. Now she felt at loose ends, uncertain where to go or what to do. Maybe she could sleep for a while, eat a quiet supper and go to bed early. *She had beaten them.* She had beaten the Russian establishment, had beaten Luchenko, Shapkin and Laev, had forced Borgov to resign. In two years she could be playing Borgov for the World Championship. She had to qualify first by winning the candidates match, but she could win it. A neutral place would be chosen, and she would meet Borgov, head to head, for a twenty-four-game match. She would be twenty-one then. She did not want to think about it now. She closed her eyes and dozed in the back of the limousine.

When she looked out, sleepily, they were stopped at a traffic signal. Up ahead, to the right, was the forested park that was visible from her room. She shook herself awake and leaned forward to the driver. "Let me off at the park."

Sunlight filtered through the trees on her. The people on the benches seemed to be the same people as before. It did not matter whether they knew who she was or not. She walked past them along the path into the clearing. Nobody was looking at her. She came to the pavilion and walked up the steps.

About halfway down the first row of concrete tables an old man was sitting alone with the pieces set up in front of him. He was in his sixties and wore the usual gray cap and gray cotton shirt with the sleeves rolled up. When she stopped at his table he looked at her inquisitively, but there was no recognition on his face. She sat behind the black pieces and said carefully in Russian, "Would you like to play chess?"

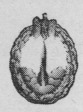